FALLEN

Patrick Abbott

Copyright 2022 Patrick Abbott

ISBN: 9781737393016

KARL PRESS

Cover by Kris Koves

Dedication

This book is dedicated to my deployment friends, the Afghans and Iraqis who cared for me, and those we left behind. However, no words can express my feelings for those who can never go home again.

One – Genesis

Every night. It is always the same visions of the past.

First is the high point of his life. The "running of the table" in Syria.

"Let's go!" Brendan yells as he leads the group forward, his rifle held out before him, guiding the group towards the enemy position.

They are breathless, grimy, and tired, but they all push on together. The last bridge! Five bridges! No casualties! It is right before them. The path to victory is wide open.

"Forward! Forward," Brendan cries. "Secure the other side and fall in the trenches over there! We've cut them off!"

The interpreter summarizes Brendan's words in Arabic. Everyone cheers and charges forward, their guns ablaze. They have completely cut off the Islamic State terrorists. Brendan is the anvil, and the terrorists are about to get the hammer. Brendan grabs his radio and dials his colleague back at the compound.

"Malcolm, we secured the fifth bridge. Let's go!"

Brendan's mind then races to his apartment in Washington, DC, where it all began to fall apart. He is standing in front of his wife, Heather. His shoulders are slouched as he stands dejected. Brendan is holding a letter of congratulations for his service and an offer for a dream assignment. He clutches it as if it is a lifeline to happiness, a happiness that threatens to fly off in the wind.

Heather laughs at him. "You're a pathetic loser who thinks this makes you a hero! Heroes don't cry when they discuss missing their daddy, Brendan. You don't even realize how little you're worth in real life beyond your work." The emphasis on his name is particularly harsh. She mocks the letter. "Brendan Sean Murphy is a hero because he can run really fast, but he can't please his wife!"

Finally, it returns as always to the last deployment to Afghanistan. Brendan is lying on his back in the dirt. The evening sun sets behind the mountains while the heat from the burning wreckage around him keeps him warm. Blood is seeping from his shirt and pooling on his chest. He is looking straight up at the clouds above him. The blue sky above him is visible, but his mind focuses on the word *failure.* He failed the mission. Because of his decisions, peace failed. Americans and Afghans suffered and died because of him. His very birth was a failure of his father, and it just continued from there. His seminary experience was a failure to both him and God if such a being exists. Lying there, he realizes there is no meaning to any part of his life. At home, in school, and in the field, it all ended the same. He is a failure in all things, on his back in the dirt half a world away from home, bleeding out all alone.

PATRICK ABBOTT

Brendan jolts awake. Looking up, he sees not the blue sky of Afghanistan but instead the apartment's ceiling. Looking at the clock next to him is unnecessary. He knows it's sometime between 0300 and 0330. *Every night. Every night I have these same nightmares, and then I wake up at the same time.* There is no drive within him to get up, let alone work out and get ready for work. Pain weighs him down to the bed. He meekly attempts to pray it away. It fails. *Like so much else.* Brendan just keeps staring at the white ceiling. Hours pass. Maybe he sleeps some during that time; maybe he doesn't. He can't tell; it all blends.

I am alone. All alone.

The alarm goes off at six, and like a rocket taking off, Brendan jumps out of bed. "Go time, let's go!" he yells to no one in particular. The cry echoes throughout the mostly void space of the apartment, which is empty by almost all standards. He is alone, and he feels it. Besides his mattress on the floor and a bookshelf, in the living room, there is the television, a sofa facing the screen, a table between the couch and television with his favorite dice game, shut the box. Additionally, an Ottoman and a furnished kitchen complete the room. Meanwhile, the dining room area is empty except for the dust and lint gathered there. The white ceiling, white walls, and white carpet blend together to form a single open space. The bathroom has a tub, one towel, a washer and dryer, a sink and mirror, and his dental supplies laid out on the sink's countertop. Finally, there is the closet, half-full of hanging button-down shirts and pants, while his T-shirts, underwear, and socks lie in various piles on the floor. What was once Heather's half

5

is starkly empty. This is not the family life he envisioned. It's a prison of the mind.

Brendan walks into the closet, grabs clothes, and starts dressing. As he does so, he talks to himself like a coach. "Okay, Brendan, lightweight. Today is lightweight. We're going to go in, rock all the assignments, and finally have the talk with Jenna, and she'll be receptive because she's a friend. No more doubting others and letting yourself get stuck. You're a hard worker, have lots of friends.

He stops as his reflection in the mirror catches his eye; a six-foot-two, brown-haired child of Irish immigrants. At first, he shakes his head and looks away. However, his fear of the likeness draws his gaze back. It's like watching a train wreck. His green eyes look back at him, calling him a liar. *You're not that. You failed. You can't help anyone, and more importantly, no one can help you.* Trying to snap the negative thoughts out of him, he yells, "No!" *I will not let these thoughts win!* However, the negative is not done with him. It responds by bringing back the things Heather would say when he was suffering anxiety attacks. Brendan feels his energy drain. He struggles to put on his tie. The design reminds Brendan of his father. *Please, no more!*

After what seems like an eternity, Brendan looks in the mirror again. "Stop the negative thoughts," he screams out loud. "Do what you need to do. Just make it through the day."

Fully dressed, he makes his way to the door and steps out. He looks at the neighbors' newspaper sitting by their door. The headlines are the same as they have been for years now. Always something about the Sabia. The aliens came about five years ago, and the initial collective panic gave way to a combination of gold rush and conspiracy theories. Some got rich and powerful, while others got left behind. This aggravated the already weak social bonds in hyperpartisan America. Militant leftist thugs rioted in the city while various far-right militias began popping up in rural areas. Brendan previously worked on the militia account, so he knew many of them—fellow veterans, no matter what the government said—and some decent people. But many, too many, were violent conspiracy nuts who wanted to murder those who disagreed with them. *Boys who want to play war as if it was glorious.*

Brendan shifts his attitude as he makes his way to the lobby. A positive, outgoing, cheery demeanor is his protection against the pain.

"Two more days 'til Friday, buddy," he calls out to the front desk clerk, Charles.

"Nah, man. Five more days until Monday! Best day of the week!" Charles responds with a hearty laugh.

As Brendan walks out into the morning sun, he calls back, "Don't put that curse on me! We all fight for the Fridays." He laughs.

Brendan steps out into the cool spring morning of Washington, DC. The gentrified neighborhood has a small-town feel, something he misses from his native Kansas. He surmises that the young people are walking their dogs and getting their coffee. *Capitol Hill staffers and work-from-home bureaucrats.* A slight sense of disdain crosses Brendan's mind as he observes these people's lackadaisical start to their day. *Not me, though, not me.* Brendan takes great pride in his job. People used to ask what he wanted to do with his geography degrees. "Teach?" His whole life, he wanted to travel the world and serve his country. So he pursued his dream job in intelligence. *But at a harsh price.*

The expanded underground railway system, still referred to by locals as the "metro," is one of the fruits of Sabia technology. It links this area directly to a northern Virginian community where the Unified Intelligence Command, other government agencies' annexes, and neighborhood shops are located. The ride is uneventful, though Brendan decides to forgo the headphones today. *I will have no music today to distract me; instead, I will only focus. So let's regain the positive mood we had in the bathroom. It's almost game time. Got to give the office the best attitude.*

The train chimes as it slows to a halt. Brendan wastes no time as he's already standing by the doors. As the doors open, he steps out, feeling like he could conquer the world. Entering the morning air once again, Brendan picks up the pace as he walks the few short blocks to the brand-new building housing the Unified Intelligence Command's operations offices.

He enters, places his phone in a locker, and walks through the turnstiles. Since it's after 0800, most of the morning rush for the workers is over, allowing Brendan to have a brief word with security. "We're going to do it today, boys. We got Max on the mound, and Washington will beat Philadelphia today!"

PATRICK ABBOTT

"You said the same thing yesterday about Michael on the mound, and look what happened, Murphy. Four to twelve. You aren't the same team anymore!" a guard cries back.

"That was yesterday! Today we're going one-and-oh. Woo!" Brendan says with a massive smile. *I need to get some tickets.* He ponders going to another game. The anxiety in him wants to stay home. It says he is not ready to go back. *Today I am going to order tickets, and this time I will go. No more letting pain control me.*

The hallway to his cubical farm is lined with familiar faces and friends. Senior Executive Jack Biro, who waves to Brendan as they pass each other, catches Brendan's eye. "When are you coming to work for me, man?" Jack asks. "If you're not doing the Sabia, your account is worthless."

Brendan just smiles and rolls his eyes.

"Come on, man. China grows its military with its economic base and everything the Sabia gives them. So that's the war that's coming. And if you want to play the longer game, we need insight into these aliens. Why do they look exactly like us? Where the heck did they learn to speak formal English fluently?"

"Yeah, I'll consider it," he lies. Acknowledging defeat, Brendan thanks Jack for his time and heads to his cubical area. On the wall is a massive map of Africa, which Brendan considers a gorgeous work of art.

"It's a beautiful day, and my people are all here," Brendan announces in an effort to lift his spirits as much as to greet the staff. Several heads look over from their

9

standing desks. He hears numerous teasing calls of "the King of Syria has finally arrived" from other officers. Brendan works his way through the group asking how they are, how their evening went, and finally follows up on their work progress. It takes an hour to go through twelve officers, but it is worth every moment for him—he lives for this positive interaction.

Once the check-ins are done, Brendan makes his way to the cubical of Jenna Two Bulls, the portly African office chief. He walks in fully charged with energy from the past hour. He knocks on the door. "Ma'am, do you have a few minutes?"

Jenna waves him in. "Of course, Murphy. How was your commute in?"

"Absolutely gorgeous," Brendan replies. "I hope the spring air was as refreshing for you as it was for me."

"Oh yeah, I had the windows open last night and didn't even mind chasing the girls around this morning. I swear it's like herding cats." Jenna shifts her posture in her chair. It creeks under her weight. "So, Murphy, how can I help you today?"

Brendan takes a gulp of air. "Well, I've put in a great four years building this team up and getting them the skills they need to be excellent officers. I've loved every moment of it. However"—*here it comes*—"I miss the field. Looking at issues about Africa doesn't get me excited, and I know none of the policy folks care about it either. I know I am not meant for office life. Give me six or nine months around the borders of Iran, and I'll have any tribal group running ops for us. Heck, if counter-gangs are still needed in Colombia or Ireland, that would be a blast. And I don't have to leave right away, so if you need a coverage plan, I can work on that and have one ready for you by the end of the day. The workload will be light today, I've checked, so making a plan is an easy day, I swear."

Jenna stares at him. Brendan tries to keep a poker face but can feel his doubt rising to the surface. Finally, she speaks. "You—you nearly died last time. And you became a widower, to boot. Do you really think you should go out again? Maybe you should build something here to cherish."

Brendan swallows hard. His hand shakes nervously. "I . . . My record out there shows—"

Jenna cuts him off. "Brendan, you used to do a heck of a great job out there. But no one survives what you did the last time in Afghanistan and comes out the same. With that and your wife, you really should get-" She stops herself and sighs. "That's enough negativity. Let's look at the reasons I want you to stay. Resources supporting operations in the field are declining. If you aren't focusing on the Sabia or the Sabia's relationship with the Chinese and Russians, no one cares."

Jenna leans back in her chair. Then, as a smile slowly spreads across her face, she leans forward again, putting her elbows on the table. "Tell you what, give me another two years, and I'll put your name in for Russian affairs. Ukraine will always be a basket case—you'll have fun on that team. There could be travel to Lviv."

Brendan's shoulders drop. Without a doubt, his body posture gives away his feelings. There is an audible pause as Brendan struggles to continue. "I can't go back to my apartment anymore after days office work. It's killing me. I'm seriously all alone in there. There's no goal, no purpose. Only bad dreams. Please, let me have a purpose again."

Jenna doesn't give an inch. "Look, I didn't want to, but I'm going, to be honest with you, kid—you're killing yourself with that attitude. And you need help. Look, post-traumatic—"

Brendan jumps out of his chair and shoots back, "I do not have PTSD!"

Jenna pivots. "Plus, you are great here. After years of negativity, we finally have someone who puts a smile on their face. I would clone you if I could. Give it a few more years here, get some help for your messed-up head, and then you can lead your own office. Just tell me where, and I will put in the paperwork. But listen to me—going back out to the field will kill you. And it wouldn't be the enemy; you'd let yourself be overwhelmed by it all and mess up. Or you'd kill the wrong people."

A nod, a word of thanks; maybe that's what happens. Brendan feels like he's not in his body, unable to register what he is doing, saying, or hearing. He stands up and shakes Jenna's hand. All smiles. Everything seems to move along as if on autopilot. Brendan goes to his computer and starts to look over emails. The sheer number would be overwhelming if he cared. He does not. *Delete, delete, save for later.* Emotionless. Throughout the day, several officers come by to chat. Brendan does his best to keep a brave face and pretend to care what they are talking about. *Do they see through me? Do they even care?* Eventually, the workday ends, and it's time for him to shut down the office. *Last in, last out.* A boost of energy aids in performing the end-of-day routine. However, thinking about going home makes him pause. *Home is where the crying will start.*

Brendan leaves the building. Going through the doors, he hears one of the guards say something to him about the baseball game tonight. Brendan can only wave in response. He fears he will cry if he starts talking.

Once outside, breathing the air of the early spring evening, Brendan puts on his headphones and plays an action movie soundtrack to try to drown out the pain. He passes various stores and heads straight to the metro. He's oblivious to the world.

Oblivious until he steps onto the platform, and someone holds a knife to his face.

Brendan's eyes focus on the blade, then on the attacker. He is a young man, in his early twenties perhaps, still with pimples and blond peach fuzz on his face. The man is yelling at Brendan, though all he can hear is the rock music blasting in his ears. The furious beat puts his heart in its highest gear. *I didn't deploy half my adult life for this crap!* Again, the knifeman yells something, but before he can finish, Brendan throat-punches him. Stunned, the man gasps for air as Brendan wrestles for the knife. Finally, prying from the dazed man's hand, Brendan grabs it and cuts the stunned young man across the face with one angry blow.

Looking up, Brendan expects to see shocked faces and perhaps someone coming to arrest him.

Instead, he finds a cop bleeding on the ground, surrounded by three people wearing all black plus two cowering people wearing white sweaters and gray pants. It takes a moment, but Brendan recognizes the white-and-gray clothing as Sabia attire and the individuals in black as politicized urban thugs.

Bastard cop killers are taking hostages! Brendan throws the knife behind him and charges the closest of the three thugs. His palm strikes the wannabe urban warrior so hard that Brendan feels the person's nose break. The second rushes at Brendan with a knife as the rock music reaches a new crescendo. This thug, a woman, gets a long-armed punch straight to the face as Brendan sidesteps the knife. Quickly, Brendan grabs her bruised head and presses his thumbs into her eyes until he hears her scream. Then his training kicks in. He subconsciously realizes she's out of action, so Brendan releases his thumbs to ensure there is no permanent damage.

Next, Brendan looks up and begins to walk toward the final black-clad figure. Brendan's heart is pumping, and his mind is raging. When he sees the thug's wide-eyed gaze, Brendan imagines the pain his father caused him that spring day at the baseball park; it makes him angrier. The thug ceases to be as the brain turns him into Joseph Murphy. Nothing else matters to his brain, which is in pure attack mode. Brendan's vision even ignores the grenade in the man's hand. With the music screaming in his head, just as his blood lust is at a maximum, the grenade goes off. All is then silent and, for a second, white. Brendan stands alone, wholly stunned. He looks around, disoriented, and realizes the last attacker lies dead on the ground. Brendan looks down and sees his left hand is now mangled. The middle, ring, and pinky fingers are missing, along with a portion of his palm. His chest feels cold, and his breathing becomes tense. Blood is starting to stain his shirt.

Movement on the ground grabs his attention. A Sabia lies writhing in pain, trying to hold his upper left leg. *Open wound!* Brendan automatically recalls the combat first aid training during his many deployments. Dropping to his knees, Brendan applies pressure on the alien's wound.

He tries to say, "It will be alright," but with blood building up in his throat, he can barely get out the first three words. In a state of shock, Brendan does not understand that he is dying. He tries to keep the pressure on the Sabia's wound, but his mind drifts, and his vision goes black.

Then, in a shock, Brendan's eyes open. The ceiling is white. *Am I back home? Was it a dream?* The goosebumps slowly forming in reaction to the cold airflow imply he is not dreaming. He holds up his left hand; it is still horribly mangled, with a putty-like substance on the end of whatever is left can be called. Brendan turns his attention to the room and sees the same male Sabia from the underground lying on a bed. The wound is still there. *Open wound,* Brendan's brain screams. Remembering the aftermath of a rocket attack, he undoes his belt and leans over to apply it as a makeshift tourniquet.

As he leans over, a force pushes him back down. Brendan can tell there is a person above him, but his eyes cannot focus on the vague profile. The image-of-a-person takes their hands and uses them to firmly grab Brendan's wrists. Brendan feels his hands, or hand and a half, being held firmly against his chest. The mystery image blends into the white background of the ceiling. Everything goes dark again.

Once more, his eyes slowly open. Brendan stays still, letting them focus. He realizes he doesn't feel anything. A quick mental check interprets the absence of cold and pain as a good sign. He holds up his left hand, amazed to find five fingers and no scars.

A woman in blue scrubs and a gray overcoat walks into view and looks down at him. The feminine figure has dark brown hair and startlingly deep brown eyes. "Better than new," the woman says. "It is my best work."

PATRICK ABBOTT

Two – A Visit to the Stars

"Squeeze," the woman commands.

Brendan closes his reformed left hand onto the woman's hand. The sensation of a working hand is there. Yet Brendan focuses on her. The doctor's skin is soft, yet it does not give way. Brendan refrains from fully clamping down to avoid causing her pain.

"I know your hand can do more," she says, "I made it. Squeeze harder." There is a sense of pride in her voice. In response, he squeezes, using his full strength. Still, the woman's hand resists; Brendan's effort barely moves her fingers. "Congratulations, you can use your hand." He detects slight condescension in her voice. Then, the woman turns her attention to a panel while announcing, "He is physically fine."

Brendan sits up to keep the woman in his field of vision as she walks around. An entire medical bay comes into view, filled with light-blue screens on freestanding panels and empty beds. The sudden shift in posture produces a migrant that prevents him from focusing on anything, so instead, he addresses the woman. "I'm sorry, but I don't understand."

"Understand what?" she replies without looking up from her work.

Brendan squints twice as if readjusting his vision will help him better understand his surroundings. He remembers his near-death experience in Afghanistan, the pain and weakness he felt as he lay dying. As Brendan recalls the events from that day, he remembers the dead lying around him. The dead he failed returns his mind to the metro. *You are forgetting the other wounded! Never leave a man behind!*

Brendan's heart races as he addresses the woman. "There was a man next to me; he was hurt worse than me. Is he getting medical care? Why are you with me but not him?" Brendan's chest aches with apprehension about the fate of the hostage he tried to save.

"I am more than fine, thank you," a male voice declares from Brendan's left. "And my name is Imran. It is a pleasure to formally meet you in this calmer setting, Brendan." Brendan can see Imran wearing a white tunic with an odd, thick red wrap around his left shoulder and waist. *Looks vaguely Indian and Persian.*

Brendan shakes his head. *I need to gather myself.* "I have to apologize, but how do you know my name? And where am I?"

"My name is Delegate Loft, and I can answer those questions," a warm, confident voice declares on Brendan's right. Brendan shifts to see the latest speaker. "Your wallet contained your identification and that of your employer as well. Once we had that information, the Unified Intelligence Command confirmed your identity. As for where you are, you are approximately three hundred thousand miles from Terra on the main Sabia mission ship."

Brendan can only whistle in awe. *I'm in space!*

Loft continues, "The reason you are here is for medical care. Your injuries were severe, and we did not want someone, even a Terran, who risked himself to save Sabia not to have the same opportunity at life as our own because of a mere difference in medical technology. Thankfully, our medic Zalta and our doctor Esfirs were able to stabilize your situation."

Another woman walks into view. Brendan notices her pale gray padded armor. As she approaches, his eyes focus long enough to realize she has dirty-brown hair in a short ponytail. *Boy, they really do look human.* Brendan thinks their appearance is almost Middle Eastern.

"It is good to see you doing well, Brendan. I am Zalta. I was worried about your condition, and your effort to place a tourniquet on Imran only aggravated your wounds." She is now a half step behind the doctor Brendan first saw.

Then the woman who fixed Brendan's hand speaks. "And I am Esfirs. Our biotech is compatible with Terran bodies. We just needed to bring you here, and it was a simple job to reform the hand and connect the nerves. We managed to repair the damage to your torso as well." Brendan looks at Esfirs. Perhaps he stares for a moment too long but remains intrigued by her black hair, which, depending on the light, seems to give off a dark red sheen. It's long, though the back half is in a clip.

Not now. This is your first contact. Don't be weird about it. Think tribal relations.

Brendan puts his hand over his heart, mimicking an Afghan gesture he learned while deployed. "I owe both of you my life—thank you." He turns to Imran and repeats the motion. "And I am glad you are well. Are your companions well?"

All three Sabia try to mimic the Afghan gesture, but each does so differently: Zalta makes her hand into a closed fist, Esfirs keeps hers more than a foot from her chest, and Imran looks at both hands before slowly completing the motion.

Loft walks over to face Brendan directly. He seemingly takes the initiative from the confused Imran. "Yes, the three are safe. The police assigned to protect Imran and the others are in critical condition at a local hospital but likely will live. You did an excellent job handling the terrorist attackers, though. Three incapacitated and one killed. We were surprised one Terran could take on four attackers until we learned of your distinguished military career."

The words "military career" ring in his head. While he is a civilian and not military, the Sabia knows much more about him than what can be learned from his wallet. *I am on an alien spaceship, unauthorized, and risk spilling intelligence. Are they going to hold me hostage? I shouldn't be here. Turn the situation, act like this is a deployment.*

He calms himself and begins, again with his hand over his heart. "Delegate Loft. I'm glad your two Sabia are safe and apologize for their poor treatment on my planet. I have no means of thanking you or paying. I must humbly request the ability to speak with a government representative so I may facilitate proper reimbursement to you and arrange my repatriation."

Esfirs and Zalta noticeably glance at each other while Loft laughs and says, "Brendan, I have interacted with Terrans for several years. I have never met one who apologizes while being helpful to us. You risked your life to save our people, and we are glad to have medically aided you. We have a representative from your State Department available to talk to you if you are willing. We wished to interact with you first merely to express our appreciation for your actions. Thank you." Loft puts his left hand on Brendan's right shoulder and then walks away.

Imran walks over to face Brendan and, like Loft, puts his hand on his shoulder. "I will always remember you, Brendan. May you be richly rewarded in life for what you did."

Without moving, Zalta speaks. "I am delighted you are well. Next time, however, please ensure your medical situation before helping others. You made your injuries worse both on Terra and while flying here because you moved around trying to help others." She puts her closed fist over her heart but stops. Instead, she smiles and walks out of the room. *She must have been trying to imitate my gesture.*

Esfirs approaches then smiles, and says, "You will never get a better left hand. Take good care of it, Brendan." She looks at him and begins to turn but stops herself. "If I may ask, why did you not take care of your own wounds before helping Imran?"

"He was wounded. I had no choice but to help him."

Esfirs squinches her eyebrows, which causes her nose to wrinkle. "You must have been aware of your own wounds. Did you think his wounds were worse? Or were you truly oblivious to your own injuries?"

How would she take "I did it because I didn't care about myself"? Is that even true? Was it because of my training? Or was it because he needed help? He scans his emotions and realizes he is too cynical about himself.

"There was an innocent person in trouble. Saving him was the right thing to do."

Brendan feels as though Esfirs is drilling into his mind as she looks him in the eyes. Finally, after a pause too long for comfort, Esfirs says, "Take care of yourself, Terran Brendan. If not for your own sake, for the hand I crafted at least."

Brendan laughs as she walks past him. He feels her pat his back and then hears her footsteps receding. He is all alone in what he guesses is a medical bay. Looking down, he realizes he is wearing a gray shirt and gray shorts. The realization that his original clothes were probably a bloody mess and disposed of hits him hard. Instead of feeling lucky to be alive, Brendan thinks back to the tie his father tried to give him in the hospital. *Why didn't I accept his apology? Ah! Why do I keep thinking of it?*

PATRICK ABBOTT

The door opens, and a sweaty, bald, paunchy man with a beard comes in at a near jogging pace. "Intelligence Officer Brendan Murphy, I'm Paxton Wheeler. I'm the number two of the US' mission to the Sabia." Paxton is incredibly sweaty and out of breath. "What . . . what did you tell them?"

Clearly, they did not have you just waiting for me outside. "Thank you for saving my life, and can I talk to a government representative so I can go home?" Brendan says dryly. The shock is wearing off. "I'm fine, by the way."

Paxton is still catching his breath from an obviously quick summons. "Did you tell the Sabia anything about your security clearance or employment background?"

"I didn't need to. The Sabia apparently identified me through the stuff in my wallet. They said the UIC confirmed my identity. Didn't DOD tell you guys at—"

Paxton nods. "Yeah, they found your badge and started asking questions about you while you were out. We provided context by saying you were a decorated veteran. Partially true, you know. Not sure whether or not we civilians get veteran status while in combat zones, though. War Veterans of America tend not to smile on civies like us. But come on, the best thing to do is get you out of the hot zone. You have a ride arranged back to Earth. Let's go."

The State Department representative leads Brendan down empty white-and-gray halls. As they move through the corridors, Paxton resumes talking. "They really train you desk jockeys to be killers over there at the UIC, eh?"

"What do you mean?" Brendan asks. His Catholic upbringing and sense of duty sicken at the thought of killing. Previously, he managed to do six deployments, including times to Iraq, Syria, and Afghanistan, in which no one died by his hands. *Even the bridges . . .*

The paunchy man interrupts Brendan's thoughts while taking deep breaths between sets of words. "Well, you completely blinded . . . a woman. The other person you slashed down to this skull. And whatever you did to the other . . . it caused him to blow himself up."

Brendan thinks back to the fight. He ponders the depth of the wound he gave the knifeman, *I was angry, but I couldn't have been that angry! Could I?* As for the woman, Brendan thinks he only gave her a flesh wound.

Troubled, he asks, "How could I have blinded the woman? I made sure to stop when I felt pressure resisting my thumbs."

"Nope," Paxton replies quickly, "you broke her eyes, and I doubt the Sabia want to repair them."

The fact that Brendan blinded someone shocks him to the core. Before he can reply, they stop walking. Paxton hits a button on a panel, and a door opens. Inside is a giant hangar with equipment on the walls. Brendan notices a craft that looks like a boxcar with oval cylinders. Leaning against it is a woman with the slightly olive complexion Brendan has seen in other Sabia. She

PATRICK ABBOTT

is wearing a gray, leather-looking flight suit and has short soft brown curling hair.

"Your ride," Paxton says. "You'll be debriefed when you land." With that, he walks away, leaving Brendan alone with what he assumes to be the pilot.

The pilot looks at him and says, "You look a bit better than when I last saw you. My regular shuttle still needs to be cleaned out from all your blood, but this one will get you home safe enough. Hop aboard."

A door opens on the side, almost out of nowhere. The pilot enters, and Brendan follows suit. He sees two rows of seats, one on each side, facing each other. The pilot is gone. *Probably to the cockpit?* He sits down and stares straight ahead. The door closing offers a momentary distraction, though Brendan quickly returns to his thoughts about what happened.

Brendan looks around at the small cabin. There are pillows leaning against the sides. As he sits, he waits for something to happen. Minutes pass without motion or sound, leaving him alone with his thoughts, but as time passes, Brendan is forced to focus on a surge of emotions instead. His eyes are constantly filled with flashing images of violence. With each repeated violent memory, his breathing becomes more labored. It is another relapse of his post-traumatic stress.

Suddenly, he hears a crackling sound. "Are you okay?" It's the woman's voice. Brendan looks around to see where it came from but cannot find the source. "Just talk like we were face to face," the voice says. "I will be able to hear you just fine."

"Yeah, thanks for asking. Just dealing with one crazy day." He tries to act normally, which slowly helps him calm down. As curiosity gets the better of him, he says, "Hey, I'm Brendan. What's your name?"

Laughter. "Trust me, Brendan, I know—pretty much everyone important on our ship knows your name by now. My name is Berina. I am the pilot who is taking you home."

Okay, this is getting somewhere. "You mentioned I looked better than when you last saw me and how my blood was in your spacecraft. I'm sorry I messed up your ride but thank you for helping to save my life."

"Ah, you are welcome, Brendan. Do not worry about the blood; it will be cleaned easily enough. I was just trying for a moment of levity."

He laughs. "No offense taken." Brendan tries to press his luck. "Say, why wasn't the police officer taken along with me for medical aid? He looked pretty bad even before the grenade went off."

"You fought for us. The cop ran away." The bluntness of the answer hangs in the air.

There is only silence after Berina discloses the Sabia's lack of care, or maybe hostility, toward the cop. *Poor bastard.* Brendan wonders how long the ride to Earth is and what time it is. He looks at the wall, the seats, his hands—including his new left hand. He can't tell where his old hand ends, and the "biotech" begins. *Biotech, whatever that means.* Sitting there, Brendan realizes he doesn't feel motion. *Are we even moving?*

PATRICK ABBOTT

Suddenly, the door swings open, and cool night air rushes in. Brendan is startled, half expecting the vacuum of space to suck him out. Instead, he can smell the air and even see headlights on the road in the distance. An interior door opens, and out comes Berina.

She looks at him and says, "You are home—well, you are where your government representative said to drop you off. It is near where we took you from, so I assume it is near where you would call home." There is a light playfulness in her voice. Berina grows quiet as if she is expecting him to say something, but finally, she breaks the silence with, "I am glad you are well, and thank you, truly, for saving my fellow Sabia earlier."

Brendan nods but does not say anything. The door scare has caused the emotional and physical stress to finally catch up with him. Energy-wise he is dragging. He puts his hand over his heart—on autopilot—and says, "You are welcome," before getting up and walking out.

As Brendan exits, a set of men in suits rush toward him. Before he can say anything, they surround him and hurry him into a van. During the sudden action, Brendan notices the large building nearby. *The Pentagon. Well, I'm just a couple stops from home . . .* As he is propelled into the van, followed by one of the men, Brendan looks at the clock and eyes 0407. *Dang, I don't think I'll be getting any sleep tonight. Is it the day after the metro incident? Or have I been gone for days? My goodness, is today a workday?! Oh, am I going to get into trouble!*

The van stops in an underground garage, and Brendan is rushed into a poorly lit room where a man with a bushy black beard sits at a table. His lips are stained with tobacco, and he is wearing a dirty polo shirt, a worn John Deere baseball cap, and sunglasses, despite being indoors at night. The man motions to the empty chair across from him. Brendan takes a seat. The dead-tired feeling is trying to take over, and the gray clothes he is wearing feel like pajamas he could sleep in.

"We are not leaving until I'm satisfied," declares the interrogator.

Countless stories exist of interrogators, referred to as "gators," who manage to break the will of terrorists and acquire valuable intelligence. There are also the stories of gators who meet their match in the village idiot who is mistakenly rolled up during an operation. No trickery in the world can get these poor souls to reveal what they don't know. After an epic effort, the gators realize it's not mental resistance but ignorance that keeps them from getting what they want, and they are made to look like fools. Meanwhile, the prisoner is released far from home, bribed to avoid seeking revenge, and left confused by the whole encounter. At this moment, Brendan realizes he is the idiot.

Most of the words out of his mouth are "what." Although Brendan freely reveals what he learned, the gator already knew these things. Finally, the gator lets out a grunt and points to the door. Brendan gets up without comment or ceremony. His eyelids are extremely heavy.

Leaving the room, Brendan is gently escorted to the van. He looks over to the clock, revealing the time is 1030. They drive into the city and toward his apartment.

PATRICK ABBOTT

As they arrive, a suit-wearing man stationed in front of his building approaches, saying, "Officer Murphy you have the rest of the week off on admin leave because of your condition. Therefore, we need you to remain at your apartment and wait to be contacted when you are more coherent. Do you have any questions?"

All Brendan can think to say is, "I think I lost my keys."

Three – The Assignment

Brendan looks at the clock. *0300 on the dot. Please, not again.* It is prayer, but it is too late to benefit him. It was worse tonight. The bridge, Heather, and the Afghan near-death experience were all there. However, there was something new as well. The fighting in the metro. During the event, the frantic action and music are replaced with gratuitous violence seen in slow motion. The blade cutting across the knifeman's face, the palm strike, and the grenade going off. What haunts him most, though, is what he did to the woman. *I'm so sorry! If I could take it back, I would.* He repeats these words, begging for forgiveness. At that moment, he could have shown the world he still had the power to disarm people with his words, but instead, Brendan proved to everyone, including an alien race, that he is a violent man.

The hours pass in a vague mental fog. Brendan's alarm goes off at 0600, but he does not move. Eventually, after a seeming eternity, the alarm stops sounding. Looking over, he sees that sunlight is beginning to move across his wall. *Heather's gone, and now I have probably lost my job as well. My own family won't take me back, so there goes the option of going back to Kansas. Would Malcolm offer me a job doing intelligence with the militia movement? Would I even want to work with them? Bunch of murderous thugs who fancy themselves a legitimate force. The Irish Republican Army thought the same thing, too, while they ran drugs and kidnapped poor widows. Perhaps I could be a moderate voice among them? No, my hands would only get innocent blood on them. Maybe I am doomed to wander the Earth as if it were the land of Nod. I wonder how many private military companies worldwide had various North and South Americans, Europeans, and Africans who could never go home? Could I be like them, making a living going from conflict to conflict? I can't imagine a worse fate for a person than that.*

A ringing disrupts his train of thought. *Phone! Someone wants to talk to me!* He leaps out of bed and rushes to the living room. He picks up his cell phone off the couch and stands at attention. "This is Murphy."

"Intelligence Officer Murphy, this is Intelligence Officer Ben Klerk with the UIC's Special Programs Office. Are you dressed?"

Brendan looks down at his shirtless torso and boxers. "Dressed enough for apartment living but nothing formal, sir." Even though he doesn't know Ben's rank, his mother and father taught him well enough to address people as sir or ma'am.

"That will work. I am about ten minutes from your apartment. The director has a new assignment for you. Klerk out."

He hears the sound of the phone disconnecting. Brendan is elated, even wobbling his knees in a bit of a dance. *The director has an assignment for me! I didn't lose my job! Maybe it will be assisting analysts with defensive training? Perhaps I can leverage the position in a few years for another deployment! Then I can go back to doing tribal affairs!* He rushes to put on clothes. *A polo and shorts will give an appropriate impression.* He doesn't stop to think about what message the practically empty apartment will convey. He is too far removed to realize that.

There is a knock at the door, and Brendan opens it. A man in a business casual button-down shirt and slacks greets him.

"Brendan, I am Ben Klerk."

"Ah, come in, come in," Brendan says, gesturing toward the living room. "Please, take a seat."

Ben notices the couch, table, television, and lack of anything else. After an awkward pause, he sits down on the edge of the sofa. Meanwhile, Brendan moves over to face him, standing back against the wall. Then, he puts his hands behind his back to fight the urge to fiddle with them.

His nervous energy keeps building. He tries to focus his brain on conversation, attempting to relieve the desire to toss his hands about. "Klerk—I knew a couple of Klerks who served in Global Outcomes. So that makes you part of the Boer mafia, eh?"

Ben nods and laughs. "Yep. Parents came over when things were getting terrible. Kind of like your own. Your mother is Rhodesian if I—"

Promptly, Brendan cuts him off. "My parents are Irish. I was born there and moved as a kid."

PATRICK ABBOTT

Doing a double-take, Ben tilts his head and squints. "Really? I read in your file that you are of mixed Irish and Rhodesian—"

Brendan firmly shakes his head. "My father was Joseph Mathew Murphy, and my mother is Alexandra Mary Byrne Murphy. Dad was from County Donegal, and Mom was born in County Fermanagh."

"Okay . . ." Ben trails off. "Anywho, I run the special programs with the UIC, and that's why I am here. We need you to help us out with the Sabia."

Brendan crosses his arms as he leans in. By sheer force of will, he finds himself able to stop his hands from shaking.

Ben continues. "You managed to get alone time with several Sabia and even discovered the reasoning why they left a cop to die during your little space adventure. This is more face time and information than we have gotten in over a year. They stonewalled us on why the cop was left but freely told to you. Meanwhile, they repeatedly have filed follow-up requests to see how you are doing. UIC told them you were fine and gave them a survey of your file. They think you are some sort of superhero now. Ambassador Bass was visited by the good idea fairy and asked if the Sabia would want you as a—get this—intelligence liaison. Now they are demanding to know when you can start. Not bad for getting blown up, eh?"

Brendan takes this all in while remaining silent. He is stunned.

Ben goes on. "So, this is what is going to happen. Next week you'll get a crash course in defense liaison, collections, and testing. Here's your coursework in a few sentences: Give them whatever is unclassified or whatever classified we give you. Play dumb, stupid, or hard to get if they ask for anything else. Meanwhile, collect on anything and everything without giving them a reason to think you are a straight-up spy. And I mean anything. Whether it's their secret to space travel or who taught them to speak our languages. Oh, and you're not a diplomat, so don't agree to anything. Got it?"

"Yes, sir!"

"Okay. Now, enjoy the weekend and stay out of trouble." Ben gets up. Looking around the empty place, he adds, "And, um . . . be sure to pack up. Next week you'll get orders at training so that you can break your lease. Don't ask me what the per diem for this will be. Good luck and stay safe, brother. This will be a thousand times more exciting and dangerous than the last time you went to Afghanistan."

Those words sit darkly inside Brendan's soul. He shakes Ben's hand as he leaves. Then, Brendan closes the door and waits a full thirty seconds for the man to walk down the hall before he lets out a yell of celebration. *Deployment! Handpicked for a deployment! They believe I can still do great work! Finally, I have a purpose again!*

The rest of the week and weekend are different. No more bad dreams. Instead, Brendan sleeps soundly. He jolts out of bed when he wakes up and starts working out. Push-ups, planks, and running. On Saturday and

PATRICK ABBOTT

Sunday, he goes to work to use the gym for the cardio equipment. The week's classes are a breeze, with most instructors remembering Brendan from the days he deployed out doing tribal affairs. The courses quickly cover the necessary topics, from rehashing the basics of liaison work to the many unknowns of the Sabia. Almost everything about them is a mystery, including their mastery of English, governance, and social structure. Brendan grabs dinner with the instructors at the end of each day. They have all previously deployed before, sometimes together in various combinations, so many stories are shared. Brendan attempts to focus on his professional successes, but the instructors ask about his personal life. Once filled in, they awkwardly offer empty platitudes. "You're doing fine," and "At least you are free of her now." Brendan swallows the pain of not being able, to tell the truth, putting on the facade he has had to uphold for the past few years.

Throughout the week, he works down a deployment checklist. The process goes well until he sees the list of required signatures. There, staring back at him is the chaplain. Brendan's doubts ended his seminary career. Briefly, he had gone back to church once he married Heather. Renewed faith even played a role in giving him a purpose when he was overseas. However, the horrors of war and his wife's betrayal all took a toll on his faith. Finally, reluctantly, he goes Friday afternoon.

Down the hall, Brendan sees the chaplain's office. Next to it is the chapel. As he approaches both, his lips begin to tremble. An odd sensation, similar to heartburn, surges in his chest. *Nerves, it has to be the nerves.*

Clenching his fists, Brendan notices a stinging sensation in his left hand. *Phantom pain—freaking nerves.* A large exhale allows Brendan to refocus.

Pushing past the anxiety, Brendan looks away to not peer inside the chapel. When he gets to the office, he sees a woman in a military uniform filing paperwork. Brendan knocks, and she identifies herself as Chaplain Frazier.

Frazier starts by congratulating Brendan on the mission. Then, without missing a beat, she says she read in his deployment forms that he is Catholic and describes how God has a specific role for him with the Sabia. She tries to play up how Brendan was ordained a deacon at seminary. The talk of faith makes Brendan's ears ring. He nods and says a few words to ensure Frazier signs the paperwork, which she does.

First, however, she hands Brendan a rosary. All he does is look at it. His heart feels cold and empty when staring at the prayer beads. His feeling flowing, a frown forms on his face. *All gone.* Politely, Brendan declines and heads out the door, but a strong arm pulls him back. Forcing the rosary into his hand, the chaplain says, "Don't forget your faith, Brendan; you'll need it."

What if it has forgotten me?

Brendan spends the weekend in his apartment. Part of him yearns to be with the people at work who greet him with their playful titles, but the loneliness he feels has become, in its own sense, company for him. *Horrible company, but it's the devil I know.*

PATRICK ABBOTT

D-Day happens on Sunday. He gets up promptly at 0700 to await the driver coming at 1300. Putting on the Unified Intelligence Command's uniform causes an odd sensation in him. Searching his heart, he realizes he is proud and patriotic right now. *The government needs me to serve America. Me. There is a golden opportunity before me right now.* Yet, as he looks in the mirror, his pride is undercut by the reflection. *What a liar I am.* Suddenly, a knock on the door brings him back to the here and now. An agent's voice commands him to come outside. *It's time; let's do this.*

The agent drives Brendan over the Potomac River to the landing pad at the Pentagon. Waiting there is a brutalist-looking shuttlecraft. Outside, leaning against it is a pilot in a gray flight suit.

A uniformed UIC officer approaches Brendan as he exits the car no more than twenty feet away from the craft. The officer, wearing a name tag reading "Mustafa," says to Brendan, "You clear on your orders? Be the lovable guy who gives them the stuff we don't mind losing and steal the keys to the castle from them."

Brendan nods and takes his two bags containing clothing, his wallet, the rosary he got from Frazier, and the Shut the Box game out of the car. As he makes his way to the craft, his brain seizes on the realization that it is a bright, sunny day with a slight breeze. *Everything seems normal. Certainly not the type of day I thought I'd be doing anything weird like going into space.*

As he approaches the craft, he notices the pilot looking at him with a broad smile. It's Berina, the same one from before.

"I remember you," Brendan says in a friendly manner.

Berina raises an eyebrow and responds, "'Oh, hello Berina, you are the pilot who saved my life and took me home, too. It is such a pleasure to see you again. I hope you are well.' Oh yes, Brendan, I am very well, thank you for asking. I hope you are well, too."

His eyes widen, and the air is filled with stunned silence. He fears he managed to insult the first Sabia he has met in his role. *I am going to be sent back in shame. That's if I am lucky enough to even get off the planet.*

Her laughter breaks the silence. "Seriously? I was told you had a sense of humor!"

He struggles to recover. "My apologies. It's just that we have a bunch of worry about giving a good first impression—"

Cutting him off, Berina waves her hand. "Relax. Putting your life on the line already has made a good first impression. Plus, if your file is accurate, you will be fine. Now, you want to take a ride on my actual shuttle?"

He looks over the ship, taking it all in. "Is this the same one I was taken in after the metro attack?"

"Yes, it is," she says in a somber voice. Then, her tone becomes playful again. "So remember what I told you, and do not bleed in it because you have no idea how much work it took to disinfect the inside. You were flopping around trying to play doctor, only making things worse." She ends with a laugh.

PATRICK ABBOTT

With a slight head movement from her, a panel appears and opens. Berina steps inside, Brendan following with his bags. The interior is different from the other spacecraft, as there is just one seat facing forward. The panel closes, and Berina turns around.

"Welcome aboard. Take a seat, and we will be back at home base in less than thirty minutes."

"Thank you. And thank you for the ride, or should I say rides? In the meantime, if you have any questions for me, just let me know."

"Ah, a true gentleman," she says teasingly. "Since you offered, tell me your thoughts on the militia movement."

Brendan goes into briefer mode. "The militia movement, like the urban leftist movement, seeks to remake America into what it wants the country to be. They see the country's legitimate problems and want to address them outside the republican political system. Some competent people are leading the national-level militia movement, like General Javier Meade. Previously, I served under him in Syria and Afghanistan. I consider him a good man who cared for his mission and country. Personally, I would say he is very much mistaken in his actions, though." Catching himself, he reverts to a more objective tone. "His popularity has united various militia groups while other militia groups have segregated themselves based on religious or regional factors. These movements generally believe the Sabia has made the situation in the country worse through increased disparity or even that they are purposefully dividing the American people."

Berina stares at him for a few seconds. Her intense look makes his head ache slightly, but the pain goes away when she closes her eyes. Then, she opens them again. "Did you just say there were legitimate problems in your country and some good, but mistaken people were running the militia movement?"

Oh crap. The most important thing is for this not to become leverage against me. If I take ownership of this and then shift it, I can manage it like anything else I have handled while deployed. "Yes, I did; it's an extraordinarily complex situation. However, it is important to see the situation for what it is, not the way we want it to be, so we can work together toward solutions. There is a saying from my country's history which goes, 'United we stated, divided we fall.'"

"Brendan, we are going to love having you. Do not be surprised if your entire time with us is just us asking you nonstop questions."

That would be a mission failure. "Glad to be of service."

PATRICK ABBOTT

Four – Integration

Brendan doesn't feel any motion during the entire ride. During the passage, Berina chats with him through the crackling air, which he is finally getting used to. He doesn't get to ask anything as she just presents him with a barrage of questions.

"What did you do during this deployment?"

"Did you work with this person while deployed?"

"Why did you volunteer for that deployment?"

"Why did you not volunteer for Sabia duty when we first appeared?"

In one way, her interest in following up on things in his file flatters him, but in another, they raise a sense of alarm. *Collection threat.* How much of this is genuine curiosity, and how much is it trying to build a profile on him? *To be fair, I am doing the same thing. Just answer the questions, and eventually, I'll get my own opportunity.* For the rest of the flight, Berina keeps up the question-and-answer session.

Finally, after a seeming eternity, a short pause allows Brendan a breather until the door opens and Berina comes out.

41

"Welcome to your new home, Brendan."

Surprised, he responds, "That was quicker than the trip back last time, wasn't it?"

"No, but time does fly when you have fun."

Such comfortableness with English phrases.

"And, let me thank you for such an enjoyable conversation. I think some of your fellow Terrans just see me as a pilot and not important enough to talk to. You, however—I learned so much in this short little ride."

Brendan decides to test her. "What did you learn besides my life story?"

"Goals of your government, how your government views different developments, personalities, how you value the same and sometimes different things than your government."

Yep, she was feeling me out. "So, I'm that transparent to you?"

"Honest. We will talk more; I am most sure of that. But you should exit—you are awaited." She motions toward the panel door.

Brendan grabs his bags and says, "Where I am from, we allow the woman to go through the door first, so please let that be a small measure of my thanks to you."

"Ha! While I am greatly pleased to learn more about your customs, if I exit first, I would be violating protocol, so we can either play 'which tradition is the better one,' or you can do me a favor and go first."

Brendan nods with a smile. Berina responds with another odd head motion, which opens the door. He steps out into a hangar and quickly notices a person dressed in a suit standing in front of Imran, also wearing human professional wear, a woman in a gray pencil skirt, and Ambassador Virag Bass. Bass is the lead American representative to the Sabia, and his face was drilled into Brendan during his training, as were the instructions to follow his commands to the letter. As such, Brendan keeps smiling as he walks up to the lead, preparing to put his bags down.

"Greetings and welcome, Brendan. I am Delegate Loft. I handle most diplomatic affairs with Terran representation here. It brings me great joy to have you aboard with us with no medical emergency this time. How was your flight?" the black-suited man says.

Before Brendan can respond, Berina walks past them and interrupts, "This one had less blood and yelling, so it was better."

Loft and the others chuckle at the joke while Berina assumes a position beside Imran. The laughter throws Brendan off guard, as this level of informality in his own first contact situation was not what he expected. He also thinks about the initial ride-up. *I don't recall yelling. It must have been worse than I thought.*

"Is this all you brought with you?" Loft asks while looking at the bags Brendan is holding.

"Yes, sir. I wanted to move fast and light."

"Brendan, please call me Loft. You are a guest who is here to help us. There is no need for titles.

Please, set your bags down. I will ensure they are delivered to your new domicile without the contents being disturbed."

"Thank you," Brendan says as he drops the luggage.

Berina falls out of formation, picks it up with a smile, and walks out of the hangar. Brendan watches her go and then faces back to Loft.

"Now," Loft continues, "I will escort you to meet Zand. Please follow me."

Brendan looks at him, confused, and Ambassador Bass's face drops. Loft takes a few steps and gestures for Brendan to follow. Imran and the woman in the gray skirt start to move as well. After doing a few double takes, Bass rushes up to Loft.

"Delegate Loft, Brendan has just arrived, and I would like to brief him about our mission here before any actions by him. He has not yet been prepared to handle liaison meetings. We do not want him misleading anyone."

"Nonsense," Loft says as he waves his hand. "Brendan has demonstrated himself enough, according to the record you gave us. The goodwill he has earned will be rewarded; we will not abuse him."

Loft takes a step forward and gently grabs Brendan's wrist, leading him out of the hangar without a word. The delegate's hand is notably soft, yet somehow Brendan senses its potential for great strength. Bass runs up alongside Brendan, out of breath, much like Paxton had that previous night.

PATRICK ABBOTT

"Alright, Brendan. Here's the crash course. Zand is their leader—well, leader of the mission. I will handle the talking and—"

Without looking at Bass, Loft says, "Zand has requested a private council with Brendan. You may meet with him during or after the meal."

While Brendan follows this back and forth, the woman in the pencil skirt approaches him.

"Hello, Brendan. I am Behnaz. I wish to thank you for saving my life. Are you doing well?"

"Yes, very well. Thank you for asking."

Bass tries to jump in and talks about how he has only met Zand once. However, just as he starts, Imran cuts him off.

"Brendan, did you think you would come back to us?"

Is this a confusion tactic? Not knowing exactly what to do in this situation, Brendan begins answering a series of rapid-fire questions from Imran and Behnaz about his health, what he did when he returned to Earth, and what he thinks about being back with the Sabia. He is unsure, but there seems to be a certain intensity whenever Bass tries to get a word in. Quickly, Bass becomes flustered, and Brendan decides to give the Sabia this one. *I will have to do better in beating these tactics if I want to actually be a benefit to the UIC.*

The cacophonous caravan approaches what appears to be a checkpoint. Two Sabia wearing boxy padding and helmets stand at the ready, eyeing everyone.

Brendan perceives both the male and female guards to be capable of defeating him in a fight if they wanted to, despite them being slightly under six feet tall. Loft stops and thanks Behnaz and Imran for being there to greet Brendan. Both wish Brendan well and walk away.

Loft turns to Bass. "And thank you, too, for being here, Ambassador. Please know we are preparing a meal to welcome Brendan, which will be ready soon. You and Representative Paxton are more than welcome to attend. Now, if you please, Brendan, is awaited." Loft looks at the female checkpoint guard. "Kimya, will you provide an escort for Ambassador Bass back to his office?"

She steps forward with a strong command presence, causing Bass to back off, his eyes full of resentment. *There is tension here.* For a moment, Loft takes hold of Brendan's wrist again and starts to move past the checkpoint. Brendan attempts to ask Loft about the protocol for what is about to happen. Loft dismisses Brendan's concerns and instructs him to handle this engagement as if it were any other. *There is a difference between meeting desert tribesmen and personal first contact with an alien race.* They approach a door that looks like every other door on the ship. Brendan can't see any identifying marks on it. It is not until Loft touches a button on a nearby panel that the door opens. Without a word, he motions for Brendan to step through.

Brendan inhales, steadies himself, and enters. The contrast between the general white theme of the ship and the blackness of the room is striking. The floor feels like carpet, the walls are dark onyx, and the dim lighting amplifies the darkness. Brendan's eye catches on a woman sitting on the floor in the middle of the room, crisscross or Indian style, as they say in Kansas. She looks about fifty, with dirty-blond hair flowing down to her shoulders. On each side of her are six others, all women, forming a semi-circle. At a glance, their approximate ages appear to range from early thirties to the oldest one, who looks to be seventy. *No men. That would have been handy to know in training. Is this something I stumbled upon, or something I am meant to see?* The women appear stoic and give off an air of authority. Brendan assumes an attentive posture. The older woman studies him as if he were a statue. Perhaps it's just his own tension, but her focus on him corresponds with his headache returning.

He decides to break the ice. "Ma'am, please allow me to introduce myself. I am Intelligence Officer Brendan Murphy of the United States Unified Intelligence Command. I have been ordered to provide my services as intelligence liaison to you. It is an honor and pleasure to be the first American in this role."

The woman softly presses her left thumb against her lips as if pondering his words. "Tell me, Brendan, is this how you normally would begin working with various groups on Terra?"

"No, ma'am. Usually, meetings are done informally, where those I am dealing with encounter me in a relaxed state, and conversation can happen naturally."

The older female looks over to the woman on her left, who gets up and moves toward the end of the semi-circle. Then, she looks back at Brendan with a smile. "It would be most enjoyable if that could occur here. I am Zand, and you are welcome here, Brendan. Please, take a seat on the pillow to my left. Let us discuss like you would with other Terrans."

"I would be honored to take a seat wherever you asked me to sit, Zand. I do wish to make known that by doing so, I mean no disrespect to anyone to whom I show my back while taking a seat. That action can be viewed as offensive in some human cultures, so I want to reassure you that is not my intention."

"Thank you for sharing that portion of cultural information. We wanted you for this very reason. Someone who can help us gain insight from your government while more importantly being able and willing to provide the cultural nuance needed to understand Terrans."

He nods. "As a Unified Intelligence Command officer I—"

Zand interrupts him, forcefully raising her left hand in a "stop" position. "Tribal affairs, cultural liaison, fighter for the Syrians, sympathetic ear to those who feel alienated with changes in America, loyal solider for his government, and one who will fight against his fellow Terrans to save Sabia. All these phrases have been used to describe you. How would you reply to these descriptors?"

He quickly scans the room. The women are looking at him intently. "I would say those who used those terms and phrases were observing traits representing my objective of achieving the common good. I believe my country's interests are best served

PATRICK ABBOTT

when we focus on what is true and fair, so I do not seek
to swindle or trick those I work with. I am open and
honest with all those I partner with and state how
working together can accomplish everyone's goals."

"And what does that mean for us?"

Her stare is intense, and again his headache
returns. This time, it feels like the pressure is pushing
against his eyes as she looks into them. "It means I will
be candid with the intelligence provided, my own
opinions, and what I am seeking in return. I will do this
because what is truly best for the United States is also
truly best for the Sabia. I will not lie to you."

"And if there were a war between the Sabia and
your government?"

He blinks for a moment from the pain. *Is it the
lighting?* "If war occurs, then one or both sides are failing
to adhere to the common good. I will work to my utmost
with both sides to ensure peace, even if it costs me my
life. In that regard, I would work with you, and I would
plead for you to work with me."

Two of the women turn their heads to each other
rapidly, betraying surprise. Zand's gaze leaves Brendan,
her eyes moving slightly down and to her left. His
headache eases, and Brendan can take a better read of
the room. The women's stoic facade has given way to a
seemingly quiet anticipation of Zand's response.

The pregnant pause makes Brendan nervous. He
does his best to keep his face free from emotion as if he
were waiting for the following order of the day. He
breathes in deeply through his nose to steady his heart,

which begins to beat faster. *Calm. Patience. They are testing me, and that's okay. Behave well, and I will have their trust.*

Zand's eyes move back to Brendan, and with a perfectly straight face, she says, "May the only blood spilled between us be what you shed earlier. I apologize, but we have many matters to attend to this evening. I do hope Delegate Loft will be an agreeable host for you."

She slowly and delicately lifts her left arm and points to the door. Understanding that this is a command, Brendan leans his head forward, bows slightly to the left, and puts his right hand over his heart all at the same time. He holds the position for two seconds and then rises. Without a word from anyone, Brendan heads over to the door. As he approaches, it opens. The whiteness from outside is blinding, but he manages to deal with it. Loft is standing outside the doorway.

"I do hope you find the meal prepared to your satisfaction. We inquired what food you may have had while you were a child in Kansas. With that knowledge, our cooks have been able to prepare bierocks, corn, salad, and tea."

Brendan laughs. "Bierocks, I haven't had those in years. But yes, those foods would provide a great welcome for me. I'm honored you thought of me in that manner. Is there time for me to see my cabin and prepare for the meal?"

Loft turns to face Brendan with a self-assured smile. "Brendan, the meal is about to begin. The guests certainly would be confused if you were not there."

"Ah, we wouldn't want that now, would we?" *Yep, they're putting me through the wringer.*

They walk down the hall together as Loft makes minor remarks about the positive relationships the Sabia have with Earth's—or as he calls it—Terra's governments and various wealthy and influential people. Brendan decides to keep the deep-seated prairie populist persuasion in him quiet. They pass a checkpoint without stopping. Loft mentions that the checkpoints delineate the area where "Terrans" are and are not allowed to go without an escort. Loft begins a story about his visit to New York when they divert left into what looks like a long dining hall.

Brendan takes in the room as everyone turns to look at him. There are three tables. The first table has Bass and Paxton, an unknown man wearing a business suit, and two empty seats. The second table has Berina, Imran, Behnaz, Zalta, and Esfirs. Imran is still wearing his Earth-looking professional wear, but the Sabia women are wearing what looks like black monk robes with oversized, drooping sleeves and bulky gray scarves. The third table features representatives from China, the European Union, India, Russia, and the United Kingdom, all wearing their countries' military uniforms. Loft makes a few opening remarks, and everyone sits down to eat. The meal does look tasty to Brendan. Before he can start, though, Loft introduces the unknown man as Kadar, the Sabia who is a direct liaison for the ambassador when Loft is unavailable.

Brendan leans over to Bass. "How are you doing, and how much of this behavior is normal?"

"Loft is on a power play today. He told us nothing about their plans for you. It's a control game." The acidity in Bass's mumbling voice is sharp.

"Uzbeks tried this on me the first time I deployed to Afghanistan. It's like a prison; you have to set the tone right away. Watch me."

Bass's eyes widen in fear of what sort of diplomatic protocol breach Brendan has in mind. But before he can react, Brendan is already making his move.

Brendan stands up, his cocky smile almost an imitation of Loft's from earlier, looks down at him and says, "Delegate, you honor me with such a Kansan meal. Let me honor you all with the Kansan custom of eating the meal at various tables."

Loft looks confused as Brendan grabs his plate and chair. He walks with purpose and half-tosses, half-slides the chair to an open spot at the second table by Berina and Esfirs. Both women jump up, unmistakably startled. Brendan puts down his plate between them.

He slides into his chair and claps his hands. In a commanding but playful voice, he says, "Hello, everyone. My name is Brendan Murphy, and I am tonight's entertainment. However, I cannot be entertaining if I sit at another table, away from you. So I am coming over to you." A part of him that could be a carnival barker comes out. "And not only that, I am coming over with a game. You all get to ask me any question about myself. The person who asks the best one wins a prize."

PATRICK ABBOTT

The Sabia's eyes light up with excitement. Apparently, either the idea of games or the prospect of asking questions seems like a fun dinner activity.

Berina jumps in with a question. "What religion are you?"

Brendan relaxes in his chair and puts on an air of complete control. It's all a show. He purposefully slouches a little in his chair to give the impression of being completely open. "Ma'am, many in my country are not religious."

The pilot claps her hands and leans in. "That is not an answer. Your file said you went to a school for clerics. So, what religion are you, and why are you not a cleric now?"

His mind leaps to the opportunity to escape. "That's cheating." He playfully laughs. "That is two questions, so you lose." He turns his face to one of the Sabia he helped rescue. "Imran, it is your turn!"

The male Sabia smiles nervously. Berina tells him to re-ask her first question, but she shakes her head when he looks at Behnaz. "Oh, I do not know." There is a pause. "Are you happy to be back with us?"

"Imran, I am thrilled to be back here. Where else could I enjoy some fine Kansas food, which I haven't even tried yet because I am with such great friends?"

The male survivor smiles bashfully and looks away. Brendan turns to Esfirs and taps the table twice to signal he is ready for her.

"How is your hand?" the doctor asks.

"See for yourself."

He offers it to her, and she takes it. Her hands are also abnormally soft. She turns his left hand over once, twice, three times. She applies pressure and studies it as if she were some sort of palm reader. Finally, after a moment's pause, she gently lets it go with a smile but without a word.

"Quality craftsmanship," he says.

Now it's Zalta's turn. He looks at her, but she smiles nervously and looks down, softly murmuring a desire not to ask a question. So Behnaz's is next. Eagerly and with almost childlike enthusiasm, she asks, "What are your family members' names? Do you have any siblings?"

Brendan ignores the double question violation for the sake of the game. "My father was Joseph, and my mother is named Alexandra. I have one brother, Michael, and two sisters, Mary and Bernadette. Unfortunately, my father passed away when . . ."

The last line drops like a nuclear bomb. The table is silent, and the expressions on the Sabia's face change from happiness to sadness. Berina, who Brendan has only seen in a good-humored state, softly says to no one in particular, "The baby."

This is unexpected and could ruin all the momentum he has gained. Brendan moves to salvage the situation. "I think those are great questions, all of which demonstrate care and interest in me. Though I wonder if Esfirs is interested in the hand or me." Laughter around the table signals the sadness has lifted. Esfirs makes a disapproving face but breaks it with a smile. "As such," Brendan continues, "you are all winners. I will arrange a party at my cabin in a few days, and I would love for you all to come. If you like this game, I will introduce you to a couple more Earth games."

The statement leaves everyone excited. Brendan bids everyone a good meal and makes his way to the foreign diplomats' table.

Five – On the First Day

Brendan wakes up when his alarm goes off. There had been no nightmares, nor waking up and lying in bed for hours before the set time. Instead, he has a purpose, a mission, a reason to be alive. He jumps up and begins the day with planking. *I'm back!* After the plank, he does a round of burpees. He finishes with stretches and ends by making the bed. A connected washroom allows him to quickly shower and change into a button-down shirt and black slacks. He looks at a wall panel that shows the ship's time displayed militarily. *Twenty minutes to spare.*

Brendan makes his way to the living room of his cabin, where there is a couch. He sits down and waits, almost motionless, for the time to pass. A thought creeps into his mind. *The stillness of waiting means I have no other purpose but the job at hand.* He bats the idea away.

At the agreed-upon time, chimes sound in the air around him, a phenomenon eerily similar to the communications on the Sabia's transport shuttle.

"Enter," Brendan calls as he stands up and walks across the plush carpeted floor.

PATRICK ABBOTT

Loft strolls right in as the door opens, with three other Sabia in tow. "Brendan, I hope you found the cabin, bed, and furniture to your liking."

"Oh yes, Loft, the room is fantastic. The bed is great, and the couch, table, chairs, and television are more than satisfactory. Compared to the converted CONEX boxes I've slept in during other deployments, living with the Sabia is like living in a castle. Say"—Brendan shifts the conversation—"were you able to acquire the treats?"

"The treats, yes. I must tell you"—Loft chuckles a bit—"the cooks were alarmed by the order at first. They have never made so much, so they assumed something grand was about to happen."

Two Sabia, a male and female, step aside to reveal a cart with a tray on top. Brendan sees congealed, transparent cubes with various fruits and nuts inside. He admires them and, with a slight smile, remembers Loft's reaction when he told the delegate he wanted as many of the best treats he could get by morning.

"Oh, my friends, I am indebted to you. What are they called?"

"Anything dealing with our own language is classified, I am sorry to say."

"Uh-huh." Brendan shifts the conversation from the classification buzzkill, as intelligence analysts call it. "Well, the cooks were correct; something grand is about to happen. I am going to play Santa Claus. Now, if everyone would please join me in partaking of one?"

Loft and a female Sabia standing beside him express surprise. Taking the initiative, Brendan grabs several pieces and gives them to Loft, the woman, and the two Sabia standing by the cart. Brendan keeps one of the treats for himself. The Sabia, meanwhile, are glancing at each other, trying to take in the situation.

"Sir"—the male Sabia by the cart speaks up—"we are just staff . . ."

Brendan cuts him off. "Ah, hello, 'Just Staff,' my name is Brendan. Will you share in my happiness of being alive by having some of this treat?"

The staff members nervously look over at Loft, who nods. Then, with big smiles, they each take a bite. The female standing by Loft takes a smaller mouthful of her piece and clearly enjoys it. Brendan takes a bite, which reveals a deeply sour taste. It takes everything he has not to suck his whole face in. Loft, meanwhile, takes two big bites and demonstratively savors the taste.

"Well"—Brendan claps his hands—"I was not expecting it to be sour, but I am glad I tried it." That is a little white lie. "Loft, would you please introduce everyone to me?"

Loft swallows the last bit of the treat. "Of course. The 'Just Staff' are Nikrad and Atosa." Both smile nervously and step back against the wall. *They weren't expecting to be called out.* "And my associate here is Leleh." He motions to the female. She looks to be in her thirties and is wearing a top with long sleeves tucked into a loose-fitting pant that opens up above the ankle. "Leleh will be your counterpart in intelligence matters and the voice of the Sabia to you."

PATRICK ABBOTT

"I look forward to working with you," Leleh says. "The council has assigned me to help orientate you to our requirements while ensuring you have all the available resources. Please do not hesitate to reach out to me when you require support."

Brendan places his right hand over his heart while Leleh watches the move intently. "Oh, I have a feeling I will be reaching out to you a lot. Shall we now bring the treats to everyone we encounter?"

He leads the caravan consisting of himself, Loft, and Leleh, while Nikrad and Atosa follow behind the cart. The first Sabia the gaggle encounters is a lightly armored man stationed outside his door. The man, named Gul, at first tries to downplay himself as a guard. Brendan's overwhelming yet oppressive friendliness and Loft's approval finally force Gul to take a treat. He consumes it in one bite and mumbles thank you with his mouth closed. As they continue on their way, the group encounters two more Sabia. At first, they try to decline but again take pieces with gusto when given permission. *Clearly, this is a hit.* Brendan introduces himself, describes what he will be doing on the ship, and tells the Sabia that they can just ask him if they have any questions about Earth. The Sabia are grateful for the classified-named treat though Brendan can tell they do not feel entirely comfortable interacting with him. *Yet. Sometimes you have to make them like you.*

Loft indicates the spot for the requested detour as they walk down the hallway. Brendan remembers these doors lead to the hangar. They open, and the group enters the massive room. Looking around, Brendan eyes an empty corner.

"That will do nicely, Loft. I do have to thank you once again. That space is perfect. And as agreed, I will arrange the funds if you can arrange the transfer."

"Of course," the delegate says.

Coming toward them as they confirm the deal is Berina.

"You cannot keep away from the pilots, Brendan? Do not feel bad; if I were not a pilot, I would want to be around them all the time, too." She then struts up to Brendan with a cocky stride, ending face-to-face with him.

Loft responds, "Pilot, do you have a flight today and, if so, what is the mission?"

Berina stands in a formal attention position and replies, "I am scheduled to fly to the United States Spaceport in Djibouti to ensure the transfer of raw materials."

The delegate looks at Brendan. "Can you arrange a pickup of your supplies there?"

"That hub? Oh yeah."

Loft turns to Berina. "Pilot, the intelligence liaison is purchasing supplies in the form of exercise equipment, which will be placed in that corner. You will see to it everything is received, transported, and erected before ending your shift tonight."

"Yes, sir!"

PATRICK ABBOTT

The formality of everything is something Brendan had not been expecting. He doesn't want to be remembered as the guy whose mere presence results in the loss of space and extra work. He decides it is essential to rectify the situation.

"And to thank you, Berina, I have brought treats for everyone here."

He motions to the tray behind him. Berina's eyes widen. She calls over a group of people, several pilots in jumpsuits like her, as well as others in matching gray tops and pants. Berina walks up to the cart and grabs handfuls of the treats, tossing them to people whose names she calls out. *No shyness in her.* She then takes two for herself. As she chews, she chats with Brendan.

"So," she says with her mouth full, "can you show us how to work the exercise equipment to ensure we correctly put it together for you?"

"Of course, and I don't mind helping out once I'm done with work today. In fact, you and your friends are welcome to it or exercise with me in the morning. It might be fun." He hopes the appeal, at the very least, can make a connection.

It does something more than that. "Really? I love to try new things. And exercising is something best done with friends. Be prepared, though; I am going to ask you so many questions about yourself and Terra!"

And hopefully, I will be able to get something out of you, too.

Brendan bids farewell to Berina and the others. The pilots and what Brendan assumes are the crew bid him goodbye. *They sure are a friendly bunch. At the very least, this has been a first impression win.*

They reach the second and last detour: the medical bay. The doors have been left wide open, and Brendan can see all the panels, beds, and various workstations as he enters. Zalta is putting together several things in a bag.

She looks up and sees the caravan. She calls out, "Esfirs, it is Brendan. Brendan has come to visit us." She turns to him. "Brendan, are you well?"

He nods. "I am very well, thank you for asking. In fact, I have something for you and anyone else here."

Esfirs then walks into the room. Her doctor's clothes differ from Zalta's medic uniform, just like a guard's uniform.

"Well, Zalta," Esfirs says, "it looks like the Terran cannot stay away from us."

Brendan chuckles. "Esfirs, it is a pleasure seeing you. I was just telling Zalta that I am indeed well."

"Excellent, and your left hand, too?"

She likes her work, time to have some fun. "Well, I did want to talk about my left hand. I've noticed since the . . . the rebuilding of it I cannot write with it."

Esfirs winces. "Has this been getting worse? Come here immediately. We need to—"

PATRICK ABBOTT

Brendan takes a step back and waves his hands. "Whoa, whoa. No need. It was a simple joke. I am right-handed, so I have never used my left hand to write."

Zalta and Loft laugh at the joke, but Esfirs looks incredulous and somewhat upset. "Of course, the hand is fine," she says.

Leleh says, "I am starting to see why your file stated you left 'strong impressions' wherever you went."

"Glad to be of service. Now please, I ordered plenty of these sour treats, which everyone seems to love. So have some while they still last."

Zalta, Esfirs, and a male doctor all take pieces. They have a brief conversation about Brendan's upcoming day, which he ends with his now well-practiced offer for the Sabia to just come and ask him if they have any questions about Earth or Earth customs.

Zalta takes him up on this by asking him to practice a handshake. The medic extends her left arm at a slightly downward angle. Brendan explains that most people shake with their right hands. He first demonstrates holding his arm and hand out several times before inviting Zalta to do the same. Next, he grips her hand, explaining the reasoning behind not squeezing too hard or shaking too limply. After that, Zalta and Brendan practice a handshake together. She is awkwardly slow and reluctant to grip.

Zalta giggles as she moves her arm up and down. *Cultural exchange, love it.* Brendan thanks everyone again, making sure to especially acknowledge Esfirs and ensure there are no hard feelings from the joke. She

63

responds that she "enjoyed the moment of levity" and tells Brendan to return any time he wants to. He places his hand over his heart, nods deeply, and wishes everyone a good day.

The diplomatic offices are less than a thirty-second walk away. Loft opens the door, allowing everyone to step in. Nikrad and Atosa rush up like a pit crew to place the remaining mystery treats on a table in the center of the room, then duck out without a word. *Probably what they prefer.* Brendan takes in the space. There is a central interior room and mini offices with desks and shelving along the sides. No one else is present.

Loft disrupts Brendan's inspection. "Brendan, this is where I leave you. Leleh will instruct from here on. Good day." With a smile, the delegate leaves.

Brendan turns to the woman. "Ma'am, it is a pleasure to be working with you." He holds out his right hand for a handshake, but Leleh puts out her left, looking confused. In response, he switches and gives her a lefthanded handshake.

"I agree; it is indeed a pleasure. We have prepared you an office over there." She motions toward one of the small rooms.

"I can't help but notice there is no one else here. Are we early?"

"The other Terran representatives sadly have decided not to perform their duties this week. Your ambassador, Virag, claimed we did not show proper protocol when you first arrived and has persuaded the other representatives not to come to work. Will this be an issue for you?"

Talk about a test! With a racing mind, he ponders what to do. *Bass did not contact me, so* . . . "No, I have not received any order to stand down, so I must assume the situation for my work is normal. I'm ready to begin. Please tell me how I may be of assistance."

Leleh slowly blinks and says, "Very good. We require a summary of the news of the day. Please have one ready by the ship clock of 1800 this evening. The computer and television screens should be adequate." She begins to walk away.

"Do you have a preferred format or template?"

As she opens the door and turns the corner, she says, "No, whatever you deem best."

This is something they did not prepare me for. In the past, each deployment featured people eager to work with Brendan. Now he must deal with a group where he has no idea whether they really want to work with him or merely pump and dump him. He remembers being told to provide anything unclassified while also attempting to collect everything. He recommits himself to that goal.

He enters his office and sees a laptop marked, "Property of the US Government." *Both Uncle Sam and the Sabia probably are tracking every key stroke on that thing. Work is work, though.* He starts by logging into his unclassified work account. Thankfully, the privileges granted to his account allowed for ordering the exercise equipment. The order note stating, "Will be picked up today via alien spacecraft," is something he never expected to write.

He then turns on his television screen and browses the news for anything of interest, internationally or domestically. Unfortunately, it's not just a slow news day but a dead one. Several hours in, all he has managed are two write-ups. The first is an update about a minor riot in Northern Ireland, the second a summary assessing an upcoming congressional hearing about militias and urban militants. *Maybe I could do a rundown of all the major players in the militia and black front movements?*

"Hey!" a voice calls. "You are still here."

He lifts his head to see Berina smiling at him.

"Do you Terrans not eat?" she asks.

He looks at her, surprised.

"Esfirs and I walked into the cafeteria and asked about you. We were told you had yet to come for a meal. We wondered if you knew how to get to the dining hall, so Esfirs suggested we check up on you. Come on. She's waiting outside."

Brendan locks his screen and gets up to follow her out.

"I found the little lost lamb," the pilot tells the doctor.

"Brendan," Esfirs says, "would you please join us for lunch?"

"I don't think I have much choice given Berina's will, but I won't turn down a meal. Thank you for thinking of me and coming back for me." They all start walking.

"You are most welcome. And thank you for the treat; it is one reserved for only the most special occasions."

"Well, I think making new friends"—he smiles at her, and she smiles back—"is a special occasion. But, say, what do you call that treat? To me, it seemed similar to something we call a Turkish delight."

Esfirs looks down at the floor. "I am sorry, Brendan, but words in our language are classified."

Worth a shot. Looks like I'm going to have to earn my Ws.

She changes the subject. "How is work treating you on your first day?"

"Ugh, let me tell you, it feels like I've been given vague orders with no understanding of what good looks like. Writing summaries while not knowing if they are on topics that interest you is difficult."

"Have you tried using your left hand to see if it is easier?"

Brendan does a double-take. Esfirs holds up her own hand and wiggles it back and forth.

He lets out a short laugh. "My good doctor, I think you just told a joke. Glad to know you have a sense of humor."

"I once heard a human expression—'tic for tat,' I believe it went. You are not the only person here who can tell a joke."

"It's tit-for-tat, a decent attempt at using the expression. As for humor, I've only had short experiences with Berina, but I can already tell she is more than capable with the comedy." Berina smiles. "And by her behavior, I can tell certain attitudes of pilots seem to be truly universal."

"Why?" Berina asks. "Do they think they are all as skilled as me?"

"One day, I will tell you the difference between God and a fighter pilot."

A broad smile spreads across Berina's face as they approach an opening in the wall, revealing a carpeted area with pillows forming several circles on the floor. Brendan follows the two ladies as they pick one of the smaller circles, and all three of them take a pad. Staff members arrive before any words can be said. They place salad bowls, fruit, silverware, glasses, and a water jug near them.

Berina and Esfirs begin to eat. Brendan lowers his head and closes his eyes. He wonders whether this food could accidentally poison him. His thoughts are quickly interrupted by a tap on the shoulder. Opening his eyes, he sees both females looking at him.

Berina asks, "A prayer?"

"Oh, uh-huh." Brendan laughs nervously. "No, I was just, uh, gathering my thoughts."

PATRICK ABBOTT

"Do Catholics pray at meals?"

He nods. "Yes, before they eat."

"But then you would not have had your food. Why would Catholics thank the divine for something you have not been given yet?"

"In Catholicism, it sanctifies the meal and invites God to figuratively join us."

Berina rests her chin in her left hand. "Truly, that is a fascinating thought. What do you think, Esfirs?"

"It is a . . . unique thought. Alien, though. Truly alien."

She's trying to be diplomatic, so I will take that as a win.

Brendan takes a few bites of his salad before Esfirs speaks up. "Brendan, I have a question for you. When we were saying what we thought was goodbye to you in the medical bay, you told me you felt you had no choice but to help Imran even though you were dying. But before that, could you not just have walked away like your law enforcement guard? Why did you get involved?"

Because those thugs started it. Because they murdered a cop. Because it was the right thing to do. "Innocent people needed help." Brendan shakes his head as memories rush back to him. "People need to stop evil. They think they have a choice; so many cower and let evil win. Choosing that route only leads to more people getting hurt. No, I have served all my life. I cannot let evil win. I had no choice because the right way is the only way."

There is silence as Esfirs puts down her fork. "What philosophy do you believe in which causes this thinking?"

"I am the son of Irish emigrants—"

Berina cuts him off. "What are those people like compared to Americans?"

"The Irish are a proud but suffering race of warrior poets."

Esfirs gives Berina a look of annoyance and then beckons Brendan to continue.

"What my parents taught me was to only do the right thing. And what's right can be summed up with the words 'common good.' It's possible for everyone to win, for no one to lose, and peace to occur. When someone favors themselves over all of us, bad things happen, whether to my people or in personal cases."

"In what situations did bad things happen to you?"

Esfirs' question hits him like a ton of bricks. He takes a moment; the past is painful. "I've buried my father, wife, and fellow intelligence officer friends, all because people chose to do evil while good people did nothing." The medical CEOs who took his father and pushed drugs with lethal side effects, the drunk philanderer who seduced his wife then killed her in the drunk driving accident, the terrorists who waited for his friends in the ambush all took from him and made him empty.

A touch stops his racing thoughts. He looks at his shoulder and sees Berina's hand there. She tries to smile, and he nods at her, embarrassed. He glances over at Esfirs and sees her eyes expressing deep pain.

"I am sorry for upsetting you, Brendan. Thank you for saving Imran and Behnaz. I wish more Terrans were like you."

Brendan wipes away a forming tear. "Nah, I am alright," he lies. "It is a true shame this is how we had to meet. But hey, I got two new friends, so that all worked out."

"Yeah," Berina says, "it is really something how it all turned out. I was surprised when the guards told me Imran and Behnaz had demanded you be brought aboard the craft. Then hearing Zalta tried to constrain you as you were giving Imran medical aid while you were dying. I—"

Brendan cuts her off. "Dying?" Then, suddenly, he loses any appetite for food.

Esfirs serenely shuts down the topic. "Your wounds were severe. We can discuss it later."

Nearly dying makes sense. Brendan saw his hand blown away, and the chest wounds had reminded him of the Afghanistan attack. That thought sends a shiver down his spine. His failure. Was the fight in the metro really another loss? *It was. I blinded a person. The cop died, and the black-front thug perished. I nearly died. Maybe I should have died?*

She calls him back, summoning him from a dark place. "Please tell me about the get-together you have planned at your new cabin. We were all excited when you told us of your plans yesterday."

Brendan's heart calms. She really pulled him back from a place where he did not want to be. With a quick gulp of air, he is back in prime form. He asks if they would be interested in games and poetry, both suggestions that receive enthusiastic responses. He takes another bite of his salad and continues to describe his plans.

PATRICK ABBOTT

Six – A Dance of Spies

Brendan hands Leleh his daily report. To be fair, the three paragraphs with assessments are all he has to show for a day's work—a slow news day with an extended lunch break. The basic document has headers for Northern Ireland, the upcoming congressional hearing, and a Canadian by-election in which natural resources being provided to the Sabia is a significant issue. He hopes for a lengthy conversation, a give and take, of his analysis and her thoughts on it. These sorts of dialogues developed into real friendships during his deployments. The tight bonds that formed have so far been lifelong.

Leleh looks over his report, and by the time she puts it down, the silence has become awkward. She thanks him for the "satisfactory work" and says the Sabia look forward to working with him. Brendan gives her a confused look. He tries to ask what she thought about the various pieces, but she attempts to redirect the conversation to his lunch.

Dang it, if an honest plea won't work, it's storytime. Brendan slides a little bit in his chair and assumes a relaxed and open posture to appear more approachable.

"Leleh, may I tell you a story?" She raises an eyebrow but does not respond, which Brendan takes as an invitation to proceed. "One of the reasons I am here is because I had such success working with tribes in Iraq, Syria, and Afghanistan. Also, various other liaisons work in the Arabian Peninsula and Scandinavia. I was well-liked on those missions because I always succeeded. I got the United States what it needed. And I did that by getting what my counterparts needed. Those allies realized I cared about and fulfilled my promises to them. Because they were happy, they worked with me. Everyone won. Whether they were happy Norwegians or skeptical Saudis, they all knew me as the man who would get things done for everyone. Now here, with the Sabia, I have gotten the impression there is tension on both sides. The human diplomatic corps and their Sabia counterparts will smile at each other, but really they do not care for each other."

Leleh's eyes zero in on him, and another headache comes on. "Who told you our alleged perspective on the Terran diplomatic delegates?"

"One"—Brendan holds up his right index finger—"it does not matter who told me what, because, two"—he holds up a second finger—"what matters isn't how we got here, but how we best work to serve everyone's interests. The Sabia requested my services, and government officials were more than happy to send me. So it seems that everyone wanted me here. Knowing my government's objectives gives me clear guidance on my deliverables to them. And I'll tell you, what they want is to know everything possible about the Sabia. The mission's degree of success depends on my personal observations and the Sabia's willingness to tell me things.

PATRICK ABBOTT

All fair. However, the Sabia haven't shared their desires for what they want from me as an intelligence liaison. You, Leleh, can help fix this. Obviously, you don't care for daily news summaries; anyone can do that for you. So what do the Sabia really want from me?"

She chuckles and looks away; his headache disappears. "Your choice of words seeks to separate me from the Sabia. Well played, but too discernable." She sticks her tongue and says, "I hear your appeal, Brendan. So let me separate you from your own. The ambassadors are rude and petty. They always want more for their masters and themselves, despite prior agreements. They only care about what we can give them. Are you different than your political masters?"

Trap. "I trust you're a good observer. You see me asking how I can help the Sabia. You know what I want for my government. How does that differ from what you described?"

"I will answer your question with one of my own: what do you personally desire?"

Brendan sits up. He thinks this demands an honest answer without pretenses. "I want to work for the common good—peace and goodwill for all Terrans and Sabia. I wish to start a process of building trust and friendship and hope that, whether through me or a future liaison, this trust will allow the United States government to learn about the Sabia and the Sabia to gain what they seek. We both know this goal is too important to fail. So please work with me." He sighs.

She blinks once, then again. Silence. He feels her eyes study him.

"My mission right now is to determine whether or not you are trustworthy. We know who you are when alone, but what do you sacrifice when you work for someone else?"

"Thank you for your honesty, truly. That is a start. You're right; you don't know anything about me besides what others have told you. But I look forward to earning your trust."

She puts out her left hand in the same awkward manner Zalta had that morning. Brendan realizes what is going on and smiles, reaching out and shaking Leleh's left hand.

"We are on the right path," she says.

PATRICK ABBOTT

Interlude – Esfirs: The Terran

Every day he has been coming here. There is no liaisoning to be done in the medical bay, yet here he is. Maybe he is bored. Well, regardless of why he is here, he certainly makes sure we are not bored.

"I kid you not," Brendan says, "I kid you not. So, I go to the clinic the next day, and I tell them, 'Hey, you remember that anthrax level one shot you gave me? Well, I think I am having a reaction I shouldn't be having.' Then, I took off my hoodie, revealing my deformed left arm. Where the shot was, I basically had a bright-red ball, an inch in size. Radiating out from there, I had a raised rash the size of my palm. Then there was a non-raised rash from my shoulder down to my fingertips. To top everything off, it all was emitting heat. And"—now Brendan begins to laugh—"guess what the doctor said?"

Probably wanted to conduct some tribal spell to make you well.

"What?" Arasto replies, her full attention on Brendan.

Esfirs looks at the nurse's rapt face. *Remember to remain stoic in front of the Terrans, Arasto. Though . . . this is an amusing story.*

Brendan continues. "The doctor said, 'Eh, are you sick?' So I looked back at the woman and said, 'No, but my arm has morphed. Could there be something wrong with that?' And the doctor just says, 'Nah. Come back in a few days if you feel sick.'" Both Brendan and Arasto laugh.

In the back of the room, Zalta shakes her head while eyeing Esfirs. "Esfirs, why would his arm react that way to the medicine?" The medic stops packing her gear as she awaits an answer.

"Terrans inoculate themselves with weakened diseases to protect against pathogens." Esfirs' voice is as emotionless as a computer's. "The reaction Brendan had demonstrated he probably had been exposed to the disease—this anthrax as he called it—and had a negative reaction to the vaccine."

Gasping, Zalta asks, "Did your condition worsen, Brendan?"

He waves his arm dismissively. "Nah, my body has taken a lickin' and can keep on tickin', as people say. The arm remained its mangled self for a few days; then, things started going back to normal. Never have had a negative experience since."

Arasto makes a sound of disbelief. "Well, Brendan, please consider coming to us versus Terran doctors if you are ever ordered to have more medical treatment. We will make sure you suffer no side effects."

Brendan winks. "Thanks, boss man." The Terran now claps and announces he must be getting back to work. Arasto and Zalta shake his hand as well as they know how to, and as Brendan tells them goodbye, he promises to teach them the greeting. Now, he comes up to Esfirs; not that she minds the company. Approaching her, he places his right hand over his heart and bows while thanking her for the morning conversation.

Ugh, such a waste of a repaired hand. Start using it; you will be surprised by how the nerves have been remapped. "Again, with the right hand, Liaison Officer? I thought part of your job was to impress us, Sabia. Your left hand is an improved model. Why not show that off?"

"You know, Doctor, since we're using titles and not names, I honestly thought about how I could show off my left hand to you, but then after the fiftieth time or so of you mentioning it, I realized it is much funnier to make use of my right hand as much as possible when I'm with you." Brendan gives her a big toothy grin.

After everything, this Terran takes pleasure in teasing me. "Uh-huh, I am sure you spend hours plotting how to taunt me."

"Actually, no." Brendan looks down at the ground as he says that. *Did he think I was serious?* "I do spend hours looking forward to having another conversation with you and Berina, as well as to having everyone over at my cabin when it's ready."

"Hey," he continues, "I always see Zalta and you busy prepping stuff, working on things, or cleaning up. Is there anything I can do to help?"

Is he trying to steal basic medical equipment? "That is quite alright, Brendan. I believe we have it down to a routine. Your help is not required."

79

Brendan's face drops. "That's alright." Brendan scratches his head with his left hand. *Maybe his brain is adapting.* "Hey, I'm having some things delivered from Earth. Is there anything you want? It would be my treat."

Could he . . . "Thank you for the offer, but I must decline."

Letting out a sigh, Brendan nods. "Okay, that's fair. Are you able to do lunch with me today?"

"Yes, I enjoy our meals together."

Now Brendan tilts his head and sucks in the corner of his lower lip. "Would you mind if I came by a little early to pick you up?"

He must not like being alone; he is still talking to me after announcing he had to leave. The poor Terran wants to spend time with someone. But . . . he is talking to me.

What would be the harm? "Sure, Brendan, I would enjoy you coming early very much. Perhaps you can think of something to tease Berina with today." *Let me tell him how I feel about this.* "You doing all that would make me happy."

Brendan smiles warmly and looks her in the eyes. *His eyes . . . such emotion is displayed in his simple joy.* Esfirs makes sure not to telegraph anything she is feeling or thinking. *Such detail in his irises. Indeed, they are creatures of the divine, too.*

Without breaking eye contact, Brendan says, "I really should get going. But . . . umm . . . I will see you soon, Esfirs."

PATRICK ABBOTT
"I look forward to it."

Seven – A Feast Amongst Friends

The party is a success. Or mostly a success. Or a failure. It all depends on one's point of view. Imran, Behnaz, Esfirs, Berina, Zalta, Leleh, Loft, and Gul, the guard from the morning, are all there. However, Loft politely turned down Brendan's invitation for Zand and the other council members to come. They did send a large bowl of strawberries, kiwis, bananas, and oranges, though. *Can't have enough of those.* The tough loss came from his own team. After a three-day boycott of official channels, Paxton reached out to Brendan to tell him to continue to write reports for the Sabia. However, the United States would not provide Brendan with intelligence to share. To make matters worse, to protest how Zand treated Bass, the ambassador would not deal directly with Brendan. The death knell came when Paxton said no one from the American delegation would come to the housewarming party due to Loft being invited. *The common good isn't so common when one side won't show up.*

The Sabia arrive within five minutes of each other, and natural habits take over. They put the chairs in a corner and use the padding to sit on. Brendan is forced to grab pillows from his bed to provide enough seating for everyone, and being an accommodating host, he sits directly on the carpeted floor.

PATRICK ABBOTT

Fresh fruit is passed around like an hors d'oeuvre. After that, conversations begin to flow as everyone starts to mill about. Berina is keen on telling everyone Brendan prays before eating, which becomes a miniature spectacle. Brendan then tries to explain the baseball game that he has on. The aliens' interest in America's pastime lasts forty-five seconds, after which they start asking why the team on defense has the ball and why nothing is happening. Brendan realizes introducing this sport to the Sabia is a fool's errand.

Thankfully one of the many packages Berina and the other pilots picked up is ready to go. Brendan brings it out from his bedroom. The cornhole boards fascinate the Sabia. The women in the monk-like robes and the men in tunics and baggy pants look like the Arcadian shepherds in Nicolas Poussin's *Et in Arcadia ego* painting as they point to the boards and try to figure them out. Once shown how they play several games. Zalta proves to be a natural from the beginning, but Berina becomes a master within a few rounds.

Sure, there's the disappointment of no Zand and her council and the lack of the ambassador. Still, Brendan considers the party a great success in demonstrating his, and therefore America's, openness and friendship.

With the party winding down, Esfirs pulls away from the crowd and approaches Brendan as he watches Berina dominate yet another round.

"Brendan, thank you for inviting me. Tell me, is it what you expected?" she asks.

"You're welcome, doctor. It's a night with friends. What more could I possibly want?"

"Very good. Berina will be on an extended mission for the next few days. Will you be willing to still join me for lunch while she is away?"

The lunches with Esfirs and Berina have been a highlight during his time here. Every day he leaves his desk like clockwork and arrives at the cafeteria just as they take their seats. Berina likes to share her thoughts about places she has flown to, and Esfirs has backed away from pressing questions. Instead, she and Brendan stick to non-threatening matters, such as teasing Berina.

"Of course, I wouldn't want to miss any lunches with you." *Uh oh, that probably came off wrong.*

Esfirs tilts her head and takes a half step toward him. "May I escort you from your office to the cafeteria?" She looks him in the eyes.

"I'd like that," he says. He lets out a long exhale through his nose. A sense of peace at the thought of . . . *Nope. Keep it professional.*

He becomes distracted as the door chimes. He calls for the visitor to enter, and in comes a wide-eyed, thin male Sabia in a gray uniform. The Sabia scans the room and shows signs of relief when Leleh approaches him. He is holding something small in his hand; Brendan cannot quite make out what it is. Leleh motions for the newly arrived Sabia to follow her. Together, the two aliens walk up to Brendan.

"Brendan," the Sabia intelligence liaison says, "a gift for you has finally arrived. This candle is made from

PATRICK ABBOTT

Terran flowers we grow here in our greenhouses. I find the smell pleasant, helping me sleep. Please accept it as a gift from me." Leleh holds it out to him.

"Thank you." He looks at the unlabeled glass jar and inspects it for a few seconds to express gratitude. "I will light it if I ever have trouble falling asleep. Thankfully, I have slept easily while I have been with you all."

More cries of joy sound as Berina wins another round. Brendan hears her pridefully boast about being a natural at gift-giving. He uses the opportunity to ingratiate himself by playfully announcing himself as Team Everyone Against Berina, challenging her to a round of the best of five bags. She accepts and says that, as the challenger, he should go first. Brendan grabs his bags to toss.

Hit. Miss. Miss. Hit. Hit.

"Three in!" he yells as he introduces Gul and Behnaz to the fist bump.

Berina grabs her bags and, with a stone-cold face, tosses her first four. *Hit. Hit. Miss. Miss.* She looks at the hole like an eagle eyeing its prey. Then, with perfect form, she underhand-tosses the bag. *Miss.* Brendan lets out a loud whoop and now fists-bumps Gul, Behnaz, Imran, Zalta, and Loft. He looks over to Leleh and Esfirs. They look back with satisfaction on their faces as he points to them.

"Had to stand up for my team; you were winning too much." He winks at Berina.

"Tomorrow, we choose my athletic challenge in the gym," she says, grinning.

"I don't know if that is a question or demand, but sure."

They both laugh.

"Dear Brendan," Imran says as he approaches, "thank you for a wonderful time. Please excuse me, though. It is getting late."

Brendan embraces Imran and promises to continue to host social events. Then Zalta, Behnaz, Loft, and Gul all bid their farewells. Brendan ponders how to rearrange the room based on Sabia sitting customs when Esfirs calls to him.

"May we stay longer? I am enjoying my time here." Esfirs' words are music to his ears, though he has to make sure not to misread her intentions. It's lonely being a widower.

"Sure, I'm enjoying having guests over. It's been a while since I've had a party at my home."

Berina expresses that she wants to stay too and asks, "Do you have any other games? Or can you only beat a rookie with one game?"

With a salesman's smile, he gestures at what he has to offer. "Madame, can I introduce you to the wonder that is Shut the Box? It is a perfect four-person game which involves short, quick play while presenting ample opportunities for conversation!"

He retrieves the Shut the Box game and demonstrates the dice, how to play, and offers suggestions for strategies. All three Sabia women agree to play. He places the box on the floor, and they all sit around it.

"Well," Brendan begins, "now I am going to have some fun because I will ask questions."

Both Esfirs and Berina look nervously at Leleh, something Brendan notices.

He starts with a simple command to the doctor. "Esfirs, tell me about your family."

She gives Leleh another look, this one tense. Leleh clearly notices.

"Family makeup is a classified topic," she proclaims, unthreatening but firm.

He responds by play-acting as the friendly tribal affairs agent. "Ah, I didn't mean to bring up something that would risk spillage of classified information. Is the fact that Sabia have mothers and fathers classified?" *Assuming what intelligence has been gathered is correct and the Sabia are mammals, this is a naturally obvious question to test their response. Unless they are lizard people, then they'll probably just eat him.*

Leleh's eyes jolt to the left, then right. *She's thinking about how to reply.* "No, we have a mother and father just like Terrans."

Jackpot. "Excellent, then we can have a conversation about that, at least. My father was an engineer who owned his own business constructing houses and office buildings. He was educated in Ireland but decided America had more opportunities for him.

While my mother was growing up, she lived on a farm in Ireland. Her family, however, left because of a conflict there. The family tipped the police off to terrorist activities, so the terrorists started targeting them. Only in Kansas were they far enough away from those thugs. Huh, I guess that's why I've always hated those who prey on the innocent." He lets those words hang in the air a moment before asking no one in particular, "What do your parents do?"

Berina jumps in without looking at Leleh. "My mother was the best pilot ever. And then she taught me." She smiles at her own joke.

Leleh offers a sigh of relief, which Esfirs appears to note.

"My mother is a doctor," Esfirs offers.

Leleh, avoiding her turn, preemptively asks, "Why is your career different from your parents'? Could they only accept your brother and sister?"

So Sabia children must follow in the path of their parents. Sort of an apprenticeship?

Brendan laughs. "No, no." He fights to stay cheerful as the memories try to push their way out. "My siblings are very much like our mother. Tight-knit, bound to the land they love. They live right near home. Mary runs a small farm with her husband, and Bernadette is studying to become a teacher."

Esfirs leans in to inquire, "So why did you move away? You said your siblings were like your mother. How are you different?"

PATRICK ABBOTT

She does have a way of asking powerful questions.
"My dad died when I was young. As much as my siblings
are like my mother, I'm even more like my father. Ah"—
he sighs to mask his pain—"my dad gave me his Irish
spirit, which still has not been satisfied yet."

"Tell me about your Irish spirit. How does it
differ from most Terrans'?"

He looks at the floor and reaches down into his
soul. Then, looking up, he locks eyes with Esfirs and
starts reciting a poem he knows from memory. His eyes
jump to Leleh, Berina, and Esfirs as he speaks in the
soft, almost forgotten accent of his dead father. Each
time he looks at one of the Sabia, he feels like a
headache is coming on.

> Oh, stick me in the old caboose this night of wind and rain,
> And let the doves of fancy loose to bill and coo again.
> I want to feel the pulse of love that warmed the blood like
> wine;
> I want to see the smile above this kind old land of mine.
>
> So come you by your parted ways that wind the wide world
> through,
> And make a ring around the blaze the way we used to do;
> The "fountain" on the sooted crane will sing the old, old
> song
> Of common joys in homely vein forgotten, ah, too long.
>
> The years have turned the rusted key, and time is on the
> jog,
> Yet spend another night with me around the boree log.
>
> Now someone driving through the rain will happen in, I
> bet;
> So fill the fountain up again, and leave the table set.
> For this was ours with pride to say—and all the world defy—

No stranger ever turned away; no neighbor passed us by.

Bedad, he'll have to stay the night; the rain is going to
pour—
So make the rattling windows tight, and close the kitchen
door,
And bring the old lopsided chair, the tattered cushion,
too—
We'll make the stranger happy there, the way we used to
do.

The years have turned the rusted key, and time is on the
jog,
Yet spend another night with me around the boree log.

He'll fill his pipe, and good and well, and all aglow within
We'll hear the news he has to tell, the yarns he has to spin;
Yarns—yes, and super-yarns, forsooth, to set the eyes agog,
And freeze the blood of trusting youth around the boree
log.

Brendan finally turns back to Esfirs and looks into
her brown eyes. This time, rather than a headache, he
feels a sensation of warmth and embrace. He allows it to
consume him as he finishes the poem.

Then stir it up and make it burn; the poker's next to you;
Come, let us poke it all in turn, the way we used to do.
There's many a memory bright and fair will tingle at a
name—
But leave unstirred the embers there we cannot fan to
flame.

For years have turned the rusted key, and time is on the
jog;
Still, spend this fleeting night with me around the boree
log.

He then gently lets the feeling pass through his body. He looks around and sees Leleh and Berina silently observing him. Meanwhile, Esfirs has an expression on her face Brendan cannot interpret.

"That was beautiful," she says, breaking the silence. The others agree.

"Thank you. It is a poem about an Irish man far from home but keeping his memories alive. To me, the poem represents a longing for what has been lost, the value of friendships, poetry, and truly loving one another. It sums up the common good, too. Good can't be just what helps one man or one side. It means nothing if you cannot share. Do the Sabia have similar poems or songs?"

Leleh shuts him down. "While we enjoyed your sharing, we must decline to answer your question. Such cultural matters are classified. I mean no offense."

He sees Berina look down while Esfirs glances over at Leleh. He changes the tone by putting down one of the last Sabia treats he has, offering it as a prize for the champion of the Shut the Box game. Leleh wins the round. She savors her victory by slowly chewing bites of the confection.

With that, Leleh stands up and announces her intention to retire. Brendan follows her out and wishes her a good night. He puts his hand over his heart and gives her a reverential nod. She tries to copy it but then holds out her left hand instead before realizing she should shift to the right. Brendan shakes it. Berina then gets up and reminds Brendan about working out together the next day. Esfirs bids him good night as well. The two women walk to the door, and Brendan starts cleaning up.

"Brendan," Esfirs softly calls.

He turns around to see her looking at him. Only one of her eyes is visible, as her hair has shifted to cover the other. Her lips part slightly, and she sings a few notes of high-pitched music. *Angelic. The first music from another planet a human has heard?* Without another word or action, Esfirs steps out, and the door closes.

Brendan looks at the doorway, considering the extraordinary event that has just occurred. He then makes his way to bed, removes a notebook and pen he has stored beneath the covers, and writes down notes. His left hand stiffens up in pain before unclenching. *It must be old age finally getting to me.*

PATRICK ABBOTT

Eight – Amen

Brendan is standing and talking—or rather, arguing—with Paxton. The heartburn is not making things easier. All weekend the pain has been cycling in and out. Paxton and Bass's games are not helping matters. Paxton spent the morning threatening to pull Brendan from the assignment because he hadn't gotten approval from Bass to have a housewarming party with Sabia. Never mind that Bass had completely ghosted Brendan and had yet to provide any official intelligence documents Brendan could share. He asks Paxton what the point of him being here is if the government won't empower him to do his job. His effort to question the reasoning fails; instead, the out-of-shape desk jockey gives Brendan the fiercest tongue-lashing of his life. Brendan thinks about how one of the enjoyable things about being deployed is being far away from the flagpole. *You can get weirdos there, though. There was that one State Departmenter who would do barefoot yoga . . .*

The rest of the chew-out is a blur as his memories form an automatic distraction shield. Once Paxton is done, Brendan walks back to his desk and monitors the day's events for anything new. Unfortunately, paying attention is proving difficult as the memories are now working against Brendan. Flashes of an embarrassing moment here, a humiliating incident there, all build up to Heather yelling at him, mocking him, bragging about how she told her lover about how Brendan's PTSD trauma prevented him from satisfying her. He squeezes his eyes hard and shakes his head. *Stop. Just stop.* He struggles against his brain, which can be his best ally or worst enemy. He battles himself, trying not to say out loud the dreaded words "I'm sorry." He knows he can't give in to the memories.

Then the new reports icon blinks. Brendan clicks the flashing button on his screen to reveal another nightmare. The social media posts come at him with dreaded hashtags: #Attack, #TerrorInChicago, #LiveShooter, #Hostage, #Sabia. He fights the memories of the incident in the metro as hard as he did the actual assailants on the day he nearly died. The memories are pushed aside by rage. The attackers have taken a Sabia hostage, identified themselves as the "Army of Saint Michael," and have taken over Saint Dymphna parish. A *Chicago Argus* news report states police are setting up a permeator and consulting with the federal government on how to move forward. This sends Brendan into action. He walks past everyone crammed in the Russian delegation office to watch the news coverage passively. Paxton calls out to Brendan, but he just keeps walking.

Brendan looks out the doorway and sees a Sabia guard standing watch.

"Guard. . . I forgot your name, sorry. I need to be taken to Leleh right away. I need to talk to her! I want to help in Chicago, and I think I can be of assistance. I just need to be taken to Leleh," Brendan rambles out.

PATRICK ABBOTT

The guard's eyes widen as he listens to Brendan's urgent histrionics. Placing his arms on Brendan's shoulders, the guard urges the intelligence officer to slow down. This only causes Brendan to speak faster. The guard then forms a giant X with his hands to get Brendan to stop. Getting the message, Brendan quiets down, allowing the guard to press a button on a panel.

"Terran Liaison Brendan is insisting on meeting with Leleh immediately. He claims he can help with the situation in Chicago."

The air crackles and Brendan hears a male voice. "Take him to the council chambers immediately."

The guard instructs Brendan to follow him, and for a second time, he is taken to the council chambers. Brendan passes the security checkpoint and sees the female guard from earlier, Kimya, eyeing him as he is ushered past. The doors open as Kimya approaches, and both she and Brendan enter the council chambers. Unlike last time, though, no one is sitting. Instead, Leleh, Loft, and several Sabia in white body armor stand around Zand. It is evident to Brendan a briefing is going on.

Without waiting, Brendan blurts out, "I can help!"

The Sabia turns to face him. Some are stoic in their expressions, while others appear skeptical. Brendan doesn't care; he is running on adrenaline. He doesn't allow a pause for the Sabia to ask questions nor grant himself the ability to catch his breath.

"The attack, the attackers, I mean—" He inhales deeply because his body forces him to. It hurts. "They're members of a group called the Army of Saint Michael. They're a known anti-government, militant Catholic sect. I know these people. They are resistant to working with other militia groups, and they are highly resistant to dialogue with the government. The police think this is a simple criminal matter. This group, however, is an extremist organization that seeks an audience for violent propaganda. If the police negotiate, they'll give the terrorists a platform, and the terrorists will use that opportunity to kill the hostage. Trust me; I've worked with members of this group before. I know what they want and what they are going to do."

Loft asks suspiciously, "You have worked with these attackers before?"

"Well, not personally. But I've interacted with this group before. They think you're godless and probably demons. They think the police are part of Satan's—the evil one in their religion's—army. Killing evil is not a sin to them. There's no way the police's standard tactics will result in an acceptable outcome. I can help. I can engage them and get whoever is being held out safely."

"Are you not one of the evil one's army to them since you are a government agent?" Leleh asks.

Brendan points to his chest and, with the smile of a bodybuilder who knows he's just won a competition, says, "I'm a baptized Catholic. They're Catholic. I know their beliefs, convictions, and terminology. I can outmaneuver them."

He looks around and notices the Sabia seem, if possible, more stoic than before. The skeptical ones are even less readable to him.

"Look," he pleads, "I can help. Let me help."

"Send him," Zand says. "Prepare a shuttle, and send a medic."

Brendan pumps his chest and lets out a war grunt, something he has not done in years. And it shows. He notices that his ears hurt afterward, and the vibration of the hit causes some discomfort in his left hand. Leleh and the guard escort him out of the room. Then, without saying anything, they take him back down the halls, through the security checkpoint, and into the hangar. Outside the boxcar-like shuttle is Berina.

"Time to fly! Just do not bleed all over my craft again, okay?" she calls out to him.

"I do that one time, and I can never live it down, cornhole girl," he yells back.

Berina and Brendan both laugh as they enter the craft. Zalta is already on board, standing in the middle of a seatless vessel. She looks incredibly nervous.

"No one dies today," Brendan tells her. "You got that, Zalta? No one dies today."

She looks blankly at him and then slowly nods.

He repeats to reassure her, "No one dies today."

Brendan hears the crackling sound and then Berina's voice. "No argument from me on that one."

Brendan squats down and starts to do some exercises to work on the tension skyrocketing in him, and Zalta leans against the wall, dead silent. The lack of motion in the shuttle is odd for Brendan. The disconnect between the rush of the situation and this stillness upsets him and aggravates his tension. *I'll be there soon enough.*

Berina's voice calls his attention back. "Hey, Esfirs says to make sure you keep your left hand safe."

He laughs. "Maybe I should just cut off my left hand and give it to her if she likes it so much!"

Silence.

"She says if you harm that work of art, she will cut your right hand off."

Now both Brendan and Zalta laugh. When it comes to easing tension, humor is always the best medicine.

Suddenly, Berina says, "We have arrived. Brendan, you are up."

Brendan awkwardly walks to the door, hoping it will open as he approaches. Zalta navigates around him and hits a button on a panel. He lifts his head in thanks. Zalta looks at him, confused. *Clearly, that nod means something else, or nothing, to her.*

He hops out and scans the scene. They have landed in a park less than a block away from a large police cordon around a church. A uniformed police officer runs up to him. He introduces himself as Deputy Chief of Police Ryne Delacruz and asks if Brendan is the Sabia representative he was told to expect. Ryne seems non-plussed after Brendan explains he is a Unified Intelligence Commander officer sent to represent the Sabia. Brendan's heartburn comes back as Ryne explains why he thinks the intelligence officer shouldn't be there. Brendan's efforts to move the situation along only result in more pushback from Ryne, which gives Brendan an upset stomach. Then it happens. In the middle of his diatribe, Ryne mentions the attackers claiming to be Franciscans.

Paxton's tongue lashing, Ryne's jerk behavior, the physical sickness, and now these terrorists claiming to be Franciscans is too much for Brendan. A righteous rage and wanting to get away from Ryne inspire Brendan to storm the church solo. He quickly breaks away from the group and purposefully moves toward the parish. A heavily armored cop steps in front of Brendan to stop him, but Brendan shoves him out of the way while barking a loud "No!"

Brendan pulls out his rosary from his pocket as he walks up the steps. His right hand forms a death grip around the beads. Approaching the church, he pushes against the door only to find it will not budge—it pulls outward. This only angers Brendan, so he yanks it open and storms in, giving off a battle cry.

"Franciscans?! You claim to be Franciscans?!" He stands enraged.

There are two people with guns in the middle of the church. They stand in awe and shock for a brief second before pointing their pistols at Brendan.

"We are Franciscans who serve the Army of Saint Michael. Who the hell—" one starts.

Brendan screams as if he were an ancient Pharisee who had just heard horrible blasphemy. "You dare to claim to be followers of the stigmatist?! The seraphic father? The one who preached to all, calling for their conversion? The one whose first rules for the brother of penance prohibited the carrying of arms? You? You who insult the House of God with violence? How many have you killed? Did you ask for their conversion? Or do you only attack like the Muslim hordes? You just leave people with their fate without trying to save them. How dare you? How dare you!"

The insults and pointed questions roll off Brendan's tongue. He is too busy to bother demanding the safety of the out-of-sight Sabia hostage. The verbal assaults that the embassy and the Sabia have directed against him have led to this counterattack. Yet even through his anger as he questions the alleged Franciscans' faith, Brendan ensures his attacks hit the terrorists' center of gravity, mind-gaming the hostage-takers to obtain the desired outcome. Finally, he decides to go for the kill shot. He says the Church does not recognize them as a Franciscan order, making them no different from "Protestants." That hits the terrorists right where Brendan wants it to. They look at each other and lower their guns.

This epic stand has released the Brendan known in seminary for being a fiery preacher. Mentally, he towers above the two terrorists, looking down on them as a god would look down on sinners caught in the act.

Then, Brendan takes two steps forward and puffs out his chest. "My name is Brendan Sean Murphy, and I am once and forever a deacon by the grace of God! Through the powers of my holy orders, given to me by Archbishop Roberto Gomez himself, I demand you hand over your hostage. Whether or not you soil this church with your blood is on your soul, but you have no right to take the hostage's life here."

The two attackers just stand dumbfounded.

"The hostage! Now!" barks Brendan.

"In . . . in the con-confessional," one of the attackers stutters.

Brendan points at the two attackers and then at the pews, instructing them to take a seat, which they do. He then calls out, "Hostage! I am Brendan Sean Murphy. I am going to get you out of here. Exit the booth now and come to me."

The confessional door opens slowly, and a woman with a bloody face comes out. The Sabia looks to be around fifty years old and has a deer-in-the-headlights look. She takes a few steps and then stops.

"Come with me," Brendan simply says. As Brendan walks up and begins to wrap his arm around her, he must momentarily stop because his shoulder begins to throb. Then, as he embraces her, he turns around and addresses the two attackers. "Go into the confessional now."

As the two make their way to the confessional, Brendan takes the Sabia's hand and walks her out of the church. He opens the door and is the first to step out. The police just look at Brendan and the hostage. A human medic runs up, but Brendan tells him the Sabia have their own physician on the shuttlecraft. Next, he yells at Ryne, telling him both attackers are in the confessional. The police storm the church as Brendan gets the woman onto the craft.

As soon he is aboard, the door automatically closes. *Why now and not when I wanted it to open?* Zalta inspects the former hostage while Brendan sits down on his rear, rubbing his temples.

"Brendan, you look pale," Zalta says to him.

"Just take care of the hostage. She's wounded. I'll be fine."

Brendan closes his eyes. He hears Zalta walk over and feels her hand on his forehead. "I . . . I just need to calm down," he whispers.

He instinctively starts moving the beads of his rosary. His migraine is now tremendously painful, and a sharp ache surges to prominence in his chest. Everything is overwhelming him in a way he has never experienced before.

He hears Zalta speaking some nonsense. "*Kvedbaischvenze!*"

He begins to feel weightless and numb. He hears frantic voices making sounds. Sobbing. Then nothing. He feels cold.

Nine – A New Creation

At first, it's just flashes of light. Then the light becomes meaningless images. Then, quickly, they transform into memories.

Brendan is leading the Arab tribals across the bridge in Syria.

He and his father are at a minor league baseball game.

Heather says, "I do" during their wedding ceremony.

Malcolm tells him Heather is cheating on him.

Alexandra tells him he is no longer welcome in the family home while Mary and Bernadette look on without uttering a word.

A colonel is giving Malcolm and Brendan crowns while the Unified Intelligence Command team jokingly hails them as kings of Syria.

News reports cover the Sabia's arrival on Earth. The vision flashes forward to the night the Sabia flew over Washington, DC. Several people at the pub were already spouting conspiracy theories. Brendan pulled rank to shut them up before they became unruly.

The mental movie then goes back to where it always does: Afghanistan. He is on his back. His blood is pooling on his chest as he stares at the sky. *But I don't want to die yet. I want to hear Esfirs sing some more.* It is a weird thought, he knows.

His eyes open to reveal a white ceiling. It looks familiar. Slowly his brain registers he is back in the Sabia medical ward. It sends signals to his muscles to get his body up but merely causes weak, barely registrable squirming. The pain from his failed attempt at rising causes him to moan.

"Ashidar, he has awakened," Brendan hears Zalta's voice say.

Zalta walks into Brendan's field of vision. There is an immense expression of worry on her face. Brendan tries moving again, but she puts her hands on his shoulders and pushes him down. Next, he tries to sit up, but she presses down even harder. Finally, he gives up and lets loose something between a sigh and a moan. Zalta looks him in the eyes, which helps ease the sensations of pain flowing through his body.

"You are safe now. Just rest. We will protect you," Zalta declares.

Brendan does not respond. The last bit confuses him. His head is still swimming from . . . whatever. He closes his eyes just to rest them.

"Brendan, are you still awake?" a voice asks.

Brendan opens his eyes and sees a male looking down on him as Zalta walks out of view.

PATRICK ABBOTT

"Yeah, just resting my eyes," Brendan responds to the person he assumes is Ashidar.

"Brendan, I am Ashidar, I am a doctor. Do you know what day it is?"

Brendan considers and then replies, "When I got the hostage out of the church, it was the fifteenth."

The doctor's eyes widen in fear, and he hurriedly asks someone out of view. "How long was he without oxygen?"

Something in Brendan wants to clarify, so he adds, "Well, if you meant the day of the week, then it should be Tuesday."

Ashidar sighs in relief.

This annoys Brendan. *Confusing day and date is hardly a reason to freak out, Doc.*

The doctor steps out of sight. Rather than stare at the ceiling, he closes his eyes. He starts experiencing motion sickness—feelings of sudden starts, stops, and lateral movements. Up and down, his stomach goes, despite him knowing he's not actually moving. He grabs on tightly to the sides of the bed. The idea of holding on helps nullify some of the pain as his nerves battle the various sensations.

The door makes a sound, causing Brendan to open his eyes again. This time he does not try to sit up. Paxton walks into view now, sweaty as always. This time he looks utterly unsure of himself. *At least now he won't yell at me.* Brendan realizes Paxton has two guards beside him, and Loft is barely visible. Loft looks at

Brendan and then sternly at Paxton. Paxton looks back timidly, unable to break away.

"Hey, Brendan—Intelligence Officer Sean—Brendan Sean Murphy. I am here to notify you that you are under arrest. You are to remain in the Sabia's custody until formally transferred to a United States authority."

Loft says, with harsh hostility in his voice, "Your duty is complete. Now get off our ship and never return."

Paxton backs away without even looking at Brendan. None of this makes sense to him. He tries to address Loft but can only cough.

"Brendan, you must rest now. You still are not well. More will be explained to you later."

Loft then shifts his gaze. Suddenly Zalta reappears with her hands extended, the left one wearing the glove with the glowing fingertips. She gently touches it to the left side of his face. Brendan faints the moment she makes contact with his cheek.

The process repeats—at first, just flashes of light. Then the meaningless images. Then, like before, they transform into memories. This time they are all painful ones. Starting as mere embarrassing reminiscences, they transform into the most tragic moments of Brendan's life.

Hearing about his father's death.

His mother refusing to say she loves him.

Driving through burned-out villages in what his government called an "unqualified victory."

PATRICK ABBOTT

Tribal elders are sitting around him. He berates them while holding pictures of elementary students. "Why did she have to die? Why did he have to die? What did he do to deserve to die? What did she do that warranted you all letting killers build a bomb in your village?"

The memories, as always, settle on the events immediately following the suicide bomber blast in Afghanistan. The blood is now being coughed out. *But I wanted to hear Esfirs sing just one more time. Please, just give me that.* He feels the sensation of dying. *I want to hear Esfirs again.*

His eyes open, and he realizes he is still on the medical bed. A quick self-diagnostic reveals he has regains some energy. He breathes deeply and swings his legs to prop himself up on the bed. *Not too shabby.* He slowly moves to put his feet on the ground, but Zalta comes into his blurry view and puts her hands on his shoulders.

"Stop," she instructs. "Just stop moving until we tell you it is safe for you to be up."

"Zalta," Brendan says surprisingly hoarsely, "no one died today?" He says it not so much as a declaration of victory but as a question.

"No one died, correct," she says. Her face betrays a pain, though.

The strange memory of Paxton appears in his head. Did he really say Brendan was under arrest? Did he give a reason? Was it just a bad dream? Brendan needs to straighten that out.

107

"Where is Esfirs?" he asks instead. He does not even think about what he is saying; it is more the soul talking than the mind.

Zalta looks away as she holds him. He scans the room for anyone else and can make out some guards, but none of them move. Brendan tries to look at Zalta, but she moves her head to avoid his gaze.

The door opens, and this time Leleh comes in. She is wearing some kind of gray coat, which makes her look vaguely militaristic. She stops at the door, allowing Brendan's eyes to focus on her. She looks pained. Brendan calls out to her in a gravelly voice, but she does not move.

"I don't understand"—Brendan finally breaks the silence—"what's happening?"

Leleh slowly walks up to him. "Sarha is safe; law enforcement captured the terrorists peacefully without loss of life. You helped. You did what you told us you were going to do, and you did it according to your own code. Everyone truly got the good you told us you desire. We cannot thank you enough for what you have done for us a second time."

He has to fight through the mental fog. "But Paxton. He said I was under arrest and—"

"Nominally, the reason is that you 'conducted an unauthorized operation for a foreign power on United States soil.'" She pauses. Her voice becomes more uncertain. "When you first came to us, your hand was maimed, and you received multiple chest wounds. The damage was from shrapnel, some of which shredded the lower quarter of your heart. You were dying. Esfirs noticed the damage. She received permission to enter your chest cavity, temporarily remove your heart, and use our biotechnology to rebuild it." Another pause. Now every word is cautiously measured. "The biotechnology uses Sabia genetic material. In all previous cases, the cells have slowly been replaced with natural Terran cells. In your case, however . . . the Sabia cells have resisted and instead are progressively assimilating your cells, creating a hybridization effect. You are becoming a mostly Sabia creature."

Brendan begins to shake.

"The American government," Leleh continues, "seeks to seize you for biological testing. Do not have any fear; we will not allow that. You carry Sabia cells and blood within you; we will not betray you."

Zalta tries to get Brendan to lie back down. "This is obviously a lot. Why not rest some more, and we will answer any questions you may have later?"

Brendan shakes her off. "I am an officer of the United States of America Unified Intelligence Command. I was born in Abilene, Kansas . . ."

Panic is setting in. The world begins to spin. Brendan stands up, then a violent cough arises, forcing him to his seat again. Zalta pleads for him to lie down while Leleh adopts a stoic stance. Zalta again places her hands on his shoulders, but he pushes her off with his right arm. She backs away while the guards take a step forward. Leleh raises a hand, causing them to stop.

"I am Brendan Sean Murphy, son of Joseph Martin Murphy, and I am an officer in the United States of America Unified Intelligence Command." It starts as a defiant statement but ends up a near plea.

The door opens, and Esfirs comes running in. Her devastated-looking eyes lock on to his. A wave of dark depression overwhelms Brendan. He places his face in his hands and cries.

Ten – Job Weeps

Brendan is lying in bed. His face turned toward the wall. It has been three days since he found out about the . . . the . . . cancer inside him. Time both flies by and stands still. Awake, asleep, neither and both at the same time. Loft and Leleh visit him separately every day. Brendan either cannot listen or chooses not to; not even he knows which one it is. Those sessions don't bother him nearly as much as Zalta's daily visits. The medic asks if he will eat or drink anything. He stays motionless, his back to her. Then, with a sympathetic voice, she begs him to have some of the food she brought. When he doesn't, she tells him the injection will hurt on an empty stomach. Not only does it hurt, it burns as well. She apologizes. This causes him to do some soul-searching. He regrets violently pushing her, but grief for himself overpowers any desire to apologize to her. Ultimately, he is stuck in a mental prison. All he can do is cry even after the burning pain subsides. She then tells him she is sorry for causing the pain. She sits with him for a while, watching over him. He knows it is friendship, but he is powerless against his intrinsically disordered mind. She leaves, saying goodbye, and the cycle repeats the next day.

Memories come to torment him, as well. Islamic State massacred children's bodies looking at Brendan with their death stares. The colonel who laughs when told the locals refer to him as a butcher. Brendan's mother telling him she doesn't understand how he can be her son. The friends who ask him why he hasn't visited Kansas in over nine years. The Afghan Taliban peace envoy who has a suicide bomb under his clothing, ready to—

He hears the door open. *And so it begins again. It must be morning now, so Loft will—*

"Hey, Brendan, guess where I was?" Berina's voice sounds carefree and throws Brendan's dour mood into jarring discombobulation.

Brendan does not respond. All of a sudden, his view bounces as the mattress does. Berina must have jumped on the bed. She leans over him, holding out her hand so he can see it. She has something in her closed fist. Brendan notices her gray leather flight suit doesn't quite smell like leather. *Some Sabia animal skin? Synthetic?*

Her hand opens up, revealing a white rock. "Cottonwood limestone from Fort Riley, Kansas. Close to your home, yes?" She slowly rotates it in her hand. Brendan's eyes are transfixed on the rock. It reminds him of home in a good way. "Tell you what, I will give you this rock if you answer a question about your religion."

He moves his head slightly to see her in his peripheral vision. She looks happy as if she were completely oblivious to his pain. So different from the stoic appearance the other Sabia have repeatedly put on when dealing with him.

"Deal?" she asks.

"Okay." He surprises himself with the response. Maybe it's the desire for what the rock represents.

"In what circumstances does your god allow for suicide?" There is a smirk on her face as she waits for his reply.

"Suicide is a forbidden thing, a sin, and is therefore never allowed."

She claps her hands and flips the rock at him, causing it to land next to his face. "Amazing! I read some of your religious passages, and they say the same thing! So, do the logical thing by appeasing your god and drink this water I have for you."

As Brendan shifts to lie on his back, he sees her pour water from a carafe into a cup.

Berina continues. "Maybe if you behave, I will tell them you ate something. That way, Zalta will not have to come in here to give you another injection."

That last bit is enough to convince Brendan to drink what she offers him. The ice-cold water feels refreshing as it flows down his throat.

Imitating the other Sabia, she triumphantly says, "Oh, we have been trying, Berina, but he will not respond to anything." She repositions herself so she is sitting on the floor, causing Brendan to shift his back to the wall so he can see her better. "All it took was one minute, a rock, and a question. Oh, and me. You should put me in for an award."

Brendan laughs briefly but then has to fight his mind. His thoughts try to shut him down. He manages to get out, "I don't understand what is happening."

"You and us both," Berina says in a suddenly sad and sympathetic voice. "There was such panic when we found out about the hybridization. Your ambassador attempted to steal you while you were unconscious. Thankfully one of the guards realized and stopped it. We still cannot understand why they would risk your life to do that. Let me tell you something we know for sure—you will risk yourself to save our lives. You will always have our friendship for that. And we will never, ever let anyone harm you."

"Thank you," he says meekly.

"We will protect you always. The behavior you have shown as a person transcends any officer role in the—the—um . . . whatever, showing the universe who you really are. What is happening to your cells will never affect that. So never forget who you are, Brendan."

A long silence allows the words to settle in his mind. Her seeming care for him is indeed a comfort. Part of him wonders if there is a psychological intelligence operation regarding the ambassador, but her other words appear genuine. He breathes and clears his head for a minute.

"May Esfirs come here to visit you?" Berina's words disturb his once growing calm. "She is so scared, thinking you never want to see her again. I told her you would see her, but she would not enter unless you gave your approval.

The strange death thoughts of wanting to hear her voice again clash violently with his mighty rage at what the Sabia's biotechnology has done to him. *She is the one who used it! She hurt me!* His heart races while his breathing becomes more rapid and shallow. His mind plays and replays Leleh's words about the hybridization and Esfirs' singing at the same time.

Berina leans over and places her hand firmly on his shoulder. She gives it a hard squeeze.

"Calm, Brendan, calm." She sits in silence for a minute without loosening her grip, making his breathing more stable. "Just give me a nod, and I will call her in."

Part of his mind tries to delay and distract. "You are trying to use persuasion skills against me."

"So far, the main persuasion skills I have seen you use are beating up people who have knives, yelling at people with guns, and somehow repeatedly finding ways to nearly die only to rebound."

He stares at her. *That's not fair. I have established relationships with you all.*

"Meanwhile," she continues, "I have demonstrated life-saving piloting skills, play an excellent cornhole game, and can even get once suicidal hunger-strikers to laugh."

Brendan laughs again.

"So, wave your hand to signify it is okay for her to come in. And if you do not want her here, still wave your hand to signify I can call her in; otherwise, I will keep bugging you about it."

Again he chuckles, despite the overall melancholy. The brief moment of lightness allows him to control his hand and wave it. Berina looks over her shoulder and yells Esfirs' name. Brendan can hear the cabin door open. Berina calls his friend over.

He closes his eyes. *I just want this to pass. Why won't it pass?* He senses someone sit next to him and then feels a hand stroking his arm. He looks up to see Esfirs. Her eyes still have the same devastated look they did in the medical bay.

He is at a loss for words but forces out, "What's happening to me?"

"Cellular hybridization. You are not becoming a Sabia, but you are not remaining Terran," she replies.

"Why? How did this happen?"

She closes her eyes and breathes deeply. "Your heart, it beat its last when I held it. We had never used biotechnology on a heart before; no tests were ever done. I assumed it would be like just another limb or organ regrowth. I had heard how you fought for Behnaz and Imran. It made me think you were a life worthy of extraordinary efforts to save. With my tools, I rebuilt your heart, placed it back inside you, restarted it, and healed the rest of your body. We thought it was successful and that your body would simply replace the Sabia cells. I am so sorry, Brendan."

PATRICK ABBOTT

"Is it reversible?"

She makes a *tsk* noise. "Your body was trying to grow human cells over the new hybrid cells. It was killing itself to prevent the change. Our medicine can ease the transformation and stop your body from killing you. This means the hybridization will continue until it is complete."

Brendan rolls onto his back. He stares straight at the ceiling. "I should have died."

"But you did not," Berina says resolutely. "You nearly died saving two Sabia, but you survived. Why? Because maybe the divine, your god, whatever supernatural force you want to call it, desired you to live. Your living allowed you to save a life in Chicago. And then you nearly died again, but you live now. Do you know what that means?"

The question resonates with Brendan. He looks up again, thinking and worrying about his future. Esfirs calls to him, but he ignores her.

Interlude – Bass: Defeated

Ambassador Bass and Delegate Loft are sitting across from each other at a large conference table. The American diplomat fidgets nervously while the Sabia delegate is relaxed in his chair, rocking gently. Behind Bass are two marines in complete battle kits, while Loft is accompanied by two towering guards in baggy white costumes that make them look like Italian Renaissance painters. Bass studies them; both the male and female are physically imposing. He ponders each culture's attempts to portray force.

Bass begins. "Intelligence Officer Murphy is a United States citizen and an officer in the United States Department of Defense. He has been recalled from his liaison duties and is under arrest. He belongs to us."

"Liaison Brendan has served us incredibly well. He peacefully ended a hostage situation resulting from a terrorist attack you allowed. He advised us on the situation, and we utilized his skills to both the Sabia's and your benefit. Your reasoning behind arresting him is beyond our understanding, but it is your own, so we do not question your motivations. Thankfully, you realized some error and allowed us to keep him in our custody instead of seizing someone we consider a hero."

PATRICK ABBOTT

Bass winces, remembering the near threats from Loft. The ambassador is in a tricky spot. Washington told him to tell the Sabia that Brendan has gone rogue. In reality, they want to run medical tests on him. That officer is a walking, talking petri dish of biomedical knowledge and possible future weapons. The Sabia almost certainly know this, but they are playing dumb for now.

The diplomat decides to press his case. "He is one of ours, and when something belongs to the United States and is being held by someone else, we know there are many options to rectify the situation.

Loft sneers. "That sounds like a threat.

"Of course not! We are friends, and friends do not threaten each other."

"Good, because we recognize a strong friendship with the United States. We appreciate you allowing us access to resources we could easily get elsewhere in exchange for our aid and technology. The ambassadors from the People's Republic of China and the Russian Federation have frequently mentioned the truth of that to me. However"—Loft turns in his chair, slightly away from Bass—"we Sabia do not play Terran powers against each other, and we respect the United States for being such a great friend, to the point of loaning us Brendan.

"This was a productive discussion, ambassador. Perhaps, we can continue it tomorrow. Please bring some proposals we would entertain. Good day."

Loft stands up and walks out of the room with his guards. Bass sits in silence while the two marines glance at each other.

PATRICK ABBOTT

Eleven – First Steps

From his bed, Brendan watches, impressed, as Berina goes into minute three of a plank. Her visits have been a highlight of his day—everything from her positive attitude to her gently pressing him to do more. He drinks plenty of water, has good conversations with her, and avoids thinking about the hybridization.

"So how does the son of a teacher become a hereditary monarch of a foreign country?" Berina pops up to do a burpee-like stretch before going down to a plank.

Brendan smiles—he realizes he has been smiling more often when she visits. "We were not real monarchs. Malcolm and I just called ourselves kings. It started as a joke between us, then a joke amongst our intelligence cohort. Then it became a widespread joke with others claiming monarch status where they worked."

She shifts to yoga-like poses. The mix of what is clearly an Earth-created routine and things that look odd to Brendan makes him wonder about the greater mysteries of the Sabia. *How did they learn to speak Earth languages so well and so much about our customs?* However, he has been banned from asking questions during Berina's visits, and each time has been told, "The answer is classified," and, "You can only ask questions when you stop dying on my shuttlecraft." Plus, there is no one to report to even if he could get answers. His government has tried to have him arrested since the hybridization . . .

"Hey!" she snaps, "you owe me an answer!"

Brendan looks at her as if suddenly awoken from a dream. "I'm sorry. What was the question?"

She rolls her eyes. "What did the Syrians think about you declaring yourselves their kings?"

"They knew it was a joke. The tribes I was working with were happy with us giving them weapons and chasing out foreign terrorists. But, most importantly to them, we were also working to make sure no occupying force was coming into their homelands. Let me tell you; my country thinks wherever we go, we will be viewed as liberators. What we don't realize is that most others view us as occupiers. It was an uphill battle fighting terrorists while also ensuring our own big military stayed out. Malcolm McAndrews and I truly made a difference over there." He pauses to reflect. "He was a great friend."

"Was? What happened?"

"General Javier Cadiz Meade happened. I went to Afghanistan while Malcolm fell under his sway. Meade saw things much as I did; the once-great meritocracy was becoming tribalized, with elites excluding the masses. However, instead of working for the common good or restoring what America was, he wanted to remake it into what he calls an 'efficient system.' It is not a good philosophy but a materialistic one that seeks order at the cost of dignity. But he grows more popular every day as the other side riots, trying to remake America into a tribal hierarchy, which they claim will bring justice. Instead, they'll tear everyone apart, just like everywhere I deployed to."

She ponders his words, obviously getting new insight into domestic Earth politics. "Have you tried reasoning with your friend?"

"I did. Then I ruined everything in Afghanistan. I thought I was so close to getting a deal with the enemy that I got sloppy and cut corners to meet with the other side. The representative they sent to talk to us was actually a suicide bomber. He killed two Americans, and I took blast damage to the chest. I was bleeding out, but the medics focused on me rather than the other two. They died while I lived. They died because of me. Nothing was the same after that day; everything became worse."

"If you had died that day, no one would have saved Behnaz and Imran. Nor could anyone have handled Chicago as you did. You are alive for a reason, Brendan. You keep coming back. Do not discount what the future has in store for you." She stands up. "Thank you for being you. You are a person who will risk himself for peace and will suffer to do the right thing. Before you met us, you were that person, and you are still that person."

The words echo in his soul.

"Same time tomorrow?" she asks.

"Please." His response is a hidden plea for a healing friendship.

Berina starts for the door and then stops. She turns to Brendan, "Want to go on a walk tomorrow?"

His post-traumatic stress surges in response to the question. Brendan has not left his room in the six days since he came back from medical. He has yet to even shave.

"I don't think I'm ready. I may need a couple of days to get ready to leave my cabin."

"Come on," Berina says with a tone of frustration.

She grabs him by the arm, pulls him off the bed, marches him from the bedroom into the living room, presses a button to open the door, and tosses him outside. The guard stationed by the entrance looks at Brendan in surprise. Berina walks out.

"Now, a walk outside your room is no big deal. I will see you same time tomorrow!"

PATRICK ABBOTT

Twelve - Reconciliation

Brendan ponders the last few days as he sits on the floor. Berina's strength, the injections that apparently keep him from going hungry or thirsty, his musings on the Sabia's language skills, the questions, the stonewalling when he wants answers, visits from Berina but not from the ambassador, the hybridization—all of it runs through his head. He has never been more confused in his life. *This is definitely the worst place to be confounded; at least when my marriage ended, I was home. All of this is increasingly making me suspect an influence operation. Are they influencing me? Or are these honest attempts at friendship?*

A sound causes him to look up. Berina walks into the bedroom. She wears a tunic with a complex geometric pattern—red on a white background—which causes Brendan to raise an eyebrow.

"Classified," she states as if she can guess what he is about to ask. "Plus, you are not allowed to ask questions until you stop dying on my ship, remember? Now, are you ready for the walk outside?"

He acknowledges and stands up. His heart begins to race as he walks toward the door. Each step feels heavier and heavier while his vision becomes narrower and narrower. Berina says something which he hears, but his brain does not comprehend. Together they step outside, which lifts his anxiety. He feels lighter, free. His breath steadies. A kind of happiness descends on him, chasing away the melancholy. *Thank you, God, for friends.* It is the first honest prayer from his heart in years. He ponders where the feeling came from as they walk down the hallways together. Two Sabia, a male and female, holding hands are about to cross their path when Brendan stops and addresses one of them.

"Excuse me, sir, but I've seen you before. You have served food to my friends and me in the cafeteria several times. I'm sorry, but I've never gotten your name."

"Oh," the male Sabia says, "my name is Kavian. I am not surprised you do not know it. I just serve in the cafeteria. I am no one interesting."

"You know, I have been all over Earth and met many humans and Sabia, and not a single one was uninteresting. That makes you really interesting."

Kavian looks bashful and waves dismissively.

"I bet she thinks you are pretty interesting," Brendan continues, nodding to his companion.

Kavian nervously smiles before the woman takes the initiative. "Greetings, I am Giti." She holds out her left hand in a stiff, awkward style.

Clearly, the handshake is not a thing wherever they are from. Brendan places his right hand over his heart and bows. "A pleasure, ma'am. Keep taking care of

Kavian; he is the most interesting uninteresting person in the universe."

Kavian laughs while Giti awkwardly tries to copy his gesture. "Why did you do that rather than shake my hand?" Her voice betrays a hunger for knowledge.

"The handshake normally is done with the right hand. However, I didn't want to be rude by telling you that, so I instead gave a very formal greeting."

Giti throws her right arm straight out toward Brendan. She does not grip or shake well, but Brendan is happy to teach her the proper procedure.

"Excellent," he offers, "you are a quick learner. And hey, if you or Kavian ever want to know about Earth customs, just let me know. Happy to be of help."

"We will," Giti replies. "How is your time with us?"

Without missing a beat, he answers, "Many challenges, but I think I'm making a difference. That's what counts, right?"

"A life well-lived is one that makes a positive contribution to the universe. May you continue to do well."

Giti and Kavian have giant smiles and offer handshakes before they all part ways. Brendan responds by wishing them well.

Berina is incredulous. "What was that?"

"What?"

"You looked like a person walking to their death on the battlefield when you left your cabin. But then, suddenly, you see some random Sabia. Without a moment's pause, you are joking with them, conducting a cultural exchange, and talking about something other than that you are undergoing an existential crisis."

Brendan looks down, the depression surging back. "It is an anxiety coping mechanism. I don't like to show my depression. I realized people like happy interactions, so I provide what they like. This way, I am not a burden to others."

"Does it help you heal?"

"Not really, no."

"Then stop it!" she snaps while pointing her index finger at him. "Focus on actual healing, not failed methods."

Berina starts walking again, and Brendan follows her. Silence dominates as they go down the empty corridor.

He turns to her. "I know you said I am not allowed to ask questions, but . . . is Esfirs well?"

"I like that question. What makes you ask?"

Open-ended questions to get me to talk more. "I miss her. She saved my life, and . . . part of me hates her because of what is happening to me. I pretty much stonewalled her when you brought her to visit. I hate myself for that. But, hell, I don't know what to do. I just— I just hope she is well." He walks on in silence. "Can I tell you something you promise not to tell anyone else?"

"Yes." Her reply is emotionless.

"She sang to me. The night of the party at my cabin. Whatever she sang was so beautiful it practically haunts me. When I was having . . . whatever you want to call my medical emergency, I . . . did not want to die because I wanted to hear her sing to me again. And it kills me that I've been a horrible friend to her since then."

"What does being a horrible friend mean to you?"

"I understand you like getting me to do soul-searching, but could you please answer the question? Is Esfirs well?"

"You think you can dictate the terms of this conversation?"

A passion grows inside him. "Look, she is a friend to both—well, I know she is a friend to you, and she has only ever been kind to me, despite what I've done recently. It's not right for you to avoid my question. I've been in the wrong lately, despite the past week giving me some reason. However, there is no reason for you to withhold how she is doing."

"And in exchange for her status, what do I get in return?"

He takes a deep breath to calm his now raging emotions. "I am in exile from my own government, my own people, for fear of arrest. I live here at what I assume is your leader's whim. You already have my friendship—it's literally all I can offer you. So I ask you,

129

pray, tell me if she is well. She never has to see me again. I just hope she is well."

Berina laughs, then smiles. "Brendan, I would have told you regardless of your response. It was only my intention to have you break through your emotional shell. I wanted passion, not an 'anxiety coping mechanism.' She misses you too. She feels your anger and worries she has lost your friendship forever. Let me take you to medical. There, you can heal all wounds. Your friendship will be so much better for it."

"Thank you." His voice breaks as he speaks the words.

"Just be yourself—passionate, friendly, not putting up a false front." She looks at him sternly for a moment. "You have shown emotions before when talking about your past. When you talk to her, show and tell the truth."

It is a lot for Brendan to take in. Since Heather and that horrible day in Afghanistan, he has been living with facades that protect him. At least he thought they were safeguarding him. *Instead, maybe they just prolonged the pain.*

They continue walking. Berina brings up the exercise routine she has started and describes what she will do tomorrow. Brendan wonders if being a pilot created this attitude where she can just declare things to be or if she was always that way. *Humans and Sabia are similar in that regard. I wonder just how deep those similarities are?*

The duo reaches the medical center. Berina motions to indicate Brendan should go first. He enters the room. Esfirs is looking at a digital tablet when she sees him. Her eyes widen with surprise while he is a combination of too afraid, ashamed, and angry to say anything.

Berina walks in to address Esfirs. "You have some time, but be ready and do not make the others wait." The pilot holds up four fingers with her palm facing out, then raises them. *What the heck is that?* Esfirs acknowledges. Berina is about to leave when she turns around and looks at Brendan. "Remember tomorrow morning. Bright and early, so you have plenty of time in the gym before you get to work." She laughs as she leaves.

"I think she had all this arranged from the beginning," he says as an aside.

"She does enjoy commanding people."

Brendan puts his hand on his forehead and then runs it through his hair. "Look, I—I'm sorry, let me begin again, please." His mouth dries. "I have been—No. I have treated you unfairly. In my pain, I projected strong anger toward you. You only did what a doctor should do: try to save my life. And you succeeded. What happened afterward was beyond your control. I'm sorry for giving you the silent treatment when you visited me, and most of all, I'm sorry for being angry at you."

"I never meant to cause the hybridization." Sadness echoes in her voice.

"I know."

They look awkwardly at each other.

"I am sorry," he says, "I understand if you never want to deal with me again. I managed to mess up this liaison job, eh? It's just . . . I want to thank you for the time at the end of the party in my cabin. That memory got me through the sickness. I didn't want to die because I wanted to hear you sing one last time."

"When you were convulsing on the table, I thought I would never hear you recite another poem."

Again, they look at each other, this time making eye contact. Gazing into her brown eyes feels like looking into deep pools of water.

"May we go to your cabin, Brendan?"

"Of course," he says, almost in a trance.

Together they walk toward his cabin.

"So," he clumsily begins, "what have you been up to these last few days?"

"The details of the last few days are classified."

Brendan nods while looking down. A new guard is watching the door. He does not acknowledge the doctor and the human intelligence liaison as they enter the cabin. The door slides closed. Esfirs walks into the now chair-less living room—Brendan having adopted the local custom—and sits on the carpet. Brendan follows suit.

"Recite another poem for me," she instructs him.

Brendan closes his eyes. An adapted classic from William Butler Yates seems appropriate for a moment like this.

PATRICK ABBOTT

> Sickness brought me this
> Thought, in that scale of hers:
> Why should I be dismayed
> Though flame had burned the whole
> World, as it were a coal,
> Now I have seen it weighed
> Against a soul?

She looks at him intensely and places her hand on his arm. Their eyes lock again, and a pleasant, engulfing warmth flows over him. Before he realizes it, she is singing to him again, what sounds like a long verse of lyricless notes. Her music sounds even better than he remembered. He longs to know anything and everything about her. However, it was a struggle to learn about her mother's career, and he doesn't dare ruin the present moment.

"I like games," she says spontaneously. "My mother would play many games with me when I was young. We also enjoyed long walks in nature together, collecting various types of rocks. I can do neither of those with her now. Your games are enjoyable, as your poetry." She smiles at him.

He smiles back and gently puts his hand on her still outstretched arm. She slowly withdraws it.

"May we play the box game, as we did at the party?" she asks.

He jumps up and runs over to the wall, where he propped up the board and dice. Running back, he places them on the floor and quickly sets up the board. Their conversation flows naturally, moving back and forth like waves as they begin. During their playtime, which Brendan loses track of, he describes his father's death as his breaking point from his family, his deployments as a means of seeking self-value, and talks about Heather. Discussing his ex-wife proves to be painful, yet he wants to be open and honest with Esfirs in this regard. Brendan tells her everything, starting with his hope for a settled life after his deployments. How she was supposed to be his island of family stability. Next, he describes how Malcolm told him about her cheating while Brendan healed in a hospital after the suicide bomber attack. He describes the emasculating divorce in which he agreed to all her demands just to end it and her sudden death in the car accident, followed by his depression.

Throughout Brendan's long spiel, Esfirs listens intently. Once he is done, all she does is nod. He figuratively kicks himself for sharing too much about a former lover. *Stupid, I am being stupid again. Why would she want to know about another woman in my life? All I do is mess things up.*

"Would you want to know a little about my childhood?"

Her question seizes Brendan. *Would I? I would love to know more about you!* "If you don't mind," he says gently.

Ever so cautiously, Esfirs describes how her mother would come home every day and show her the tools of the medical profession. Then, when she was a little bit older, her mother would take her to the hospital and describe how she treated people. Esfirs' face lights up when she talks about her, a striking contrast to how she looks as she recounts memories about her father and his career. "He was an engineer and spent little time with me," is all she says about him. When Brendan asks a clarifying question, Esfirs weakly shrugs and says she cannot share much. Whether that means her answer is classified or that he was not a factor in her life is unclear.

"My six beats your eight, Brendan," she says.

Brendan looks down at the board. He has been so wrapped up in conversation that he has practically been on autopilot with the game. They both turn toward the door and hear the ship's time chimes gently play.

"I must be going; I am glad you are well. Please see me tomorrow in the medical bay," Esfirs says.

"Will do. Can we still do our lunches together?"

"Of course."

Brendan's heart leaps. *I didn't ruin everything, thank goodness.* He thinks back to Berina warning Esfirs about time. "Hey, one last thing before you leave. What is the deal with Berina's outfit? Is there some particular celebration or reasoning behind it?"

"Classified." She smiles as she gets up to leave.

He watches her run out. *Crap, I've fallen for a foreign national!*

Interlude – Esfirs: Ashes

Esfirs' hands are cupped as she approaches Brendan's cabin. At this hour, Almas, a friendly enough guard who has had security postings throughout the ship, is standing outside. She makes eye contact, which he responds to with a nod.

"Greetings, Almas. Will you allow me passage to visit Brendan? I desire to arrange details and say good night to him."

Almas raises an eyebrow. "It is late. He may be asleep already."

"He assured me he would be up late tonight." Esfirs hopes her lie is convincing.

Almas's eyes look down and dart around.

Just let me through, guard! Since when do you care about his sleep cycle?

"Go ahead," he finally says.

She uses her elbow to bump the panel and reads off a security code, allowing the door to open without disturbing the occupant inside. Then, she walks in and gives a verbal command for the door to close. Brendan is visible in the living room; his eyes are shut, leaning on a pillow against the wall. The sounds of his sport with the club and ball are barely audible. *Such a weird thing to be fascinated by. They stand around the whole game yet act like winning is a huge challenge.* She steps toward him and bends down to level her head with his.

"Brendan, are you awake?"

He opens his eyes slowly and rubs them without saying a thing.

"Hold out your hands."

He looks confused, so she repeats the order. As a result, he stretches out both his hands chest-width apart. *You have to be fooling with me!* She rolls her eyes at him and instructs him to cup both hands together. After a moment's pause, he does so. Finally, she pours the contents of her hands—ashes—into his. A huge smile appears on her face.

"Sleep well, Dear Brendan," she whispers to him.

With that, she stands up and rushes toward the door. *Oh, Watchers, protect him!*

Thirteen – Eliezer's Word

Brendan is on the elliptical while Berina uses the rowing machine perpendicular to it. It has been a week since he, or really Berina, got himself back out of the depression. Working out feels great; he can tell he missed it. Just working his muscles, expending energy, and doing it with a partner to cheer on and keep him accountable feels excellent. Of course, he would be perfectly happy to just do cardio on the machine, but Berina has convinced—sort of forced—him to mix it up with upper and lower body routines.

He is not allowed to listen to music, as Berina uses this time to ask him endless questions. *Who knows what file they are building on me.* The exercise routine is the highlight of his day now that Bass has banned him from the office, and the Sabia have yet to give him a task. Every time he is on the floor, he is safe from the acedia that drains him of meaning.

"Brendan," she says as she pulls the handle of the rowing machine, "how did your first day with us compare to your first day with the Unified Intelligence Command? Let me guess: we were out of this world, right?" A massive grin forms on her face as if she is silently laughing at her joke.

PATRICK ABBOTT

"Puns are learned behavior, so don't start those with me." He chuckles. "Obviously, going to live with the Sabia was an epic decision which still is overwhelming. I know this will be forever life-altering, no matter how long or short my stay is here. Starting with the UIC was different. It seemed as if I were just starting a new job. I didn't know how long I would be there, nor did I understand the complexities of life in general. I came in, attended some assemblies, signed many forms, was briefed on things I didn't comprehend and said the oath of service. Then I went home, made a rice dish, slept, and started a lifelong cycle of working."

"Do you remember your oath? How seriously do you live by it?"

"Berina, the oath is a solemn vow. I would never break it without formally declaring my intentions. No one can ever doubt my word, and I plan on living it out for the rest of my life. Let me recite it for you; it is drilled into my soul. 'I, Brendan Sean Murphy, do solemnly affirm that I will support and defend the Constitution of the United States against all enemies, foreign and domestic; that I will bear true faith and allegiance to the same; and that I will obey the orders of the President of the United States and the orders of the officers appointed over me. So help me, God.' Because of that oath, I could never join a militia movement like Malcolm or my other friends. I still believe it."

"Wow. Would you bind yourself to any other oaths?"

He stops on the elliptical to drink some water and wipe down the sweat. "Depends. Does it complement, conflict, or stand apart from my current oath? For example, I have no issue with taking additional vows, my wedding vows which died with my marriage, but I couldn't do something that would make me an enemy to the United States."

"Interesting, fascinating even, Terran man." She now stops. "I am flying out today, so no lunch with me. Do you want me to get you anything while I am on your planet?"

"Whoa, whoa, slow down there, Ms. Changes-the-topic. What is so interesting about my ideas on oaths?"

"The reasoning behind my thoughts is classified," she playfully says as she gets off the rowing machine.

"Okay, where are you going on Earth?"

"Mission details are classified."

"Do you enjoy digging into the lives of others while rebuffing them when asked simple questions?"

"My motivations are classified. Not by the Legion but by me."

Legion! Was that a slipup?

"I must prepare for my mission, Brendan," she continues. "Get yourself washed and presentable. You never know who will visit you or when."

That's cryptic.

Berina and Brendan high five as they bid each other goodbye. Back at his cabin, Brendan washes up in the shower. Once dry, he puts on his uniform, valuing the outfit as a lifeline to normality. Brendan looks at the clock and decides to lie down briefly before heading off to work. Daydreaming on his bed, he imagines Bass and Paxton coming in, praising him for his hard work earning the Sabia's trust, debriefing him on what he has found out, and giving further orders. How he pines for orders and for others to know he is working hard for his country.

The door chimes. "Enter," Brendan calls out. In walk Loft and Leleh. Wanting to be presentable, Brendan pops to attention and greets them in the living room. He offers them pillows from the couch, and together they sit in a circle on the floor.

"Thank you for the cushions, Brendan. Thank you for considering our comforts," Delegate Loft says.

"Not a problem at all, sir. I am glad to be in a position to consider your needs."

"You look much better than when I saw you last. Has Berina aided you in your recovery?"

"Very much so, and thank you both for visiting me now. I think I needed some time to comprehend all that was happening. I still am troubled by it, I will not deny that, but I'm ready to get out and do my job again."

"Berina was very vocal about how our initial methods were ineffective," Leleh offers. "I am glad she proved to be correct."

Loft takes over. "It is good you are ready to do your job again. Unfortunately, developments have complicated accomplishing our goals, but a new opportunity presents itself.

"Your service in Chicago was masterful. Relying on the local Terran law enforcement would surely have led to the terrorists killing Sarha. The United States originally tried to take you from us, claiming we illegally conducted an operation on its territory." Brendan makes a mental note of the pronoun usage, trying to separate him from the government. "However, we were able to resolve this yesterday. You are no longer under arrest. Instead, they have recalled you from your liaison duty and are trying to arrange your transfer back to Washington. This is a trick to capture you again, and we will not allow it. We are concerned you would not receive the proper medical care and . . . deteriorate over time."

Now it's Leleh's turn to speak. "We have no interest in working with another Terran representative. Another Ambassador Virag or Delegate Paxton would not offer the insight and conduct action the way you do. Instead of ending your duties and returning to Terra, would you be willing to assist us?"

Solicitation? Were Berina's questions earlier laying the groundwork for this? Now would be a heck of a good time to touch base with the UIC or Bass.

"How so?" Brendan asks.

"Zand has noted how you provide deeper insight into the various militia and other groups who oppose not only our presence but our working with legitimate factions of your government and society. I must personally admit you have a rare knowledge of the groups. We are willing to offer you an auxiliary officer position in exchange for your continued help. You would continue to assist us and help your people achieve a mutually beneficial peace for the common good. You may stay, and we will continue to protect you as one of us. May we have this deal?"

Leleh awkwardly holds out her right hand.

Oh, they are good, but I've been in corners before. The pronoun usage, playing up my abilities, utilizing the term "common good," and attempted handshake are all meant to influence me . . .

Brendan stretches out his feet and places them between Loft and Leleh. Leaning back, he props himself up on his hands in a relaxed position he knows portrays strength.

"I had an inkling Berina's questions at the gym were leading up to something." *That's right; I figured out she isn't just an interested pilot.*

The Sabia are emotionless, waiting for Brendan to say more. Leleh still has her hand frozen in midair.

"So," he continues, "I am interested in working with you as an auxiliary officer. However, I imagine I would need to make some sort of promise of working toward your goals. I need to know what vow I would have to take. Furthermore, I need to discuss this with my government. Being an officer in the Unified Intelligence Command has placed a multitude of requirements on me. One of them is obtaining their permission when accepting an additional job."

Leleh withdraws her hand while Loft repositions himself. She sounds almost hurt when she says, "The

American government wishes to harm you and tried to arrest you. What is their permission to you?"

"I have successfully worked with various tribes and organizations because I keep my promises. There is nothing I will abandon that I have pledged my word to. In fact, you value my analysis because you know what I give you is the truth. If I break my commitments to the United States, I break my word. If I break my word, I am not valuable to you, and you wouldn't want me."

Leleh and Loft give each other side glances, locking eyes for a few seconds. Loft sits up straight on the pillow.

"I will personally inquire with Zand to see if your requests are reasonable. Please see to your health in the meantime. Additionally, continue to enjoy your freedom of movement within the Terran-allowed portions of the ship. I hope you are allowed to stay."

That's the passive-aggressive Loft I saw that first day. He's kind of a jerk to say, "Work with us," and then, "we may kick you out," because of your requests. This is turning out to be one heck of a deployment.

PATRICK ABBOTT

Interlude – Berina: Knock, and the Door Will Not Be Opened

Again, Brendan is standing in front of the closed door. Berina can't tell if he is trying to drill a hole with his gaze or if he is staring past it into oblivion. Meanwhile, Bavird shifts back and forth, making his guard uniform rattle. Brendan's soft tapping on the door forms a beat to the annoying clatter Bavird is causing.

If you do not want to be here, you do not have to be, Bavird. "Guard, I do not believe your assistance will be required anymore. You are dismissed."

The guard requires no more encouragement and books it away from the embassy office. Berina's eyes follow him down the hall until he turns a corner. Shaking her head, she is glad to be rid of such a useless addition to a sensitive situation. Now, as she turns her attention to the matter at hand, the muscles in her chest, especially around the heart, feel as if they are contracting.

Oh, Brendan, how long are you going to wait? I would never criticize you for trying, but at this point, you are only hurting yourself.

"Brendan," Berina calls to him, "you have been pouring your energies into trying to use telekinesis to open the ambassador's door. The last time I checked, Terrans did not have that ability. So you are only stressing yourself out. Why not go back to your cabin and write another letter? I will personally see to it that Loft demarches these jerks tomorrow. In the meantime, maybe we can play another game?" *Come on, Brendan, take the bait and let us relax.* "I will invite Esfirs over." *Now I got him.*

Instead, Brendan remains motionless, his gaze still on the door. Berina thinks she can hear a sniffle or two coming from him, ever so softly.

"I gave them the best years of my life. Everything I did was because of them. And now they won't even talk to me. If I could . . . if I could just talk to them, maybe I could . . ." Brendan's voice trails off.

Poor guy doesn't know how to liaison his way out of this situation.

Approaching him, Berina puts both her hands on his shoulders. Whispering in his ear, she says, "Let us go back to your cabin. You should rest, friend."

Still, Brendan does not move. Facing the door, he says, "I don't understand."

"That is an excellent thought, Brendan. Keep the conversation going in your mind, do not give up. Hey, let us go back and turn it into a prayer. Maybe your god will answer you soon."

Brendan squeezes his eyes shut. "Thank you for helping me."

PATRICK ABBOTT

"What are friends for? Now, let us get you back home."

Fourteen – Patriot's Game

Brendan is walking down the hallway with a male guard escorting him. It has been two days of wearing the UIC uniform and hoping for official word from the United States delegation concerning the Sabia's offer. Finally, Brendan has been given a chance to discuss the situation. His attention is torn between different scenarios of how this meeting could play out. *Maybe they'll apologize for the misunderstandings and grant me the ability to stay. Perhaps they will tell me the Sabia have been lying, and we must fight our way to a shuttlecraft. Man, I hope someone can fly that thing. Maybe they just say "no," and I am ordered back to Earth. What do I do then? Orders are orders, but I don't want to end up in some hybrid autopsy video in Area 51.*

As they approach the diplomatic cabins, a United States marine in battle rattle is waiting for them. Brendan quickly scans for insignia and identification. He assumes an alert military posture when he sees the E-9 rank of Master Gunnery Sergeant. Brendan offers a salute which the marine flawlessly mirrors.

"Intelligence Officer Brendan Murphy reporting for duty, Master Gunnery Sergeant."

PATRICK ABBOTT

"At ease, Murphy. Ambassador Bass and Delegate Wheeler are currently off ship; this makes me the top-ranking man here. Director Wilson, Secretary Nicholson, Secretary Patel, and even POTUS have reviewed the Sabia's request for you. Do you remember your standing orders?"

"Yes, Master Gunnery Sergeant, I was ordered to—"

"No, no, no! I just asked if you remembered your orders."

"Yes, Master Gunnery Sergeant."

"Drop the rank crap, Murphy. You're a civie, and my name is Anthony. Anyways, I'm to tell you to continue your mission. Now get out of here, as you no longer have status with the mission."

Brendan does an about-face and starts walking past his guard. Confusion reigns inside him. On the one hand, he remembers his command to integrate with the Sabia and gain as much information as possible. However, neither Paxton nor Bass have bothered reaching out to him, and Master Guns' behavior indicates they probably won't try in the future. *Are they writing me off? Or are they letting me stay merely to appease the Sabia and then plan to dispose of me? Anthony did not give me an official yes. This way, no matter what, I will be held responsible for what happens. Talk about profiles in government leadership.* His thoughts go to dark places. Even the guard is perplexed, and he pesters Brendan about Anthony's behavior.

"Brendan, wait for me!" Berina's familiar voice cries.

He turns around to see her running up to him, her flight suit making a leather-on-leather sound.

"Hey," he says.

"I just got back from taking your ambassador and delegate to Terra. Complete silence, no conversation whatsoever. I even tried talking to them about baseball. Not a peep. Finally, I asked about you, and they said that if I continued to ask questions, they would file an 'official diplomatic complaint' against me." She speaks the last five words in a mocking tone. "Hey, what is wrong? You look sad again."

Brendan forces a smile and then drops it. *She will be able to tell if I lie.* "Had an odd experience with the acting head of mission here. It looks like I have permission to become an auxiliary officer, though I have a feeling my own government does not like me."

"The first part is great news! The latter just proves they are idiots. If you are anywhere near as helpful to your government as you are to us, then they are fools for not liking you. Third, let us both work on pronouns. Becoming an auxiliary officer makes the Legion your government, too. Your new role makes you one of us and . . . well . . . your transformation, too. When are you going to do the ceremony to join us?"

Legion? "Wait, what?"

"What what?" Berina rejoins with a convincing but overly theatrical British accent. Her grin makes evident the mockery in her response.

PATRICK ABBOTT

"Playing with accents, eh? Do you speak like that when you fly to England?"

"That is classified," she says. Brendan notices a devilish grin on her face.

This is as close as an admission they use languages and accents to influence people as I'll ever get. I bet they are strategic about who can interact with who based on language skills. Shifting his mind to the conversation, he says, "You said Legion; what is that?"

"You need help putting that together?" Berina rolls her eyes and crosses her arms. "There are Terrans, and then the United States of America or even your native Éire." She gives him a wink after demonstrating her Gaelic knowledge. "It kind of would be awkward to call our government 'Sabia.'"

"So the Legion is your government?"

"And so much more!" She waves her arms wildly. *She isn't taking this conversation very seriously. She sounds like she's seen too many commercials.* "The Legion is the all-encompassing system which guides us, takes care of us, and evolves us. When I was on Terra one time, I met some people called the Amish. One unified system controlled their religion, government, and social structure." She nods as if thinking something through. "That is, say, a close but not perfect comparison. If I were you, I would not write any doctoral dissertations making that claim, but it gives you a good rule of thumb."

"Huh," Brendan replies, "interesting. Is the Legion the only government for the Sabia? Or are there other factions of Sabia that have their own forms of government?"

Berina flips her hair. Taking a step back, she places her left hand on her chest and gives him a seductive wink. "Lean in as if you are going to kiss my neck."

"What?" Brendan says, aghast.

Then, like a ventriloquist speaking without moving her lips, she says, "So I can answer your question without speaking too loudly."

Brendan looks up and down the empty corridors. With a queasy stomach, he starts to lean toward Berina.

Suddenly, the pilot grabs his head and yanks it toward her. Then, yelling with the full force of both her lungs, she declares, "It is classified!"

The ringing in Brendan's ears nearly blocks out her riotous laughter. He closes his eyes and puts his hand over his right ear. Brendan thinks he gives off a few sounds of distress, but he is unsure because of the pain. Within a minute, his hearing comes back—conveniently as Berina's laughter is finally dying off.

"That really hurt," Brendan says as he fights the constant involuntary brain signals to close his eyes in pain.

"Like I am going to tell you that detail, auxiliary-officer-to-be." She laughs some more. "Okay, okay, I am sorry for the pain I caused you, though I am not sorry for getting you like that. But, hey, when are you going to bite the bullet and have the initiation ceremony?"

PATRICK ABBOTT

"To be honest, planning a party is probably the last thing my mind is capable of doing right now."

"May I be the one who conducts it?"

He was not expecting her question. But, thinking on his feet, he decides it's best to have personal allies, even ones who yell in his ear as a joke. "Sure."

"Great! We will have the ceremony in your cabin tomorrow. I will arrange everything since your mind is probably going to be scrambled for a while. This is going to be fun!"

I was not expecting today to happen this way at all.

Fifteen – The Oath

Brendan straightens out his uniform, turns, and gives Berina a nervous nod. Meanwhile, she is in her own white uniform, which includes a boxy top and a beret, its long side hanging down to the end of her ear. Berina puts her feet together, straightens her back, and instructs him to hold out his left palm. He does, and she places a thin blade on top of it. Then, putting her own right hand on top of the dagger, she uses her left to slice the weapon across his palm, causing sharp, hot pain. He knows he is bleeding, but he keeps his hand there.

"Repeat after me: We vow—"

"We vow—"

"To protect, assist, and advance the Sabia Legion—"

"To protect, assist, and advance the Sabia Legion—"

"We bind our promise—"

"We bind our promise—"

"To the divine and all the divine's creations."

"To the divine and all the divine's creations."

PATRICK ABBOTT

Brendan withdraws his hand. Before the event, he was worried about his blood mixing with Berina's. Now though, his mind is wholly preoccupied with the deep cut on his palm. The blood is pooling rapidly and beginning to spill onto the floor. He stares at it as his breathing becomes quicker. Images of Afghanistan flash before him.

"Be calm, Brendan, calm." Esfirs' voice snaps him out of his trance.

Zalta presses a cloth to the wound, seemingly absorbing the blood while causing a tightening sucking sensation. She removes it, revealing a completely dry hand, tightened skin, and a large gash down the middle. Esfirs then spreads a wet jelly over the cut. She instructs Brendan to open and close his palm three times. This causes the jelly to work its way into the wound while numbing his nerves.

"It will be like new in a few minutes, I promise you." Esfirs looks into his eyes. He finds it incredibly calming.

The crowd claps as Berina introduces Brendan as their newest auxiliary officer while simultaneously wrapping her hand in a bandage. Besides her and the duo providing medical help, Gul and his wife Nema are there, as is Leleh. Each one of them comes over to congratulate Brendan. Following the kudos, two groups form. The first is the soccer-watching section—Gul, Nema, and Zalta—while the second clique gathers separately and is composed of Berina, Esfirs, and Leleh. Initially, Brendan tries to sit with the soccer group. This is a futile effort, though, as he hates soccer. His annoyance is made worse by the fact that the Sabia like it. Brendan stays to answer a few questions about the rules and explain the rivalry between the Celtics and the Rangers, but he manages to excuse himself in short order.

As Brendan approaches the more senior-level Sabia, he overhears Berina say, "I am not joking; Ambassador Virag threatened me. At first, when we were flying down to Terra, I thought maybe I could talk to him and at least give him a positive impression on the way out. But instead, he then tried to intimidate me. What a small man he is."

"What dishonorable trash they send us," Esfirs adds. "Then again, just look at what stock he comes from."

"Well," Brendan adds as he joins the circle, "that is a little bit of a dig. The ambo certainly was no friend of mine, but he has a long record of serving his country, which just so happens to be my country. So, I'm not sure what you mean by the 'stock he comes from.'" He ends his sentence with a lighter tone hoping Esfirs will take it as a humorous out.

She doesn't. "Do not defend him. You are nothing like him nor his ilk."

Berina looks at Brendan, then Esfirs, and back to Brendan. "Well," Berina begins, "on that lovely note, we have our newest auxiliary officer. So tell us, Auxiliary Officer Brendan, how does it feel to be part of the Legion?"

PATRICK ABBOTT

Now is the time to set boundaries. "Well, my government has made no objection to me taking the oath in addition to my standing UIC oath; it feels great to have a foot in both camps and being the bridge."

Esfirs makes a *tsk* sound and wrinkles her nose, her face upset. "How can you say that? You were disowned."

She's furious. Brendan has not seen Esfirs like this before; it's quite unsettling to him. "The order I received from the United States government was to continue my mission. My mission is to be a liaison and work with you. Taking the Legion's oath is another step toward that."

Leleh opines, "It was a unique solution which personally I was against; however, approval from Zand settles the matter for me."

"Brendan"—Esfirs sounds desperate—"the local Terran government you came from is not your friend. They tried removing you from us at a stage where any complication would have meant your death. Do you not understand that you owe them nothing?"

Brendan sends a "help me" glance toward Berina.

"Well," Berina interrupts, "now that we have everyone's opinion on the matter, I have another question for you, Auxiliary Officer. What is one thing you want to do that you could not before?"

"Oh, that's easy; I want to go to Earth's moon and then Mars. The moon's Sea of Tranquility appeals to me because that is where our first astronauts landed." Leleh snickers at the term astronaut; Brendan chooses to ignore her. "As for Mars, I want to be in the morning fog of Valles Marineris and stand on the edge of Olympus Mons, looking out over the rest of the planet."

"You are aware those are dead planets, right?" Berina asks. "Nothing compared to Terra."

"Oh, I know. It's just I remember learning about those places as a child. The way my teachers described them made me want to see them. I guess the fact that I know they are there, just out of reach, draws me to them. It's a simple reason, I know, but that's just me."

"Brendan!" The scream cuts across the room. The senior group turns around and sees the soccer fans sitting alert and pointing at the screen. On the television, images flash of riots in the street, the Capitol building under assault, and people doing weapons drills in the forest. A logo then appears. "Militia: The Splitting of America."

"You were on the screen!" Gul cries.

Brendan closes his eyes. The pain is starting to come back. Esfirs asks how it was displayed. Eagerly, Gul describes an advertisement showing a picture of people, including Brendan, as well as a piece of paper with "The Meade Report" on the cover. The title makes Brendan feel like he has been kicked in the gut. Various Sabia begin talking at once, making the sickening feeling worse. Suddenly, someone tugs his hand gently and leads him to sit on the floor. Esfirs.

"Everyone, Brendan is going to teach us a new game."

PATRICK ABBOTT

In their excitement, the soccer group stops asking questions about the advertainment and forms a circle. Brendan whispers a thank you to Esfirs.

She looks at him. "Tell us, Brendan, what game will we learn today?

Options quickly come up and are shot down in his head. He has no board or cards, so he needs to think of something else. Finally, thankfully, an idea comes to him.

"The game is called 'Guess.' The rules are simple. Each of us takes a turn; I will start by thinking of someone on the ship. Next, we will go around the circle asking a yes/no question about the person. Go ahead and guess who you think it is if you have enough information. If you correctly guess who I am thinking of, you win. You can no longer participate in the round if you're wrong, though. As I said, I will start things off. Okay. I have someone in mind. Berina, since you are sitting on my right and the right hand is dominant on Earth, you get to guess first."

"Are you thinking of me, your favorite pilot?"

"That counts as a guess and not a question. And no, I am not thinking of you."

The room bursts into laughter. Everyone takes turns guessing until Gul figures out Brendan is thinking about Loft. When it is Berina's turn, Esfirs solves it immediately by saying the pilot is thinking of Brendan. Esfirs' round is solved immediately by Berina, who guesses Zand.

"How did you two gang up?" Brendan asks.

"That is classified," Berina replies. Both she and Esfirs laugh.

"You were sent to tease me, weren't you? Tell me, how did the universe put you two together?"

"Classified!" Berina bounces in her seat with joy at her own response.

"I guess my auxiliary officer role doesn't come with a higher clearance. Nice to know I will still be denied the ability to get to know you."

Esfirs winces. "You should not think of it that way. Instead, cherish the fun we are having now."

A chime occurs, and Nema announces that it is time to leave. Berina yips, causing Brendan to give her a double-take. She jumps up, runs out of the room, and just as quickly as she exits, comes back with something in her hands. Her rush to get to Brendan nearly causes her to run into him.

"We got this for you, Auxiliary Officer. It is a communication device simple enough for you to use. Using the body of a Terran cell phone, we made this gadget to communicate with each other. It works whether you are on Terra or elsewhere on the ship. Of course, I programmed it with quick contacts for myself and the medical bay, Leleh, Loft, and Esfirs. Additionally, it can also be used to dial any Terran phone number."

She hands the device to Brendan. *Great, they are giving me a SIGINT device to spy on me and give me tasks. Double trouble.*

PATRICK ABBOTT

"Thank you," he says.

Nema welcomes Brendan into the Legion and begins to leave again, taking Gul with her. He doesn't say a word during the goodbye. Meanwhile, Zalta offers Brendan a hug while Leleh does the awkward handshake. Much to Brendan's delight, Esfirs declares she intends to help clean up, and Berina gives her a playful, doubting look. Finally, as a means of farewell, Berina reminds Brendan of their daily workout session in the morning.

Esfirs watches her leave, waiting for the door to close. "We have been friends since our first assignment together."

This is a positive development for Brendan. *Esfirs wants to tell me more about herself. Now I really need someone to report to!* He keeps a poker face and stays quiet, hoping Esfirs will say more.

She walks toward Brendan. "When Berina was selected to be a lead pilot on this mission, I made sure we would work in the same division." She looks at him and studies his straight face. Then, she wraps her arms around herself and walks closer to him. "Please tell me of your home, Kansas. I want to see it."

His professional desire for more information and his personal longing for a connection with her surge. "The hills of grass stretch in every direction. Sometimes in the spring, you can smell the fires farmers set to clear the fields. Animal life ranges from domesticated cattle to wild buffalo and birds of all types. It all makes for a beautiful state with a small population. The people are great there. My dad knew he was home when he first came to Kansas. You would absolutely love it there, too, Esfirs. I would show you a buffalo herd and—" His mind cuts off. Groups like the Kansas State Defenders and the New Jayhawkers would target her.

"What is it, Brendan? Why did you stop?"

"That ad on the television mentioned the *Meade Report.* That was my effort to show I was useful after Afghanistan. My command ordered me to make all these connections with militias in the South and Midwest. And what happens? My best friend betrays me while the commander of the whole operation goes rogue by using the information we gathered to form his own militia. If I took you to Kansas, you would be in danger because of them. Damn fools. What makes matters worse is they're good people, but they'll do horrible things if given a chance. Everything I worked on with that report made things worse." He looks at Esfirs, who is in a stoic pose. *How I hate those.* "I'm sorry." He looks away. "That ad is bringing out bad memories in me." Still, she stands motionless. "Dang it, I am so sorry for ruining . . .""

When they lock eyes, his mind stops. He looks at Esfirs in silence, no longer thinking of the report and its failure.

"Do you remember the song I sang you?"

"Only the first few bars," he answers, incredibly embarrassed.

"Then sing what you can with me."

Together, they sing. After the opening notes, Brendan stops, but Esfirs continues. He remains enraptured by her eyes, holding her gaze for what seems like a blissful eternity. Eventually, the song finishes while his eyes begin to feel heavy.

"Remember the song—do it for me, Dear Brendan."

He can only nod.

She slowly turns away and leaves. Brendan just stands there looking at the door. *Wow. I think I love her.*

Sixteen – Kentucky Rifles

Week after week passes slowly. The days are monotonous; ever-changing duos of Sabia intelligence officers come to question Brendan on the United States' thoughts about other countries, international events, and the militia movement. He bases his analysis on open-source news, commentary, and various social media reports. Every attempt to reach the new American diplomatic mission has been answered with deafening silence. The initial enthusiasm he had for the job is slipping away.

Berina's activities help keep him afloat, but just barely. Her initial teasing concerning the state department's treatment of him has become a thinly veiled way to ask how he is every day. To make matters worse, group lunches with her and Esfirs are becoming less common, as all three have duties that keep them occupied. Brendan also catches himself using "anxiety coping techniques," putting on a brave face when interacting with Sabia in the hallways. They are happy to talk to him, and it's enjoyable until they walk away and reality sets in. The nail in the coffin, though, is Esfirs. Her behavior toward him has become more stoic. He sees her every day for lunch and every three days to take medicine for his hybridization, but the spark they initially shared seems lost. *Maybe she didn't want to move too fast, perhaps someone talked to her, or I was just desperate for female attention and misunderstood her intentions. Or maybe she doesn't want to be with a genetic freak.* Depression is starting to worm its way back into his soul.

Brendan is sitting in his new workroom, in a different part of the ship from the human diplomatic offices. News reports cross the screen as he prepares for another day of monitoring, report writing, and—if he's lucky—questions and answers. As he reads the updates, Leleh enters the room. He sits up straight in his chair.

"Brendan, what can you tell me about the militia that refers to itself as The Kentucky Rifles?"

"Independent group dedicated to preserving states' rights against perceived federal government encroachment. Not as radical as the other militia movements, as it does not seek the overthrow of elected government. I am unaware of any violent actions by the group, just protests, and shows of force. I worked with their leadership a few years back, but I am sure there's been turnover since then."

"What do militia members think of you?"

"The leaders at the time I was there probably thought I was a somewhat reasonable federal agent. Not saying much, but they trusted me for what I was."

Leleh studies him for a moment. "The Kentucky Rifles militia has been blockading a shipment of minerals. Last night the local governor sent the National Guard to secure the minerals, but those units now claim the militia is besieging them. We cannot allow them to block our agenda. The council has debated how to resolve the situation. Several members initially favored a small demonstration of force. However, Zand believes sending you along with a force of guards may prevent violence while successfully obtaining our objectives. I cannot stress enough how important it is that you not disappoint her, Auxiliary Officer."

Purpose flows back into his mind, body, and soul. "I will succeed. Do we have any additional information concerning the situation on the ground? What personalities are involved in this operation? What is the physical geography of the scene of action? Have there been any acts of violence thus far?"

"Everything we have is in here." She hands him an Earth-made tablet. *Clearly, they don't trust me with most of their tech.* "You have an hour to prepare. We will send someone to retrieve you then."

Brendan hurriedly scans the file. The siege is more of a road blockade at a mining site than anything close to medieval warfare. A river and bridge separate the semi-trucks full of fluorite and zinc from over three hundred reported militia members with small arms. *The National Guard are justified in their worry; I wouldn't want to challenge that either.* Perusing the file, Brendan sees a contact number for Lieutenant Colonel Saul Paulides, the operation commander. Deciding to put his Sabia phone to good use, he calls Paulides. It takes Brendan some effort to convince Paulides that he is not prank-calling. Finally, the commander shares an intelligence report stating that the Kentucky Rifles believe the Sabia are kidnapping children, using the mining operation as cover. As Brendan finishes the call, a male

PATRICK ABBOTT

Sabia approaches. The newly arrived Sabia introduces himself as Apahvez.

"I am the lead for the operation down to the state of Kentucky. You will serve under me as my delegate to all Terran factions in the immediate area. Your orders are to secure a peaceful transit for our shipment. If you fail, we will consider it a security operation, and I will be forced to entrust the successful transit of our shipment to Guard Bahram."

"Yes, sir."

"Very good. If you complete your mission, I promise you no Terrans will be harmed. Now come with me; everyone else is ready."

Walking to the shuttle bay gives Brendan a chance to get ready for this mission. *Maybe I can have a roundtrip without a medical emergency this time.* He smiles wryly at that thought. When he arrives, he sees a dozen guards, all in the white uniform and wearing what looks to be body armor. *How similar the armor is to the medical uniform. I wonder if it is a derivative of a standard cultural costume.* Near the shuttlecraft, he sees Zalta standing next to another female medic. She waves him over.

"First mission as one of us! This is Nashifran," Zalta introduces the other medic. "She was with me on the evacuation mission when we first encountered you."

"You look much better now than you did then. Personally, I thought you were going to die; you had so much blood coming out of your mouth." Nashifran's emotionless response makes what she says even more jarring.

"Well, like I told Zalta before Chicago, no one dies today."

Zalta's eyes widen.

"In fact, that gives me an idea."

Brendan runs up to Apahvez and whispers in his ear. Apahvez then stands back and motions to the guards and medics with an open hand.

Brendan calls for everyone's attention. "No one dies today—no one. Because I'm the deputy lead for this part of the mission, I request that all guards remain near the shuttlecraft. Apahvez and I will meet with the local National Guard commander, Lieutenant Colonel Paulides, and inspect the situation. Medics, stay at the ready, but we'll do our best to keep you bored. Alright, let's roll!"

Brendan takes two steps toward the shuttlecraft's open door but stops when he notices no one else is moving. He looks around, gently motioning for others to board the vessel, but everyone else is still. Then, from behind him, Brendan hears the clearing of a throat. Turning around, he sees a fully suited-up Berina looking out of the shuttlecraft's door. She stares at him, then turns to address the rest of the group. "You all have permission to board *my* craft." The group starts loading into the ship. All Brendan can do is be embarrassed.

The door closes automatically, and the weird motionless motion begins—or at least, Brendan assumes it begins. He focuses on the chance to make a positive impact as he takes a seat.

The air crackles around him. "How we feeling about this one, Auxiliary Officer?" Berina's voice is a welcome sound.

"Okay, overall. You know, if I don't almost die on this mission, I can ask you all the questions I want because I will have fulfilled your requirement."

"Oh, dear." She laughs. After a moment, she comes back. "New order from medical; you need to put your hand in a well-armored gauntlet."

Now Brendan laughs. *Esfirs is thinking of me.* "Negative, going to go commando with my hands. Gonna get Kentucky weeds to cut them all up. It will give them character."

A long pause. "I told you-know-who you will protect it."

He laughs again; several guards look at him as if he is insane. Brendan does not care.

As the door opens, one of the guards exits so quickly that he barely gets out without hitting it. Brendan sees a dark sky and feels a drizzle as he jumps out. Apahvez comes out, as does another guard. Thankfully, the rest of the unit stays inside the shuttlecraft.

The fresh air sweeps over him like a welcoming wave. *Mountain dew, sweet freedom, that's good air!* For a split second, he pauses, remembering that this is the first time he's been back since everything in his world collapsed. *Here's hoping no one tries to grab me. Or . . .*

169

He imagines himself making a break for it, running away from the Sabia to . . . wherever his legs will carry him. *Would the Sabia just let me go? How far would they chase me? Heck, could I even make it as far as the militia on the other side of the bridge? For all I know, these aliens can leap a football field if push comes to shove. No, I can help with this situation right here. So, let me focus on that for now.*

Brendan walks over to a tent but stops when he sees a man in military camouflage running toward them. Brendan instructs Apahvez to stand on his right. He quickly explains that this is not a slight but a position of honor and peerage on Earth. The uniformed man reaches the two delegates with barely any breath left. Brendan can see the O-5 rank and the name tag "Paulides." The man has bloodshot eyes and is clearly worse for wear.

"Hard night, Colonel?" Brendan asks.

"Sir, you Officer Murphy? Glad to have you here, but let me tell you, these folks ain't budging. We're dug into the mud. Finally got some quiet to rest, but then you showed up."

"Yep, that's me," Brendan replies. "How are you all holding up morale-wise?"

"Not well. I came out here alone because half my guys are ready to walk away while the other half might as well just join the natives. People think the aliens are kidnapping children."

Apahvez interjects, "I assure you that is not true." Apahvez sounds annoyed.

PATRICK ABBOTT

"Uh-huh," Paulides says before spitting. "Meanwhile, the only one I really trust out here is a Hersey Bar first lieutenant. I have him back in the tent. He's capable, but I don't know if he can keep my men from getting restless. So if you don't mind, we can head over there now."

As they walk, Brendan gets a view of the bridge and sees the barricade on the other side. There is a National Guardsman on the near side, and on the far side, two people are standing behind a dumpster placed in the middle of the road. Inspiration hits him hard. Spurring into action, he asks Apahvez for permission to approach the bridge. The Sabia is hesitant for a moment but allows Brendan to take the short walk to the span. Brendan is off as soon as he gets the okay, making his way to the bridge as Apahvez and Paulides continue toward the tent.

From the edge, Brendan can count at least a dozen armed people starting to gather, likely checking him out, wondering who exited from the Sabia craft. The United States and Kentucky flags are visible in a makeshift tent city nearby, but Brendan can't see any specific militia flags. *That is a most welcoming sign.* Several militia members are gathering around one individual and pointing at Brendan. As their conversation goes on, Brendan talks to the lone guardsman on the near side of the bridge. Brendan learns that Private First Class Jordyn Cole is wet, miserable, nervous, and worried about whether she'll have to shoot someone. He promises her that won't be necessary. When she asks if the militia will try to storm the bridge, he tells her that he will do everything in his power to make sure that doesn't happen. Jordyn nods quickly. While she is acting as if he has reassured her, Brendan can see that all-too-familiar desire to run and hide in her eyes.

"My king!" the man at the center of the small gaggle of militia members calls. "King of Syria! It's me, John Parks! It's me, my king!"

Laughing and with a leaping heart, Brendan waves back. "Parks! The last time I saw you, I was telling you about my bucket of pad thai! We're a long way from Afghanistan; what the heck are you doing here?"

"How do you like my blockade? Chokepoints covered on all three sides, plus constant appeals for people to walk away. Works like a charm!"

"Ha! It dang well should because you learned it from me! Come over here, bring a couple of chairs, and let's get all caught up!"

"Uh"—John sounds nervous—"I would, but I think there's a siege going on. Plus, the guardsmen on your side threatened to shoot us if we came too close again."

"John, I'm Brendan freaking Murphy, King of Syria—your king, mind you. No one will shoot you because people do what I tell them to do. So, on that note, come on over!"

Brendan quickly instructs Jordyn not to shoot. It takes a couple of minutes, a couple of minutes too long in the rain, for John to grab chairs for himself and a small entourage. They walk across the bridge, ready to set up camp on the National Guard's side, but Brendan stops them by taking one of the chairs and setting up just on the edge of the bridge. Four militia members and John set up facing Brendan while the one who lost his chair to Brendan runs back to grab another one. Brendan tells Jordyn to bring a United States flag and plant it in the soil alongside the road next to him. Then, he invites John to have a flag walker bring over a Kentucky flag.

"See, everything is awesome. Just like the day I brought Costco pizza to the office."

John laughs, sparking an hour-long conversation in which he and Brendan get caught up on the last few years. John, a Korean American, served in the Unified Intelligence Command before he came to believe the system was too flawed to save. He returned to his native state and quickly rose the ranks of the local armed groups because of his intelligence and combat skills. When asked about Heather, Brendan starts recounting his life since the men last saw each other. This time, he does not use an "anxiety coping mechanism" as he shares the positives and negatives of the last few years. Finally, he gives a version of events with the government ordering him to work with the Sabia to ensure peace. By the time they are caught up, at least thirty more militia members are standing behind John's seated group. Several interrupt Brendan's story to ask if he is a Sabia. John gets more annoyed each time and yells at them that, no, Brendan is a war hero who was John's boss back in the Unified Intelligence Command. *If only they knew.*

"So," Brendan says once storytime is over, "tell me why all of you are here."

173

During the next hour, he hears conspiracy theories so insane that only crazies on the internet would think them up. Finally, after asking a few clarifying questions, Brendan gets up and takes PFC Jordyn with him as he slowly walks back to the command. A terribly angry lieutenant colonel is waiting for him.

"What the hell are you doing? You gave them control of the bridge! Now those loons can swarm us all at will!" Angry-looking veins appear across Paulides's bright red forehead. Apahvez, meanwhile, stares stoically at Brendan.

"Relax, Colonel, their officer in command, is a friend of mine. He won't do anything while I'm here. They are absolutely convinced children are being hidden in these shipments. Freaking social media has them seeing conspiracies everywhere. So I must ask—just to be sure—what's in the trucks?"

"Freaking rocks, that's it. Look, Officer"— Paulides says the title with a dismissive tone—"I know the people who work the mining and shipping. They live here, for Heaven's sake, they ain't about to be kidnapping children and moving them in rock shipments."

Brendan turns to address his Sabia commander. "Apahvez, this is your show. Would you have any objections to a limited number of militia inspecting each truck to ensure no kids are hidden inside? I will make sure they don't take anything, just examine the goods."

Apahvez exhales deeply. Paulides pleads with him, saying the Sabia can't give in to terrorism, but Brendan counters that this is about establishing trust.

PATRICK ABBOTT

The Sabia ponders this and gives Brendan approval to proceed.

Brendan salutes his commander and runs out of the tent. Just as quickly, he returns with John and four other armed locals. Brendan senses the alarm felt by Apahvez, his guards, Paulides, and the guardsmen.

"Apahvez, sir. My friend John Parks here, and some of his men, have never seen a Sabia before," Brendan offers as an introduction. "They also have a question for you, sir."

Parks takes one small, cautious step forward. He looks down to the left of Apahvez's feet as he speaks. "Hello. Greetings from the Kentucky Rifles. We heard rumors that children are on these trucks. Would you allow us to ensure the safety of our families by inspecting the goods?" Parks then glances up at Apahvez only to quickly look away.

Apahvez breaks his stoic facade. He says, sounding high and mighty, "Kentucky Rifles, you have my permission to inspect the trucks under the supervision of Auxiliary Officer Brendan."

"Ramblers, let's get rambling." Brendan waves his fingers in the air as if he were an umpire signaling a home run. They head toward the trucks.

A quick inspection reveals nothing but mined rocks. John expresses his relief at the lack of kidnapped children, while the other amateur inspectors seem disappointed.

"I'm going to start calling the Sabia 'rock lovers' because they sure do love their rocks," Brendan says.

"No crap. It's weird, though; these are pretty meaningless in terms of materials compared to other stuff. So what do you think they want them for, my king?"

"Man, for all I know, they come from a planet made of gold and silver. This junk material could be their equivalent of wealth minerals or rare earth elements. I might call zinc a 'rare Sabiaistan element' just to see if I can get a reaction out of them."

"That's what they call their home planet? Sabiaistan?"

"Dude, they don't share crap with Washington or me. They could very easily be mole men flying their UFOs out of Earth's pole. I'm pleasantly surprised they let us look at these shipments, however. It must be imperative to them to have this stuff. Speaking of which, a deal is a deal. You have to lift the blockade now."

"Yeah, I'll call it in." Within a minute, John texts out an explanation of what is in the trucks. Next, he shoots down a theory posed in a chat application that the children have been pulverized into rocks. Finally, he puts down his cell phone and studies Brendan closely.

Does he suspect something? "What's up, buddy?"

"You want to catch a meal and hang out with the wife and me? Tonight's Wednesday, so there's a Bible study at my church. Afterward, I'll take you out for dinner with some of the boys and let you play with the kiddos."

Brendan thinks about the offer. A little personal time could ensure friendly, or at least non-hostile, relations between the Sabia and Kentucky Rifles. Plus, other groups may want to talk to Brendan about the aliens. He agrees.

The National Guardsmen watch in awe as the militia dismantle their roadblocks. Back in the command tent, Brendan declares, "Great news, Apahvez—the blockade is over, and the trucks should have a clear shot to go wherever they need to. But personally, I recommend they get moving immediately because who knows what other yahoos in the hills might want to veto the end of the standoff."

"Very good," Apahvez replies without emotion.

"And, uh, one more thing. I will spend the night with the militia commander to ensure we establish working relations that outlast our brief time here. Can I get a lift tomorrow morning, say 0900 or 1000?"

Apahvez looks dumbfounded. "I . . . I . . ."

"Sir," Brendan starts, "if I go with them, I can guarantee they will go from believing any random theory on the internet about the Sabia to leaving this operation alone for years to come. I can't divulge any secrets because you haven't given any to me. I'll be fine, they like me, and because of what I'll do, they will like you, too."

The Sabia commander gives his approval and instructs the two guards to follow him back to the shuttlecraft. Brendan, meanwhile, heads to join John. His communication device vibrates and chimes as they make their way to an old, battered pickup that has seen hard years in the mountains.

Berina: <u>ARE YOU INSANE!</u>

Brendan texts back, "Making a better universe for you and everyone else."

He hops aboard the truck, which starts to make its way down the road. Looking back, he sees the first of the container trucks begin to move. The device chimes again.

Berina: <u>CALL IMMEDIATELY WHEN YOU NEED HELP!</u>

Brendan smiles. "I love this job," he says out loud.

PATRICK ABBOTT

Seventeen – Rules of Engagement

The morning is sunny and slightly warmer than the previous rainy, overcast day. Brendan and John are leaning against the militia commander's truck. Brendan is still in his office clothes but has a satchel filled with things he acquired throughout the night. A classic country song is playing on the radio, providing a gentle background soundtrack. John is waxing on about how the America he knew as a child is gone. Lines such as "We go to war, and these power players tear us apart so they can stay on top" are a common refrain. According to John, the Sabia are responsible because they give technology and power to the elites, worsening the problem. Brendan listens but tries to get John to focus on positive solutions that don't promote a cycle of violence.

Brendan's communicator device vibrates. Because of the incessant noise it made the previous day; he had turned off the chime. Requesting a moment to check the message, he sees the screen.

Berina: Almost there.

Simple and to the point. Brendan scrolls up to read the past twenty-or-so hours of messages again.

Berina: Tell us when you need us to come!

Brendan: I am fine. Tomorrow will work as planned.

Berina: Are you okay?

Brendan: Yes.

Berina: Can you leave early?

Brendan: 0900 is still a good time. That will allow me to have breakfast with my friend.

Berina: Are you really staying overnight?

Brendan: Yes.

Berina: Are you okay?

Brendan: I am fine. I promise.

Berina: We are all geared up, so send a message if you need us to get you tonight. This channel is being monitored, so someone will see it.

Brendan: Seriously, I am fine.

Berina: Crafts on standby.

Brendan: Good to know. Still fine. No need to send them early.

Berina: It is almost dawn. Are you still safe?

Berina: Please message me when you wake up. We are worried.

Brendan: I just woke up. Everything is fine.

Berina: Thank you.

Brendan: You are most welcome.

Berina: We will leave in ten minutes.

Brendan: See you soon.

Brendan chuckles and shows the messages to John.

"Jeez, man. Who is this Berina? Sounds like a crazy girlfriend I used to know." John laughs.

"She's a pilot, the one who dropped us off here. I must give the Sabia credit; they show strong affinity for those they consider friends. And I do have to admit I've been treated really well." Brendan fights off a desire to talk about Esfirs.

There is a moment of silence. Then, Brendan brings up the elephant in the room. "John, we both took vows for our country. We need to stick together. I know the Kentucky Rifles aren't part of Meade's group, and they are definitely not like the radical groups out west, but John, we need smart people like you to fight for America inside the system."

John shakes his head no. "The system gives us politicians who turn punks into organized political enforcers. Hell, man, you live in DC. You know they attack any right-wing people who show up. There hasn't been a Christian or conservative rally there in years because the Black Front attacks them while the police sit back and watch us get the snot knocked out of us. What sort of democracy allows that?"

"Yeah, don't forget the attack on the Capitol."

"Seriously, Brendan," John retorts, "when war comes, will you help the elites and their Sabia allies? Or will you help the people?"

"John, you know I will never betray the American people. That being said, I will die before I allow another civil war to occur."

John grunts and nods. "Patriot to the end."

They shake hands as Brendan's device goes off again. This time it's audio.

"Three craft and over thirty of us to get you. Hold on!" Berina's voice declares.

Brendan looks at John. "You guys may want to back away; these aliens act like crazy girlfriends."

As they laugh and hug, the shuttlecraft rapidly but silently descends in front of them. Brendan keeps John in the embrace, partly to enjoy the goodbye but also to ensure no over-eager Sabia thinks he is being held hostage. As he walks toward the craft, a side door opens. He turns around, lifts his hat to John, and turns back to board the vessel. As he is about to enter, a guard reaches out for him. Expecting a helping hand, Brendan is instead grabbed by the shoulder, the hard yank nearly sending him flying into the aircraft. Zalta practically catches him, preventing a collision with another guard standing against the far wall.

"Up!" Zalta yells. As the door seals shut, Brendan guesses the motionless travel begins. "Are you alright?" she asks as she quickly feels around for any wounds and then checks his eyes.

PATRICK ABBOTT

"I'm fine," Brendan says in a voice that tries to allay the Sabia's concern. "The Kentucky Rifles treated me fine, so there's no need to worry. I served with one of their commanders, and they're primarily angry at the government, not the Sabia."

Zalta is trying to conduct more checks, but he gently waves her off. Another guard comes up to him, inquiring about immediate threats.

"To us?" Brendan asks. "I imagine we're in space now, and I doubt they have anti-spacecraft missiles; we should be safe." The dry humor is lost on the alien, so he decides to answer honestly. "None whatsoever on the ground. The Rifles have agreed to leave future shipments alone. Additionally, I met with some other group representatives—they all promised not to interfere with your operations there."

The guard walks away without saying anything. Looking around, Brendan sees about ten of them; all dressed for combat, packed into the shuttle. Not finding any space to sit down, he leans against the cockpit door. There is a knock on the other side, followed by a crackle.

"Welcome back," Berina's voice says. "You should have heard the rant Esfirs gave us yesterday when we returned without you. You have orders to meet with Zand and the council, but they need some time to assemble. I will escort you to medical first and then Zand when she's ready. I cannot comment on the council's opinion, though I can assure you Esfirs is very mad at you."

Joy.

The craft lands, and everyone debarks. The guards do not display any interest in Brendan apart from one Brendan met earlier named Kimya. She gives him a hard pat on the back as she walks by. Last off the ship, Zalta runs up to him and tells him she's glad he is alright.

"Boo!" Berina yells from behind him. She laughs as he turns around. "You ready to see the boss? Her bark is fierce, but she cares for you."

Brendan gives her a wide-eyed look and motions for her to lead the way.

"Wait here," she tells him as they arrive. She enters medical. In a few seconds, she walks back out with two other Sabia doctors.

Crap, she's emptying the room. This is going to be unpleasant.

Brendan sighs hard and then puffs up his chest. He confidently walks in with a smile. Esfirs has her arms crossed and a stern look on her face. He starts to talk but is cut off.

"What is your hybrid expansion rate? How did your immune system react to a Terran atmosphere without medical care overnight? What if you had had another attack? Who would have helped you? Even care? Well? Do you?"

He steps back. "It's okay. Everything worked out—"

"I asked you a question. Answer it."

PATRICK ABBOTT

"Well, you asked me several questions . . ."

A primal, guttural sound exits through Esfirs' now clenched teeth, preventing Brendan from continuing. A shade of red he's never seen on a human flows up and down her face as if something were moving underneath her skin.

"You must take care of yourself!" she screams. "The work you do is not worth it if you die! You do not realize how much your life is worth beyond your work!" While she talks, Brendan is taken aback by how those words compare to what Heather used to yell at him. "The rocks were successfully taken to the spaceport without incident. But what would that be worth if you had another attack? Do you think we would say, 'We lost Brendan, but at least we got our rocks?' Do you think I would be fine with that outcome? Please, Brendan, please put things in perspective before you act!" She stops, out of breath.

Brendan lets silence have its turn as he digests what she has said. Then, he calmly tells her, "I will, next time. I promise. My mission was to help the Sabia, and I did so. Please acknowledge that."

He can see her battle a wave of conflicting emotions. "Yessssss"—she struggles to use words—"you did. Thank you. Please know Zalta, Berina, and I are also Sabia. Help us by not robbing us of your life."

He nods. "Okay. I can do that."

He puts out his hand for a handshake, but Esfirs takes a step back and, instead of shaking it, slowly and awkwardly places her right hand over her heart and nods.

"Thank you," she manages to get out.

Her eyes dart around; her face follows their movement with a slight lag. Brendan is shocked by the alienness of the action. *Of course, she is an alien after all, but still, it's freaky.* The action slows down along with her breathing. *Was she trying to control her emotions?*

"Thank you," she repeats. "I am glad you are back with us."

How much of their behavior is truly theirs, and how much is mimicry?

She closes her eyes for a moment and breathes out. "I am sorry for yelling at you. I could not sleep last night. Berina told me you would be alright, but I envisioned you having a medical problem and dying. She kept contacting you because she forbade me from reaching out."

"Thank you," he replies, "and I am sorry for not thinking about you and the others when I planned my mission. Sometimes I do what we call 'going into the zone.' I was eager to do a good job for you all. And hey, I managed to interact with Sabia and humans without any medical issues. That's something to take pride in, eh?"

Esfirs laughs and clasps her hands together. "Welcome home."

Berina enters and addresses Brendan in a formal tone. "Auxiliary Officer, you are summoned to appear now before the council."

Without even acknowledging Esfirs' presence, she takes him by the arm. As they leave, Brendan feels the stress building. Finally, it becomes too much. Taking a moment, he leans against a wall to catch his breath.

"Hey, are you okay?" Berina asks more naturally.

He tries to wave her off. The mission was a success, but instead of acknowledging a job well done, Esfirs gave him major crap. It will probably be easy to rebuff criticism from the council, but Esfirs' yelling wounded him more than it should have.

"Do you need me to take you back to medical? Are you having another attack?"

"No, no. Seriously. I . . . I wasn't expecting what happened back there with Esfirs, I guess."

Berina laughs. "Well, now we can sympathize with each other. She was not happy with me—at all. She seriously was demanding we go back for you. Rank had to be pulled to get her to stop. She cares, Brendan. Now, can we please go? I would take you back to your cabin to rest, but Zand and the council are not people you should keep waiting."

Brendan, approaching the checkpoint, sees several guards in the middle of a conversation. Some of them are wearing body armor, others just padding. Kimya, the one who pulled him into the shuttle, steps in front of them.

"Greetings, Berina. I have been ordered to escort Brendan to the chambers. You are relieved."

"Ha"—the laugh from Berina is shockingly harsh—"good for you. Too bad you cannot give me orders. Stand aside. I relayed I would escort Auxiliary Officer

Brendan"—Berina stresses the title for extra emphasis—
"and that is what I will do." Berina looks over to the
others. "And who here will enforce orders of this . . .
guard?"

This is oddly intense.

Berina grabs Brendan's arm and maneuvers
around Kimya while the rest of the guards watch. After
they turn a corner, Brendan tries to ask what the standoff
was all about, but Berina harshly shushes him, and they
walk on in silence.

They approach the council chamber, a guard
flanking each side of the door. One of them opens it as
they arrive. Berina lets go of Brendan's arm but follows
him inside. She announces his presence as "the auxiliary
officer" and leaves in a formal manner. Brendan looks
around the room. The council is arranged in a semi-
circle with Zand in the center, farthest away from
Brendan. There is an empty pillow facing her. Brendan
realizes he is going to be front and center during this
interrogation. Meanwhile, younger Sabia of both sexes sit
along the back wall.

"That's not good," Brendan mutters to himself.

Zand motions for him to take a seat. "Please
explain what you think is not good here and why."

He sits down cross-legged. In his head, he argues
with her, criticizing the tone of his retrieval, Esfirs,
Berina's standoff with the guard, and how he is not sitting
at anyone's left. Part of him wants to ask if Zand truly
plans to inquire about his thoughts or is merely trying to
set him up for a stream of insults. This doesn't happen,

though. The resolution with Esfirs has leveled him off significantly. He decides to push aside his emotions and handle the situation with frankness.

"Zand, this setup is different than last time when I had a decent conversation with you. Clearly, this meeting is about how I handled the situation on the ground. So please, tell me your thoughts so I can explain my actions to your satisfaction."

The Sabia female at Zand's right leans over to whisper something. Not knowing if this is a genuine inquiry or a powerplay to demonstrate Brendan does not control the meeting, he counters by laying out his case. "The mission was a complete success." The Sabia woman stops whispering, and both she and Zand look at Brendan, surprised by the interruption. "My actions secured the mineral shipments, and not one Sabia or ally was harmed. The Kentucky Rifles and other neighboring militias no longer suspect the Sabia of kidnapping children and thus are much less likely to target the mining operation or shipments. I left the situation better than when I arrived. By all definitions, that is a positive outcome. What do you think?"

Zand sits motionless. The Sabia female leans in toward Brendan, but as if he missed some cue, she returns to her original position. Brendan quickly glances at the other Sabia. He sees that they are watching their leader more than paying attention to him. *The ball's in your court, Zand.*

"Disapproval does not lie with the outcome. Accept our gratitude for the result you secured. What upsets us is that the militia that stopped the shipment was given the power to inspect material that belonged to us. You gave the vigilantes this authority. This puts us at greater risk of attack in the future as it demonstrates our weakness to others. The message is 'interfere with our business, and we will accommodate you.' Do you not have a policy of 'no negotiating with terrorists?'"

He stretches out his legs and feet not only to get more comfortable but also to display confidence. "I understand you're worried my actions displayed weakness toward a hostile entity. I don't believe that is the case, though. The Kentucky Rifles were afraid, not adversarial. They believed a mysterious force was kidnapping children: you Sabia. In your name, I demonstrated that the Sabia are peaceful and transparent, not some unknown. Furthermore, the inspection proved the lies they had been told were false.

"Meanwhile, the inspection has created a bond of trust that didn't exist before. Because of my actions on the ground, the Kentucky Rifles and smaller groups nearby are no longer interested in interfering with the mining operation. Thus, the blockade has not only been resolved but future problems have also been prevented before they can manifest. Is this not what you desire, too?"

Zand looks down. Both Sabia sitting beside her, look to her for some response.

"I hope you are right, Auxiliary Officer." She does not look up as she speaks. "Tell me, Brendan—your government was weak in handling the situation. Apahvez tells me the leader of the military on site did not trust his own personnel. What are your intentions when open conflict emerges among your people?"

Brendan shakes his head like an Afghan refusing to believe something said at a *shura*. "That is a loaded question and unfair. What I will tell you is that all the Sabia's thoughts and talk about 'when war comes' suggest one future outcome as the only possibility. This blinds thinking. One way to avoid conflict is to think about other possibilities and work toward them. People internalize single-future talk. Too much single-future thinking makes the dire outcome a reality."

Brendan studies Zand intensely for some sort of visual clues as to what she is thinking. When she looks up, they lock eyes. Her gaze is soft and passive, but Brendan feels his head start aching again. He suspects he looks intellectually and emotionally naked to her. He tries to look away but can't. The headache grows more intense.

"Words for us to consider." Leleh's voice breaks Brendan's concentration, allowing him to look at her. His counterpart sits several seats down from Zand. "We gave the auxiliary a task with few parameters, and he accomplished it in a way that makes sense to his Terran reasoning. Our reasoning would accomplish the same goal, but the Terrans might have misinterpreted it, resulting in casualties and further violence. We have accepted Brendan's participation because he does things differently than us. Is that not what he did here?"

Leleh for the save!

She continues. "Perhaps we can all work together to communicate our understanding, give clearer parameters, and ensure we can complete our missions without putting our faith in those who may harm us."

"That is more than fair," Brendan replies. His previous conversation with Esfirs serves as a sort of antibody, keeping him from negatively reacting to the barb at the end of Leleh's statement.

Zand leans over to discuss matters with the flanking Sabia. She thanks Brendan for his time and instructs him to leave.

"Wait." A voice stops him as he stands up. Turning, he sees a Sabia with flowing golden hair. She looks like she is in her mid-to-late twenties. "What did you do when you were with the Terrans?"

Brendan replays the events in his mind, trying to keep it to things the Sabia would be interested in. "Well, ma'am"—he places his hand over his heart and bows slightly—"first we drove into the nearby town. I visited with my friend's family and played with their kids. We then went to an evening religious service; they are a splinter sect from my religion, but it is close enough to allow joint worship. Afterward, I was famished, so we all went to a small community restaurant where we ate, and I met with various community members and militias. Back at my friend's house, I played with their kids again, and we spent a few hours discussing life and Earth politics. I woke up in the morning, had breakfast, and was picked up. And now I am here."

Brendan braces himself for a conversation about what politics were discussed.

PATRICK ABBOTT

"Please, tell me"—there is urgency in her voice—"how many children does your friend have? What are their ages?"

"Oh, he has five children. The oldest is twelve; then there is a ten-year-old, a seven-year-old, a five-year-old, and one child about eighteen months old."

The young council member's face beams with happiness.

"Thank you," Zand now says, "you may go."

As if on autopilot, Brendan stands at attention and salutes. He turns and walks out.

Eighteen – The Scream

Brendan has collapsed on his bed. He stares up at the ceiling, allowing his mind to wander. Resentment over the lack of praise for his success is growing inside him. *Esfirs criticized me, and Zand thinks I gave in to terrorists. Forget that crap.* He compares his return to the Sabia with how John and the others treated him. *Man, if I did that Kentucky mission for the UIC, I would be freaking employee of the month.*

Chimes. It is the door. Startled, Brendan calls out permission to enter.

"Do you Terrans not eat?" Berina yells from the doorway. "Where are you?"

"In the bedroom!"

"Come out here near your television. We brought dinner!"

We. That means . . .

The bedroom door opens. Esfirs is in a striking midi-dress patterned with bright, colorful symbols on a white background. *Many of their outfits look Central Asian, Tajik-like.* She slowly walks in, holding her left arm. *It must be a habit when she is nervous.* She does not make eye contact, and her shoulders are hunched over. She stops halfway between the bed and door. Brendan reacts by sitting up, taking in her appearance.

"Hey," he says.

"Hey," she replies, "now that we got you back home, I bet you have an appetite."

Home, she said, I am home. "Not really, but I'll always take the company. And, ah, it's great to be here."

She smiles at him. Walking up, she puts her left hand on his cheek for a moment, and they look at each other for what feels like hours. "Come, Dear Brendan, we must not keep Berina waiting."

He is in too much of a state of awe to object. A deep longing ignored for years arises in his heart. *I've missed being loved. Is this love, though? Is she playing me? Why did she act indifferent to me for so many weeks?*

"Brendan"—her voice calls him back—"come. Berina will know." There is a slight tone of playfulness in her voice.

He gets up and follows her to the living room. Facing the television, Berina has laid out pillows, a mat, and various food dishes. She gives Esfirs and Brendan a suspicious look. When she asks what they've been doing, Esfirs responds she was telling him she was glad he got back safe. However, Brendan can tell Berina suspects more. They take seats on pillows, and Berina asks him to pray, which he does. Berina respectfully lowers her head, but Esfirs merely waits for him to finish. They then eat a spread of vegetables, hummus, and what looks like a fire-grilled chicken.

"Brendan," Berina starts, "I realized I have been remiss in congratulating you on a job well done on Terra. It was a great victory for the common good."

Trying too hard, but nice nonetheless. "Thank you; I am glad you see what I tried to do."

"And Esfirs has had an eventful day as well." She looks over to Esfirs, who puts down her plate.

"I have been authorized leave to return home." Esfirs pauses as Brendan's jaw drops. Then, she continues, "This is what you refer to as rest and relaxation leave."

"How—how long will you be gone?" *Not after what we just shared. Please don't go.*

"Length of leave is classified." The quickness of her response hurts Brendan.

His heart races. *But I do not want to be away from you.* "Will I get to see you again?"

Esfirs' eyes dart to Berina, over to Brendan, and back to Berina.

Berina answers for Esfirs. "She will return to the ship and will have the same role. Personally, unless you insist on returning to Terra in the immediate future, I would assess you two very likely will be back together in a few weeks." The two women look at each other for a moment.

PATRICK ABBOTT

Exhaling deeply, Brendan remembers his satchel. "Would you two be interested in receiving some gifts I picked up in Kentucky?"

Berina is eager, while Esfirs demonstrates restraint with a lifted eyebrow. Clapping his hands together, he brings back the bag from his bedroom.

"For you, Berina, I got these aviator sunglasses so you can look the part of a pilot."

Berina puts them on and poses proudly.

He digs further into the bag. "For you, Esfirs, I got this fluorite quartz crystal. It's a neat rock from the mining site. What I really like about it is it gives off a prism effect."

Esfirs takes the stone without a word and starts studying it. *She must like it, the way she is looking at it transfixed. Geology, or whatever she called it, must really have been something she and her mother enjoyed.*

Berina asks if there are any more gifts in the bag. Brendan looks down and sees the cross John gave him when he stayed with him. *The man wanted me to know I wasn't alone, even with the Sabia.* Unsure whether to show it to them, time passes as the cross and he have a sort of staring contest. Finally, he starts to pull it out when Esfirs suddenly screams. Looking up, he sees the crystal flying across the room.

"What's wrong?" he asks in alarm.

"She's fine; it was nothing," Berina tells him as Esfirs hyperventilates, staring at the rock.

Asking again gets no response. Esfirs' skin has gone pale. Brendan starts to move toward her, but Berina pulls him back. She assures him Esfirs will be fine in a minute.

There is a back and forth between them while Esfirs calms down. Throughout the incident, the sunglasses-wearing pilot surprises Brendan with her placid demeanor. She places her hand on his shoulder and calmly repeats, "Esfirs is fine," in response to all his questions.

"I . . . I . . . I am fine, Brendan," Esfirs finally manages to say. "Thank you for the gift. I just had – a moment. I am fine, I assure you."

Confusing, to say the least. Brendan gently pulls out the cross to ensure she is not reacting to the religious object. Nothing happens. *Okay, they're not demons. We can cross that conspiracy theory off the list. Too bad I can't write that in a report.* The humorous thought leaves as quickly as it came. *Something has spooked Esfirs, but what is it?* Brendan examines both women. Esfirs is still visibly upset. Berina has taken off her glasses, and the women are looking each other in the eyes. The silence is palpable. *First, my reaction to her leaving and now her reaction to who knows what. This is a disaster of a dinner. Time to save this night.*

"Berina, would Esfirs and you like to go for a stroll to the areas on the ship I'm allowed in? It might be nice for us to take a walk together."

"Yes," Berina says without breaking eye contact with Esfirs, "a walk would do us all good. Let us go to the gardens. Esfirs loves the gardens."

PATRICK ABBOTT

The three of them stand up in unison. Berina effortlessly slides on her sunglasses with a flick of her wrist, looking like the epitome of a cocky pilot. When Esfirs asks Berina if she will take the rock, she says yes. She takes a cloth from the dinner set, picks up the mineral, and slips it into her pocket.

Meanwhile, Esfirs tries and mostly fails to meekly smile at Brendan. "Thank you for the kind gift. It reminds me of my youth."

They then set out toward one of the ship's hydroponic gardens.

Later that night, Brendan returns to his room. The walk had been much needed and enjoyed. He looks at the food spread and ponders how to clean up. But first, he goes to his satchel bag and pulls out another fluorite crystal. He looks at the rock, moving it back and forth in his hands. Refracted light moves across his arms like a rainbow as he manipulates the mineral. *Interesting.*

Nineteen – The Elixir

Brendan is hanging up a jump rope while Berina slips on her boots. Working out has robbed him of much of his breath, and dealing with Berina's semi-gains in human religious knowledge has been strenuous.

"Okay, seminarian, so your religion teaches you the one who saves is God-Man-Jesus-Son-of-God, He-Who-Is-His-Own-Father is—"

"No," he interrupts, "you are messing up the Trinity again."

"Three people, one body!" Berina shoots back. "So your God-Man-Jesus-Son-of-God-Holy Spirit . . ."

He groans, and Berina responds with laughter. Brendan uses the break to try to flip the conversation. "It's clear you are not a trinitarian. So, what are you? You have expressed enough interest in my faith—now I am interested in what you believe." He grins widely.

"Nice try." She wags a finger. "You may not have died on the last ride with me, but classified information remains classified. My turn again! Imagine your Jesus-Son-of-God-Man comes to you and says you could ask him any question. What would you ask your god?"

PATRICK ABBOTT

Why? Was it because I left seminary? How much more must I lose? Brendan thinks about the pain he has felt; the many times he told God that he didn't understand why He was letting the divorce happen. However, enough seminary teaching remains in him. He knows what he would say. "I wouldn't ask anything. I would just apologize for all the wrongs I have done in my life."

"That is not a question, though!" Berina meets his somberness with an air of jest.

"It's what I would do."

"You think you are so bad you would need to apologize on the spot? After all, you have done?"

"All the good done is but trinkets to God. All the bad separates me from God." He sighs. Reflecting on his soul upsets his stomach. "What would you do if your 'divine' were to give you the same chance?"

She shakes her head. "Religious matters are classified."

My faith life is not a joke! he wants to snap back, but the thought catches him. *My faith.* The idea rings in his head. Brendan rolls his eyes and picks up his backpack. Suddenly, he feels two hands on his shoulders, pulling him back.

Berina whispers, "I would ask for a large family."

She slowly releases him. There is a twinkle in her eye. Then, she assumes a formal military pose. "I believe you have an appointment in medical today, Auxiliary Officer. I will escort you."

Small victories. This claiming everything is classified is annoying. Eventually, I should be able to have something to report back about the Sabia. Now, if only I had someone to report back to.

Together they walk down the halls. After a little prodding, Berina drops the military airs and reverts her playful tone to discuss Earth-related matters. Her interest in soccer far surpasses Brendan's level of caring for the sport. Her repeated questions about the next match are answered with, "I'll have to look into it."

Medical is open, and there are several doctors and medics inside. Zalta is the first one to see them.

"Hello, Brendan and Berina. Are you here to say goodbye to Esfirs?" Her voice is bubbly.

"Sadly so," Brendan replies, "but it has also been ten days since the last time I was here. You know what that means." Just hearing his own words sinks his spirits.

Nodding somberly, Zalta walks into a back room. At the same time, Berina gently pats Brendan's back. He looks over, lifts his eyebrows, and lets out an exaggerated sigh.

"Shot at, bombed, knifed in the face, but ultimately the thing you fear is a think drink. Odd how life works," Berina states.

Looking around, Brendan takes in the scene, appreciating the busyness of the medical bay. Four doctors are at their respective alcoves. Various tasks are being performed, ranging from looking over images on screens to typing on tablets. Brendan has no idea what sort of work is being accomplished. He notices Nashifran in one of the alcoves, packing up things a doctor gives her.

Zalta waves them into the back room. Inside, Esfirs is waiting for him with the cursed drink in her hands. The thick black liquid has become the bane of his existence, a reminder of what he has become. He attempts small talk, but Esfirs' tapping of the cup shuts him up. He sits on the bed and tries to prepare for what is coming. The first thing he does is grab the glass and close his eyes before chugging down the thick, oily medicine. *The countdown begins.*

"Sure am going to miss you, but have fun. Can you share anything about what you plan to do while away?" he asks.

Esfirs' mouth moves back and forth as if deciding what she can reveal. "I intend to see some old friends. No intention to travel once I arrive. Rest without worries is what I look forward to the most."

"That's great. Any outdoor activities or spending time with the family?"

"I cannot reveal anything classified; I am sorry." Her eyes focus on him.

These dang hands are already shaking, and she knows it. This is hell. "Oookay . . ." He swallows hard. *Not yet.* "That's okay. I bet everyone will ask you what us T-t-t-Terrans are like." He tries to do air quotes around "Terran," but his arms do not cooperate. This is it. As he lies back on the bed, he lets himself drift off. Cold sweat begins to pour from his skin within seconds, and his vision goes blurry. He feels Zalta lift his head to place a pillow underneath it. Meanwhile, he can sense Esfirs standing above him. Surging pain in his teeth and feet disrupt any thinking he can do.

"I wish it didn't hurt so much," he forces out through the pain. He feels an alien hand on his, soft, though the grip becomes iron tight. "Thank you," he says to his unknown hand holder. Full body convulsions begin. "Esfirs," he calls out, "I hope—I hope to, to . . . see you off."

The pain wanes, his body stops shaking, and the only thing audible in the room is his breathing. His vision slowly returns, but the person holding his hand lets go before he can see who it is. Zalta pulls a blanket over him.

"Thank you, thank you," he whispers.

First, Zalta and then Berina leave. The lights dim. Esfirs remains to watch silently over him.

"How much . . . how much more of this?" he asks.

"Until you are safe," she somberly replies.

"I hate this change. I'm scared, Esfirs, I am so scared." Then, quietly, he begins to cry.

She shushes him. "Do not fear this, Dear Brendan. You would have physically changed if your hand had not been repaired. No one thought you would become something you were not. Remember, you will always be you. The thing you can control is how you grow to your full potential. That has always been true. Do not let outside events change you."

PATRICK ABBOTT

He takes in her words. She begins to leave.

"Wait," he calls out, stopping her. "If I'm not up, grab me before you leave. I want to see you off. It's a tradition for deployed personnel, so you can't rob me of it."

"Doubtful logic," she says stoically. "But yes, I will make sure you are up, Dear Brendan." She smiles as she leaves.

Interlude – Esfirs: Departure

Esfirs laughs. The efforts the Terran Brendan makes to entertain her while she waits are admirable. *However, he should rest; he looks tired. It is comforting to see him up so soon after his treatment.*

"And did you see them again?" she asks.

"I actually met up with Benjamin randomly on another deployment in a chow hall. That's, umm . . . like the cafeteria, but with food of a lot lower quality. Mohammed, however, I stayed in touch with him a bit, but then he moved, and since then, I haven't heard from him in years. I will forever be grateful for the morning we spent together the day I left. The breakfast, chatting about a birthday party in the village, and him carrying my bags to the helicopter." Brendan slightly lifts the straps of the two bags of Esfirs' he has set down near him.

"Ah, so your insistence on all this is because you feel indebted to him. Are you using me as a proxy to return the favor?"

Brendan shakes his head. "No, I learned that day what friends do for each other. I want to emulate what he taught me."

PATRICK ABBOTT

A group of new Legionaries passes by. *They get younger and younger.* She looks over to Brendan and wonders what he notices about them.

"Do something fun for me while you are away, eh? As a Kansan, I miss the prairie. If you can, walk barefoot outside for me." He laughs. "Let me or Berina know how you are or if you need us to do anything while you're away. If you want to talk or send photos, I would be more than game for that."

She feels sad. "I am not allowed to communicate with you while on leave, Brendan."

He looks down. Esfirs feels sorry for him. *He really will be lonely without me. Oh divine, send a Watcher to care for him.* She wants to reach out, but not here. *Who knows what Berina has relayed, but I cannot be so open here.*

"I understand. I didn't mean to get you to break any rules; just trying to stay connected. Being without you will be hard. Ever since—well, you know, I haven't had many friends I can talk to."

Ugh, so many contractions. "Thank you for your understanding. And it will be hard to be without my friend, too. However, I will return. Wait for me."

Brendan's eyes open widely when she calls him a friend. "I will! I can't wait for you to come back, though." He sounds like he misses her already.

The air crackles. Esfirs' shuttle is called. She reaches for her bags, but Brendan is up the moment she makes a move for them. He swings both onto his back.

"Let's go," he says, "I will walk you out."

Twenty - Preparation

Looking around, Brendan can't help but take in the situation with a bit of mirth. To his right, Zalta is—successfully, he thinks—peacocking herself to several young Sabia men. He can't make out everything, but he has repeatedly heard Zalta name-drop him, referring to their friendship. To his left, Berina is standing around with what he concludes to be senior officers. Brendan notes how sometimes she can appear immature and other times the model of a professional officer. She and the other seniors talk to the new Sabia, who keep pointing at him. Intrigued by this behavior, he asks Berina about it. She tells him she invited him to this party in the restricted part of the ship to acculturate the new Sabia to Terrans. *Glad to know I'm the test monkey.*

Guard Ishan and his girlfriend Ayra sit next to Brendan on pillows watching baseball as they play a card game that Berina instructs them to call the "Sabia card game." Their open displays of affection certainly differ from what Brendan has seen on his previous deployments. He wonders if the Sabia's culture tolerates it or if it just occurs on long, interstellar missions. Ishan inquires whether the latest action in the baseball game signifies that Brendan's team scored. Brendan tells him no. Ishan asks if the other team scored. Brendan says that the last play was a ground ball foul, so nothing happened. Ishan mutters that he does not understand baseball.

The "Sabia card game" is its own epic event. First, it was the use of a deck of cards he picked up in Kentucky. The base ten of the suites works fine, but the court cards cause the first snafu. Ayra asks about the order of precedence; Brendan explains it goes jack, queen, king. A discussion ensues. Things fall apart when the Sabia discover male-headed monarchies are a thing on Earth. In the verbal ruckus, Brendan gets a laughing Berina to admit women head Sabia governments. This is a significant difference from the supposed gender equality the UIC believe the Sabia to have. It also implies that the Sabia intentionally gave a false impression by having Loft lead most delegation matters. *If only I had someone to report this to* has become a repeated theme in his head.

Noshen sits beside him. The female ship engineer looks to be in her mid-twenties and is barely five feet tall. Her white uniform almost consumes her. She motions to a card on the floor and then to his second of three rows.

"No helping him," Ayra cries.

Noshen moves two scoots away but then back toward Brendan. He thanks her with a wink. In response, she smiles nervously and buries her face in her arms. She tried talking to Brendan earlier but only offered up a few heavily accented, broken words before giving up. *Makes sense—she is on-ship staff. They probably thought she'd never need to speak to humans, so they didn't give her the same training as those who do deal with delegates from Terra. She seems friendly enough, though.* Thankfully, no one has been hostile to him. *If that changes, I'm in trouble.*

Brendan studies the totals of the three rows and decides to boost the sum of the first one. In an instant, both Ayra and Ishan place cards in their third rows, laughing joyfully.

"I don't get it. I just don't get it," Brendan says. He takes out his communicator and snaps a photo for Berina to send to Esfirs. His cards are then divided between the young couple, who take turns trying to work against each other's piles.

On the screen, he sees Washington's rally cut short via a strikeout. The team can't seem to get started post-break. As a commercial plays, he hears Berina laugh and yell, "Nice set of rows you lost with, Brendan." The event is an enjoyable change from the monotony of the slow nights after work. However, he feels lonely without Esfirs' company.

The next day Brendan is up and ready for another grind. The nightmares are gone, but in their stead, there's a waking race that has no end. Initially, the idea of being a liaison gave him purpose. He was going to provide basic intelligence assessments while collecting everything he could. However, he feels a lack of accomplishment since the new ambassador has yet to reach out to him. As he puts on his gym clothes, he reflects on the lack of support from his own country and his mixed relationship with the Sabia. On the positive side, Berina is a great friend, and Esfirs is, well, very lovely. They have even told him things that they initially claimed were classified.

On the other hand, Leleh will not reveal the motivations behind her requests for information during their semi-weekly meetings, and he has been made to feel like a man without loyalties the two times he has met with the council. He closes his eyes and breathes deeply. *I must get in the zone.*

"No zero days!" he yells, pumping his chest twice.

Leaving his cabin, he sees a guard.

"Two more days to Friday, Resra. You know what that means—upper body day!"

The male guard Resra fist-bumps him and smiles. "The best is yet to come, Brendan. Five more days to the best day of the week: Monday!"

Brendan laughs. Teaching them this joke has added a lighthearted sense of normalcy to an extreme situation. He starts walking to the gym backward, so he still faces Resra. "Nah, man, don't you put that on me!" They both laugh heartily.

He enters the hangar and takes in the view. Over time, the Sabia have acquired multiple ellipticals, treadmills, rowing machines, exercise bikes, spin bikes, weight machines, and free weights. What started as an effort to get a few pieces of equipment for himself has grown as Berina and others have joined in the daily workouts. *Some of it must be her willful personality, but she must be more than just a pilot.* He doesn't discount the novelty some Sabia must feel spending time with a "Terran," though. Most Sabia he has talked to have never been to Earth, so he's the only one they can interact with. *But how much of a Terran am I?*

Upper body day begins with sets of five chest presses. After a few iterations, Berina and Apahvez come in. Berina is dressed in the green T-shirt and black shorts the UIC wears, copying Brendan's look. Apahvez, meanwhile, is dressed in his white service uniform.

"Hey, you two. Where are you flying today, Berina? Somewhere nice, like a beach where I can work remotely?" Brendan jokes.

"I am taking you home so you can introduce me to all your friends," she retorts with a smile.

"What?" Brendan is confused.

The pilot motions toward Apahvez. He looks annoyed, perhaps more so than during the Kentucky mission.

"Yes, you have been selected for a mission later this morning," Apahvez begins. "Your assignment is to assist Delegate Loft when he travels to the Washington, District of Columbia area. In addition, I will oversee overall security. Please return to your cabin to prepare and for Leleh to brief you."

"Whoa, whoa now. A mission this morning? Where in DC? Who are we meeting? How long has this been planned? No offense, but things like doing liaison work and intelligence matters take time. You just can't rush it."

"Further details are classified until you are formally briefed," Apahvez responds without emotion, and Berina laughs.

The laughter sets Brendan off. "That is really not fair. How do you expect me—"

Berina comes up to him, grabs his right calf, and pulls it up above his head, causing him to fall backward onto the padded floor. She jumps on him, pounds the floor three times, and then lets off him.

"The hell, Berina?" he curses.

"When it comes to missions, classified is classified. So do not worry; you will be fully briefed. We can work out together tomorrow." Her tone is both playful and deadly serious.

It feels to Brendan like she is trivializing him. *It's as if my concerns don't matter to her. I am like a musical instrument that can be played on demand.* He gets up and lets out a sort of snort as he rises. Holding back an urge to lash out at Berina, he gives her an upset look and walks out of the hangar toward his cabin. Berina yells something as he leaves, but he doesn't bother to give it the attention needed to comprehend what she is saying.

A newer male guard, Berzo, is talking to Leleh as he approaches. Both Sabia turn to face him.

"Brendan, I am here to brief you about the mission today. May we discuss the matter alone in your cabin?" Leleh inquires.

PATRICK ABBOTT

"Sure, get it in." Brendan's voice betrays his annoyance, and his brisk nod toward the door only reinforces his hostile tone.

Leleh gives him a perplexed look. Brendan opens the door, allowing them both to enter. He closes it and leans up against it, waiting for her to make the first move. She, in turn, remains silent.

"Okay, I blink." He throws his arms up. "Go ahead and tell me everything. I only ask that you not throw me to the freaking floor."

She looks even more confused and then regains her stoic composure. "In two hours, you will depart from here to join Delegate Loft on a mission to the Unified Intelligence Command. We have, with growing concern, observed increasing tensions both among Terran countries and within them. Powers such as the Russian Federation and the People's Republic of China have aided us immensely in understanding these developments. However, we are worried they are giving us biased analysis despite their claims of being objective. Thankfully, the United States of America has offered us its own perspective. Today, we will be meeting various American experts and the director of the Unified Intelligence Command, Michael. You know these people well, Brendan. Please assist Loft in the meetings. Afterward, we can all work together to analyze whether what the UIC has told us is true or not."

The pronoun game again. This is some sort of real-world field test designed to see how I play ball.

"Leleh, why was I not told about this earlier? I could have prepared for the mission and helped Loft as well."

"The mission details were classified. Now was deemed an appropriate time for you to be authorized access to the information."

"Was it planned before today to have me as part of this trip?"

"Yes." Her voice is entirely without emotion.

"Then why wasn't I trusted earlier on? Keeping things classified from me can be perfectly valid; I don't need to have access to everything because there are some things you simply cannot trust many people with. That's fair. But you purposefully kept plans involving myself secret from me. You're paying the highest price for that. I could have created biographies, discussed what the UIC might say if they were stonewalling you, and even helped plan out the schedule so we could maximize what the Sabia could get out of it. Why was I not trusted with this information?"

"Where do your loyalties lie, Brendan?"

"Not this, Leleh! I have sworn an oath that was mutually agreed upon by all of us. No one can question that I have served with honor and distinction, saving Sabia lives while risking my own. As an officer, my actions have already answered your question." Every word is painful, as he wants to erupt in righteous anger. But he knows Leleh will come back with something else if he leaves it at that, so he asks an open-ended question. "What have I done to make you doubt my honesty?"

"Brendan"—she starts to mull over her words, causing her to lose her stony composure—"there is nothing you have done to make us doubt you. Your situation is . . . unique. It would be fair for all of us to say we are . . . adapting . . . to the situation, yes?"

Got you off your A-game. "It's an adaptation, alright." He means his words to be acceptable to Leleh without accepting what she said.

She responds with a slow downward nod, forty-five degrees to the left of the center of her face. *That's new behavior.*

"By the way, Leleh, while I am eager to see the old office, how do I know I won't be captured and arrested for medical testing?"

"We have thought about those concerns despite the United States government promising us you are no longer under arrest. You and Loft will each have your own security details."

"Thank you." He is surprised by how worried he is about his own government capturing him. *Is it a question of loyalties? No—never!*

"You leave in three hours. Please be in the hangar in two and a half."

With that, she leaves. Brendan is fuming as he puts on professional clothes—including a jacket and tie. *It has been a while since I've had to put on a full suit. When was it last? Briefing the senator, maybe?* Once dressed, he makes his way toward the television only to slump to the floor. The dark thoughts weigh him down.

217

The last time he was in the office was when, well, he was told he couldn't deploy and then nearly died in the metro knife-fist-bomb battle. Would his friends be there to welcome him? Would they think him a turncoat? He is trapped within an endless loop of negative contemplation. The fierce fangs of depression sink in. The Sabia do not trust him, and his government has cut him off. Meanwhile, Berina assaulted him without warning when he protested the Sabia's doubts about his loyalty. All this has led him to doubt himself. He is alone in a universe where both human and Sabia genetics comprise his physical being.

Twenty-One – A Cherubim and Flaming Sword

The door chimes once and then again after a pause. Brendan chooses to ignore it. It rings a third time, and still, he doesn't respond. He hears the door open and footsteps coming toward him. Trying to avoid the situation, he puts his head in his hands.

"Brendan? Sir?" the guard Berzo cautiously calls out to him.

Brendan nods, stands up, and mutters a "thanks" to Berzo. Without another word, he walks out toward the hangar. He arrives, silent and weighed down with emotion. The inside of the hangar is quiet as Berina is looking at a checklist on her tablet. He avoids her by going to the makeshift gym and sitting on a bench. Then, in the corner of his eye, he sees Berina walking up to him.

"Hey, you! You ready to go back to your old office?" Her voice is excited and happy.

Brendan responds with just a slight headshake. Berina, in turn, sits down next to him on the bench.

"I understand," she says in a somber voice, "you are upset we did not inform you earlier about these plans." *She and Leleh must have talked. However, I*

219

would rather have an apology from her. "I should have understood that earlier. Instead, I laughed at you. I apologize." She holds out her left hand for a handshake in the Sabia manner.

Instead of accepting her hand, he starts ranting at her. "What am I doing here, Berina? I am reporting and analyzing everything Leleh asks me to. I put myself in harm's way to help the Sabia accomplish missions, sometimes even saving lives in imminent danger. And for what? I'm not even told about upcoming missions until a few hours beforehand. Then, my loyalties are questioned. Plus, a friend flips me on my back when I protest this unfair treatment. Why am I not trusted?"

"You should be trusted more, yes." Her hand is still waiting to be shaken.

"That's it? I should be trusted more?"

"Remember Esfirs saying you are not like most Terrans. Many Sabia are more closed-minded than you. They are slow to recognize friends not born into the Legion." Her hand remains outstretched.

He takes it and tries his best to shake it. Berina responds with a gleeful noise and a warm embrace.

"Brendan, my friend Brendan." She passes her fingers through her hair. "Do not worry. In time you will convert the last few remaining doubters. Just the other day, I was discussing you with a council member. Your actions in Kentucky shocked her. She could not understand why you would risk yourself without protection. I told her you were given a mission and would do anything to accomplish it. Then, I asked her if she was shocked a person who risked his life twice for the Legion was willing to risk it a third time. She replied her first impressions were wrong about you."

"And who was that?"

"Classified!" She laughs after yelling the cursed word. "Not really. It was a personal conversation, so I should not share too much. What I can share, though, is some of what Esfirs and I have talked about."

Brendan sits up straight. "Esfirs? How is she?"

"Oh, I see this has gotten you excited." She slyly smiles. "She is well—I will tell her you asked. But, more importantly, she has gotten approval for trips to Terra when she gets back. She asked me about certain things to see if she should seek to do them with you."

Brendan wonders what Berina is hinting at. However, he is too wrapped up waiting to hear more about Esfirs to say anything.

"She asked if you still watch your baseball games. When I said yes, she asked me if she could withstand a full baseball game. Long story short, I have obtained permission to attend the evening game tonight as a sort of experiment. We have to be incognito, away from the rest of the crowd. Think of it as a gift from us Sabia who know you are trustworthy."

"Wow, that"—he almost begins to break down but fights it off with a laugh—"would be a huge way to end the night. A day in the office with an after-work baseball game. It's been too long since that last happened."

She slaps him on the back. Then, without a word, she stands up and holds out her hand. He takes it, allowing her to pull him up. She twirls a finger vertically by her face.

"Home run," Brendan says.

She smiles and heads back to her craft. Loft and six guards walk in. *Just in time.* The guards are wearing heavy body armor. Brendan approaches the delegate.

"Sir, are we expecting any trouble today?"

"No, Brendan, we are not. Just an insurance policy, as the Terrans would say."

"Good to hear. I figure, though, if anyone were to be targeted for capture, it would be me."

Brendan looks over the guards. The division into two groups is apparent enough. An intense-looking male leads one, a female the other. The female leader looks at Brendan with fire in her eyes. *Hope I get the guy.*

Loft calls everyone over for the briefing. Berina explains the breakdown of seating and general facts about Virginia. Loft explains that the male guard, Aban, will protect him while Dena, the female guard, will "secure" Brendan. Brendan looks over to acknowledge Dena, only to see her disgusted look has turned into direct hostility. Delegate Loft explains the necessity of ensuring they are not separated from one another, as the United States has demonstrated that it will use deceptive tactics to acquire information by any means possible. After the briefing, he tells everyone to board. Brendan stretches one last time and enters the craft.

PATRICK ABBOTT

Inside, the seats are arranged against the two long walls. As Brendan sits down, Dena walks up and towers over him with a stern look.

She barks commands at him. "At all times, you will stay within five feet of one of my team or me. You will under no circumstance attempt to skirt away from us. I will have no problem detaining you and bringing you back to this craft. I am not your friend, and I do not want to be your friend, so do not try any of your tricks on me."

Shocked, Brendan weakly salutes her. "Roger that."

Dena leans down, coming face to face with him. "I did not ask if you understood."

She turns around and walks to her seat, several down from him. Brendan can hear the air crackle in the distance.

"That is an officer you just addressed," Berina's voice declares.

"An auxiliary," he hears Dena dismissively reply.

In response to the slight, he looks over at Loft to see his reaction. The delegate acts as if he hadn't heard a thing. While observing the various guards, Brendan can see a general disinterested look in them. Aban is the exception, with what Brendan interprets as an intensely focused look on his face. *Really wish I had him rather than Dena. As for the others, better disinterested than hostile.*

The air crackles and Berina's voice announces to everyone they have arrived. Brendan rocks back and forth in his chair slightly to get himself pumped.

Loft looks over to him and says, "Let us go together. They will see we are equal then." His voice gives away his nervousness.

What? Not sure what you mean, but okay, boss man.

"Please, charm them all, Brendan." Loft honestly sounds worried.

He responds with a wink. "Game time, Loft. Easy day, brother."

The door opens, and the late Virginia morning sunshine nearly blinds Brendan. He slowly walks forward as his eyes adjust to the brightness of the sky. A delegation waiting for them becomes visible first as shapes, then as individual people.

The sight of the delegation's head thrills Brendan. "Sarah? Same-Birthday Sarah? Heck yeah! We're a long way from the wadi, eh?" All his cares and worries fade away. He runs to her, leaving Loft behind.

"The agency hasn't been the same without you, kid," she replies. They embrace as old friends.

"We're old, Sarah. 'Agency'—ha! It hasn't been an agency for years. But yes, it will always be our agency."

He laughs joyfully. Fears about this being a trap fade away. He takes a step back to take in the rest of the delegates. All smiling faces. Ones he doesn't know but still friendly looking.

PATRICK ABBOTT

He turns around and motions toward Loft. "Sarah, this is Delegate Loft and our security teams. Delegate Loft, please allow me to introduce you to Intelligence Officer Sarah. Sarah deployed with me the first time. Loft, meanwhile, is the lead delegate for Earth matters."

While Sarah and Loft greet each other, Brendan has a moment of being cross with himself. *First names only—really? I have been with the Sabia too long. Dang thing of theirs is rubbing off on me.* Sarah introduces the UIC's security team that will escort Loft and Brendan. Three guards are assigned to each of them. *Three on one. Six people guarding me with two agendas in the group. Lovely.*

The gaggle of Sabia and humans enter the UIC headquarters to a large crowd of gawkers. Brendan knows practically everyone in the front row and does his best to briefly chat or shout something at them. Whether it's about baseball or not putting a leave request in before going to live with the Sabia, everyone has something to say to Brendan, and he has something to say back. An odd realization hits him as he makes his way through the turnstiles. He is truly happy. These people gave him purpose, and he was part of a team. Now, here they are, all glad to see him again. *Am I . . . home? Do I belong here? Should I ask to stay? Maybe I should make a run for it.*

Loft and Brendan are led to a conference room where old teammates who are subject matter experts on various topics are waiting for them.

"Don't all get up at once." Brendan's words are greeted with laughter. "Hey y'all, you all know me, so I'll spare you the introduction. However, this is Delegate Loft, and he is the lead Sabia interlocutor here. I'm just tagging along to be a sort of cultural translator for him."

While Brendan speaks, there is an awkward shuffle as the various guards jockey for position in the cramped room. It gets to be such a spectacle that Brendan offers to limit the security presence in the room to two guards, one Sabia, and one human. An intense pause occurs as Dena, and a sunglasses-wearing UIC police officer get in each other's face and refuse to budge. Finally, an annoyed Loft politely but firmly orders all Sabia guards but Dena to leave the room. Following Loft's lead, the sunglasses-wearing UIC police officer orders all the other cops to get out. He stands in the far corner of the room while Dena positions herself immediately adjacent to Brendan.

Loft addresses the group, still sounding nervous. "American friends, thank you for coming. We desire to foster a close relationship. This intelligence briefing is a demonstration of our cooperation. Brendan, will you lead this off?"

What an incredibly odd introduction. Brendan decides to keep things casual instead of intimidating. He also wants to show that he is the same old Brendan while demonstrating his ease using his craft.

Brendan starts with a joke. "I leave for a couple of months, and suddenly, you kiddos are the subject matter experts. I swear your tradecraft better be up to snuff, or I'm going to beat you all with the third rule of the office."

PATRICK ABBOTT

The table erupts in laughter while Loft forces a smile. He looks lost.

Brendan continues. "The gist of our visit here is that the Chinese, Russians, Indians, and even some of our closer 'friends' are smack-talking America nonstop. This is where my Sabia friend Loft comes in. He is responsible for communicating what's really going on on Earth to his leadership. But he knows he can't give his belief—note I said belief and not assessment because of tradecraft people . . ." The room laughs again while Loft looks perfectly confused. "—his belief without providing full insight from everyone. And since we, Americans, use an actual methodology and not just propaganda lies like the Chinese, the stuff we give him will be better than anything else he has received. So now, entertain us." Brendan leans back in his chair like a Roman emperor and waves a hand.

The briefings on countries and issues begin. Loft asks many questions, and the analysts provide detailed responses. Brendan can tell many of the briefings are watered down, though he smiles at everything. *The foreign disclosure process for giving intel to space aliens must be hell.*

As the briefings are wrapping up, Guy Chasè, Brendan's former center chief, comes in and asks Brendan and Loft if they want to eat lunch with the analysts or alone. Loft expresses his desire to eat with the analysts to talk further before the meeting with the director. Brendan asks to use the restroom before eating. Guy gives his permission and states the washrooms have been reserved for Loft and Brendan's sole use.

"Hope the disinfectant sprays applied today don't burn your bum off," jokes one of the intelligence officers.

"It's not the rear I'm worried about," Brendan flippantly replies.

A police officer steps into the room to tell Brendan that he will escort him. Dena follows Brendan out so closely her body armor bumps into him several times. When they reach the lavatory, a handful of guards are protecting the entrance. They allow Brendan to pass. Dena moves to enter, too, but the guards block her way.

"Men's bathroom only," one explains dryly.

She gets in his face and tells him, "Move aside."

"No," the cop replies defiantly.

"I will hurt you, Terran."

Brendan slips through the guards to get in between Dena and the officer.

"Hey, hey, hey!" He turns to Dena. "Look, it's a restroom. There's only one entrance, one exit. I'm not escaping. How about we keep the door open? That way, you know I'm not doing anything amiss. I will take a few minutes in the stall to do things you probably don't want to see, anyways. You'll hear me flush, and then you'll see me wash my hands. This way, I can do my business in peace, and you know I'm not escaping, okay?"

Dena silently steps back. Brendan thanks the officers, tells them to keep the door open, and explains he will not take too long.

PATRICK ABBOTT

Upon entering the bathroom, he sees it has three stalls, sinks, and urinals. *Home sweet home.* How many times has he hidden in one of these because of his depression? He enters a stall and sees a whiteboard hanging on the side wall with a marker on a string taped to it. The board has a message: "Murphy, any info you can report will help your country." A sign below it reads, "Quantum texting phone. Secure comms. Don't let Sabia know. Default delete rule. You have to select messages you want to keep." A rush of thoughts enters Brendan's mind. The loyalty oaths to the UIC and Sabia seem to conflict. *How to balance both?* He quickly realizes his first loyalty is to his home. *Home.* He slips the phone into one of his pants pockets. He grabs the marker and writes on the board, "Still loyal. God bless the USA! Sabia leadership is all female. Call themselves the Legion. NFI on that. Mothers are more important than fathers, at least to the females. Most social, personal background info they won't share. Integrating myself to gain trust. Some wins. Some hard to get."

"It does not take this long to take care of bodily functions, Brendan!" Dena sounds furious.

"Just wiping up!"

He flushes the still clean bowl and walks out of the stall. After washing his hands, he heads out to the waiting group of guards. Dena glowers at him.

"Thank you for waiting; I had to take care of some things," he says politely.

She lets him pass only to shove him forward as if instructing him to move faster. A cop responds by putting his hand on her shoulder.

"You want to go?" the cop says, challenging her.

She bats the officer's arm off her and starts to reach out for him.

"Peace, please!" Brendan yells. "It was a trip to the restroom, not an excuse for war." *This is insane. She's going to kill someone.*

Both the cop and Dena stare at each other. The other police form a circle around the Sabia guard.

Brendan speaks up again. "Okay, I will walk back to the conference room now. I will be unescorted unless you decide not to fight."

Dena looks at Brendan, the guards, then Brendan again. She instructs him to start walking. An awkwardly silent, tense convoy begins with Brendan in the lead, followed by Dena and then the police officers. They all walk back to the room, and Brendan and Dena enter.

The room's atmosphere has calmed down noticeably since Brendan left, so he decides to seize the group's attention. "I spent how much on sweets and treats, and you can't even feed your poor king? Woe, does the King of Syria have no place to fill his stomach?"

Emotions in the room pick up. One of the analysts offers Brendan her plate. He feigns magnanimity by turning it down and is handed a prepackaged meal. Small talk dominates the lunch half-hour. Various people jockey to talk to Brendan, who makes sure to

PATRICK ABBOTT

repeatedly put his arm around Loft, include Loft in conversations, and explain different aspects of the discussions to the delegate. Toward the end of the meal, the efforts pay off as several analysts start engaging Loft directly. Brendan does fear intelligence spillage, but he hopes the friendliness felt here today can make his life easier with the Sabia.

"Brendan!" a familiar voice calls out, "I'm not supposed to be here, but give me a call. I'll have you in the field in no time working for me!"

Senior Executive Jack Biro maneuvers through the room and puts his business card in Brendan's shirt pocket. Then, just as quickly, he walks away.

"Love ya, babe!" he yells as he exits the room.

"A very close friend," Brendan explains to Loft. The delegate nods.

The guards say nothing during the whole meal, though Brendan can feel the hate Dena directs toward him. Her gaze worries him to such an extent he won't even look at the business card. Eventually, an analyst declares it's time to meet the director. Everyone in the room stands up and starts giving Brendan tight hugs while Loft gets a few nods and even a handshake or two. As they walk out, Loft whispers his thanks to Brendan. Being greeted by old friends, accomplishing a mission, and receiving positive feedback fill Brendan with a sense of reward he has not felt in years.

Once they reach the director's office, Loft instructs Aban to be the sole guard while everyone else is ordered into the lobby. Dena protests, warning that no one will be "securing" Brendan. Waving his hand, Loft silences her. The three men enter the Director Michael Wilson's office, with Loft and Brendan taking seats while Aban stands in the back.

"Director Michael, we Sabia are very thankful for the wealth of knowledge freely shared with us," Loft states.

"Delegate Loft, the United States of America is happy to provide you, our close ally, with the intelligence you requested. Today proved a great success. Therefore, I will fully recommend to the National Security Council that the United States and the Sabia sign an intelligence-sharing agreement immediately. I will also push for an attaché from the UIC to be assigned as soon as possible."

"Thank you, Michael. We are greatly pleased with the work Brendan has done for us. We hope you can increase the necessary powers he needs to be an attaché."

The director stiffens in his chair. "Delegate Loft, Unified Intelligence Command officers swear to uphold certain values so they may be prime representatives of our government. Unfortunately, former Intelligence Officer Murphy has repeatedly acted in ways that represented something other than the United States and its constitution. He acted without express permission from his proper chain of command, and I find that sickening. He is a disgrace to his uniform. His . . . presence . . . is tolerated here merely because of you. If he stays longer than this specific trip, I will personally see to his arrest. Good day." The director stands up, looks directly at Brendan with disdain, and points. "There's the door."

Despair. *Was this whole day a lie? Did the UIC just use me for one last intelligence dump? So much for loyalty to home.* Brendan's throat goes dry while his vision becomes blurry and sounds become muffled. He meekly stands up as Loft says something to the director. Even Aban looks at him with surprise. Cautiously, Brendan makes for the door. On the other side, he sees Dena. She says something to him, but he cannot understand her. The director disowning him proves to be overwhelming. Loft tries to engage with Brendan, but he cannot respond. Instead, the delegate takes Brendan's arm and walks him down the hallway.

The corridors are empty as they make their way back to the landing pad. A man in a police uniform makes a beeline straight for Dena. Brendan can hear but does not understand the yelling between them. She brutally launches her whole weight into the policeman, sending him flying. Instinct kicks in as Brendan puts his hand on her shoulder to turn her away from the now downed officer. Dena responds with a sudden twist, grabs him, and spins him around and down toward the floor. Brendan's head slams hard onto the marble. He can hear a crack.

The rest is a bunch of nonsense to him. Aban picks him up. He can feel a sensation of vertigo and running. He hears Berina yelling, "What sort of guard attacks the person they were assigned to protect?" The next thing he knows, he is sitting in his seat, throwing up on himself. All these sensations are too much. He has brief moments of clarity, but they are lost to the director's words repeating in his mind. *The Sabia and the government just want to use me. Once they are done with me, they will likely discard me. My life will probably end on a government autopsy table or in an alien airlock.* The commotion of lights and noise on the shuttlecraft hurt his head. All Brendan can do is cry.

Twenty-Two – The Land of Nod

Aban and Zalta help Brendan deboard the craft. He wants to stay to clean up his vomit, but Zalta convinces him to come with her. It's not so much her words as her kind tone that Brendan finds persuasive. While walking down the corridors, Brendan finds Aban surprisingly personal. Aban holds Brendan tightly while sharing a few words of motivation and reassurance. Brendan can't focus on exactly what is said, but he thinks Aban would be an officer he'd love to serve under.

What the Hell was that? I serve and am abandoned. Meanwhile, Dena attacked me!

The medical bay is a familiar sight—however, it reminds him how much he misses Esfirs. The doctors take him to a back room where the lights are off. They place him on a bed that has a hole for his face. He feels the doctors repeatedly touch the back of his head. Simultaneously, Zalta engages him by talking about baseball. It strikes him as odd, especially since she has consistently demonstrated a lack of understanding of the sport, using terms like "person with the wood" and "person with the ball." This conversation gives Brendan the impression something is wrong, which gives way to the realization he was rushed to medical. *Why am I thinking so slowly?*

Over time, his eyes adjust to the darkness, and his ears become aware of the slight hum and buzzing of various parts of the ship. Unfortunately, the dark thoughts also return. *How many times have I been defeated? How many times have I had to be saved in this job? It's too much for me. I failed. I am a fraud. The Sabia see it, and the UIC probably wouldn't even take me back because I'd have nothing to offer them.*

Ever so quietly, he hears someone slowly moving in the room.

"Hello?" he calls out gently.

"It is I, Brendan," Berina responds. "How are you feeling, dear friend?"

"I'm not going to lie to you," he says, still looking down through the hole in the bed. "Today, two Sabia physically attacked me, and my previous boss threatened to arrest me. I feel horrible."

He hears her footsteps approach. Brendan feels her hand on his back.

"Dena is being removed from this mission completely. Attacking a fellow officer! If you ask me, she should face prison time, not a demotion. But praise the divine, you are alright. Tonight when I offer prayers, I will make sure they center on your health."

"She slammed me rather down hard. Did I get a concussion?"

PATRICK ABBOTT

"Brendan"—Berina sounds hesitant—"she cracked your head open." She pauses before continuing. "It really was the hardened hybrid bone that saved your life. But even still, we had to reconstruct your skull with more biotech . . ."

The swear words pour out of him like water. At first, they're not aimed at anyone or anything in particular. However, Berina soon becomes the target of his animosity.

"Why? Huh? Why? Seriously? I gave years of my life to my country. Now they threaten me with arrest. If I hadn't been of use to them, I probably wouldn't have made it out of Virginia. And today, you, Sabia, have tried to kill me. From the very beginning, Dena was hostile to me. Hell, Loft said her job was to secure me. What the hell am I doing here, Berina? My father and mother lost their homes and tried to make one for us children. Now I am displaced from the place I grew up. Did you know that? My mother has disowned me—she won't even allow me to go home.

"Meanwhile, I do everything my country asks me to do. But do you know what it got me? A wife who left me and a guilty conscience. I followed orders and let prisoners go in the middle of the desert. Did they live or die? I don't know! And now I'm just a tool for my country to threaten. The moment they think I can't gather more information is when I'm locked away forever.

"But you Sabia—oh, here comes the good part! You bring me along to help you. But I need to be 'secured' by a guard who hates me because I can't be trusted with plans about myself. Because of this lack of trust, my skull gets cracked open.

"So Berina, I ask you: where is my home where I can rest and be welcomed? I'll tell you where—it doesn't exist! I am in a universe full of life, yet I'm all alone!" He stops and becomes much more somber. "There is no home for me. No hope."

His face is swollen, and he begins to cry. His depression has reached a climax he hasn't experienced before. In between the tears, he pleads for Berina to let him die.

The tears continue to flow. He pulls his head out of the hole, wipes his face, and sees the blurry image of Berina sitting next to him. Through his blurry vision, he can see a look of compassion on her face. They lock eyes. Brendan instantly feels a wave of sadness flow over him.

"Brendan, oh, Dear Brendan. I am so sorry. My whole life, I have always had the bonds you lacked. Please do not lose hope." She leans in and holds his hands. "I can only do so much for you, but ask what you need, and I will try to deliver it."

He exhales. After his rant, all the energy has been sucked out of him, and now looking into Berina's sad eyes, he feels powerless. She squeezes his hands.

"Tell me, Brendan. What can I do for you?"

"I want to go to church." He barely gets the words out. His answer surprises him, as he was not even thinking about church. It's as if it came from a long-forgotten part of his damaged soul.

Leaning back, she withdraws her hand. She breaks the eye-lock and looks down, studying the floor, then she nods her head.

"Yes, I will. I will somehow get you the spiritual care you need. I must learn some things first, but I will not fail you." She looks back up at him. "Please do not lose hope. I will talk to a few people. What we thought was acceptable clearly is not to you. Let me prove your fears wrong. You are not alone, Brendan. You have us. Esfirs, myself, Zalta, Gul, Imran, Behnaz. We all consider you one of us because we have gotten to know you. Perhaps the time for you to prove yourself is over. Now should be the time we prove ourselves to you."

Esfirs' name changes the direction of Brendan's thoughts. As if sensing this, Berina says, "Esfirs would be so enraged at Dena if she were here right now."

Brendan breaks out laughing.

"I miss her singing," he mumbles. *I shouldn't have said that!*

Berina says as if she can tell what he's thinking, "She told me she sung to you. I had a talk with her about that. However, she always has done what she wants to do."

Together they sit in silence. Seconds become minutes. Despite staring into Berina's eyes, Brendan does not feel a headache. In fact, he finds the whole experience calming.

"Thank you," he says, finally breaking the silence.

"Rest now, dear friend. I will go to fulfill my promises."

She gets up and walks out. Alone in the room, Brendan is at peace. Moving, he feels the business card in his pocket. He reaches in and pulls it out. On the front is Jack's standard information. On the back are two phone numbers written in pen. One is labeled "REPORT INTEL," and the other is "MALCOLM." *Was everything a facade to make the Sabia not suspect me? Is Malcolm trying to reach me?* The peace falls away.

Twenty-Three — Kimya

> Brendan: Jack, I'm alive. Got a concussion but well. Guard removed. Sabia treating me well.

He looks at the phone for about the tenth time in an hour. There is no response from Jack. Strangely, he feels slightly dirty looking at the message. They told him to liaison, not to spy. Serving the common good doesn't seem possible this way.

Suddenly, an envelope icon flashes in the corner of the screen. A response from Malcolm opens as Brendan touches the icon.

> Malcolm: Brother, about time I heard from you. Heard they attacked you. Collect everything you can on the leadership decision-making hierarchy.

Exhaling deeply, Brendan puts away the Earth-made spy device and instead pulls out the cellphone-like machine the Sabia gave him. A text without a reply is waiting there to mock him.

> Brendan: Happy birthday, Mom! Anything planned for the day?

The lack of response tears at him. *It was worth a try. Better to have been loved by a parent and lost than never been loved.* He looks at the message some more. *I'm sorry I was born. You never asked for me.* He throws the device across the room. The night is lonely. Closing his eyes, he drifts back to sleep.

His alarm cuts through the darkness. *Another long night; at least I didn't have a nightmare.* Getting out of bed proves difficult, but he manages to slither from the sheets and prop himself up. Soon it will be time to go to the gym, but first, a deep desire leads him to grab his rosary, but he cannot initiate the prayer. Instead, he plops onto the floor and, with a sorrowful voice, says, "God, help me." His actions confuse him. How long has he fought to stay indifferent to God? Now Brendan finds himself crying out for God. *Lord, I don't understand!*

As he looks at the rosary in silence, the door chimes. *What the heck?* Dropping the prayer beads, he presses the button causing the door to open. On the other side is a female Sabia in full body armor. Half expecting Dena's glower, he instead encounters a smiling face.

"Hey! My name is Kimya. I was on the Kentucky mission with you. You might remember me lifting you into the shuttlecraft." Her eyes are bright with excitement.

"Yeah, I remember you. You escorted Ambassador Bass away when he wanted to come with me when I first met Zand."

Kimya looks briefly confused but quickly recovers. "Ah! You mean Virag." Another smile forms on her face. "He should have listened to Loft. Oh, where are my manners?" She holds her left arm straight out.

PATRICK ABBOTT

They can master English, but every one of them struggles with a freaking basic greeting! Brendan takes her hand and shakes it. She does not grip firmly and allows him to control the up-and-down motions. He notices her looking intently at his clasped hand as if trying to learn.

Kimya continues. "I am taking over the full spectrum of safety operations for you. Not only am I the new officer in charge of the aides who are stationed here, but I also will personally take care of your physical protection when you are out on missions."

"Thank you so much. It is nice to formally meet you," Brendan replies diplomatically.

"I have also changed your pass status. You now have access to most of the ship. Just arrange with me to clear any area you wish to go. This means you no longer need to be summoned to access the more restricted areas. Maybe you will join some parties at our cabins." Brendan notices she is beaming.

Berina really must have been convincing on the trust level. "Thank you, I—"

She cuts him off. "For lunch, I was wondering if you wanted to join me in the cafeteria I eat in, it is called 'Amdar.' I think you will find the food more appealing and exotic than what is served in the one you are used to. Afterward, I would love to take you to the firing range. You can try out my railer." She holds out a compact rifle-like object. Brendan cannot tell where she pulled the weapon from. *Her armor, maybe?* She puts the gun behind her back before he can get an adequate look at it.

"Sounds fun." He tries to balance the collection opportunity and potential outreach of trust from the Sabia against his worry that using a weapon could also be messaging from the Legion.

"Great." Kimya slaps his arm so hard that he's knocked off balance for a moment. "I can pick you up from work." She starts to walk away but abruptly stops. "I want to apologize for how you were treated the other day on Terra. You will find me different. Your record demands respect. In fact, I would love to chat with you about your war experience in Syria. The idea of anyone taking those bridges with a tenth of what the enemy had is thrilling."

"Thanks." Brendan tries to fight off the praise, reminding him of the combat. He also can't tell if it's genuine flattery or just an act.

Kimya then proceeds to do the oddest thing Brendan has seen this whole trip. She makes a sucking sound out of the side of her mouth, winks, then gives a thumbs up. Brendan slowly responds with a similar series of gestures. She smiles and walks off. *That was the weirdest Sabia attempt yet to mimic what they think Earth culture is.*

Once Kimya leaves, Brendan heads to the gym. Berina is off on a mission, so Imran and Gul are his primary workout partners. Several newer Sabia join the group, but their lack of effort indicates their main reason for being there is seeing a Terran in real life. One of the more recently arrived medical staff, a male named Siahmoak, admits as much by saying that he doesn't like the Terran equipment but wants to learn more about Earth culture from Brendan.

Once he gets to his office, the daily routine of boredom is broken up by Zand's aide Havar arriving. *I wonder what Zand wants to know today.*

"Greetings, Brendan," Havar starts, "I come with a question."

"Hey buddy, how can I help you today?"

"How fair is the democratic system in Western countries?"

Brendan stares in response. He wants to respond with a "Come on, really?" but instead uses an old government trick. *Time to play "talking out of both sides of my mouth."*

"Wow, that's a complex question because each country is different. But tell you what, I'll make a note and wargame this problem into a paper idea. The process is complex and will take some time. However, I'm sure thinking about this question will produce some interesting results."

Havar stares, uncomprehending. *Bet you didn't expect that pocket veto.*

"Umm . . . thank you . . . Brendan. I will be sure to relay what you said to me."

"Not a problem, brother. Make sure you tell Zand and the others exactly what I told you. Precision is the key here."

The aide turns to leave and walks away slowly. The rest of the morning is spent reading news reports. Meade's new Patriot Alliance coalition won a special election in the House of Representatives. This is the first candidate the militias have funded themselves. Meanwhile, crime rates are up in New York City as armed leftist gangs have made whole blocks no-go areas for cops. There is talk about private security organizations uniting to protect specific neighborhoods. Meanwhile, the federal government is warning that various militia groups may seek to establish a presence in the area. *Things are getting insane.*

He hears the midday chimes. Like clockwork, Kimya walks in. This time she is without her armor; instead, she wears Earth clothing—a V-neck shirt and jeans. However, a technologically-advanced-looking wrist guard is prominent on her left arm.

"Hey! Bet you thought I was a Terran for a second!" There is an almost childlike eagerness in her voice.

Brendan considers his response for a moment. "You know, you did look like a Terran for a split second before I recognized you."

"You joke, Brendan," she says laughingly. "Come on; I will get you some filling food. No more salads."

The thought of finally having a meal of something other than greens appeals to Brendan. He gets up and allows her to lead the way. As they walk, Kimya starts talking about what she learned about him from the Sabia's personnel file on him. Brendan tries to ask questions, but she's speaking too quickly.

PATRICK ABBOTT

"Will you answer something for me?" she says.

Brendan nods.

"When you first fought those terrorists at the train station, how worried were you about being outnumbered?"

An interesting twist, not focusing on the why but something else. "I probably was worried, but I really don't recall. What I do remember is being very angry."

"Wow," she remarks with a whistle, "you really are a warrior. Those murderers did not think they would encounter a killer like you. Woo!" Brendan finds her smile disturbing.

Desperate to get away from recalling the time he killed someone, he reflects the question onto Kimya. "If I may inquire, how much combat experience do you have?"

"My personal history is classified. Even if it was not classified, I still dislike talking much about my own past. Just know I will do my utmost to protect you, and I know how to handle myself." She waves at a checkpoint guard as they pass. "So tell me, do you like noodles? A dish at this cafeteria combines your cereal grains with some of our spices and creams, which I love but should not have too often. We can share, so it does not count against my diet!" She grins mischievously.

"That last part didn't sound like a question, so I'll just trust the will of my host."

She bursts out laughing. "I like you so much already. Everyone told me you are so friendly."

Laying it on rather thick, aren't we? Brendan takes note of that little bit of intelligence as they arrive at the dining facility. The room features a garden in the middle and a small pond. An extremely plush carpet covers the floor. Kimya leads Brendan to a set of pillows, and they sit down, facing each other. Kimya takes a deep breath and slowly exhales.

"Ah! This reminds me of a place where my mother would take me to have meals with my extended family. It is important to be reminded of home when so far away." Brendan notices a hint of longing in her voice.

Brendan decides to pursue that personal line. "My own native home is called Kansas. But sadly, I haven't been able to visit it in years." He sighs. "Have you gone back home lately? Maybe on a leave trip like Esfirs is doing now?"

"I am saving up leave. It is difficult, as different positions provide leave credit at different rates. Moreover, a lonely guard like me does not get the same time off as senior officers."

As a waiter passes by, Kimya signals in some sort of complex sign language with her right hand. The interaction seems to give her new energy.

"So," she continues, "I want to know about Syria. How do you take two colleagues, gather about thirty locals, and then successfully take on three hundred religious zealots to seize four bridges? I read several reports from your military, and they are all vague."

"Well"—he pauses to swallow—"the two special forces operators, that's what we call elite soldiers, were all that could be spared. We knew we needed to flank the Islamic State fighters attempting to take over the compound. However, as long as they held the bridges, they could get all the reinforcements in the world. It might as well have been three versus a billion at that point. But, I had contact with the various Arab tribes in the city. So while the special forces were setting up a distraction, I organized a motley group of local fighters. Realizing the need to go on the offense, we fought bridge to bridge, using our momentum to roll over ISIS—that's the nickname for the Islamic State. Once the bridges were secure, the fighters attacking our compound had to disperse and flee."

Kimya shakes her head. "No, that is not right, Brendan. There had to be over double your force at each bridge. It does not make any tactical sense. How did you win those fights? You can tell me the truth."

Repressed feelings begin to surge in Brendan. His throat goes dry, and a sickening feeling rises in his stomach. *Is she collecting on me, or does she see through the story?*

The waiter returns and places two small, empty bowls in front of them and the food in a larger bowl between them. With an eager look, Kimya divides up the food, giving herself a larger portion. *She must really enjoy these.* Her enthusiasm for the noodles is further demonstrated by her scarfing down two forkfuls. Her gluttony provides him a few moments of silence until she slows down.

"Are you excited Esfirs will soon return?" She gives him a sly look.

"Oh yes, I could always use a person who can repair my hand," he replies dryly.

"You are avoiding the question. Your feelings for Esfirs are not a secret."

Brendan chokes briefly. *Crap.* He feels like he has been caught stealing. Trying to eat more is a failed effort—he can barely hold his fork.

"Ah, do not worry about it." Her words snap Brendan out of his trance.

Brendan does his best to move on. After a few minutes of not touching his food, Kimya asks if he is ready to "have some fun." They get up and leave the cafeteria, walking deeper into the ship.

She asks, "With all your battle experience, what is your favorite weapon? The M4 rifle? A carbine? How about a pistol? Some heavy machine gun? Maybe rockets?"

Brendan takes her to be a bit of a gun nut. "My mouth is my favorite weapon. It has solved so many problems long before anyone started shooting."

Kimya looks at him inquisitively. "Well, let me show you something that comes in handy when people do not want to listen to your mouth."

They enter a narrow but long room filled with gray crates of various sizes. Looking at the boxes, Brendan doesn't notice when Kimya pulls out her railer. Seeing the weapon in her hands, he makes a surprised sound that causes her to roll her eyes. "It is called a railer, not 'ahhh!'"

PATRICK ABBOTT

She hands it to him. Taking the weapon, Brendan is awed by its lightness. There is no pistol grip, no muzzle, and no trigger. While fiddling with it, pointing downrange, he notices a red targeting triangle in the area where its end stub is aimed.

"Sabia biotech." Kimya's voice is proud. "The railer interacts with Sabia genetic material. No need for sights because it will display all necessary information directly to the user. It can only be fired by one of us. No Terran can use it."

She walks behind him and puts her hands on his arms. She softly maneuvers his aim onto one of the boxes about twenty-five feet away. "Imagine the railer firing a bullet."

As he does, the box he is aiming at reacts as if it has been hit. Looking at the target, he sees a hole. Kimya gently takes the weapon out of his hands and sets herself up in a fighting stance.

"I am going to vocalize my thoughts so you can follow along. Same box, .50 caliber."

The box crumples in the middle while the back of it blows out.

"Same box, grenade round." The box explodes with bits of it flying about.

Kimya lowers the railer, holding it in her left hand. "Fusion-powered plasma. Enough matter in this thing that you will never run out in a battle."

Kimya beams with joy while Brendan is torn between awe and horror.

"Is that standard issue for guards on this ship?"

"Standard issue for every guard and defense force member in the Sabia Legion. You have to be qualified on the railer to be a member." She hands back the weapon to Brendan. "Shoot it off for a while."

Deciding it best to get more experience, Brendan begins target practice. He first aims as if there were sights. Then, he shoots from various angles as well as from the hip. Throughout the whole process, he feels no kickback whatsoever.

"Do you enjoy combat tours?" Kimya asks. Behind her cheerfulness, there is a seriousness in her voice.

"Deployments are awesome in hindsight. Food is prepared for you, laundry is taken care of, everyone is working on the same mission, and the outside world fades away. It's just you, your friends, and the mission. The happiest I've ever been is when I've been deployed." As he speaks those last words, Kimya nods her head. "But it's not real, you know? Family issues don't really go away. They just wait for you. Problems at home and work still fester even if you don't think about them. You can earn all the awards in the world, but they won't make you whole or save a family on the verge of collapse."

He lowers the gun. Silence dominates the room as both human and Sabia ponder those words.

"We have a lot in common, Brendan."

PATRICK ABBOTT

She reaches for the railer. Brendan silently hands it to her. Then, wrapping her arm around his shoulder, she leads him out of the room and down the hall.

"What are you doing after work?" she asks.

"Washington is playing against Miami tonight. I think the game will be broadcast on a channel I get here, so that will be my evening." He stops in the hallway. "Hey, you wouldn't be interested in joining me, would you?"

"Oh no!" She chuckles. "I have read all about that game. Do you know what we call baseball in our reports? 'The boring game.' Do I want to be bored? No, thank you!"

They arrive back at his auxiliary office. Kimya bids him good day and tells him they will see more of each other. Brendan notes the railer is nowhere to be seen as she walks away.

Noticing the guard Aras, he turns to address him. "How's your day going, brother?"

"New commander." Aras motions in the direction Kimya left.

"What do you think of her?"

Aras eyes Brendan. He then turns his face toward the hallway Kimya walked down. "Classified."

Interlude – Jack: Message from the Front

Jack Biro reads the printed message the analyst hands to him. He has to strain his eyes in the dim light of the office.

> Brendan: Compact weapon called railer. Seeming near-endless ammo. Ejects fusion power plasma. Can scale damage. At least from small round to grenade launcher.

"What do you think?" the analyst asks.

"They either are trusting him more or trying to message us a threat through him."

"Helluva gap."

"Damn right."

"This is the first message from him. Should we have the embassy reach out and give him further orders?"

Jack laughs. "Are you kidding? Hell no! The kid is under deep cover right now. Heck, he doesn't even know it. All we can do is hope he gets triggered to report back to us once in a while." Jack stretches in his chair, putting his legs on the table. "Thankfully," he says as he grabs a water bottle, "the kid is enough of a basket case that he'll bounce around and send us something every so often."

Twenty-Four – The Beauty of Bathsheba

"The Chinese demographic imbalance between males and females, combined with the growing north/south political split, fuels the country's largest economic recession since the Communist Revolution nearly one hundred years ago." Brendan pauses to let the facts settle in before continuing his brief. "Beijing is implementing a strategy which primarily focuses on domestic matters such as family planning and social control. A secondary portion of this strategy is designed to destabilize adversaries for the period China views itself as weak. The Chinese government is funding extremists in France and the United Kingdom. Against India, Beijing is providing intelligence support to Pakistan for covert operations. Like the United States, China has provided resources to various leftist urban movements. China very likely will begin efforts to aid the militia movement as another means to apply pressure on the United States."

"Why would the Chinese empower a potentially anti-Chinese force?" Leleh asks. "The figurehead leader Javier is a self-described patriot and has denounced the Chinese before. I do not understand the logic of this."

"If General Meade, or Javier as you say, seizes power, various elements of the United States will resist him. He really could only assert power in the central, southern, and western parts of the country. He is so toxic of a figure that states and elites in the Northeast, on the Pacific coast, and in the city of Chicago would resist him. His overall rise weakens the United States. A Meade presidency would fracture the country, accomplishing China's goal."

Loft inquires, "What do the governors of the regions where Javier is most popular think?"

Brendan walks over to the map. "In these states"— he points to Oregon and Colorado—"the governors oppose Meade's ideology. On the other hand, the governors and the general populations of Utah, Idaho, Montana, North Dakota, and South Dakota support Meade and his goals. Here, Meade feels safe and can build and train various militia groups. The rest of the Interior West governors will be politically astute and not openly condemn Meade. The general carries a lot of sway amongst the voting population."

"What about his number two," Leleh probes, "Malcolm McAndrews?"

Brendan sighs. *Now they decide to include the last name.* "McAndrews worked with me in Iraq and Syria. I know him and his style well. He is much more action-oriented while remaining very loyal to Meade. If McAndrews had his way, the militia movement would seek direct confrontations. They would attack the Sabia to rally any wavering groups, thus securing strength before taking the government on directly. McAndrews is a fighter, while Meade is a politician. The more influence

McAndrews has, the more likely there will be some form of armed conflict."

The tag-teaming turns back to Loft. "Describe your current thoughts about Malcolm."

"We worked well together." Brendan tries to fight off emotions. "We see—saw—eye to eye on many different issues. Together, my diplomatic skills and his ability to sometimes push through trouble spots balanced each other out. I miss him. I miss the person he was, the patriot."

Leleh nods. "Thank you; you have presented well on the Chinese situation and the militias. I am sure we will have follow-up questions after studying the matter further. Have a good evening, Brendan."

Brendan thanks them, puts his hand over his heart, and bows slightly. He then exits the room and starts heading back toward his cabin. He is looking forward to changing out of his professional outfit into something more casual to enjoy the rest of the night. One of the Sabia pilots was able to acquire a copy of a new history of the Revolutionary War that Brendan asked for. He quickens his pace as he thinks about sitting down with a good book.

Turning the corner, he sees Berina in conversation with a couple of guards. *Odd that there are two.* She is moving her hands rapidly while one of the guards says, " . . . and that's all she told me." Brendan's approach causes the guards to alert, prompting Berina to turn around.

PATRICK ABBOTT

"How long were they going to keep you in that room?" Her voice is full of exasperation.

Before he can reply, she grabs his wrist and leads him down the hallway toward the meeting room he just left.

"What's going on? Is everything okay?" he asks.

"Everything is fine now you are out of that endless meeting."

She leads him past a checkpoint Brendan has not encountered before. Upon approaching, Berina greets the two guards on duty without stopping. Neither of them responds, nor do they say anything about her dragging him along.

"Will you tell me what's happening?"

"Do not worry, Brendan, you will enjoy this." He can make out a smile forming on her face.

Deciding to engage in an indirect route to secure more information, he says, "Thank you for what you've done recently. Communication with the leadership has greatly improved."

"No need to mention it. What are friends for?"

"And Kimya is definitely an improvement from Dena."

Berina slows down and turns her head halfway toward Brendan. "No need to mention it." This time, there is resentment in her tone.

She exhales deeply. Brendan is worried he has somehow crossed a line. He begins to apologize, but Berina stops abruptly and winks at him before resuming walking and talking cheerfully again. She asks if he's excited, and he asks what he should be excited about.

They arrive at one of the many doors, which all look the same. Brendan can't see any distinguishing markings on it. Berina begins to rock back and forth on her heels and bouncing a little.

"This is the most excited and energetic I have ever seen you," he says. "Seriously, what's up?"

"Well..." She motions toward the closed door.

"Well, what?" Brendan stares at Berina.

She rolls her eyes and hits a button on the panel; she pushes him through the open doorway as it opens.

"Have fun!" she yells.

The door closes behind Brendan. Looking around, he sees a richly decorated room that reminds him of Persian and Turkic motifs. It is laid out like his cabin, but the carpet is emerald-green with an odd gold pattern of interlocking diamonds. The room is devoid of any pillows or other signs of habitation. He walks into the area where the television would be in his own cabin, but nothing is visible.

"Brendan?" a voice softly says behind him.

Esfirs! His heart sores as her voice shoots through his heart.

PATRICK ABBOTT

He turns around to look at her. The sight is shocking. He pays little attention to her flowing silver gown, which has a hood draping over her left front side. Instead, his vision locks on her stunning, golden eyes. Her pupils are dark, the irises bright, and the scleras a lighter gold. Her breathing is causing slight ripples of color across her iridescent skin.

Esfirs moves slowly toward him. "I heard about what happened when I was away. We all want you to trust us, so I volunteered to show you our true selves. This is us. This is what we Sabia look like."

He stands in awe like a statue.

She continues. "I received permission to return without taking the steroids that dull some of our physical traits." She pauses. "May I touch you, Brendan?"

Again he is stuck in a state of shock. She calls his name, and he notices her locking onto his eyes. His head begins to hurt. Trying to fight it, he imagines a brick wall . . .

"I am not attacking you, Brendan. You do not need to fear me," she says to him.

She puts her left hand gently on his right cheek. As she traces her fingers against his skin, he feels the urge to sit down. Then, almost in sync, they lower themselves to the carpet.

Is this some sort of psychic empathic persuasion?

"It is not a weapon," she says reassuringly, "just look at me."

Brendan focuses on her eyes, studying the rich shades of gold and the slight details that emerge—faint spots in the iris, the way they light up the eyelid's iridescence, and soft lines coming from the pupil. He imagines—no, he hears—her singing to him but notices her mouth remains motionless.

"Ah!" He leaps back. *She's in my head!* Despite a mental struggle, he manages to close his eyes. In the blackness, a calming feeling enters him. Everything becomes quiet and safe. For some reason, he is convinced it's okay to open his eyes.

Esfirs continues to look at him but no longer straight into his eyes.

"I am sorry, Brendan. I did not mean to upset you. Please allow me to start again. This is what we look like. In our language, 'Sabia' means beautiful children. If Terrans saw us like this, they would fear us even more than you did. You know they fear and hate anything different. So we have no choice but to hide what we look like from Terrans. We trust you, though; we trust you to see us and understand us as we are."

Everything still overawes Brendan, but he manages to say, "You may."

Esfirs laughs. "Brendan, you just answered a question I asked minutes ago." She places her hand back on his cheek.

"I'm-I'm—I don't know. I don't know; I don't know, I don't know. Wow. This is . . . dang."

"Berina told me all about your former leader, how he disowned you. We will never do that to you. You are one of us."

Her words weigh on him. He looks down. Thinking about his latest message to Jack makes his head spin. The scale weighing the Sabia and the government has been broken. Everything is falling apart.

"I did not mean to upset you. Please, tell me something pleasant that has happened to you lately." Esfirs gently removes her hand from Brendan's cheek, resting it in her lap.

"Nothing, really," Brendan mumbles.

Esfirs' shoulders drop.

"You came back," he finally says. "How about you? Did you walk barefoot outside for me?"

"Yes, I did." Her eyes meet his.

They smile warmly at each other.

Interlude — Behnaz: The Letter

These rooms are small, but you cannot ask for anything larger for a trip back home. Being an engineer allows Behnaz to do the mental math in her head. *Too much private room equals too large a ship equals too high an energy requirement to get us back home. Allotting more space to a common area allows for more social activity anyways. What use is a bedroom other than to sleep in? Plus, my room back home is big enough for a single woman like me, anyways.*

The thought of home brings a smile to Behnaz's weary and wrinkled face. Throwing her bag into her small cubical sleeping area, Behnaz heads back to the shared space. *Everyone in here is probably going back to one or two places. Thank goodness I live off-planet. All the open space I want with only my type of people.* She chuckles at that thought. *Even the most annoying Sabia is ten times more preferable than the average Terran.*

Remembering the Terrans she encountered brings the Virginia incident back to her mind. What Behnaz remembers most is not the initial fear she felt but the Terran who saved her. *Anyone willing to intervene is cool in my book. Pity about his condition. He is too Terran for the Sabia and too Sabia for the Terrans.*

PATRICK ABBOTT

Behnaz looks around the common area. In a corner, she eyes Imran sitting alone, reading something on Terran paper. Intrigued, she approaches her gray-robe-wearing fellow survivor.

"Imran, what do you have there?"

The botanist looks up, the usual cheerful look missing from his face. Rather than explaining what he's holding, he hands the paper to the woman he once dated.

Flipping the paper over, Behnaz sees that it's a short letter from Brendan addressed to Imran. The concise message hides deep emotions, she can tell.

Brother,

I heard you're redeploying to your home. My apologies that we could not get to know each other more. I wanted you to know that if you ever need to talk about the first time we met, I will always be available to chat. No matter where I am, I will make time for you. Just reach back here, and I am sure whoever is in charge can find me.

Your friend,

Brendan Sean Murphy

Behnaz raises her eyes from the paper to look at Imran. Then, handing him the letter, she says, "Is he writing to offer you healing or pleading for his own?"

"Tell me about it," Imran says, rolling his eyes. "He has received no care for combat illness from his own kind. Heck, there is no care for combat illness amongst any Terran polity. Headed for a fall, if you ask me."

"Brendan or the Terrans?"

"Both."

PATRICK ABBOTT

Interlude – Esfirs: Cancer

Please, just understand. Why are you so resistant? Since we met, I have only worked for your health and betterment. Trust me now, Brendan, please! Esfirs' internal thoughts stay in her as Brendan looks down. *If you would only trust me, I could comfort you right now.*

Brendan sighs. He makes a pathetic figure as he sits on the floor in medical, but he straightens his back, which restores his dignity. He says, "But in a physical sense, it's me. How can I allow myself to be thrown away?"

That is not true, though. How lucky you are, Brendan! The divine is taking you and making you anew. You are here because that must be part of the divine's plan. We are here to take care of you, protecting you as you become one of us. Not even Namziah– no, that is blasphemous.

"Brendan," Esfirs begins, "I am only recommending the best for you. Your stem cells are trying to fight off your Sabia genetic material. This is causing cancers that will kill you unless we take care of them. Please, trust us. Trust me."

The Terran turns to face Esfirs. *His eyes, they seem so tired.* Brendan takes a moment before speaking. "I do trust you, Esfirs. I will do what I must to save my life. I am asking you, though, is there another choice besides cutting away the last fully human part of me? I believe you when you say doing so will stop the cancer. But is there another choice?"

Lie. If I lie to Brendan, he will believe me. He can be stripped of his Terraness. Later on, I can tell him the truth when it is more appropriate. He will be sure to understand why I lied after he realizes why the surgery was the better choice. However, Brendan saying he trusts her tugs at Esfirs' heart. Deep down in her soul, she knows what she needs to do. *Protecting him includes not lying to him.*

"Brendan," she says, "there may be a way. But it involves frequent treatments, and they may not work. But–" thoughts pull at her to stop. Still, she fights through them. "I am willing to try to let your body develop however it chooses, even if that means part of the Terran genetic material remains." She sighs.

Brendan's smile makes it all worth it, though. Esfirs looks back at his eyes. *They look so happy underneath.*

Twenty-Five – A Song of Solomon

Brendan is struggling to tell the story without laughing. "So, we all look at him and go, 'Dude, what is the point of your long-winded story?' And do you know what he said? 'I like stories.'"

Leleh and Apahvez exchange alarmed looks as Brendan breaks down laughing.

"I am glad Terrans can find humor in such different situations," Leleh struggles to say diplomatically.

"Leleh," Brendan replies while trying to regain control of himself, "are you sure you don't want to join me as a liaison officer? Your tactful reply was perfect." Again, he fails to stop an outbreak of hearty laughter.

Apahvez looks worried. "Did your friend have brain damage?"

"No, no," Brendan reassures, "he was fine after a while. Though, we did send him home after that."

"That is good to hear. I would not want anyone to have such a life-altering injury. Tell me, please, where is Jules now?"

Reality, like always, catches up, ruining the memory for Brendan. "Jules, like many of us veterans, could not get a normal, private industry job. Instead, he started serving his community as a sheriff's deputy. Soon enough, he was elected sheriff in a nearby Florida county. He keeps the peace between the government and the growing militia outfits. I read about allegations concerning him tipping off people to federal raids in the county."

Leleh asks, "People like Jules seem to be straddling the lines of loyalty among various factions in the United States. This is a phenomenon we are encountering on a level that surprises us. So tell us, how open are such people to peaceful relations with us?"

Stroking his chin stubble, Brendan says, "Almost everyone on the lower levels of government, and outside organizations like militias and leftist groups, are good people. Most people want peace with the Sabia, of that, I have no doubt. The problem is society has been so tribalized it only takes one strong leader to cause people who would initially desire peace to seek war."

"And if there is war?"

"Then many good people, including those I value as friends, will fight." The words weigh heavily on Brendan.

Apahvez interjects, "Well, it is reassuring you are advocating for reason and peace. We will use you in ways that will benefit everyone, especially your friends."

"And we have just the way for you to do so," Leleh takes over the conversation. "Recent polling has revealed growing anti-Sabia sentiment in the Rocky Mountain portion of the United States. Zand wants us to cultivate relationships with local governors to secure goodwill and help combat this, as well as securing future resource extraction rights. We need biographies of the governors and a breakdown of various militia groups in the western United States to help shape our planning."

"Sure thing. When do you need it by?"

"In three days, we would appreciate a complete breakdown. First, however, we request an overview of every group and governor by this evening."

Brendan jerks up on his pillow. Within an hour, the midday chimes will occur, signaling lunchtime. *I'm going to have to work fast.* Brendan accepts the task; Leleh and Apahvez express their gratitude and leave the office. Brendan grabs his laptop and immediately starts working.

Outlining his thoughts, Brendan decides to tackle the governors first and then turn to the militias. He keeps things basic, focusing on the biographic and demographic factors, political history, and known opinions about the Sabia. During the initial drafting, Berina comes in, but he waves her off, explaining he is too busy to talk. She exits without a word. Once he's done with the governors, he starts writing about the militias. Time is a factor, so he writes a top-level overview.

> **Patriot Assembly:** Confederation of groups aligned with General Meade. Meade is turning once independent factions into a united force and a political party. Poses the greatest organized

threat to government rule. Seeks to remake the United States into a corporatist state on a Francoist model. Views Sabia as enablers of ruling elites in government, politics, and business.

New Sons of Freedom: Second largest militia group behind Patriot Assembly. Seeks to "ensure" liberties promised by the Constitution. Opposes Patriot Assembly and views its ideology as foreign to the United States. Has no organized political wing. Leadership believes the Sabia and government conspire together to enrich the elites while keeping the rest of the country poor.

Nationalist Sons of Freedom: Off-shoot of the New Sons of Freedom. Largely white supremacist in ideology. Potential for fracturing in the future. Funded mainly through criminal activity. Unreconcilable racist beliefs against Sabia. Believe the darker skin of the Sabia is a sign of inferiority.

Idaho Freedom Militia: Formed by members of the Idaho National Guard who resigned after the White House riots. Working on expanding into neighboring states. Attempting to create a professional force on the model of the United States military. Not in principle against Sabia. Fears leftist groups are taking over the country. Primarily focused on "defensive" capabilities against federal government overreach.

Sons of the Shepherd: Violent, neo-Protestant conspiracy group. Poorly organized. More of a movement than an actual group. Has conducted the most anti-Sabia attacks of all militia groups.

PATRICK ABBOTT

Unwilling to enter discussions with the government or Sabia. Views both as controlled by the devil.

A quick scan of what he wrote leads Brendan to flesh out a few sections. He quickly proofreads, makes minor edits, and sends the document to Leleh. Brendan removes his seat pillow to lie on the carpet of his office. *That was exhausting.* His stomach rumbles. Not knowing what time it is, he gets up, hoping it's either dinnertime or there will at least be something in the cafeteria to grab. Walking out of his office, he is surprised to see the spot where the guard usually stands is empty. *Did I work so late the guard went home?*

The cafeteria itself is empty sans one server, a male named Oshin, wiping down the wooden disks that larger meals are served on.

Oshin looks up but appears nervous. "Sorry, Brendan, special event tonight. We are closed."

"I got that impression. So what is the event, buddy?"

The server shakes his head. "Sorry, that is classified."

Brendan fights to control his frustration. "That's fine. Don't suppose you have anything in storage you can give me? I can eat it in my cabin."

"We have no food to give, sorry."

"Wowza," Brendan says in defeat. "Well, brother, have a great night."

273

They exchange a handshake, which Brendan once demonstrated to the waitstaff, much to their delight. As he begins to leave, Gul runs into the dining hall.

"I found him!" he screams.

Uh oh.

Berina comes rushing in, maneuvering around Gul. Her pristine white smock, worn with a black stole, stands out as rather puritanical compared to the other clothing he has seen on the Sabia.

Pointing wildly at Brendan, she addresses Oshin. "You did not feed him, did you?"

"No food was served. As I told Brendan, we are closed," Oshin answers.

Eagerly she turns to Brendan. "I tried talking to you earlier, but no worries. Tonight is an exceptional night—come on!"

She waves for him to follow her. Berina leads, with Brendan tailing closely behind and Gul bringing up the rear.

"I take it the classified reason the cafeteria is closed is because of where you're taking me." He phrases it almost as a rhetorical question.

"It is not classified, Brendan. Happy New Year. I organized a celebration for a few friends. Had to make sure you did not eat first, though. One has to fast for such things." Her voice sounds excited.

An actual party! Wow! Looks like I needed to just take a few lugs, and now I have reached some new level of trust with them. A desire to shake his hands in excitement causes him to tuck them into his pockets. *Keep calm, son.*

They walk down the corridors taking multiple twists and turns along the way. This is the deepest he thinks he has ever been on the ship. Eventually turning into a corridor with dimmed lights, they pass through a door into a massive hall. Something large and black initially blocks his vision. He quickly determines it's some sort of hydroponic garden. The air smells of vegetation, and flowing water can be heard everywhere.

He hears clapping and then the commotion of many people. As he reaches the end of the maze of hanging plants, he sees a fire in the center of an ample open space. Gul leads Brendan to a large circle of Sabia and sits him down between the guard Ishan and another male. Brendan enjoys the heat of the flames as it radiates toward him. The experience reminds him of camping with his father. Loft walks around, passing out pieces of naan-looking bread. Gul takes two, one for himself and one for Brendan. Whispering, he tells Brendan not to eat his portion.

A tall Ottoman-looking cushion is placed in a gap in the circle. Berina walks over to it and sits down with her legs crossed. Looking around, Brendan sees Loft seated along with everyone else. *What the heck rank does she have?* As he observes the various Sabia in the dim light, Brendan notices males and females are separated, with females on Berina's left and males on her right. Counting, he views about two dozen present.

"Blessings of the divine, everyone," Berina starts, "and Happy New Year. Here we, all bodily members of the Legion, are gathered. Whether we are senior officers or auxiliaries, we set aside our ranks, deny our sinful selves, give thanks for what has come, and look forward to what may come."

Holy crap, this is a cultural intelligence goldmine!

Berina continues. "I am an unabashed braggart. This I hate about myself."

She tosses a piece of bread into the fire. The room is silent, everyone still as church mice, as the bread burns. Brendan watches the flames illuminate Berina's face. He can see tears forming as she sits deep in thought.

"I have helped many of you in times of need. This I love about myself."

She tosses another piece of bread into the flames. Brendan continues to observe her. Berina still looks sad, but a slight smile fights through her manifest melancholy. Once the fire consumes the second morsel, her more familiar cheerfulness returns.

"I look forward to seeing many of you off as you rotate out. Oh! And I look forward to helping many of those who replace you."

The third section of bread is thrown into the blaze. With this last statement, there is murmuring among the participants. *I know that redeployment feeling. It looks like Sabia and humans are not so different in this regard.*

PATRICK ABBOTT

The females on Berina's left start their turns. Many confess personality flaws, give thanks for each other, and while some are looking forward to an end of their tours, most offer up hopes of aiding the Legion in completing its "goals." All appear emotional yet uniform until the turn comes to a Sabia with auburn hair.

"I hate Terrans. After all we have done for those backward, sororicidal monsters, they just hate, and hate, and hate. I cannot sleep some nights because all I hear are my friends crying as the doctors reconstruct mangled limbs. I hate them, and I hate that I hate them."

She stares at Brendan. He wants to say something. The pressure of dozens of eyes lies upon him. He feels the repressed pain of him insulting his dying father, using horrible slurs against Muslims, and mocking the Islamic State dead. Part of him wants to reassure the Sabia woman, but these flashbacks distract him. She looks down, breaks off a piece of bread, and puts it in her mouth. She sucks in her face as she eats it, indicating a sour taste. Everyone is silent as she chews. She says nothing more.

Next, Brendan hears Esfirs start to speak. "I . . ." There is a long pause. "I am a person who has yelled at friends. This I hate about myself."

The first piece of bread is tossed in. Brendan is deeply interested in the rest of what she has to say. He wonders if it is wrong to be curious, but he hungers to hear more. *Will she be thankful for me?*

"I have been challenged and changed by my friends. This I love about myself." She pitches the second portion of bread. Finally, she says, "I look forward to being told we have been successful in our mission."

Brendan dwells on Esfirs words. He cannot help but be proud of her. He wishes he could be as self-reflective as she is with his own shortcomings, thankfulness, and goals. *Crap, they are going to expect the same from me!* The rest of the females finish their statements. Looking up, he sees the auburn-haired Sabia looking down, her face resting in her hands. Tears flow down her arms. *She looks like hell.*

After a short silence, the males start. Like the females', most of their confessions deal with personality flaws. However, Sabia males differ from their counterparts in that their thankfulness is centered on things they have personally done. The delta continues with the males overall looking forward to beating personal challenges.

It becomes Brendan's turn to talk. Pressure mounts, though he sees no one looking at him. Butterflies begin to fly in his stomach. His eyes dart around, and his brain draws up quick exit plans. Finally, squeezing his eyes shut, he wills himself to remain seated.

"Well, I . . ." He knows verbal pauses will only gain him so much time. "Looking back at my year—and it has been a heck of a year—on the negative side, well, here it is: it has been pointed out to me, and it's true, I do not deal with anxiety well. I wasn't always this way. I try to fake being happy. It works to get me out of situations, but I always, and I mean always, break down. I can't count the times I've lost my cool when dealing with some of you. It's because I don't confront stress well. Not since . . . well . . . it has been a long decay. On the day I fought in the metro, I pretended I was happy in front of my coworkers. Yet, that very morning I begged myself not to break down. So many days ended with me crying. I need to be more honest. I hate being dishonest with myself and mistreating friends."

He tears off a piece of bread and throws it in the general direction of the fire. His words make him think about how the stress in his life has been building up. *I have PTSD.* It is the first time he confronts the painful truth. He has thought about it for a while but never wanted to get help because that meant others would know.

Gul's gentle hand pats him on the back. Covertly reporting back to the Unified Intelligence Command makes him feel terrible. *It would be one thing if the Sabia and the UIC were just large organizations, not people who cared for me.* He's never had to keep his collection secret before. Everyone knew liaison officers were collectors. Here, though, the Sabia are opening up to him. *Or are they? How many 'classified' stonewalls do I run into?* He feels another pat on the back. Gul whispers that it's time for the second statement.

"I have worked hard for both humans and Sabia. Certainly, I have not always been successful, but I love that I can try."

He watches the second bit of bread fly into the fire and burn. Speaking the truth lifts a heavy burden off him. The humid, plant-filled air enlivens his lungs. *I do not have to pretend.*

"Now, time to say what I look forward to. Not knowing how long one of your years is gives me a vague deadline. Hmm. I guess I look forward to every day I am given to work with you all."

The third piece of bread is enveloped by the flame. Like the others, Brendan has about half his bread left and is unsure what to do with it.

After Brendan is finished, the rest of the males complete their ceremonies. After the last Sabia speaks, Berina comes off her ottoman. She walks over to each person, places her hands on their cheeks, and briefly says something. When Berina reaches the auburn-haired Sabia, the once angry female's eyes are now bloodshot, and her skin is becoming paler by the minute. Rather than provide comfort, Berina looks down and passes over her without saying a word.

When Berina approaches Brendan, she smiles, places her hands on his cheeks, and says, "Bless the divine for giving you to us."

Once done with everyone, Berina sits back on top of the ottoman-like cushion. From behind her, she pulls out a dark bowl. She dips her remaining bread into the bowl and eats it. The bowl is then passed to her left. Brendan notices the auburn-haired Sabia is passed over. He feels horrible for her but does not move to do anything. Fear of breaking up the ceremony overrides his desire to comfort her. Soon the bowl reaches him. He dips his bread into the clear syrup. Taking a bite, he finds it tastes like honey combined with citrus. There is a slight sourness, but the syrup masks any unpleasantness. Next, Gul takes the bowl, and then the rest of the males dip and eat their bread.

Finally, the ceremony ends with everyone getting up and walking away. Brendan stands around, unsure what to do until Esfirs walks up to him.

She whispers, "Come with me; I will take you back."

She leads him through the dark maze of plants and into the hallway. As they make their way back, Brendan thinks about all the things he should report back from the ceremony—the fact that this is a year new for the Sabia, Loft's position compared to Berina's, the one who hated humans . . . However, a mental snap breaks off that line of thinking. *Were you there as a spy or a friend?*

His thoughts are interrupted again as he looks over to Esfirs. The way her brown hair rests in the clip is, for some reason, incredibly fascinating. How something as mundane as hair in a clip can belong to something so alien. He tries to make some remarks about the evening but cannot form anything intelligent. The way she moves in her sari-like gray outfit is more pleasing to ponder than anything he could say.

"Well?" She stops to ask him the question.

"Well, what?" *Dang it, I wasn't paying attention to her. Well, I was paying attention to her, but not—*

"What I asked you. What did you think about the ceremony?"

"Oh, that." He chuckles nervously. "Happy New Year. Whether it was you or Berina, thank you for inviting me."

"Happy New Year to you too, Brendan." Her voice sounds genuinely happy. "You were invited because of your role here. We did nothing extraordinary."

They spend the rest of the walk chatting about their days. Brendan focuses on the paper he drafted while Esfirs discusses minor medical checkups involving several Sabia. He steals glances at Esfirs as they walk side by side. *She is beautiful. Both in her human and Sabia forms.* When they arrive at his cabin, Brendan asks if she wants to celebrate the New Year with a game. Rather than answering, she smiles, causing him to wink back. Brendan greets the guard, opens the door, and they both enter.

When he turns to her, their eyes lock. *She is so beautiful. I really hope she gets what she wants this year. Just to see her happy, to see her like this . . . What a lovely person.* His heart speeds up. More air is pumped in and out with each of his breaths. Simultaneously, Esfirs tilts her head slightly, and her eyes adopt a sly look. *Does she know what I am thinking?* They both turn away. Shame overwhelms him.

"Look, I am so, so sorry. I didn't mean to—" Brendan starts.

"The fault is all mine, Brendan. I should not have been so bold in my thoughts when we bonded." Her face is turning red.

PATRICK ABBOTT

Bond. They call it a Bond.

"Your thoughts?" he asks.

She shoots him a surprised look. "You mean you did not hear what I was thinking?"

"I, uh, thought you may have figured out what I was thinking."

Nervous laughter first comes from him, then her.

"What were you thinking?" she asks.

Brendan closes his eyes and builds up the strength to be truthful. "I was thinking how much I like seeing you happy."

Silence reigns in the room. His heart sinks. *I was too bold.*

Finally, she speaks. "I was thinking how I love having you be a part of us." He shrugs sheepishly. "And how I never want you to leave."

Slowly Brendan locks eyes with Esfirs, creating a new Bond. Emotionally he reaches out and feels as if she's embracing him. He gulps hard, unsure of what is happening.

"Calm, be calm, Brendan," she says. "You said you hated being dishonest with yourself. It is because you are trying to be something you are not. You fear being yourself means you will be alone. But being fake is what makes you alone.

"I fear you deceiving yourself, too. The Terrans will lie to you, Brendan. First, they will tell you sweet things to confuse you, get you to work against us, and make you return to them. Then they will betray you. All because you lie to yourself, thinking you are a Terran.

"You are Sabia, Brendan. And the great thing about being Sabia is you are not alone. You are with us, you serve us now, and the Unified Intelligence Command has disowned you. So, look into my soul and see the truth."

First, it is emotions he senses in her brown eyes, then thoughts. *Kindness. Friendship. Partnership. Love.* The last one is so jarring that he tries to back away.

"No, look at me, Brendan," she commands. "Those emotions I have, what I want for, and from you— do you want the same from me?"

Life experiences flash before him. He thinks of all the ways in which he has suffered. How Heather hurt him so. About how the next few seconds could decide the fate of the rest of his life. Esfirs asks the same question again, this time with more force.

"The last time I told any woman I loved her, she betrayed me and hollowed out my soul."

"Then let me make you whole," she answers.

Years of stress, fear, and panic come crashing down on Brendan. He wants to run. He wants to hide. He needs to get away. Thoughts of running out the door become louder. He's going to do it. His muscles tighten in anticipation.

"I love you."

Her words are simple, soft, and cause the world to fade away. His muscles feel like popcorn. Then, without thinking but meaning every word, he says, "I love you."

They look deeply into each other. Brendan thinks he can feel the warmth of her soul, or at the very least, her love for him. Gazing at her brings a primordial joy better and more meaningful than any lust for her body. So he closes his eyes, leans forward, and kisses her. The moistness of a woman's kiss is a long-forgotten joy to him.

Slam! His head is jarred to the side as Esfirs' fist knocks him to the floor. Looking up, he sees pure rage in her eyes. A new Bond forms. This time he feels only hostility.

"Freak!" she shouts.

She jolts back as if something has startled her. She might have said something, but Brendan's ears are ringing too loudly to hear.

"You did not know?" Her eyes are wide open as she speaks. "Brendan, males should not be so bold with such things." Her response is as much as an explanation to her as to him.

"What the heck was that?" Brendan can only just manage to say the words without screaming in pain.

"Females lead in such things. Male Sabia who do are it—different—wrong."

The brutal knockdown response is the weirdest reaction to a cultural faux pas Brendan has ever

285

experienced. At least the Afghans thought it was hilarious when he accidentally challenged everyone to a fight with a thumbs up.

"Got it. Tell you what. Next time one of us commits a cultural no-no, let's just tell each other that's a no-no and not hit each other, okay?"

Esfirs nervously laughs. She offers her hand, which Brendan takes. Her Sabia strength allows her to easily lift Brendan back up. Still, the right side of his face is numb. Brendan tries to feel it with his hand but only senses numbness. *This is going to hurt in the morning.*

"Will you allow me to help you heal?" Esfirs asks.

He doesn't know if she is referring to his face or if she means the PTSD-related stresses in his life. He looks her in the eyes to form another Bond.

"Yes," he replies, unsure.

"I meant both."

She walks up to him, allowing their bodies to touch. Then, using her right hand to bend down his head, she kisses him on the lips.

PATRICK ABBOTT

Twenty-Six – A Night to Remember

Brendan feels alive as he rests his head on the floor pillow. From getting walloped for taking the lead to ending up on second base. He looks over to his right to see Esfirs. She is smiling, her hair loose from the clip. It is long and beautiful. While he studies her profile, she gazes toward the ceiling. *I wonder what she is thinking about.* All he can do, all he wants to do, is admire her in this position. However, thoughts from previous deployments slowly start to trickle into his mind.

"Esfirs, are we—did we—do something that will get us in trouble?"

She laughs. "Brendanshe, have you not paid attention to this whole ship? Have you not noticed couples on the ship? Relationships are perfectly natural."

Brendan is too enraptured to question immediately why Esfirs added a -she to his name. Instead, he instinctively desires to answer her question. "Well, when I was deployed out to, say, Iraq or Afghanistan, relationships which . . . got more physical were forbidden by General Order Number One. The very fact the order was named 'General Order Number One' says a lot about its importance."

"Are you going to tell the Unified Intelligence Command director to get me in trouble?" she asks playfully, staring into his eyes.

Crap! Does she know I have sent messages back? The idea of such paralyzes him with fear. Brendan catches her glancing at him, her pupils dilated wide and a deeper brown color than usual. She appears genuinely, uncomfortably alien to him.

Before his panic can manifest, Esfirs turns her gaze to the ceiling while laughter erupts from her. "Calm, Brendanshe, calm," she says. After she speaks, she turns back to him and gives Brendan a gentle kiss. After the kiss, she pulls away.

"You were not afraid when I showed you how Sabia looked; why do you fear me now?"

"I'm not afraid—I am just really overwhelmed." *A partial lie. Already bringing lying to a relationship. Stupid, Brendan, stupid!*

His words cause her to laugh some more. "Stop being dishonest, Brendanshe. You are afraid."

"Okay, you're right, I am afraid. For — many reasons — I fear getting in trouble. I have no idea how any would view us being together."

As if some sort of talisman, the words work. After a moment, Esfirs sits up straight with a surprised look on her face. She adjusts her gaze, and her eyes go back to their usual color.

"I am sorry, Brendan. I did not intend to scare you. I thought what we were doing was enjoyable. You having fear is understandable, but we are free to be together, an officer and an auxiliary officer. Only in your head are you an alien to us. Sabia blood runs in your veins." Esfirs voice trails off. "Brendan, you do think you are one of us, yes? You are comfortable with us, with me?"

Brendan sits up. Using his left hand, he grasps hers. He doesn't want to chase her away, not now. "There is nothing to apologize for. It's like when I was too bold in kissing you—we should work on making ourselves comfortable with each other. Our cultures are going to . . . make things difficult, but I want to make us work."

"What may I do to help you be comfortable?" she asks.

"Earlier, you called me 'Brendanshe.' What does that mean?"

Her olive-hued face turns red again. Then, gently wiggling, she first looks away, then back toward Brendan. "It is a term of endearment. A special one. One that is not said in public."

"I understand, Esfirshe."

Her laughter is so loud Brendan is worried it will attract the guard's attention outside. She holds her sides as if they are going to split. Her riant fit is so intense she starts to cough. "No, no, no, no, no," she manages to say in between gasps for air. "Never, ever add -she to the name of a woman. Never. I would hit you again if your innocence were not so lovely!"

Brendan gives her time to recover, which she needs. As she calms down, she looks at him, and another Bond forms. The sensation is warm and loving. The only time he felt something similar was when he would hold Heather close on their earlier dates. That, though, was not as rapturous as what he feels now. To love and lose, only to love again, makes the experience richer.

"What may I do to help you to be comfortable?" Brendan mirrors her question.

"I need the real you. Please help me by getting rid of the lies you tell yourself."

It is now Brendan's turn to laugh nervously. "I have a real problem. What I said I hated about myself back at the New Year's gathering, yeah. I have a terrible case of post-traumatic stress disorder. During my deployments, I saw horrible things: dead bodies, terrorist attacks against schools, pointless missions that people died in for no reason, corruption, and people treating each other horribly for the sake of being cruel. I convinced myself of the righteousness of our missions until I realized I was an accessory to terrible crimes. My whole identity was invested in them. They became more and more a part of me as my family life collapsed and work in the States became pointless. I really was losing my identity outside deployments. And to tell you the truth, I am scared—so scared—about this mission. I have no idea what I'll do after this. I live every day in fear. I'm so scared." A light bulb goes off in his head. "Huh, that's it. I'm scared. That makes sense, but I never thought about it that way."

PATRICK ABBOTT

"Brendanshe"—her voice and the Bond move Brendan to sense a deep, compassionate sadness—"I feel your pain. May I tell you a story?"

Brendan nods.

She continues. "There was a woman named Namziah. Her family disowned her because she was free of false rules, unwilling to conform to her people's ways. They beat her and drove her into the desert to die. As she lay there, from above, a beautiful spirit named Remel heard her cries. When Remel finally found her, she was dying of thirst. Remel rescued her, gave her a drink, and made her well. They were then devoted to one another and founded a mighty nation together. Their children are us. Our name, Sabia, means 'children of beauty,' because we are the children of the beautiful spirit who saved Namziah."

Brendan's eyes are wide open as the story ends. He ponders the macro-level meaning behind it. The immediate meaning, however, escapes him. "Esfirs, I don't understand the point of your story."

She closes her eyes and breathes deeply. "I have told you several times that you are not the same anymore. You are not Terran anymore. You are a child of beauty because you are one of us. Let me be your Remel. Let me help you shed yourself to aid you in shedding the lies you hate. No more will you fear being honest with yourself. Will you allow me to do this?"

He looks away, searching for an answer in a room without them. Words fail him. The idea of being free of his "anxiety coping mechanisms" is thrilling, yet the notion that his humanity is tied to his problem is offensive. *How to say yes and no to the woman I love?* The question is one he's never had to face before.

"Brendanshe, if you cannot commit, please just take my hand and promise me that you will at least let me show you what I mean. Do not fight me on this!" Esfirs pleads.

Cautiously and slowly, Brendan puts out his hand. Esfirs clasps it just as he pulls it back slightly in a moment of self-doubt. Next, she pulls him into a tight hug.

"Thank you," she says. "I love you."

They hold each other tightly. Brendan feels completely alive as he embraces Esfirs. Long-forgotten masculinity awakens in him. Her smell, the touch of her skin, and the hot breath coming from her all enliven him. He feels parts of himself come alive again. A particular surge propels him further into the embrace. Brendan rests his head tightly against Esfris as he smells her hair, the loveliest scent he has ever breathed in. Desire continues to grow within him. *Would she allow me to—*

"Brendanshe, I have a busy day ahead of me tomorrow. You must sleep, too. Good night, my love."

He starts to protest, but a look from her comforts him. He watches her put her beautiful hair back into the clip and walk out. Closing his eyes, he can still sense her around him. Whether it's perfume or just how she smells to him, it's intoxicating. After lying down for a few minutes, the weight of his eyelids makes keeping them open difficult. Getting up off the floor, he makes his way to the bed. Plopping down, he feels the UIC's phone-like device underneath the mattress. He pulls it out. The flashing light indicates a message is waiting for him.

UIC-X2: Report.

The anonymous demand fills him with dread. The warmness he felt moments before has all but escaped him. Part of him wants to help his country, while the other doesn't want to betray those who trust him. Up has become down, and down is now up. *Is this what being compromised is like? Or is this just love? This is something I should consult with seniors on.* Thinking it through, he decides it is best to report the situation while begging for help.

Brendan: Embedding efforts working with Sabia. They are trusting me more and more. However, I worry PTSD from past deployments is degrading my effectiveness. I need help. Is it safe for me to return?

He hits send after rereading the message. Looking at the screen, he is unsure what will happen. *Will the UIC try to extract me? Am I going to be ordered to escape from the Sabia? Will the government cut me off as a nut case? God, please help me.* He catches himself. *Another prayer.* This time, though, he does not feel odd thinking about it.

The device pings.

UIC-X2: Good. Stay on mission. Remember to get rest.

He looks at the screen in disbelief. The magic letters "PTSD" should have been a red flag to any officer. Brendan types out a new message to see if he can force a response.

> Brendan: PTSD is interfering with decision-making. I am scared.

Within seconds there is a reply.

> UIC-X2: Are you in immediate danger?

Brendan slaps the bed hard.

> Brendan: No. But worried I might make wrong decisions. I feel uncomfortable working behind Sabia's backs. My mission was to be a liaison and, therefore, an overt collector.

There is no initial reply. *They must need to deliberate on my situation. That's progress. I just need to sleep.* Brendan puts his head down.

Ping.

> UIC-X2: Roles change. Stay on mission.

Brendan screams into his pillow. That night is extra dark, and the room is claustrophobic.

PATRICK ABBOTT

Twenty-Seven – Putting the Pieces on the Board

Brendan wakes up groggy. Last night started so well but then collapsed into another panic. The only dream he had involved being buried under an ocean of sand. He knows he needs more sleep, but his mind screams for him to get up. Looking at the clock display, he panics. *It's late! Why did the alarm fail?* He pushes himself off the bed and rushes to get dressed. The result is a so-so success of T-shirt and slacks. Racing out the door, he sidesteps both a guard and Kimya.

"Brendan, hey! Where are you going?" she calls out to him.

"Work!" he cries back, adjusting his tie as he leaps down the hall.

"Wait!" Kimya shouts after him.

He pays no attention as he rushes through the hallways. The corridors are lively, with various Sabia going about their day. Anyone nearby can follow his progress; his passing acts like a wave rippling a peaceful shore. Apologizing as he goes, Brendan finally ends up at his office. The Sabia don't require him to be on a schedule per se, but he worries his consistency has created a de facto one. *If I am of no use to them . . .* He stops and starts to control his breathing. *No. Esfirs keeps talking to me about this. I shouldn't fear being abandoned. I just need a moment to breathe. Focus, Brendan, focus!* This allows him to calm down. He sits down on his pillow and opens his laptop. There is a lot of news, but nothing stands out to him.

"Hey!" Kimya enters the room, out of breath. "You are not supposed to be here. You have to go back."

"What?" Brendan asks, perplexed.

"Esfirs put you on medical leave. She said you were up all night and needed rest. I personally made sure your alarm was canceled. When you ran by us, I told poor Nosha you were not to leave your room. It is her first day, and already she is worried about failing as a guard. Come on; I will take you back to your room."

Before Brendan can protest, Leleh enters the office. "Ah, Brendan, after last night, I thought you would stay in bed for a while." A prominent smirk on her face rises once she is done talking.

Her words catch Brendan off guard. *How much do they know?* "Oh yeah, this. Last night, after all the fun, I was up late just chatting with Esfirs" He laughs nervously.

Kimya launches into a tizzy. "You were choking? Why did you not summon the guard right outside your door? We would have gotten medical for you! Brendan, you could have died!"

Kimya looks at Brendan with squinted eyes while Leleh drops her smirk for a stoic stance.

PATRICK ABBOTT

"Very well," Leleh says without emotion. "Zand believes we should speed up our pursuit of better relations with the governors of the western United States of America. In compliance with her wishes, Loft is arranging a conference between them and a senior council member. Additionally, we plan on offering medical care to demonstrate our benevolence. Your paper yesterday was very well received and has helped us understand what to expect. Would you be willing to aid us in a practice exercise?"

"Of course!" Brendan says, eager to help. "When do you want to do the wargaming?"

Leleh looks at him quizzically. "We are not expecting a war to erupt due to this conference."

"Never mind, it is a human expression. So, what timeline are you thinking of for this dry run? I think I'd need two days to put together a full report and then a day to prepare."

"Such interesting terms you use, Brendan," Leleh says as she glances over at Kimya. "There is no need to finish the longer report as your preliminary report, and upcoming discussion should accomplish our ends. The council member in charge wishes to conduct the meeting tonight. I can escort you to dinner with her, and then afterward, you can have the briefing. This way, you may be at ease with each other."

"Actually," Brendan begins, "I would strongly advise against that plan. The council member and I would form a connection if we had dinner together. If they want the best possible practice, they should meet with someone they are not fully comfortable with. In fact, it may help to have multiple people there for it to be more realistic. Could I form a team? Some could play friendly governors, others could be neutral, and we could have one or two hostile governors? This way, the council member would be prepared for a range of responses. We could even set it up as it will be on Earth. Have us sit on chairs at a long table." Brendan's heart jumps in excitement at what he's envisioning. "This is going to be fun."

Leleh ponders his words. "Is this how you prepare for new situations? Making it a game?"

He nods vigorously. "Oh yeah, we role-play these all the time. It gives us a more realistic experience of what to expect than a simple question-and-answer session. Rarely is something educational and fun, but this easily can be both.

"I should caveat this, though. It could get intense. Role players should not be treated according to their ranks here on the ship but as if they really were governors on Earth."

"Acknowledged."

"Would you permit me to recruit the team? Also, they will need to be excused from their duties to prepare."

Leleh thinks it over and then says, "Of course. Assemble your cohort and have them here in your office at the end of shift chimes. I will escort you all from here. Good day."

PATRICK ABBOTT

She places her left hand over her heart and bows slightly. *She's a talented mimic.*

Brendan turns to Kimya, studying her for a moment as she becomes slightly uncomfortable with his silent stare. "How do you like the sound of Governor Kimberly Yancey?"

"Me? Oh no, I would not know what to do. I would be a distraction. No one could think I was a Terran governor."

"Drat. Tell you what, if you can't do the role-playing, I want two guards. Who do you—"

Interrupting him, Kimya says, "Gul and Ishan."

"Dang, that was quick. No love for them, eh?"

She rolls her eyes. "Security forces have their own way of doing things. They have been trained from the beginning to guard rooms and key personnel who will never be threatened. And they do not like taking orders from . . . me. Thankfully, the new rotation is full of people willing to learn. New arrivals are young and with heads not full of 'we always did it this way.'"

"Okay . . ." Brendan wonders what was behind that remark. "I think you would have made a great governor. But I will draft some others. If you don't mind, I'll send you instructions for Gul and Ishan. Have them get some professional Earth clothing."

Kimya makes her sucking sound, wink, and thumbs up. Brendan responds by doing all three things at the same time. *I don't think she gets it.*

Making his way to the medical bay, he finds Esfirs studying a pad with another doctor. She looks up, astonished as he approaches.

"Brendan, why are you here?" She sounds incredulous. "You are supposed to be on medical leave. Kimya was ordered not to let you out. Can she do nothing right?"

"Calm down, Esfirs. I didn't know I was put on leave, so have pity on those I can outrun. I was wondering if we could talk alone."

She tilts her head upward like an alert bird. Then she looks over and sends the other doctor away with a nod. "Of course, let us go to the back room."

She excuses herself from the rest of the medical staff and makes her way to the back, with Brendan following closely behind. To his surprise, the lights are on. Previously, the lights have been dimmed every time he has been in here. *With the lights on, this room is a thousand times less intimidating. Or maybe it is the context.*

"What is the matter?" Esfirs asks.

"Nothing, nothing," Brendan says as he waves his hand dismissively. "First, I just want to thank you for last night. For everything, really. I . . . it—it was really nice having someone . . . there with me."

She stands there studying him. Brendan hopes she will say something, but she doesn't. Brendan squirms a little bit.

PATRICK ABBOTT

"Well, anyway," he says to recover, "how would you like to be a governor on Earth?"

Her eyebrows squinch together. She vocalizes nothing, but her face says tons of skeptical things.

"What I mean is, how would you like to be part of a role-playing game where you pretend to be a governor?"

She now crosses her arms and leans toward Brendan with the same facial expression.

"Okay then, under the authority of Leleh, I am drafting you to be part of a practice session I am putting on for a council member who is traveling to Earth. You're excused from your duties to prepare for this. I need you to show up in, uhm . . . Terran clothing at my office when the end of shift chimes go off. I will make sure to send you a copy of the report I did on the governors. This will be a fun game, I promise."

Her eyes widen. "Brendan, one does not just play a game with a council member. Berina, I, and the others have been willing to play games with you, but that is because our ranks allow our friendship. Council members are above us. I do not think—"

"Esfirs, please. It will be fine. This will help the council member learn what to expect. You might enjoy yourself, as well. I'll make things easy for you—you can play a pro-Sabia governor. Just show up in Terran clothing. I'll manage everything. It will all work out. No worries!"

She studies him in silence. "I trust you, Brendan." Her voice betrays doubt.

He chooses to ignore her tone and instead focuses on her words. "Thank you, Esfirs. This will be fun, you'll see. By the way, we'll need another partner. Where's Berina?"

"We really must do something about your repeated use of contractions."

"What?"

"Terrans use contractions. It is grating to our ears. Can you please talk formally?"

"I ain't gonna promise ya, buh I'll try." Brendan plays up a hillbilly accent for effect.

It's more successful than he intended. Esfirs face drops, and she says, "Never speak like that again."

"And why not, deary?"

"I did not spend half my life, over two decades here, learning multiple Terran languages so I could communicate with people who talk like that."

Jackpot! "Natch." He winks at her.

Esfirs sighs. "Anyways, Berina is off flying around somewhere. I doubt she would be able to join us for whatever you have planned."

Brendan claps his hands. "Dang! Wait a tick; maybe I can reach her with the communicator you gave me. Again, thank you for everything." He begins to turn away but then stops. "Oh, and I will work on my contractions if it is an issue for you. See what I did there?"

She slightly shakes her head. "I do not understand you sometimes."

"Being from another planet will do that. But seriously, thank you for last night. I loved . . . it and you," he says.

His last sentence comes from deep within his soul, unplanned and uncensored. The profound seriousness of his words hangs in the air, breaking Esfirs' confused stare. She silently nods her head. He slowly leaves the room, unsure if he wants more of a response from her.

Deliberately he maneuvers through the hallways back to his room. Calling Berina on the communication device is his only hope. *But hope is hope. Otherwise, I might not have enough for this wargame; I would have no idea what to do then.* He sees two guards speaking by his door, one male and the other female. Brendan thinks the female guard is the one he buzzed by in his initial morning panic run.

"Auxiliary Officer Brendan, you have to go back inside your cabin. You are on medical leave. You must rest today," the female guard says.

"No worries, guard—guard . . . what is your name?" Brendan replies.

"My name is Khawa, sir."

"Ah, Khawa, nice to meet you. I plan to rest a little bit today, but please understand I am acting under indirect orders from a council member to prepare an important meeting for them. So later today, I will be leaving my room again."

Brendan waits for her reply. She looks over at the male guard. Her grimace shows a lack of confidence; the male's downward gaze indicates uncertainty. Standing there in silence, Brendan waits for someone to say something. Finally, when no one speaks, he bids them both a goodbye and enters his cabin. As his door closes, he hears the female say, "We need to contact Kimya to find out what we should do."

Brendan grabs the Sabia communication device from under his mattress. Scrolling through the list of contacts on the screen, he clicks on Berina's name. It connects instantaneously. Her voice comes through crystal clear.

"Brendan! Did you have too much New Year's fun last night?"

"Last night was great, thank you. And yes, I had more fun than I budgeted for. Thankfully, today I can share some fun with you. But first, where are you right now?"

"I am sitting under a moonless sky waiting for Terrans to offload trucks so they can load supplies onto our heavy lifts. Once they do that, my crew can sign off on everything, get back on board, and we can finally head on back home to you all."

"Interesting. Are you going to be back in time for the end-of-shift chimes in the evening?"

"Yes, why?"

PATRICK ABBOTT

"How would you like to role-play a slightly Sabia-skeptical Earth governor in an effort to train a council member on how to deal with multiple governors in a meeting? Of course, you will have to pretend to be a human in all things, including wardrobe."

"I will do if you answer one question for me."

Simple enough. "What is that?"

"Did you really add the suffix -she to the name of our mutual friend?"

Brendan's jaw drops, his throat dries, and his face turns red. *Berina knows! How much does she know? Does she know about the physical activity, too? She must know I said I love her. How would she know otherwise?* Brendan becomes sick to his stomach. *Esfirs must have told everyone everything. This is Heather all over again! They must have laughed, saying I was a fool.*

Berina erupts in loud and long laughter. "Brendan, you cannot say such a thing! Never to a woman!" She laughs even harder.

"She . . . told you?" Brendan's question comes out as tears begin to form. His mind laughs at him. *It's Heather all over again, fool!*

More laughter from Berina. Brendan collapses on the bed. A meek *why* comes deep from his gut. His mind wanders until Berina's voice calls him back to reality.

"Hey! Brendan? Can you hear me!"

"Yeah," he says weakly.

"Are you alright?"

"Do not lie to me—am I in trouble?"

"What?" Berina shoots back quickly. "I am incredibly happy for both of you. She deserves some fun after all her hard years of work. You, meanwhile, have someone who cares about you. Great job, you kids. Why would I think any differently?"

Brendan still can't reply.

"Hey, Brendan. Everything is fine. Do not worry. Would it help if I said I will be part of your role-play?"

He nods, then realizes she can't see him.

"Yeah, sure. End of shift. My office."

He hangs up. Getting out of bed, he sets the alarm for an hour before the chimes. Then, heading back to bed, he collapses on it. His muscles ache, his ears hurt, and he wants to die. All he can do is cry.

Twenty-Eight – War Games

Brendan stares at the ceiling. Ever since the crying stopped, he's been unable to move. The alarm has been going off for minutes; still, his body refuses to budge. *Everything was a lie. I'm a toy to play with, one to mock. Esfirs used me and my vulnerabilities. I fell for another Heather. The UIC is my only hope at this stage.* His hands instinctively reach under his mattress. Pulling out the UIC device, he types a message.

> Brendan: Jack, setting up an exercise for the Sabia. They are getting ready to meet with western governors to discuss resource access and Gen Meade. No idea on a date.

Playing the anti-Sabia governor will not be hard. Not today, anyway. Anger toward Esfirs and Berina builds in his heart. He imagines Esfirs calling him Brendanshe, only to walk over to Berina's room and dish it all out. In his mind, Berina then writes everything down in a report, sending it off to all the senior Sabia. *All that talk about integrating more was just to make me weak to give up kompromat!* He pauses. *No, that can't be right. One springs blackmail on a person. To let it linger is not logical. Well, not logical for humans . . .* His thoughts go back and forth between visions of Esfirs betraying him and being blackmailed. He takes a deep breath, deciding what to do. Getting up, he starts the walk to the office.

He arrives at his workspace as Governor Murphy. Rather than regretting having to wear a suit and tie, his alter ego loves the high-tailored clothing. Milling outside of his office are the sources of his mental grief. He sees Berina wearing a business casual outfit—a loose black blazer over a blue dress. Meanwhile, Esfirs wears a blue blazer over a navy-blue button-down and black slacks. *They probably mocked humans and me, especially while trying on the clothing.*

The two female Sabia watch Brendan sit on the carpet. They approach Brendan as he behaves as if nothing was amiss.

"Brendan!" greets Berina. "How do we look?" Her voice is friendly and warm.

He turns to examine them for a second, only to look away.

"Governor, you look adequate. Am I mistaken in thinking that is the same outfit you wore when we last feuded over your damming of the river? My farmers and ranchers still suffer from your decision."

Berina takes a step back while gasping slightly. Then, after a few moments of frozen animation, she looks over at Esfirs.

The doctor then addresses him. "Governor, greetings. So nice of you to join us. We have been most generously offered refreshments from our Sabia friends. Shall I obtain some for you?"

PATRICK ABBOTT

Oh, she's having fun with this one. Heat flashes through Brendan as he ponders how Esfirs is enjoying herself. All he can do to avoid exploding at her is to clench his fists to the point where it hurts as his heart does.

Brendan avoids eye contact when addressing his former paramour. "Governor Johnson, a pleasure. Did you see the Sabia eat or drink any of the refreshments?"

Esfirs sends a confused glance to Berina and then says to Brendan, "No, governor, the food and drink were here when I arrived."

Snapping back, Brendan says, "The Native Americans in my state have a saying: only a fool eats his foe's food."

"Do you consider the Sabia the enemy . . . Governor?"

"Never said that . . . Governor." The pause before the title barely masks his disdain. "I only quoted a proverb."

Brendan gets up and walks to the pillow he usually uses when working his auxiliary job. Berina and Esfirs begin to whisper to each other. *Probably trying to figure out if I'm role-playing or actually upset. What's the matter? We Terrans have feelings, too!*

Brendan hears Gul and Ishan chatter as they enter. The two male guards look absolutely ridiculous. Gul has on a suit meant for a person at least fifty pounds heavier and a few inches taller, while Ishan wears a red polo and khakis. Berina playfully teases him about being inappropriately dressed. *Is her teasing friendly, or is that how she establishes dominance over someone? How long has her so-called playing with me actually been her putting me down?*

Finally, Leleh walks into the room and states, "Governors, Council Member Mon will now see you. Please follow me."

I will have to talk to Leleh about that. The Sabia are going to meet the governors, not vice versa. Brendan bites down hard on his lip. *Still loyal to the mission, I guess.* He shakes his head gently to himself.

Brendan focuses on his emotional turmoil as they make their way down the corridors. It makes him strong and gives him purpose. Tapping into it gives him the drive to challenge anyone. He goes back and forth on whether to focus his ire on Esfirs or spend it on yelling at the council member first.

Before he has time to think further, they stop at a doorway. Brendan notices they are near the cafeteria Berina and Esfirs usually take him to. They enter a carpeted room with a long conference table and chairs. The Sabia actors take their seats; Brendan makes sure he is the last to sit down. As he looks around, the Sabia delegation arrives. At the head of the table is the same golden-haired twenty-something who previously asked him about the children he encountered during the Kentucky mission. She has a beaming smile that lights up her face. Her seeming innocence gives Brendan pause. *To fight something like that with my hatred . . .* With youthful joy, she takes in the room.

PATRICK ABBOTT

"Hello, dear friends, I am Mon," the head Sabia says. "It is an honor to meet such leaders as yourselves. Your people have selected you to represent them in all things, including instances such as this day. It is a wonderful honor for you, which I hope to do great homage to."

Bit clunky, but I get the point. Zand walks into the room and sits against a wall. *Good, now I have an audience.*

Mon faces Brendan from across the table. "Dear Governor Brendan, please have a seat to my left. To sit next to me is considered a great honor, and I wish it upon you."

Brendan makes a *tsk* sound and rolls his eyes. *Arrogant she-alien.* "Hello Mon, I am Governor Brendan Sean Murphy of Kansas. You may refer to me as Governor Murphy. I will not be treated like a dog who has the 'honor' of sitting next to its master. Yes, the people of our respective states have selected us to lead them, but we will handle ourselves as a bloc, not to be piecemealed or divided up."

The other governor role-players look at each other. Brendan can practically taste the thickening of the air in the room. Then, in his peripheral vision, he can see the eyes of everyone start to settle on him.

Mon recovers without missing a beat. "My apologies, dear Governor. Please take no offense at my social failure. I merely meant to honor you according to my culture. It is an honor to sit in a manner which respects all the governors here."

311

Mon takes her seat as the only Sabia representative at the table. Then, she begins to greet each of the role players as governors of their respective states. Brendan rotates his chair forty-five degrees to look at an empty corner of the room.

Throughout Mon's over-the-top pleasantries, Brendan attempts to think through what Esfirs did. Weighing the thought of betrayal against the desire to excuse her behavior causes his stomach to rise and fall repeatedly. Inside his mind, his anger yells at his desire to love. He tries to shake it off. *Keep it together; now is not the time to get distracted.* Brendan feels his hands shake. For the first time, he starts to doubt whether tapping into his rage is a wise idea. Yet, his mind keeps replaying him, making excuses for Heather. *Goodness. I'm not even in control of myself right now.* Again, he bites his lip to force himself to focus. *There's a war game going on!*

Now, Mon is listing all the great things the Sabia have offered "Terrans" lately, including trade, friendship, and medical support. The various governors offer their praise and thanks to Mon. Unfortunately, their assigned roles aren't clear, as they are all thanking her for "such great things." *Come the heck on. You are not supposed to all be pro-Sabia.* Brendan grunts his disapproval.

"Governor Murphy, I did not understand what you said. Could you please repeat it for me?" Mon asks. Her giant smile is prominent on her face.

Brendan makes a fist and starts to bring it down. He slows his hand down, opens it into a palm, and firmly places it on the table.

PATRICK ABBOTT

"Oh, I have your permission to ask a question now?" He turns to face Mon while she tilts her head like a pug trying to understand. "I have sat here listening to you puff yourself up and telling us how great the Sabia are, how lucky we are to have the Sabia visit Earth—our home that, for some reason, you insist on calling something else. But you know what? The people of Kansas have no idea why you are here. You will not tell us. What makes your time on Earth successful for you? Surely you did not come halfway across the universe to just take rocks from us in exchange for basic medical supplies. What is your agenda here?" The intensity of his voice rises.

Esfirs jumps in, "This sort of tone does not—"

"No one asked you for your thoughts," he fires back with acid animosity. "Keep things to yourself." Yelling at her releases pressure which quickly builds back up. Brendan wants to do it again.

Esfirs' lips part and she tilts her head in that now-familiar Sabia way. Brendan wonders if she realizes how much of his passion is related to what she did. Mon, meanwhile, starts and stops talking several times, each time catching herself after her first word.

Finally, she coughs, gaining everyone's attention. "Governor Murphy, thank you for your question . . . questions. By the end of the evening, I hope to earn all your—"

"No! That is not what I asked. I never asked for your trust. Let me simplify it for you because I can only imagine your failure to be truthful with me is because of

313

your lack of skill in our language: what are you doing with all the limestone you have taken out of my state?"

He stares at her, making sure to avoid a Bond forming. *Don't want these liars in my head.* It's no longer about teaching the Sabia a hard lesson in a war game. This is about revenge. The thought of a Sabia uncomfortable is sweet to him.

She gulps. "Governor Murphy, in exchange for the minerals we have given your federal—"

"No!" Brendan screams. "Let me try again! What are you doing with all the limestone you have taken out of my state?"

Esfirs loudly interjects, "One does not address a council member in—"

"What do I care about a council member?" Brendan slams the table. "And when did you start caring about how to respect others' dignity?"

Brendan leans back definitively in his chair. Suddenly, Esfirs shoots up.

"Is this about last night?" she asks.

Meanwhile, Mon is still trying to play the game. "Governor Murphy, I—we—regret to inform you that what we do with the materials your federal government has traded with us is classified."

"What?" Brendan feels like a bicyclist stuck between gears as Mon and Esfirs simultaneously pull him in and out of the role-playing exercise.

PATRICK ABBOTT

"Yes, Governor Brendan, I am not authorized to share such knowledge," Mon repeats.

His brain locks back into the war game. Making a mental note, he takes a small pride, knowing he flustered her to the point where she forgot to address him by his last name.

He ups the ante even more. "You call us to this meeting where you make us sit before you as if we should be awed by your mere presence. You insult us with claims of how lucky we are to have you. Then, when we ask you a simple question, you refuse to answer it. Tell me, Mon, how much does it take to bribe officials to do your bidding?"

Mon's mouth hangs open. She looks over to Zalta, but the elder does not recognize the plea for help.

Mon struggles for words. "Governor Murphy . . . We do not bribe . . . We—we—"

Brendan interrupts again. "I have even gotten accounts from trusted sources that you smuggle children to sacrifice in your religious rituals. Do you deny it?"

"Stop it now!" Esfirs screams. Brendan sees her seething while Berina looks away in obvious discomfort. Drops of spit are visible on Esfirs' face—she is practically foaming at the mouth.

As Brendan takes in her rage, Mon still attempts to keep the game going. Brendan doesn't know whether she's simply committed to learning or if she is oblivious to Esfirs' real-world anger.

"I can assure you we have not harmed any of your children," Mon says.

She is off her game. She forgot my title.

"A miracle! We have an answer." Brendan waves his wide-open arms. "Speaking of which, what is your religion?"

"Why are you doing this?!" Esfirs stomps her feet, taking three steps toward Brendan. He can tell she is trying to force a Bond on him. But, doing his utmost to look away, he successfully thwarts her plan.

Mon closes her eyes and robotically recites, "Matters related to culture are classified and thus cannot be shared."

Her words call him away from Esfirs. Brendan now stands up and laughs darkly at Mon. "Your kind is notorious for wanting to know cultural, religious, and personal matters concerning everyone they meet. And then you share and gossip all about them"—Esfirs storms out as he talks—"but you will not share anything concerning your own backgrounds. Everything is on your terms. You claim to want the best for us, but you do not. Do you want to know how we know? Want to know how we are onto you? It is because we see you acting in the dark. We know you are liars. You will promise us much, pretend to be our friends, and then betray us. Admit it!" He points angrily at Mon as he finishes.

Brendan physically braces himself for her response. She tries to mouth words, but only air comes out. Watching her shake, Brendan realizes she is terrified. Instead of seeing the face of a lying alien, he sees a woman out of her depth. Her expression acts like liquid nitrogen on a fire. Instinctively, he looks Mon in the eyes. He senses a fleeting feeling of defeat before she looks away.

Zand stands up. "Everyone is dismissed," she declares without emotion. "Mon, you will say."

Brendan freezes; it is all he can do to stop his muscles from giving way. Additionally, he is shocked as his range of vision seemingly expands and colors become more vivid. Looking at the remaining role-players, he sees Gul in shock, tears on Ishan's face, and notices Berina is absent.

"Auxiliary Officer," Zand says, "you should go to your room now."

Brendan heads out without acknowledgment. His own behavior mortifies him. At first, he felt empowered. But now, he realizes he hurt people for his own sense of vengeance. Without warning, his chest tightens, his vision contracts, and the world begins to go gray. Once his brain figures out what is happening, he firmly places his hand over his heart and squeezes. Walking out of the room, he goes on high alert when his breathing stops. *Heart attack! Just like Dad!*

"You are a horrible person, Brendan!" Esfirs comes up from behind and slaps him. "It is no wonder to me your wife left you if this is how you behaved."

Esfirs' slap is so hard it restarts Brendan's breathing, restores his vision, and eases his chest pain.

Esfirs screams. "What is wrong with you?!" Quickly, she forces a Bond. To Brendan, it feels as if brick walls are repeatedly collapsing on him. *If last night was love, this is brutal sexual assault.*

"Me? What is wrong with me? I opened myself up to you. I told you all my weaknesses. I confessed my love to you. And what do you do? You run and tell Berina! Turns out I am just some fun for you. A deployment hook-up. Who else knows? When will you all blackmail me? Might as well just throw me out of the airlock now because I will not allow myself to be used anymore."

His muscles tighten, readying for a blow from her hand or mouth. Instead, a loud popping sound goes off in his head; the Bond between them has been severed. Esfirs just looks at him.

"No response?" he challenges. "Are you just going to stare at me? Pretend to be stoic, uncaring, heartless?"

They maintain eye contact, yet no Bond forms.

Brendan's jaw begins to tremble. Not receiving blowback from Esfirs makes him unsteady on his feet. "Guess you made a fool out of me. Is that what you wanted?" He chokes up a little. "How many soldiers did I know who got with local girls? All those women thought they were loved. But instead, they were just playthings for lust to be released on." Brendan's heart beats rapidly. "Is that what I am to you?"

Esfirs scoffs. "Is that how you believe I think of you?"

"Yes, yes it is." A single tear runs down his cheek. *Please don't be another Heather.*

They both take a moment to breathe. Brendan looks deep into her eyes. While no Bond has formed, the liveliness of them beckons to him.

"Brendan, I told Berina what happened because I wanted to. Have you never wanted to share something exciting with another?"

"I told you everything, and you told it to Berina! I bared everything to you, all my joys, sorrows, and burdens, only you! Now she knows, and it does not take a genius to know she tells seniors about her interactions with me. What I shared was meant only for you. And now it is going into a report that will likely be used against me!"

"Berina would never betray you." Her words are measured and controlled.

"I am not saying Berina would use my words against me—someone else would." The pressure in his body is escaping like air from a leaky balloon. At this moment, Brendan realizes tears have been streaming from his eyes.

"Brendan, she would not tell anyone the details I told her, which was very little."

"Did she promise you?" Brendan replies, choking up.

"I never asked. Brendan, we, Sabia, do not view you as a Terran liaison or hybrid. You are one of us. Not just a friend of ours but one of us. Do you not understand that?"

He senses an all-encompassing embrace.

"Get out of my head!"

Esfirs takes a step toward him. "You have been hurt so deeply. Heather, your old comrades—they were Terrans. However, we are not them. We know you were brought to us for a reason. Do you not see this? You must confront your pain, Brendanshe. Otherwise, you will do horrible things to yourself and others, like how you treated Mon."

"I said get out of my head!"

They look at each other intently. It reminds Brendan of two medieval warriors in a standoff, having to take a breather.

She breaks the silence. "What were you expecting to accomplish in there? You behaved like a beast, not the Sabia you are—not even like a Terran governor." Through the Bond, he can feel both intense heat and a comforting coolness.

As Brendan ponders a response, he can see Berina running on the edge of his peripheral vision.

"Thank goodness I found you. We have to go now! Zand is calling for your return. Just be quiet and let me do all the talking. Now is not the time to play the hero." Berina takes his hand with determined force.

"Wait!" Esfirs interjects. "I will come, too."

PATRICK ABBOTT

"Absolutely not"—Berina shoots her down—"the last thing you want is to be associated with this. I can weather this out, but you have nothing to fall back on. Stay here!"

Berina tugs on Brendan and leads him to the doorway. He turns around to catch one last look at Esfirs. She bites her lips intensely, and Brendan sees a fire in her eyes. His heart tears apart seeing this, knowing her feelings for him. Mentally he is done. His will to resist what is about to happen is non-existent. Berina chides him, but he doesn't bother trying to understand what she says. Brendan sighs and resigns himself to what he imagines is his end. *My hubris brought this on me. I deserve it.* He laughs bitterly at the thought.

"Hey!" Berina waves her hand in front of his face. "Pay attention! Let me do all the talking, please! You did not know Mon's rank nor her importance. Be quiet. If not for yourself, then for me!"

Thundering footsteps announce the arrival of Kimya. The guard is wearing what looks like quickly donned armor. The various parts rattle together as she brings herself to a halt.

Berina pounds on Kimya's chest. "Nope, too slow, guard. Go back to your quarters." She snickers as a stunned Kimya stands there motionless.

Then, Berina touches the panel, causing the door to open. Walking in, Brendan sees the table and chairs have been removed. In the center, Zand is sitting on a pillow with Mon standing on her left. Mon's bloodshot eyes provide ample evidence of crying.

"Zand, I have brought—" Berina begins before Zand cuts her off.

"You were not summoned here. Nor did I ask you to bring the auxiliary officer." Even to Brendan, Zand's voice bears the sound of weight and authority.

Berina's response comes out in a single breath as if she wants to get everything out before she can be interrupted. "Auxiliary Officer Brendan's behavior was unacceptable, but it is important to remember the context of what he was doing. As a senior officer, I have the right to ensure any punishment is just and not overly harsh, and as such, I wish to advocate for restraint."

"You are dismissed," Zand replies simply.

Berina slowly backs out. Brendan hears the door open, then close. He is on his own now. He rolls his shoulders and tightens his stomach.

Mon speaks. "I—I was prepared for this event. At least I thought I was." She gulps. "Ever since I was a child, I have watched my grandmother and mother lead delegations. They have such great ways of conversation and persuasion." She begins to smile. "I often think about what they would do if they were with me." She looks down at her feet. "However, what I thought they would do was not satisfactory for you."

Brendan puts his hand over his heart and tries to mimic the diplomatic wording Mon used during the role play. "Dear Mon, I was preparing to give you a difficult scenario. To do so, I tapped into some personal anger I was harboring. But I got way too carried away. What happened was not a personal attack against you or your capabilities. For what I did wrong, I am sorry. I accept whatever you decide to do."

"Everything, everything I hoped to do was crushed today. A mere set of questions destroyed so much preparation."

"Yep." He nods a few more times than necessary. "Yep," is all he can manage to say. Brendan feels as though he is watching the scene unfold from outside his own body.

Zand raises her left hand. This catches both Mon and Brendan off guard. Mon bends down, and the two begin to whisper. After something is communicated, Mon sits down cross-legged directly on the carpet.

Zand speaks. "Your exercise has been most educational, Auxiliary Officer. It tested a theory that Mon proposed concerning our outreach. Fortunately, it has proven the failure of such ideas."

"I am . . . sorry. What are you trying to say, Zand?"

"Tell me, Auxiliary Officer, what peace can be made with such hate? Is not preparation for other outcomes better than trying to broker an impossible truce?"

Uh oh. "Whoa, let us not get too carried away. This was one dry run to test for flaws in order to adjust approaches. What matters is not the failure of Mon's preparations but what we do about it. Come up with a truthful line about what the mission of the Sabia is. The truth would shut up the worst of any assault. More importantly, it would get neutral governors on your side. They would probably silence the hostile governors if those people attempted to press the issue. Problem solved. See, the game worked."

"Are your words not a means to protect Terrans? You even used the second person to refer to us Sabia."

Brendan's will to fight back awakens. "Okay, game time is over. I gave you my honest assessment. If you think I am working against you, stop wasting everyone's time and have me arrested, shot, thrown into space, or whatever you do as a punishment for betrayal. I can assure you; I hate betrayal." He pauses to shake off memories of the snafu with Esfirs. "I am done. Yeah, I am done. My whole time here has led to an identity crisis. I have become some sort of genetic hybrid whom the United States does not trust, and the Sabia say I am one of you all, but then you doubt my intentions. I have been trying to get a footing my whole time here, but everything keeps changing. Maybe this is the end of me, but fair is fair." Brendan waves his hand as if tossing the will to argue away. "I offered my help and gave it. I still can if you want it. You do not have to take it, but stop giving me crap when something you do not like happens." He remembers giving Esfirs crap. As the mental video plays and replays, his stomach begins to churn. Wrapping his arms around his gut, he continues. "If this is unacceptable, either kill me or let me go back to Earth. They will do whatever they will do. But at least it will be over for me."

After a pause that feels like an eternity, Zand stands. "I am amused with how your behavior reveals your true self. You strive to negotiate and take on great burdens to accomplish goals assigned to you in the manner you want. However, when the resistance becomes too great, you are a fierce warrior. I wonder how many those who resisted your peace efforts you killed."

"Offensive, boring, and wrong. That is what your effort to mind-game me is. Stop playing around and tell me if you are going to kill me or let me go back to Earth."

"It's the latter, with a modification. I prefer to send you back to Terra as an advisor for Mon. Indeed, you are correct; we need to adjust our strategy for handling hostile actors. Your assistance is required on this before the actual meeting. Additionally, we need to know how to prepare for any militia-caused disruptions."

This certainly is unexpected. He feels as though everything was turned upside down. Brendan grapples with how to process what's being said. "I would love to help Mon." He turns to address the younger Sabia. "I look forward to working with you. I promise you that our cooperation can solve many difficulties. It will take some work, but it will be worth it." He then looks at Zand. "As for the militias, you should work with the governors to arrange security. I can use my own contacts to reduce the threat."

"Very well, Brendan," Zand says. "Leave us now; we have work to do."

Brendan stands at attention, salutes, and walks out of the room. *How the heck did that happen?*

Interlude – Mon: Seeing into the Flames

Mon is catching her breath. After Brendan left, she started having a panic attack. Zand sat next to her, gently rubbing her back until her breathing returned to normal.

It has been ages since someone has shown her such platonic love and care. *Mother used to be that way with me. She would stay with me when these episodes would occur.* But those were only memories now. *Mother left me.* That horrible night had been a death sentence for Mon. The doctors, the tears, the family members who consoled Merjine and not her! *Enough self-pity, Mon. Your Watchers cared enough to bring you here on this mission. Serve the divine now!* She closes her eyes and retreats from the present moment, allowing Zand's rubs to turn her focus away from the outside toward her inner self. Then, opening her eyes, Mon is renewed and ready to face whatever comes next.

Zand gets up and walks to the far side of the room as Mon silently watches. The elder Sabia opens a panel and removes a small urn along with black and white stones. She walks back and sets the pot down about a yard away from Mon. Sitting down next to the young Sabia, Zand knocks the two rocks together above the urn. Sparks fall from the stones and ignite a substance in the vessel. Both women look into the flame. Peacefulness reigns in the room as they search for meaning in the fire.

Zand is the first to break the stillness. "Brendan is a broken man. Everything he does is because of his pain. His interfering with the terrorist attack, what Brendan did to his friends and you today, is all because he is hurting. He is in so much pain he cannot save himself. It is only a matter of time before this will kill him."

"Why would the divine make him like this?" Mon asks.

"No, Dear Mon. Our great divine made him a Terran. They are complete and whole by the standards the divine saw fit for them. However, war and his wife broke his body and mind. That is ancient history, as the Terrans will say. For some reason, neither the Terrans nor Brendan himself would recognize this problem. All glory to the divine; he then was given to us to mend. But we can only heal his body—only he can choose to cooperate with the divine and the Watchers to heal his soul."

Mon looks into the flame. Nothing this clear has come to her. She searches for more. Finally, she asks, "But why would the divine change him to be like us? Why would the divine give us something broken? If something will not mend, are we not taught to throw it away?"

Zand puts her left hand above the fire.

"What would your mother say?" the elder asks.

327

Mon closes her eyes. She pictures herself being seven again, sitting with her mother beside the great river. Oh, how often they would discuss matters that Mon would eventually grow up to deal with. The vision is full of colors, sounds, and smells. Allowing it to take its own path, Mon sees Merjine and herself sitting together, discussing the poor broken Terran.

Hearing her mother's voice, Mon replies, "She would say we must pray for him."

PATRICK ABBOTT

Twenty-Nine – Homo Novus

How the heck did that happen? Brendan thinks back to how he stood up for himself. *I could have folded, but I didn't. I have been a whiny little wimp, but no more! When things get hard, I'm going to be open and stand my ground. Zand thinks I am a killer? Well, I am no murderer, but I will fight to defend myself!*

Turning the corner, Brendan encounters Kimya. She looks both ways before cautiously approaching him. "I heard what happened during your demonstration," she whispers. "How could you say such things? There is making a point, and then there is abuse!"

Brendan shrugs. "Did I cross the line? Sure, I owned up to it and apologized. Did Zand cross the line just now? She sure as heck did. Did I push back? Yes, and I am proud of it."

"What?" Her shocked response tells Brendan she was talking about his actions toward Mon, not what occurred later.

"Never mind, Kimya. It was me just playing the role of a governor."

She leans in and, with a concerned voice, asks, "Could the governors be that hostile?"

"About half will act extremely friendly so that they can get more Sabia technology and aid. The other half will want answers about why the Sabia are staying near Earth long-term. I can think of one or two governors out of the fifty total who would outright oppose you."

Kimya nods as he talks, taking it all in.

"Brendan, this is very disturbing. I thought the political aspects were taken care of, leaving only those on the periphery of society opposing us. What would you recommend we do?"

What a pleasant question; her interest is entirely transparent. "Tell the truth. One's own secrecy drives others' paranoia." Brendan takes a step and stops. *I wonder how honest she will be with me.* "Wait a minute, how did you find out what happened?"

"Ishan. I caught him running and was going to reprimand him for abandoning his assignment. Instead, he told me about the meeting. Knowing him, I suspect he told his girlfriend, so now the whole ship will know. Speaking of which"—she leans in even closer to Brendan — "are you going to be okay? What did Zand say that you consider crossing the line?"

"Well, I am either going to be punished or going back to Earth."

The guard cups her hands over her mouth in shock. "No! You are leaving us? Brendan, it is not safe for you on Terra! I will talk to my leadership. They can address the council—"

Huh, she suspects Zand would kick me out before harming me. Brendan raises his hand to stop her.

"No need. Apparently, I am going to accompany Mon on the trip. No idea when it is, but hey, another chance to visit Earth."

Kimya gives him a double-take. Brendan feels a Bond form as they lock eyes. He passively lets it happen with hopes he can study the experience. *No more weakness. Everything is an opportunity to learn.* He feels Kimya search inside him, moving as if from room to room.

He asks, "What are you looking for?"

"Why are you in so much pain?"

He looks away and closes his eyes to sever the Bond. *That hit too close to home.*

"I do not want to talk about it right now." He starts toward his cabin again but stops himself. "But I want to thank you for saying you would talk to your superiors for me. I really appreciate that." *A person who cares . . . like Esfirs. I really need to apologize to her.*

He gently taps Kimya's arm to demonstrate his friendship. Despite this effort, she frowns at him. Once he lowers his arm, she mimics his gesture. Brendan senses both he and she are unsatisfied with their interaction. Not wanting to leave on such a sorrowful note, he forces a smile, thanks her again for everything, and then bids her a good day.

Passing the hangar, he eyes a young—almost too young—guard standing next to the door. The guard makes nervous eye contact with Brendan and then whistles. In a flash, Berina appears from out of view.

331

"Kerdar, watch the door!" Berina yells at the guard as she approaches Brendan.

Then, quickly, she grabs Brendan by the wrist, opens the door to the hangar, and drags him inside. As he enters, he hears Esfirs' voice address the guard from somewhere behind him. The doors then immediately swoosh closed. Turning around, he sees two faces, unnaturally pale for Sabia, with eager-looking eyes.

Berina releases her grip on Brendan. Before she has the chance to speak, Esfirs walks up and places her palms on his cheeks. *Nope, this is the dominance thing again.* He gently pushes them away. Esfirs quietly asks, "What happened?"

"Hey, umm. Yeah. Not sure what to do," Brendan says, scratching his head. "I can say that I am fine. Zand has asked me to help retool Mon's approach."

Esfirs releases a massive sigh, but Berina remains tense.

"Thank everything holy," Esfirs proclaims.

"Amen to that," replies Brendan. "Which leads me to my second point. My behavior at the role-play was—ah hell. I was so hurt when you, Berina, told me what Esfirs said to you. Look, I am not well. I probably am really screwed up. No, I am screwed up in the head. I realized that at New Year's during . . . whatever we did. I should have come to you, Esfirs, to talk about it beforehand. But instead, I embraced my anger and let it get the best of me. Fudge, I did not give you the benefit of the doubt; instead, I assumed you were just like Heather. I am sorry." He chokes up. "I am so sorry."

Brendan and Esfirs look at each other, a broken man staring at a scrutinizing woman.

Berina coughs, which gets both their attention. "Let me apologize for my part. I misspoke when I used the term 'fun.' I deserve the blame for that one; please, do not take it out on Esfirs. I was trying to say that I am glad that Esfirs has someone she can be with. There was no intent to diminish you to a—a— 'fling' is the word I think you would use."

"Okay, okay." Brendan breathes. "Who else have you told about Esfirs and me?"

Berina gives off an exclamation of shock. "What are you insinuating, Brendan?"

"That whenever I talk to you about problems, things change. You report on what I say and do to others."

"Because I care about you, you ass!" Berina says while stomping her foot.

Brendan has never seen this level of anger from her before. Her face flushes a deep red while her hands clench into fists.

"I have not told a single person about you and Esfirs, and I am not going to! Esfirs came to me happy, so I pressed her for information. She tried not telling me but was so excited that I got her to talk. She has never told any man she loves him! No man has ever said he loves her! And look what you managed to do with it in less than a day!"

Suddenly, the door opens, surprising everyone in the room. Kimya comes running inside.

"What is going on in here?" she demands.

Both Esfirs and Berina yell at her to get out. Kimya yells back. The room fills with noise as the three women viciously scream at each other. Finally, Berina escalates it. She points her extended hand toward the door, saying, "You are relieved!"

"Stupid black hat bug!" Kimya yells back.

Berina ferociously slaps her chest and storms up to Kimya. "What did you say? I did not hear you over your disrespect of a superior officer! Get out; your husband is not here!"

Kimya gasps. Even Esfirs apprehensively eyes Brendan before taking two steps back. Whether it was a quick mental message or not, Brendan does so as well. Meanwhile, Kimya's facial muscles twitch. Brendan notices she is avoiding eye contact with Berina. The guard mutters something and then backs out of the room. Her exit leaves them in stunned silence.

Berina turns toward Esfirs. "Did she call me a 'bug'?" She then breaks out laughing.

Esfirs' expression drops in surprise, and then she also laughs. "I came up with better insults in school."

"Hey, uh, on the subject"—Brendan pauses to gather strength—"ignoring whatever the heck just happened . . ." His throat tickles, so he coughs. "Okay, here I go. It was wrong to assume you had harmful intentions, and I apologize. All I want is forgiveness from you, but I know I do not deserve it. Please know, though, I am sorry. All the mistakes I made were because of me not loving you as I should have."

Esfirs assumes a ramrod-straight posture. No emotion can be seen on her face. "And what do you think of me now, Auxiliary Officer?"

His heart sinks in his chest while simultaneously beating faster and faster. *And this is where it ends.* "You are such a wonderful woman. And that is why my ruining our relationship will always haunt me. I hate myself for making me unworthy of your love. So I will not bother you anymore. Goodbye, Esfirs. I love you."

He nods at both women. No goodbyes, neither the Afghan gesture nor handshakes, are exchanged. Instead, making his way to the door, he prepares for a much lonelier time with the Sabia. *Maybe, just maybe, being cut off from others will keep any painful drama to a minimum.*

"Brendanshe," Esfirs calls, "I love you."

Esfirs' words ring out just as Brendan reaches for the door panel. Stopping in his tracks, Brendan cannot bring himself to turn around. Instead, the welled-up emotions start to boil over as he begins to cry. *No, not here.* Taking a deep breath through the nose, he wipes his tears away and turns back to face Esfirs.

As Brendan turns around, Esfirs continues. "Remember when you said we would have to work to make ourselves more comfortable with our differences? That means doing more than me not punching you."

Berina interjects, "Wait, what?"

Ignoring her, Esfirs continues. "As for your actual behavior, promise me you will be more respectful to council members, even when playing your games. Their roles mean something to us Sabia. Mon is . . . well, Mon is essential to us as a species. She outranks Zand in the Legion. She is not just a military officer; her family has important meaning for us. To be cruel to her, well . . . it would be like me insulting . . . things which have meaning to you."

"Yes, Esfirs, I promise you."

"Thank you, Brendanshe."

Berina looks at them both. "Can someone please tell me about this hitting incident?"

Brendan sits down on a workout bench. He looks over at the two women, friends whom he has tested time and time again. Their beautiful friendship draws him closer, though his feeling of unworthiness tries to repel him away from them. It hurts to look at them; instead, he chooses to look at the floor.

"Esfirs"—he calls out to her, originally intending to address them both—"I do not deserve you. But really, I should get back to Earth and face the music there. Can you help me do that?"

His love sits down next to him. "No more of that. You took my hand last night, remember? That allows me to show you what you are and can become. So stay, and talk no more of leaving us.

"Now, Brendanshe, let us get you back home." Esfirs gently stands him up.

Leaving the hangar, the group makes their short way down the hallway. Brendan's mind tries to take everything in. *I am loved, thank God, I am loved. Please, Lord, don't let me mess this up.*

Wanting to move on from his internal struggle, he asks, "May I ask exactly what Mon's role is? Or is the answer classified."

"She is . . . us." Esfirs looks up as if seeing something beautiful on the ceiling. "From her line came the first Sabia, the first Legion, the first"—she looks at Berina, who remains silent—"the first one who gave us the holy fire. Without her family, we would not exist. Without her family to guide us, we would have fallen to chaos."

Berina chips in. "Think Momma President Pope."

Brendan laughs. "I never meant to insult what Mon represented during the game," he says.

The group arrives at Brendan's door. The older male guard near does not acknowledge their presence. Esfirs turns to Berina, then makes a quick motion with her head. A slight smile appears on Berina's face.

"Have fun, you two," she says. "Esfirs, make sure he is aware we have a workout appointment tomorrow."

Then, without another word, Berina turns and presses the button to open the door.

Esfirs and Brendan enter his darkened cabin. Allowing the door to close behind them, they embrace. Brendan thinks about saying something but feels the urge not to. Ending the hug, she reaches out and touches his cheek. They stare at each other. He feels another Bond sensation, this one of water flowing into him through his eyes and down his spine.

He feels a growing desire to be emotionally naked with her. *Is she guiding me to do this?* A strange acknowledgment vibrates within him. To start, he envisions the suicide bomber in Afghanistan, Heather's betrayal, and his father's death. He paints his life, dead to everything but his job. His heart speeds up, pounding harder and harder as the mental video plays. Then, abruptly, the film stops, and a new one starts. He is in the first-person perspective of someone crying on the floor. The carpet looks Sabia in design. This body is smaller than his own. *Esfirs?* No words are said, nor is anything read. Nevertheless, he knows the person has received the worst news. Brendan feels a strong longing for a loved one's embrace. *But she will not come. I, Esfirs, the child Esfirs, am all alone. I-her-we are alone.* Now he views himself yelling at Mon earlier today. Mon looks saintly in this vision. It feels as if he is being torn apart as the yelling continues. The verbal assault against Mon is much more dramatic than he remembers. In Esfirs' body, he feels himself get up. The screams he hears himself utter are not hostile but pleas for Brendan to stop. He does not. *Brendan is rejecting the Sabia, me—Esfirs.* The lonely feeling begins again. The images then cease. He is back in the room.

PATRICK ABBOTT

For the next hour, Brendan and Esfirs sit together near the television in silence, communicating their emotions through the Bond. Fear of being hurt again meets the fear of being alone. At first, they share their experiences of emotional trauma. After a while, slowly but surely, they counter the negative emotions with moments of support. Knowing he can look at her without shame, Brendan is repeatedly brought to tears by the thought that someone truly loves him and doesn't wish to harm him. Meanwhile, when he is feeling strong, he messages Esfirs that she is not alone. Brendan is studious, wiping away any tears on Esfirs' face.

"Will you stay forever?" she finally vocalizes.

Brendan's mind becomes a chaotic mess hearing those words. Managing mental and verbal communication is like paying attention to a thousand different television screens.

"I am sorry," she says, looking away, "I did not mean—it is too soon." She starts to stand up.

Brendan can feel her fear of being alone grow.

"Esfirs, let us go to the garden," he says calmly.

She nods and smiles.

"Yes . . . Brendanshe."

Thirty – Game Redux

Brendan shifts in his seat as he waits for Mon, sitting across the table, to respond. His suit is tight as he moves. He envies her loose-fitting azure robe.

"Hello, sir; it is an honor to meet you." She puts her right hand over her heart and bows, copying Brendan's Afghanistan-acquired habit. "Please allow the introduction—I am Mon, and I am here to represent the Sabia."

Not perfect, somewhat stiff, but her confidence is much higher.

"Hello, Mon. I am Governor Brendan Murphy of the great state of Kansas. Before we begin, tell me, what is your relationship to the Sabia?"

Mon grins with the joy of someone who has practiced for such a pitch. "Dear Governor Murphy, my mother is a major official in our structure of government. I hope to one day follow in her footsteps and honor her with years of service to my people. All Sabia hold her in high esteem. It is my hope you people of Earth"—she emphasizes the planet's name—"may one day trust me as Sabia trust my mother."

PATRICK ABBOTT

Her face beams with a radiant glow. *Thoughts about her mother, probably.*

"Interesting, she must have quite the position. Same for you, no doubt. What is your title, by the way?"

"Oh, Dear Governor Murphy, I have several titles because of the various positions I hold. Titles imply command and authorities; I wish to avoid such things among friends."

Mon steals a look at Zand. It reminds Brendan of a child accomplishing a task and then looking to its mother for approval. *Let's see how you handle a little bit of pressure, Mon.*

"Interesting, and thank you for avoiding the rigidness of officiality. Will you, as a friend"—he loads the term with mild sarcasm—"tell me what the Sabia are doing here, not only in my state but in my country? For example, the federal government has given the Sabia a substantial amount of granite from Colorado, while private contractors have taken much of my state's native limestone. I cannot help but feel you can get these resources elsewhere in the universe. Why here? Why from us?"

Brendan can hear Esfirs prop herself up in her chair as he speaks. Though he does not look over to see his fellow role players, he imagines Berina leaning over the table and Esfirs tensing up. *Do not worry, my friends.*

"I am most happy to answer your question, Dear Governor Murphy. The rocks we acquire from you and your fellow governors have various minerals, which we extract. It is true these resources are available elsewhere,

341

yes. However, they come in different . . . shall we say, combinations, other than the convenient form they exist here on your Earth. Additionally, you are here. Therefore, we—how do you say—kill two birds with one stone by acquiring them here while engaging in cultural exchange with you."

Brendan makes a "timeout" gesture with his hands and says, "You really do not want to say 'kill two birds with one stone.' I understood what you meant, but others could take that as a threat."

Mon seems surprised and quickly apologizes. Brendan nods.

Back in character, he continues. "Uh-huh. I must admit many of my constituents doubt what you have told me. General Meade and other fine patriots are warning my people, claiming you have a hidden agenda. Farmers have told me cattle are being mutilated in areas where your UFOs fly overhead. Some even point to evidence showing an increase in children being kidnapped in areas where Sabia visit. Is this true?"

Even from a distance, Esfirs' breathing is audible to him. Or at least he thinks it is. He looks to his left and finds her intently staring at him. Berina, meanwhile, is indeed leaning over the table.

"We would never harm any children, Dear Governor Murphy. Please take my word in this matter." Her tone is adamant. "Your Javier and others are great patriots, but they are mistaken. By the way"—she shifts stances—"are you aware the United States has given us UIC Intelligence Officer Brendan as a liaison? He has told us much about the militia movement—the good and where they have erred. Would you care to meet him? I am sure he could address any concerns you may have as a fellow Earthan."

An interesting new word, but not too shabby.

"End scene!" Brendan holds his hands like a clapperboard and claps them together, hard. "How do you feel?"

Mon blows air out of her mouth. "Very well now, thank you. I have practiced for hours. My concerns over possible attacks motivate me to represent the Sabia to the best of my ability. Thankfully, preparation makes perfection."

Okay . . .

She continues. "With you at my side, I am certain we will do well. Did you like how I brought you up?" She smiles. "The governors will see our intentions and limit their support to those who oppose us."

"I know the concern about Meade and the militias is driving this meeting; that much is clear. However, why the Interior West?"

Zand interrupts. "Thank you for your help in this matter, Brendan."

He understands when the Sabia's polite responses stand-in for the dreaded "classified." The best course of action is to put his hand over his heart and do a slight bow. Then, he moves on without pushing either Sabia for an answer.

Zand continues, "We have obtained progress in arranging the conference. Governor Julie of Montana has offered her state to host us. What do you think of Montana as a location?"

Brendan's mind flashes with an idea. "Montana? That will work. The militia movement respects the governor and the legislature and would be hesitant to do anything there. In fact, I would like to arrive before the official delegation. I know someone in the state who could assist in assuring a peaceful conference."

As Mon starts asking who Brendan knows that could be so influential, Zand cuts her off, accepting Brendan's proposal. Mon knits her eyebrows, looking peeved. *Interesting dynamics between those two.*

"Thank you, everyone, for assisting with this second round," Zand says. "Brendan, we will likely require your assistance on some additional points later. We will let you know when you are needed. Everyone is dismissed."

Brendan gets up and stretches. Loosening his tie with the ease of an experienced government bureaucrat, he watches in amusement as Esfirs struggles to remove hers. She looks like she is wearing a military Class B outfit with her khaki shirt and pants. He walks over to her and undoes the knot with quick hand movements.

"Any particular reason you are dressed as if you were a co-worker of mine back in the UIC?" he asks jovially.

Esfirs grunts in response. "I have no idea why Terrans think this costume improves work. I wanted to wear something which they would recognize as commanding respect. I do not like this costume, though."

"Well, if I were in your shoes, I would wear either your doctor's outfit or something graceful. Anyone who sees a doctor will automatically respect them. Something more . . . elegant, meanwhile, will have people viewing you as similar enough to Terran to respect you as a person."

She rolls her eyes. Flight-suit-wearing Berina comes up and embraces them in a playful group hug.

"That certainly went better than the last one! I could not help but admire the growing tenseness in Esfirs when you first started speaking. Thank you for behaving this time." Berina laughs.

"Glad to know I provide entertainment for you," Brendan quips back. "What is the deal with the flight suit? Too busy gallivanting around to join the pre-brief and get changed?"

"I had much better things to do this morning. My day was so eventful there was no time for lunch. So you know what I want to do first."

Brendan circles his finger in the air like an umpire signaling a home run. They exit the conference room, and Brendan inquires if Berina was able to acquire "the item." She eagerly nods, pulling out a paperback book titled *Orthodoxy and Orthopraxy Equals Love: The Homilies of Pope Leo XIV*. Berina says she's eager to know Brendan's thoughts on it. He promises to give her a running commentary every day during their morning workout. Esfirs starts walking a few steps ahead of the two as they talk about the book.

Arriving at the cafeteria, they take seats on pillows. A new female Sabia runs up to provide fresh salad bowls before running back to fetch water. Brendan makes a mental note to learn more about the newer and much younger-looking recently arrived Sabia. *There has to be some reason they are getting younger. Youth also screw up more when talking, so getting information shouldn't be too hard.* After the water arrives, Berina stops Esfirs from drinking until Brendan finishes his prayers. This time, she didn't have to remind him to pray.

"Okay," Brendan says before his first bite, "where did you fly today?"

Berina places her hands on her hips. Then, with grossly exaggerated motions and a playful and mocking tone, she replies, "Oh, did I mention I was out today? I flew to the wonderful and ancient land home to the glorious and modern People's Republic of China. Chairman Du himself paid homage to Delegate Foround and me. Afterward, we toured the spaceport they were building. I had a long chat with several of their officers. Of course, they found me fascinating."

"You speak Chinese, eh? What did you all talk about?" Brendan asks.

"Oh no, you are not getting that out of me, you spy!" She laughs.

Brendan's heart skips. *What? Does she know about me writing messages back to the UIC? Does she know about the other device?*

"Wha—what do you mean by that?" he asks with a slight stutter.

"If I tell you, you will run away the first chance you get when we are back on Terra. You will then inform all your friends you have a Sabia willing to give you intel on the Chinese. I can hear them now"—she adopts another mocking tone—"'we love Berina so much because she tells Brendan everything!'"

She's just playing with me.

Relieved, he pushes back. "Nice to know in your fantasy world everyone loves you."

"Naturally." Again, she laughs. "And because everyone loves me, guess who just scored one of the pilot spots for your fun time in Montana?"

"Really?" Esfirs lights up. "Perhaps we can spend some time together exploring the area."

"Some time? How about almost all the time together! When you are off doing your clinic, I can be there as well. Little kids love two things: aliens and pilots. I have both bases covered. Yeah, I am your perfect mascot for that."

Brendan chuckles. "We really have to do something about that ego."

"Enough making fun of me; let us look at you, Mr. I-Have-Ideas," Berina retorts. "Who is the secret weapon to keep the militias at bay? The one Mon wanted to know about?"

"To borrow a phrase from Mon, Father Baldwin is my means to 'kill two birds with one stone.' He was known as Intelligence Officer Dan Saleh back in my younger days. Dan worked with Malcolm, me, and a few others under General Meade's staff. Dan was one of the best we had, working with Palestinians while Malcolm and I were still in school. He designed much of our tradecraft and doctrine. Real friendly guy, ready to mentor those he worked with. Toward the end of his career, he wrote a paper that many think encouraged Meade to leave the government and become the man he is now."

Brendan slows down, becoming more thoughtful. "When Malcolm and I were clearing eastern Syria of jihadists, Dan was horribly wounded in a car bombing." The memories weigh on Brendan. "He was mutilated pretty bad. I remember when Dan reached out to Malcolm and me after our falling out. He warned us that our paths would get both of us killed." He pauses; the weight of everything slows his mind down.

Brendan hums to himself to push past the hurt, then starts again. "I did not listen at the time. I was too angry at Malcolm and myself as my world collapsed around me. I should have paid attention to Dan. He was already evolving in his perceptions. Despite the horrible wounds, he was accepted into a Franciscan community as a lay brother. They realized he was meant for even greater things, and within a year, they sent him to seminary. Kinda something, right? I left seminary for the UIC, and here is Dan leaving the UIC for seminary. Now he is a priest in Montana. I can arrange things with him remotely. However, if the conference is there, I should go see him." Brendan then states his deeper intention. "He can offer me confession and Mass if the timing works out."

"Actual religious rites? May I attend both?" Berina practically jumps off her pillow in excitement. Meanwhile, Esfirs focuses her attention on her salad.

"With the Mass, you are all welcome to attend and even participate. However, I would strongly advise against taking communion because you basically have made yourself a lifelong member of the Catholic Church if you take it. That is a pretty big commitment. I imagine that is not something you are attempting to do."

"Your magician priests would be offended when I go back to my own faith after I eat the cracker, right?" Berina's joke causes Esfirs to laugh.

That stings. "I did not appreciate the joke."

Berina stuffs salad in her mouth while waving her arms as if to downplay the joke. Brendan keeps staring at her, waiting for a response. Finally, after she swallows the salad, she says, "Mea culpa."

Berina's crassness stings Brendan. *Guess she sees treating me with respect different than respecting my beliefs.* A light dawns in Brendan's mind. *My beliefs.* He had toyed with going back to church and confession before. However, it never really was a part of him since seminary. *It's different now.* Nodding to himself, Brendan decides to forgive Berina. *God, forgive her.* The simple prayer comes naturally to him.

They idly chit-chat about the previous and upcoming events during the rest of the meal. Brendan recounts his impressions of Mon from the one-on-ones he had with her. He believes Mon is a quick learner but has some concerns about a haughtiness that sometimes comes through. However, Esfirs quickly shuts down any such criticism. Instead, Esfirs talks about how she has been brought onto a team that will offer children free medical care. It'll be a goodwill mission near the governor's conference. Berina then ponders aloud her schedule for the next day but slows down and eventually stops as she repeatedly yawns. As the three of them finish, Brendan says he has a video about Montana. Berina hesitates, but Esfirs persuades her to watch it in Brendan's cabin.

When they arrive, they grab pillows and place them near the television. Berina lies down with her head on hers while Brendan and Esfirs place their cushions next to each other against the far wall. Brendan plays a show titled *Montana from the Air*. It features high-definition aerial shots of the entire state.

Berina lets out a massive yawn and shifts to her side, indicating to Esfirs and Brendan that she has fallen asleep. They share a muffled giggle. Brendan considers watching more of the show but becomes too transfixed looking at Esfirs to care about drone footage of a creek. The fact that she is looking back is even better. Her olive-colored skin, dark hair, and beautiful brown eyes remind him of the Arab and Afghan women who would watch him from afar. Looking at her causes emotions and needs to arise in him. He slowly starts inching his hand toward her. *Just one touch . . .*

Suddenly, Brendan imagines holding a shield against a gentle, sweet breeze. *Why am I preventing the air from flowing?* In his mind, he lowers the shield so the wind can freely move across his body. The Bond flows through his soul. He can feel Esfirs in every part of him. For a second, it overwhelms him until he senses her essence embrace him from within.

Esfirs brings her left hand up to her face. Without breaking the eye lock, she gently blows on her wrist. Brendan feels the sensation on his left wrist. Next, she gently rubs it with her right index finger. Brendan not only feels the motion but thinks he can see his nerves and muscles react.

"May I teach you something?" Esfirs asks.

"Please," he practically begs.

She begins. "Picture yourself, alone in the dark. There is nothing. Only a cold emptiness surrounds you. You cannot even see yourself."

Brendan's vision transforms, first becoming blurry, then black.

"In the darkness, you hear a voice coming from within you. Listening to it, you know it is ours—not my voice and your voice but our single voice. It sings our song. Listen to it. Feed it with your strength. Let it build inside you like a fire."

Being a celibate widower, Brendan had gone years without feeling this alive and masculine. Esfirs' voice has intoxicated him to the point where he is ready for whatever she asks of him.

"Feel the voice. As it moves, realize it is a fire inside you. Let the fire consume its way out of you and become a bright flame that lightens the dark. Release yourself, become the light . . ."

Brendan jolts awake. The room is dark, the lamps set to their dim nighttime level. Esfirs is gone. So is Berina. The television is off as well. Looking down, he sees a blanket covering him. *They must have tucked me in.* He stares into the darkness of the room. Whatever happened was beyond comprehension. The wonderful feelings fight with a strange sense of guilt.

He lies there in shock. *Maybe if I touch my wrist Esfirs will feel it—perhaps she will even come back.* He rubs his wrist softly for minutes. She does not return. Feeling dejected, he goes to bed. His UIC device underneath his pillow annoys him, so he reaches to hide it elsewhere. Before he can, however, he sees he has a message from Malcolm.

Thirty-One – Matthew 6:24

Brendan pulls two kiwis out of his pocket and offers them to Firos. The flight-suited pilot eagerly accepts them. Then, without pausing or doing anything to remove the skin, he bites one into two, chewing his food with a loudness that Brendan finds slightly disgusting. *Eh, at least he is a friendly enough guy.* Before taking another bite, Firos gives him a nod of appreciation.

Kimya's entrance into the hangar causes the guards to straighten their backs while the remainder of the crowd, comprised primarily of medical staff, move in to ensure they can hear the upcoming brief. Only Berina, Esfirs, and Gul hang back. Gul makes a comment which causes snickering among them.

Kimya begins by giving an overall rundown of the situation in Montana. She explains the group will land at the makeshift spaceport at a military base. There will be three chalks, with most Sabia going straight to the hotel. Guard Aban will lead this team. The guards will secure the hotel as soon as they arrive while the doctors offload their gear and rest. The second chalk of guards will stay with the shuttlecraft.

Meanwhile, Kimya will lead the minority group heading to Saint Lazarus Chapel. Kimya will take the lead upon arrival, followed by Brendan and everyone else. She will stay within five feet of Brendan at all times, except during his confession. During "the ritual," she will stand ten feet back. After the rites are concluded, Brendan and the priest will finalize negotiations to ensure the safety of the conference. However, if at any time Kimya believes the group to be at risk, she reserves the right to immediately recall the chalk and fall back to the hotel or spaceport. When she asks if anyone has any questions, everyone remains silent. When she asks for everyone's agreement, the guards give a loud, grunt-like response.

Berina grabs an Earth-made duffle bag while Esfirs picks up a case of medical gear. Gul boards Berina's shuttlecraft first, then Esfirs, and finally Brendan.

"Brendan, no, you fly with me," Kimya shouts from a distance as she approaches.

Brendan expects her to grab his wrist, but instead, Kimya motions to Firos's craft. A slight smile shines on her face as she locks eyes with him. Brendan feels a warm invitation trying to persuade him.

This warmth clashes with Berina's sudden response. "Absolutely not! He has always ridden with me! I have a full medical crew that is familiar with him. What if something were to happen? What are you going to do, Kimya?" Her voice is defiant.

PATRICK ABBOTT

"My operation, my rules," Kimya calmly counters. "If this is unacceptable to you, then I can relieve you. No burden then, right Berina?"

Berina turns around and heads back to her ship without saying another word. Brendan watches as Kimya stares daggers at Berina's back. Then, quickly pivoting to Brendan, her face again turns pleasant.

"Shall we go together?" Her tone is that of one asking a friend.

Brendan gives off an Army "hooah" and follows her onto Firos's craft. The doors close behind him, and he takes a cushion on the floor. Examining his surroundings, Brendan eyes unfamiliar guards. *Kimya's hand-picked own.* The mysterious animosity between Kimya and his two friends weighs on him and makes him curious to learn more. Pushing past the anxiety-driven fear of a socially awkward conversation that attempts to keep him in his place, he takes a knee next to the gently smiling Kimya.

"Hey, I got to ask, what is the deal between you and Berina?"

Her smile drops. "Not now," she says and turns away from Brendan.

"If not now, then when?" he presses. "Fighting between friends is something I do not like seeing. I will be the first to admit I cannot solve everything, but having people get hostile concerning me is no bueno."

Kimya looks at him, confused. *Looks like these two weren't taught Spanish.*

"It means 'not good.' But, hey, can you just tell me why there is animosity between you and Berina?"

She makes eye contact. Through the Bond, he feels sympathy emanating from her, what he thinks is a desire to share. However, he also senses a new feeling, a particular type of pain—remorse. He does his best to convey a sense of compassion, hoping she will open up to him.

With sadness in her voice, she says, "It is classified," then turns away again.

He gets up and goes back to his cushion. *Dejection.* Blowing air out of his mouth, he waits for the shuttlecraft to land. The surrealness of the craft's imperceptible movement combined with the "conversation" with Kimya makes him uneasy. *Not a good feeling to have before a mission.* Then, as if on cue, his right hand begins to shake.

Firos announces their arrival at the "Terran Malstrom Air Force Base." Kimya comes over to help him get up. Not needing it doesn't stop Brendan from accepting the friendly offer. He hears a beeping sound, and the door to the outside opens. Fresh mountain air comes rushing in. *Got to love the pollution-free Sabia craft.* Brendan steps out to take in the view.

The other craft disembarks as well. Esfirs approaches Brendan wearing a gray outfit similar to a guard's uniform, armor included. He looks for Berina but can't find her. Suddenly, a tap on his shoulder causes him to spin around. He sees the pilot holding her flight suit, wearing a conservative black top with a long black skirt. On her head is a white mantilla. She grins at Brendan.

"Did my research for how to dress for your rituals," she says.

"No kidding," Brendan dryly remarks. "Here is a question for you, and I do not want 'it is classified' for an answer, okay?"

"Oh?" Berina smiles devilishly. "I promise I will not say 'it is classified.' Any other answer is appropriate, however."

"Back about sixty years ago, this military base had multiple nuclear-armed missiles, which were deactivated while an unidentified flying object was seen hovering above the base. Were the Sabia already on, or above, Earth doing things back then?"

She begins with a serious tone, "Brendan, for as long as your Terrans ancestors could think, I imagine they looked up at the night sky and thought, 'There are lights up there!'" She starts laughing. "We Sabia have words for such phenomena. Translated into English, they are 'stars,' 'meteors,' 'swamp gas,' 'your own dang aircraft!'" She slaps him hard on the back. "Truth is, we only discovered Terra right before we initiated first contact. It was a crazy couple of months in between."

That is a lie. Esfirs said she has been learning English for decades. "I cannot help but note you did not answer my question," he prods.

"I cannot help but note your powers of observation are correct," she retorts and winks.

Esfirs joins in, "I would think my grandparents would have had better things to do than fly around and deactivate your missiles," she says with a laugh.

That helps confirm a near-parity with life spans. Thanks, Esfirs!

"Touché," he replies.

"What does that word mean?" Esfirs asks.

"He is admitting you are right," Berina says as her gaze is drawn elsewhere.

Looks like Berina is at least trilingual.

Brendan is about to say something to Esfirs, but Berina putting her arm around his waist, stops him. He sees the pilot's eyes fixed on a commotion up past a row of guards.

"Stay close to my side," she says as she locks her arm around his.

Kimya's voice can be heard in the distance. She says something is "unacceptable" and is yelling at an Air Force officer. Aban comes around the group and stands behind Brendan.

"Auxiliary, do you want to have a private meeting with a Hyder?" Aban mutters underneath his breath.

"Who is Hyder?" Brendan shoots back.

"He apparently oversees the Air Force here. Claims he wants to debrief you. He demands you be alone. Furthermore, he says you are under arrest, but they will return you to our 'custody.'"

PATRICK ABBOTT

Brendan tries to think through his options. *How can I accept without making a scene—or ensure it is not a trap? But, man, that 'under arrest' line was an excellent way to ruin things right off the bat.*

Berina's voice snaps him out of the thought. "He does not wish to go with them, Aban."

"Right answer," replies Aban. The guard pats Brendan on the back before running up to Kimya.

Berina tightens her armlock. Listening to her heavy breathing, he can tell she is in fight-or-flight mode. *I would put down big money that she is already deciding how best to fight it out. Got to give her credit; she's always been there when things look bad for me.* Part of Brendan longs to accept the offer. Is it the desire to help his country through an intelligence debriefing or a forlorn hope that maybe he can get away from the Sabia and return to being fully human? He doesn't know. He watches as Aban calmly but firmly addresses uniformed Air Force personnel.

Esfirs leans over and whispers in his ear. "Do not go with them, Dear Brendan. They are not your friends. You are not like them anymore."

Her words make him queasy. Longing for home, longing for his military friends, he is forced to remain with the Sabia. The government gets a say in the matter, as do the Sabia, but Brendan has no choice.

Esfirs now gets on his other side. Locking her arm around his free one, she whispers, "Calm, be calm. I have you. We will not let them take you."

Despite his efforts to be more assertive, he realizes there is nothing he can do in this situation. He is merely a rope being tugged in two different directions. No effort from him would even register. He wants to help everyone, but his own country has sent mixed signals. Meanwhile, his Sabia friends deny his very humanity.

An Air Force officer notably retreats three steps, ground which a proud Kimya seizes by following. Then, in triumph, she turns around and heads toward Brendan. Her head tilts in surprise when she sees the human-Sabia chain that has formed.

Kindly, she says, "Everything is fine. They have ended their demand for private time with Brendan. I see he was well protected." She sighs. "Brendan, please come with me. Esfirs, you may join us." She turns to Berina. "You may ride with Aban."

The large gathering of Sabia breaks up. Most go into vehicles headed toward the hotel while a group of guards stays with the spacecraft. Kimya's group enters the last two SUVs headed to the church.

The travelers keep their bags with them. Brendan sits in the back with Esfirs while Kimya and another guard sit in the middle row. Both the driver and person riding shotgun are enlisted Air Force personnel. To Brendan, they look like kids in their early twenties. Both remain motionless until a go code is given over the radio.

"Just a couple minutes to the church, sir," the driver declares. After a moment's pause, he speaks up again. "So, um, Officer Murphy, I was wondering—"

Kimya interrupts with, "I am the senior officer in this vehicle. If you have anything to say, you will address it to me."

The driver looks in his rearview mirror to study Kimya. The front passenger turns his head to look as well.

"Ma'am, I am sorry, but I did not catch your name. Are you with the UIC?" the driver asks.

"I am Sabia," Kimya answers with noted hostility, "and I did not offer you my name, enlisted. Now, do your job ensuring our protection while remaining silent. Any further insults will be mentioned to your chain of command."

Both Air Force members remain silent for the rest of the trip. During the ride, Brendan attempts to get his mind ready for the meeting with Dan and his confession. The desire to set things right with God is something he hasn't felt for a while. *Maybe I'm trying to compensate for the upheaval in my life, but I really think I need this.*

Assessing the scenery and Brendan's anxiousness, Esfirs softly takes his hand. She begins to tap her nails against it, an unfamiliar beat. He looks at her, expecting some playful expression, but instead finds her watching her fingers dance on his palm. Brendan is reminded of how little kids will play with their parents' hair when bored in the car. Contemplating this, he sees just how comfortable Esfirs is with him. Could Brendan ever be at ease—at home—with her and the Sabia? Her asking him to stay forever tugs at his heart, battling the lack of choice he felt just minutes ago.

Time passes for Brendan in a dream-like state. Eventually, the vehicles pull up in front of a church. Brendan reads the sign. "Saint Lazarus Chapel – Franciscan Order of St Lazarus." On the door, another sign says the church is closed today for an event. Kimya, the other guard, Brendan, and Esfirs all get out, carrying their bags. The Air Force men don't turn around to look at them as they exit. The other SUV pulls up behind them within moments. The Sabia guards get out, but so does the Air Force member riding shotgun. He opens the left side door and even offers a hand to Berina to assist her. She says something to the airman, which causes all three to laugh. The airman demonstrates some sort of a complex handshake to Berina, who then walks up to Brendan, smiling widely.

"Pleasant ride?" Brendan asks.

"Very much so. Airman Frederiksen told me all about his time here in Montana and what his family does locally to relax. I would very much like to hike the woods sometime. Already I love this place," Berina says.

Kimya looks at her with disdain, but the pilot either does not notice or does not care.

"Shall we go?" Brendan asks, hoping to move things along.

The group gathers, with Kimya in the lead. She cautiously opens the door, looks in, and then waves for the rest of the group to follow. Inside the church, Brendan's breath is taken away by its beauty. The

PATRICK ABBOTT

Franciscan design has merged a traditional Italian look with a Middle Eastern motif. A lone figure at the front of the church stands up. Brendan can make out the man's brown habit as Brendan walks toward the robed man. Next, he notices the silver face mask. Kimya moves to step in between Brendan and the incoming man but steps back when Brendan tells her that it is Father Baldwin approaching.

An unnaturally hoarse voice greets Brendan. "It has been too long, friend."

Brendan bows his head in respect. "Father Baldwin. Yes, it has." He then motions to the group. "These are my friends. They are Sabia, who have looked after me while I have lived with them. Please allow me to introduce Esfirs, Berina, and Kimya." The three females adopt stoic looks while the guard, who Brendan does not know, moves back to position himself near the door.

Baldwin's eyes are the only part of his face visible underneath his mask. There is an intensity, a fire, in them that one would not suspect from hearing his voice.

"May God's peace be with you. Welcome to this little House of God. Please make yourself comfortable here—you are always welcome," Baldwin states.

The Sabia remain silent. The priest does not move. *It is an awkward standoff.* Then, suddenly, Berina breaks the silence with, "And with your spirit," which causes Baldwin to stare at her. After that, she reverts to her stoic posture. *This could go on for a while.*

Finally, Baldwin breaks the stalemate by addressing Brendan. "Brendan, I understand you need

363

reconciliation. Come with me to the railing." His orders are quick and to the point, much like when he was Dan Saleh.

Baldwin turns his back and starts toward the front of the church, with Brendan following close behind. Berina trails Brendan while Kimya tries to get in between them. Baldwin stops to look at both Sabia females, but neither will retreat.

"The Rite of Reconciliation is one of the most important of the seven sacraments of the Church. Please respect your friend's right to confession by giving him privacy. I ask you to wait outside." Berina silently backs away while Kimya holds her position. "I promise you I will not harm your friend," Baldwin says to her. The priest and Kimya lock eyes. She then turns around and leaves the building.

I wonder what she felt in him?

At the front of the church, Baldwin takes a seat on the communion railing and invites Brendan to sit next to him. Brendan takes a seat and looks at the silver mask he and Malcolm helped purchase for the then-Dan. It provides facial features such as lips, nose, chin, and eyebrows. Holes for the eyes and nostrils allow Baldwin to see and breathe. A slight parting of the lips permits Baldwin's speech to be readily intelligible. Because of his facial deformities, Dan chose "Baldwin" in honor of the leper King Baldwin IV of Jerusalem. Before entering seminary, the Veterans Affairs hospital once asked if Dan wanted facial reconstruction surgery. He rejected the offer, saying his face reflected the damage his sins had caused to his soul. At first, Brendan respected Dan's faith, but Heather's betrayal caused him to become envious of it. *To have gone through all that and be stronger for it. Wow. I wish I had that.*

Father Baldwin starts the sacrament of confession. "In the name of the Father, Son, and Holy Spirit"—he makes the sign of the cross—"may the Lord be in your heart and help you to confess your sins with true sorrow."

"Thank you, Father; it has been a long time since my last confession. I really do not know what to confess—"

"Stop," Baldwin interrupts, catching Brendan off guard. "You are here for a reason, even if you do not know why. God has called you here, of that I have no doubt. God has brought the Sabia here, which I have no doubt of either. So let us use our God-given thinking skills to find out."

Brendan grows afraid. *How much can I share?* "Well, I think my identity as a human has been challenged during my time with the Sabia. I—"

"It is a sin to lie in confession," the priest says dryly. "Yesterday, FBI agents came and told me how your genetic makeup has changed and how you led illegal operations for the Sabia on Earth, among other things. They instructed me to tell you that you must turn yourself in as an act of penance."

The whites of Baldwin's eyes become prominent through the mask. Brendan looks on in shock. He glances toward the door where the Sabia exited and then back at Father Baldwin.

Baldwin laughs and then says, "As if I would follow the orders of the FBI. They are the domestic terrorists they hunt for. I am a priest of God. No secular Caesar will tell me what another man's penance will be. Just be honest with me, Brendan. Jesus, in chapter eight of the Gospel of John, says, 'The truth will set you free.' You have spent too much time playing liaison. Be honest."

Brendan takes a moment and sighs. "Yeah, things got crazy. Their medical care started a hybridization process in me, and I have no idea if the government wants me to work for them or to arrest me. After years working for them, they freaking betrayed me, man."

"And what about the Sabia?"

"Yeah." Brendan nods his head. "Oh, ha, I am sorry. I mean, dang. At first, I was not sure how they saw me. Some of the leaders view me as a tool. They will accommodate me when I am overwhelmed, but they will just use me otherwise to obtain information about Earth. However . . . among them, some are friends who actually care for me."

"You talk differently than the last time we worked together."

Brendan laughs. "Yeah, trying to impress a Sabia who hates contractions."

Baldwin tilts his head. "Okay, then. Back to my inquiry. How do you relate to the government and the Sabia?"

Brendan pauses. He searches for an answer, yet every internal examination reveals a complete void.

Finally, he starts scanning the floor as if the answer were there. "Man, I will tell you. I work hard for both, yet it is the same crap I have always gotten. Whether it is my dad or Heather in the past or work and the Sabia now, it is the same thing."

Baldwin sighs, touches his mask, and looks up at Brendan. "My friend, confessions I hear mostly involve sexual sins. Then comes what the criminal code would call minor crimes. The remainder is from the very pious who confess things such as malign thoughts toward their fellow man or using the Lord's name in vain. Extremely rarely will I hear someone say they did not honor the Sabbath. Your sin is a common one, yet it's one I sadly never hear confessed. Do you know what sin it is?"

Brendan looks into Baldwin's eyes in silence. Baldwin is reading him like a book.

"You hold onto the wrongs others have done to you. Because of your possessive nature of these memories, you see everyone wronging you repeatedly. All this builds up a pride within yourself. So when someone sins against you, you hold it against them, becoming an acid eating your sanity and soul. And when you sin, because you view yourself so mightily, it also eats away at you. It's a pride, Brendan. I can only imagine the constant anxiety attacks which are killing you inside out. Want to know what makes things even worse? You probably have friends trying to help you, but you overblow their wrongs to the point you are working to kill their love for you."

Baldwin's words have left Brendan dumbstruck. The liaison starts to cry as he sits on the altar rail steps.

Not hyperventilating, he nonetheless shakes as his nerves begin to twitch. Baldwin has called him out, and through the rite of confession, Jesus Christ Himself is calling him out. Brendan has religiously awakened to find God is not pleased with him.

"What can I do?" Brendan asks.

"You can do nothing. Your fallen nature will do everything to keep you there." Brendan's heart collapses. "But with God's grace, everything is possible. So confess this sin and ask God to help you with the situation. Ask Him to help you let go of the pain, to forgive, to open yourself up to love."

"Yes, yes, oh God, yes." Brendan grabs Baldwin's robes. "Yes, I confess, I confess!"

"I must warn you, Brendan. This rite will take away your guilt, renewing your graces with the Lord. However, you will still be broken. Over time, grace may heal you. But, I fear you must go down the same penitential path of redemption. God may allow you to be shattered completely. If He does allow this, it will happen soon. Your moving toward God will not go unchallenged by things in this fallen universe. Pray you allow yourself to be healed; pray for protection against those who would consume you."

Brendan sobs. "I do not understand. Why does God not heal me now?"

As Brendan looks down to wipe his eyes, Baldwin looks toward the door.

"We have an audience," he says, not so much to Brendan as to the air.

PATRICK ABBOTT

Brendan sees the door slightly ajar, Berina peering through the opening.

"Is Brendan okay?" she asks in a voice that carries across the church.

"Have you been listening in?" Baldwin asks.

"No, I was watching because I wanted to see what was happening. I promise you I could hear nothing."

Brendan says to Baldwin as he clears his throat, "It's fine if she watches. She's been curious about my faith, asking questions and whatnot."

Baldwin looks at Brendan for a moment and then back at Berina. "Do you believe in a divinity in any way, shape, or form?"

"I do, father." The reverence is audible in her tone.

"Very good," Baldwin replies, "please respect Brendan's longing for the divine by giving him privacy. He is coming to terms with things. He will be with you soon."

Berina nods and backs out of view, shutting the door. Baldwin watches the entrance intently. After a moment, Brendan wipes his eyes turns to look too, and they both stare at it for a minute to ensure there is no sign of anyone propping it ajar to peek through the crack.

The priest continues. "I can't tell you why the Holy Spirit doesn't come and heal you now, friend. Only God knows the reasoning behind His plans. But I suspect, with as minimal confidence as a mere mortal can have, He is preparing you for a test to come."

"What test would that be?"

"The one where you fail, where you are broken. From that, you will have the freedom to choose a painful purgation of yourself, saying yes to God. Or, if you prefer, damnation.

"But take heart, Brendan. He will not abandon you now. Open your heart to His will, do not guess it or try to force it. Pray and discern. But first, do you confess your sin of pride?"

"I do, old friend, I do."

"Then say your act of contrition."

Brendan looks forward. He remembers his last confession in seminary, the last one in his life. Whatever prayer he used to express sorrow escapes him. Thinking back to other confessions also draws blanks. So, he decides to speak from the heart. "God, I am so very sorry. Help me."

Baldwin raises his right hand. "God, the Father of mercies, through the death and resurrection of his Son, has reconciled the world to himself and sent the Holy Spirit among us for the forgiveness of sins; through the ministry of the Church, may God give you pardon and peace, and I absolve you from your sins in the name of the Father, the Son, and the Holy Spirit. Amen." Making the sign of the cross, Baldwin ends the rite of reconciliation.

PATRICK ABBOTT

The load flies off Brendan's soul like a sparrow released from a cage. He opens his arms up to the ceiling, using his body to offer a prayer of thanksgiving. Sitting there, Brendan realizes all his sins did come from his pride: refusal to confront what happened in Afghanistan and at home, refusal to go to Church, playing all sides as if he had to master everything. He knows growing spiritually is a process, and he realizes there will be relapses, but he is in an excellent place for now. Father Baldwin gets up and walks across the church to the door. Popping in as if they'd been leaning against it, Berina and Esfirs quickly move past the priest to Brendan. Meanwhile, Kimya and the other guard enter but remain near the door.

"What happened?!" Berina hurriedly asks.

Esfirs places her hands on his cheeks, moving his head around while studying him like a hawk. Then, placing her little fingers on his neck arteries, she counts softly to herself.

Brendan waits to talk until Esfirs removes her hands. "Thank you for checking my vitals. However, I needed that confession more than any medical care in my life. I am going to be fine. Just give me a moment, and I will get up."

Brendan is wobbly getting back on his feet. Kimya comes up and feels his face. She asks if he needs to head out, but Brendan declines—he wants to stay for Mass. While he takes a seat in the pew, Berina quickly plops herself down immediately to his left. Kimya takes Brendan's right. He's trapped by two Sabia, one at least curious about his faith and the other protecting him from nothing in particular.

During Father Baldwin's Mass, Brendan enters a dreamlike state. Confession has left him feeling lighter and a bit outside of his body. The Catholic autopilot kicks in as he changes between standing, sitting and kneeling throughout the service. Berina follows his movements closely while Kimya remains sitting, scanning the empty church. During the sign of peace, Brendan turns around to see Esfirs sitting against the far wall with her arms crossed, clearly nonplussed. Brendan feels a sense of sadness concerning her perceived attitude. He realizes he doesn't want to be without his faith anymore, however imperfect it may be. Yet, he fears what it could mean for their relationship. When it comes time to take communion, Brendan and Berina go up to the priest. Brendan takes the wafer and cup while Berina crosses her arms for a blessing, which Baldwin gives her. Both participants give a loud *amen* at the end of the service.

Brendan practically falls into the pew. He has much to think about, to discern, to determine. He barely notices Berina run up to the sacristy where Baldwin went. At the same time, Esfirs comes up to him, but her presence doesn't really register. Gently, she rubs his arm. He turns to her, and their eyes lock, forming a Bond.

"Are you okay, Brendan?" In his dreamlike state, he doesn't reply. "Brendanshe, are you alright?"

PATRICK ABBOTT

Interlude – Esfirs: The Reception

Esfirs takes in the ballroom reception as she enters. The Terrans here have been exceptionally friendly. *They all see me as a means to gain an edge over each other.* Governors, businessmen, lawyers, and other politicians mill about amongst themselves. *Yet, they are the self-serving creatures I knew they would be. Brendan says it is these people who have such distrust in his country. What impresses me is how such creatures have not caused their civilization to collapse centuries ago.*

As she moves, her gold lace gown flows down to the floor. *The look on Brendanshe's face when he saw me was to die for.* She thinks back to this morning when he was so distracted. *That damnable cleric, what did he say to him? It ruined the whole night and morning for him. The sooner we can remove Brendan from this planet, the sooner we will be happy. He needs to let this place go.*

A gentle hand rubs her back. Berina appears at her side in her flight suit and the aviator glasses Brendan gave her.

"Why are you dressed like a pilot?" Esfirs asks with some dismissiveness.

"Because I am a pilot," Berina says laughingly. "Anyways, Terrans love aliens and love pilots. I am running up the score with them here. They have given me items from their own pilot's uniforms—caps and other things as gifts. Everyone wants a photo with me. Plus, your colleague Farmin has a thing for pilots." She bites her bottom lip and playfully raises her eyebrows.

Esfirs expresses her disapproval through a quick Bond.

"At least I am not like Mon, who dresses in a fancy Terran suit," Berina continues. "She could have chosen any Sabia outfit to display power; instead, she spent all morning dressing so she could get the attention of every Terran male here." Berina leans in. "I, meanwhile, have my sites on one Sabia—for now."

"Mon knows what must be done," Esfirs says, ignoring Berina. *Just because we are far from home does not mean we act like mountain folk.* Her mind shifts back to Mon's inspired leadership. If Mon said they all had to march into the sea, Esfirs would do so. When Esfirs sees Mon or another member of the holy family, she practically feels the strength of the Watchers guiding them.

Berina takes in the scene some more. "Well, if any of us knew what should be done here, we would have just have Brendan in this room. The moment Mon gave him the floor, the governors were done with her. Those politicians just wanted him to tell them how different it was living in space. They even had the gall to ask him if they could visit. I must give Mon credit; she played it off so well. Got her points across, got the assurances we needed, let Brendan have the spotlight, and let him take some of the heat."

"She was born for such moments," Esfirs says.

"Literally true," Berina acknowledges. "So, how was your time at the hospital?"

"I loved every moment of it. So many beautiful children. Did you know one Terran boy told me he had five brothers and sisters?" Esfirs' eyes sparkle as she recalls the day's events.

"Praise the divine for such a great gift." Berina reverently lifts her hands into the air.

"Indeed, praise the divine and all the Watchers who have loved those children. The poor boy had diabetes. Five minutes with him, and he was cured. Such a planet of potential, but these Terrans . . ."

"Look on the bright side before you start musing again, sister. That family will never believe militia lies about us now."

"Yes, and many others as well. I spent a few hours there. The last doctors should be finishing up their shift soon. There was a decent crowd when we started, but it only got busier as people learned what we could do. I figure more medical missions will be conducted soon to capitalize on these gains."

"I imagine Brendan would warn us that the militias will only tolerate us making inroads for so long before they take steps to stop us. If I, a mid-level cleric, can figure that one out, there are probably plans already. Speaking of which, where is your Brendan? I would have thought he would be here pining for you, especially in that regalia."

Esfirs looks around the room full of Terrans and a few Sabia. She is nowhere in sight. This disturbs her somewhat. *If Brendan is still upset because of that priest, I will give the minister more body parts to hide away.* She shakes off her feelings. *This anger is not conducive to the mission, despite it being deserved.* She adopts the stoic manner they all have been taught since youth. *Do not let the lesser know or use your emotions against you.* She glides effortlessly from one group to another, looking for Brendan. Terran eyes—lustful males and awed females—are gawking at her and her dress. She does not care. *Lesser things. That is all you are, lesser things.*

Approaching select groups, she introduces herself and allows them to offer praises to the Sabia's magnificence. Various members then try to advance personal causes with her, attempting to gain her support for their own endeavors. *You genuinely value your individual selves over your own race. Disgusting.* But she needs these self-serving Terrans to find Brendan. Yet, none of them know where he is. *Am I wasting my time with you?* Some even go as far as to claim distant professional or personal connections to Brendan. *Will you stop at no lie to advance yourselves? How did Brendan even come from your kind?*

As she mills about the Terrans, all her thoughts lead to Brendan. When men look at her, she imagines his loving eyes when he first saw her tonight. While Terrans discuss their personal histories, she goes back to the times Brendan told her war stories while they played Shut the Box. Soon she tires of the Terrans and walks out to the roof patio. Even this tiny settlement makes her think of Brendan. How she wants to take him back home and show him what an actual city looks like at night. *How I will show him its beauty!*

The desire, want—no, the need—to rip out those last remaining Terran bits in him screams at her to do so. *They are cancerous! Why does he resist it?* She resolves to do it. The treatments have not helped. They just reset the clock. *Remel gave new life to Namziah; I will do the same. Remel loved Namziah. Their passion saved each other. I will save Brendan, and we will love each other for the rest of our lives.* Esfirs catches herself. *Calm yourself. I will just love him more, show him the beauty of being a Sabia. He will accept it then. Together, we will make the choice to remove the taint inside him. He has only been unsure about doing it because of how he has been treated.* Now is the time for her to be honest, open, and loving.

She quickly spins around after hearing a female Terran say the name "Murphy." *Why do Terrans have so many names? Because they are so divided. They need their names to claim multiple allegiances for their own survival. Weakness!* Again assuming a stoic pose, she gracefully makes her way to the group to which the female belongs.

"Dear friends," Esfirs intrudes into their conversation, "pardon me." The Terrans stand formally erect, their awe at being addressed by an alien self-evident. "I heard you refer to our Auxiliary Officer Brendan. Are you aware of his current location?"

The Terran woman bows awkwardly before addressing Esfirs. Esfirs keeps her face expressionless.

"Yes, I do, Officer—or is it Delegate . . . ?"

Esfirs knows the female's prolonged uncertainty is meant to get her to help her out with an introduction. However, Esfirs refuses to take the bait; instead, she merely blinks at her.

The woman breaks first, as Esfirs expected. "My apologies, ma'am. Please allow me to introduce myself. I am Lieutenant Governor Maryam Foster. It is a pleasure to meet you!"

Petty fief lord. The lieutenant governor holds out her hand for a handshake. Again, Esfirs remains stoic and unmoving, and Maryam slowly withdraws it. She leans back a bit, away from Esfirs. Grimacing, she looks around at the other members of the group.

"I believe you were going to tell me where Brendan is." Esfirs does everything in her power to hide her frustration. *Do not ruin what Mon has started.*

"Oh yes, of course, yes. Well, Governor Hayes and I were really intrigued by what he had to say at the conference. So we intercepted him as he was coming into the reception hall here and asked him if he could talk to us one-on-one—well, one-on-two, I guess." Maryam laughs. Esfirs is not amused but does not show it. "Well, we took a walk around the block to stretch our legs when these fascist militia types suddenly showed up and started harassing us. Murphy was able to calm them down and, get this, invited them to the bar downstairs! Michael—sorry, Governor Hayes—and I didn't want to be seen with those people, so we decided to leave. I was just telling our staff that poor Murphy was down there with at least three rednecks."

Esfirs eyes widen, and Maryam takes another two steps back. *You left him behind?* She breaks her stoic pose to give a fake smile of thanks. It is all she can muster for the coward. With the required niceties over with, she turns quickly and makes her way toward Mon and her security detail. Next to the heir, Aban stands in his guard uniform. Kimya is dressed in Terran civilian clothes. *You make for an uglier Terran than you do Sabia, you failure.*

Aban must notice Esfirs' concern because he asks her what is wrong.

"Brendan is alone in the pub in the custody of militia members." Esfirs voice is controlled, holding back the panic. She feels her heart pounding hard and fast. Everything in her wants to scream, but she dares not lose control in front of Mon.

Aban nods in acknowledgment. He moves over to Kimya and whispers in her ear. *You are getting her involved? She should already be watching him. She is failing, again!* Kimya lights up, and she and Aban look into each other's eyes. Kimya then says something short to him before running out of the room.

Thirty-Two – The Violation

The word Brendan can best describe Alex Maddoff with is "crazy." At a table in the hotel bar, he has listened to Alex list his ideas for ten minutes straight. All the conspiracy theories are "documented" in the two five-hundred-page binders Alex has given him. Alex's corpus wraps the Illuminati, lizard people, rival international cabals of pedophiles, and Sabia all up together in a hollow-Earth theory. Every time Brendan tries to move Alex along, the man mistakes it for interest and begins anew on another conspiracy point. Thankfully, the two militia members Brendan is having drinks with have had enough. Marty Babbit, a six-foot-six, two-hundred-fifty-pound behemoth of a Native American, gets up and places his large hands on Alex.

"Come on, Al, I think the man wants to get some words in with my lady," Marty says.

"Oh, yeah? I mean, sure." Alex's disjointed response is pretty much on par with his rapid monologue. "It was an honor meeting you, Mr. Murphy. Please know I have no disrespect for you, but the Rothschild people want you to be a mindless tool for the Sabia. They are all interconnected and work toward the same ends. In my book, which I am about to publish, I talk about how CERN allowed—"

PATRICK ABBOTT

"Come on, Al, time to go." Marty practically picks him off his chair and places him ten feet away from the table, proceeding to walk the nerdy conspiracy theorist out of the bar.

"Boy, I'm glad he is gone," Marty's wife Aisling wryly remarks.

The muscular brunette of hearty stock adjusts her orange New Sons of Freedom sash. Watching her husband exit the hotel lobby with Alex, she starts to tap the table to the beat of the country music playing in the background. Brendan wonders what made a former sheriff's deputy walk away from her career to take up arms and threaten federal and state-level authorities. GDP and the stock markets have seen year after year of growth. However, so has the Gini coefficient. *Life outside the Washington bubble is different indeed.* Brendan respects her silence and waits for time to pass.

"That guy wouldn't shut up," Marty says, returning to his chair.

"The media portrays you all as a bunch of Alexes, you know. It is also how the Sabia think of you. They only get one story," responds Brendan.

"Bunch of fake news propaganda setting us up for war. How do we fight it?" Aisling asks.

"You actually did well tonight. First, you came up to me with grievances but made it clear you wanted to talk, not fight. Then, you accepted my invitation to have a peaceful conversation here. We shared opinions, mutually rolled our eyes at the crazy guy, and had a nice laugh or two." He changes topics to demonstrate

381

transparency. "I will not lie to you. I think you are wrong on several important points. But I hear your concerns, see where they are coming from and will remember how you treated me. Just promise me this: you can take all the defensive actions you want, that is your right, but do not go out and start things like the Nationalist Sons of Freedom."

The Babbits both have physical reactions when Brendan mentions the violent, criminal, racist group.

"Those racists are not part of the movement. They were kicked out!" Aisling declares.

"Alright, then make sure you do not copy them. This country will not be able to survive if more on the left and right tear at it."

Marty nods and asks, "So, brother, what are you going to do about it all?"

Brendan sighs. "I do not know, to be truthful. Working with the government and Sabia on this kind of mission is draining. A pastor called me out, lovingly, mind you, on my motivations. That, of course, plays into all my actions. I think I need to get right with God before I do anything else."

"I hear ya, brother," Marty says. "Keep praying that the blood of Jesus covers you. That will protect you from everything."

As Brendan takes a drink, he sees Kimya in her undercover outfit walk a distant circle around the table. She eyes him, the Babbits, and then the entire room. Brendan focuses on her face, noticing her eyes lock on a target, hold it for a moment, and then lock on to something else. Even though the militia folks are just enjoying themselves, Brendan is worried Kimya may decide they are threats to be "solved." Quickly, he needs to end the crisis before it starts.

"Well," he shouts loud enough for Kimya to hear, "it was great meeting you all. Now I swear if I take too long to get back, I will get in trouble. So, I should get along now. Just remember everyone"—the militia members elsewhere in the bar turn to look at him—"I will always enjoy the New Sons of Freedom's company any day. Orange Power!"

"Orange Power!" the militia members cheerfully chant.

With this declaration, Brendan picks up Alex's printed rantings, steps away, and makes his way to the elevator. Before he can reach it, Kimya intercepts him.

"Come with me now." Her words send chills down Brendan's spine.

They enter an open elevator. Another guest attempts to enter, but Kimya growls the word "out." *Oh, she is mad.* He is about to hit the top floor reception hall button when she reaches past him to press for the floor their rooms are on. The ride is painfully uncomfortable as Kimya breathes heavily. Looking over, Brendan can see her hands are in tight fists. The doors open, revealing two Sabia guards playing a card game on the floor.

"Get up! You"—she indicates one of the guards—"tell Aban security downstairs is compromised. You," she says to the other guard, "get the next shift out here.

Both of you are relieved. Auxiliary Officer"—she addresses Brendan—"our room, now!"

Kimya had insisted they share a room so she could provide protection throughout the night. Upon arrival, she commands him to sit on the edge of his twin bed, which he does, placing the conspiracy propaganda next to him. He prepares for her to erupt, perhaps even threatening resignation. *I stood up to Zand; I can push back against you.* She walks up to him and stands by the bed, towering over him. This is where her facade breaks.

"Brendan! Why did you leave the room without protection? You could have been injured. Yesterday people tried to steal you from us. There are hostiles out there who want to harm you. Please let me protect you." She gets down on one knee, eye level with him.

Brendan is dumbfounded by this emotional reversal. He does not need a Bond to tell Kimya is being genuine. He merely nods.

"You asked why there is animosity between me and . . . some others. It is because of an incident like this." She now has Brendan's absolute attention. "I was with two—three—friends: Jooji, Parastu, and Mehr. Mehr was . . . a truly great man. You and he would have gotten along so well, Brendan. One day, a day like any other, we were on a mission, and . . . he liked leading from the front, so I let him. Soon enough, though, the three of them were dead on the ground. What happened that day still haunts me."

The similarities between what Kimya tells Brendan and his own near-death experience in Afghanistan strike him deeply. He is unsure how Berina and Esfirs' animosity toward her relates to this, perhaps through Berina knowing one of the three dead Sabia. However, what matters more is that Brendan knows the hell Kimya has experienced and that he has brought that memory back. Having her relive it is like mentally kicking himself below the belt.

"I am sorry," he manages. "When I was in Afghanistan, my eagerness got two friends of mine killed. Everyone thinks my being injured that day was the reason I changed. They do not understand the weight of having had friends die because of decisions I made."

"What were their names?" Brendan and Kimya look into each other's eyes, forming a Bond.

"Nicholas Bellefontaine and Ace. Ace was my interpreter. I did not even bother learning his full name." Brendan weighs the guilt over his prideful use of others to further his own goals. He senses something as if Kimya was holding his heart. It is odd yet strangely comforting. It encourages him to continue. "Because I was so messed up, my wife turned her hidden infidelities into open affairs. A proud man who thinks he is above getting to know the surname of his interpreter deserves that sort of wife, eh?"

He senses her sympathy, her pain, her care for him. *She knows.* Both nod at each other and then stand up.

"War is hell," Brendan says.

"It ruins everything," Kimya replies.

He has confirmed the Sabia have war. In the past, this was something he would write back to the UIC about as soon as possible. Not now, though. He surveys his thoughts. Esfirs comes to mind. *I need to tell her how I wrote to the UIC when I was upset with her. She has a right to now know. Coming clean is the only way I can move forward.*

"Kimya, I am ready to go upstairs."

She steps aside so he can lead them both to the elevators. No words are said. A younger version of him would have felt pride at discovering a key thing about the Sabia. His maturing self now knows pride is a trap. *Pride only serves to isolate me. Relationships with others are what matter.*

Arriving at the ballroom, he is met first by Aban, then Mon. Aban is ready for battle while Mon expresses concern. Brendan manages to assure them all is well. He then makes his way to the one person in this entire hall who matters to him: Esfirs. Brendan finds her standing back, observing him through the various groups of Terrans milling about the room. He approaches the most beautiful woman in the universe. While pleased to have gotten here, the idea of having this conversation fills him with dread.

"Can we go outside and talk, Esfirs?"

She smiles and takes his hand. The silky-smooth touch of her fingers feels so loving. Her golden dress reminds him of what her eyes look like without the medicine the Sabia take to suppress their unique traits.

PATRICK ABBOTT

Once outside, almost in slow motion, Esfirs' pupils lock on his. Instantaneously, his whole self is wrapped in the warmth of a Bond. However, her expression changes almost as speedily. *She knows something is wrong.* She leads him onto the patio as if he were in a dream state, to a secluded part where no one can see them. In his periphery, he can see the night sky. Everything in his view is beautiful.

"Dear Brendanshe, what is wrong?"

He closes his eyes to break the Bond. This is the hardest thing he's ever done. It is more painful than suffering through what Heather did to him, more challenging than learning about his change, and more brutal than war.

"Esfirs, I . . . love you." She smiles hearing this, and his heart tries to rebel against what he needs to do. "I realize that I have been too prideful, using others to serve what I think best. I think I need—"

"No," she passionately declares.

She tries to look him in the eyes, but he avoids her direct gaze. Holding his face in a vice-like grip, she forces eye contact, allowing a Bond to form.

She presses herself against him and, with a strong voice, says, "You once took my hand when I asked you to let me show you your potential as a Sabia. Now listen to me as a Sabia man would. Let me show you us."

Brendan feels as if he is being drawn into her. Suddenly, it feels like the floor beneath him gives way; the sensation of falling turns into one of flooding every part of Esfirs. As he flows through her, he feels her being displaced into him. He is stretched like a leather glove being fitted. Currents of emotion swirl within him. At first, he feels himself pressing against her, then her pressing against him. Their hands begin moving up and down each other's backs. Everything is sensual and enjoyable. He sees her, and he views himself through her eyes. The effect compounds. Everything speeds up. Desirous thoughts are released, which he is unable to put back. He is losing control, and he knows it. Panic sets in.

Calm, be calm.

The voice in his head startles him. It is not his own but Esfirs'. *Did I just hear her thoughts?*

Brendanshe, be calm. I will hold us together. This is us. Feel the pleasure of us.

Her hand begins rubbing his cheek again. She smiles. Brendan feels like he is both being touched and touching. He is unsure precisely what his role is in this. *Whatever "this" is.* As a sort of experiment, he gently presses his pelvis against her. The strange response is that he feels the pleasure of receiving it. Again, his pelvis moves forward, but this time without him even thinking about it. The whole situation is both confusing and enjoyable.

Then, the violation is realized. Brendan's body leans over to whisper into Esfirs' ear. "I love you -she," his voice says into her. Before he can even think to scream about being controlled by someone else, his lips kiss hers.

PATRICK ABBOTT

He struggles to think of the word "stop." Instead, his mind lashes out in a thousand different directions. Suddenly, it feels like he is both sucking himself out from Esfirs and her from him. During this, she digs her nails into his back in a most painful way. The last thought he has through the Bond is from Esfirs, who is telling him to stop the disconnection.

Brendan collapses into her arms. With her Sabia strength, she moves him into a chair.

He hears but does not see Esfirs ask, "Was I too quick, -she?"

Brendan pants, out of breath. The only thing he can sense is the taste of salt in his mouth as perspiration pours over his parted lips.

Thirty-Three – The Black Hats

Shaking, Brendan has soaked the bed with his sweat. Yes, she stopped, but it still felt like a violation. *To have robbed me of my body. How much of that was me? How much of it was her? Did I enjoy the things she did, thinking I did them? Was I raped?* The last question lingers in his mind. It was not sexual in the physical sense, so he decides to walk back the term. *It was a violation. Can a person violate another person if she doesn't mean to? Did she mean to? She said she wanted to show me things. Is that what Sabia do with each other? Can I ask Berina about it? That would be hypocritical since I got upset at Esfirs for talking to her about us. Can I ask Esfirs about what happened? We agreed to give each other the benefit of the doubt.* But worst of all is what he has done. *How can I expect anything from her when I betrayed her and the Sabia with that message to the UIC?*

He rolls over and looks at Kimya in the opposite bed. *The Sabia apparently sleep just like humans.* She moved a little bit throughout the night, but she has been chiefly still. Earlier, when she came in, Brendan had his back to her and pretended to be asleep. *She would be a good person to talk to if there wasn't animosity between her and Esfirs and Berina.*

PATRICK ABBOTT

Repositioning himself, Brendan stares at the ceiling. The hotel room feels like a prison. He knows he cannot go outside, as the Sabia have the hotel on lockdown until morning. *Those guards in the hallway probably wouldn't even let me go to the lobby for a late-night snack.* He is trapped.

Visions of him being told to leave Kansas, Loft telling him he is losing his humanity, and being monitored while taking pills for his depression parade around him. *I was never given a choice, then or now.* His anger grows. He battles it. *To let my emotions control me is to remain stuck in my own mental prison. Here is something I can discern: asserting myself is more than just standing up against slights—it is also standing up against my own disorders.* The pain of depression breaks as he thinks those words. The fevered sensation making him sweat also lifts. Suddenly, it feels as if he's gone from the desert to a cool, misty glen. Alcoholics would call this a moment of clarity. The way ahead still has its unknowns, but it's more straightforward than before. *No more letting emotions get the better of me.*

The train of thought from the violation to his way forward stuns Brendan. He sits up; the energy now flowing in his body refuses to let him sleep. Looking around, he sees the door of the nightstand. Opening it cautiously to not disturb Kimya, he spots the Gideon Bible. Brendan ponders it as he thinks about everything that has happened since the talk with Father Baldwin. Anxious thoughts about his father and the collapse of his marriage press him to put away the book, but he does not give in to the negativity.

Opening the holy text, he decides the Gospel of Mark is an excellent place to start. In seminary, he gave a mock sermon on how the quickness and immediacy of the gospel made it the best one. *I might as well start with something quick with Jesus.* Brendan reads it. After his earlier breakthrough, Mark proves to be a bit of a disappointment. No angels, no choir, no light from on high comes down to him. Lacking the feeling that radically changed Dan into Baldwin drags Brendan down into a funk. *Maybe if I start from the beginning.* Brendan flips to the Book of Genesis. Creation, the Fall because of sin, fallen angels marrying women to create a race of evil giants known as the Nephilim, and Noah all keep his fascination. However, as the Flood occurs, he gets tired until a wave of sleep washes over him.

Light presses against Brendan's eyelids. Its shimmer and warmth cause him to open his eyes. *Must have fallen asleep . . .* From the slight incline in the bed, he can tell someone else's weight is pressing against the mattress. Turning over, he sees Esfirs with the Bible in her hand. Watching her, he notices she is reading the same section he did last night. Her eyes are locked on the text, her head leaning in intensely. Upon looking over and seeing Brendan looking at her, she snaps the book closed.

"Morning, Brendanshe. Did you sleep well?"

He struggles to prop himself up. Esfirs gently puts his head back down on the pillow and softly begins to caress him. *She doesn't suspect anything is wrong.* Brendan tries to say something, but his head is swimming. Finally, he removes his hands and looks at her.

"Your eyes give the appearance of one starved for sleep, -she," she declares. "I will get your things packed for you and some clothes as well. Stay in bed."

Esfirs rises to her feet. As she moves around the room, she starts to hum. Brendan's heart warms as he hears the familiar melody. Pain from the bright wakeup dissipates with each note Esfirs gives off. This allows him to get out of bed with minimal bodily resistance.

Going through his bag, Esfirs pulls out a black polo and pants. She watches him as he swaps his pajama shirt and sleeping shorts for the clothing. Brendan would consider this a win for his relationship with her, but his tiredness and recovery from last night's event have muted him.

"Is everything alright, Brendan?"

He catches the use of his name instead of the diminutive. *She realizes something is up. I need to confess everything.*

In an exhausted voice, he says, "Last night took a lot out of me. I was not ready for that. Losing control of my body. I love you, but that was horrifying. Truly, I do not think I have ever been that afraid."

Brendan's mind presses him not to end it here. *I need to tell her about the message I sent . . .* But instead, he looks at her, too afraid to open his mouth. He can't control himself against fear, especially after being this drained.

"I . . . understand"—she chooses her words deliberately—"I . . . can only imagine how different being

Sabia is for you. First, we really need to get the Terran cancer and bone marrow out of you. I will arrange the procedure and schedule some rest so you can adjust. Second, a new doctor is coming who can assist with the psychological help you need."

"Esfirs, in all honesty, what the hell?" Brendan curses. "What gives you the right to make these decisions without input from me? Do you know how insulting what you said is? I opened my vulnerabilities up to you so you could understand me, and –" He waves his hand, holds it stretched out, and silently counts to five. "Could you help me as a partner? Let us give each other the benefit of the doubt. You care for me. Also, you almost certainly said what you said because you want to help me. But let me say, recommending surgery and psychological treatment is not a loving response."

She breathes hard, in and out. Closing her eyes, she assumes the all-to-familiar stoic pose. "I understand. The only thing I want for you, -she, is the best we can give. Last night, I—I thought you would see . . ." Brendan waits for more, but nothing else comes. Instead, she places her left hand over her heart and bows. Then, she turns and exits the hotel room. He can hear a loud slamming nose from the hallway.

Crap. I probably should have said something. Brendan considers what to do. When nothing comes to mind, he gives up and exits into the hallway. The only Sabia out there is Gul, sitting on the floor near the elevator.

"Hey, brother," Brendan starts, "lying down on the job?"

PATRICK ABBOTT

Gul gets up while giving off a grunting sound. "Long night, no relief, and Kimya is in charge. All that is a recipe for disaster. I figure as long she is downstairs and there is no elevator approaching, I can take it easy."

"I hear that, Brendan." They fist-bump. "Anything going on?"

"Well, the complete failure of security last night to keep protesters away has us pulling even more security. I hope the time with those militia members was worth it because it freaked out so many people. Your Terran friends had to call in sheriff personnel, which meant we had to pull in more guards from the ship because of all the Terrans with guns. Additionally, we will not be traveling back to the spaceport. All pickups will be done in the nearby parking lot. Fun times, I believe, is the Terran expression."

"Dude, sorry about that. Sheriffs and their deputies are typically accommodating people, so we should not have any problem with them." Brendan catches the first-person plural pronoun use referring to him and the Sabia. "Is everyone else downstairs?"

Gul nods. "Yes, sir. The rally point is the lobby. I was going to get you up in the next few minutes if you were still asleep."

"Sleeping some more might have been for the best," Brendan concedes.

"I figured as much. It was impossible not to hear because of the door being open. As one man to another, I sympathize. Nema would not tolerate me talking back to her, even in the polite manner you just did. I gave up a long time ago on that front."

"Did you, um . . . hear what we were talking about?" Brendan asks.

"Heard and understood. I will tell you, as a Sabia to, um—however you identify; communication is key. Both of you got your points across, yes. However, neither one of you actively listened to the other. You have valid concerns, and she has valid worries. Might I recommend a couple of doctors and priestesses you can talk to about these sorts of things? Berina, in fact, is a—"

"Thanks," Brendan says to shut him up. *Grunts universally have a bluntness to them, apparently.*

Brendan again fist-bumps Gul before getting in the elevator and taking it down to the lobby.

Various Sabia are milling about downstairs. Brendan catches a flight-suited Berina leaning against a wall. As he approaches, he sees her mouthing the lyrics to the bluegrass song playing over the speakers. She nods her head to the beat, keeping up the routine as she notices him approaching.

"Good morning, Berina. How are you doing today?"

"You know," she starts, "I have been wondering if you willingly seek danger or if danger finds you. Yesterday, with the yokels—which is a word I learned last night, by the way—crashing your evening walk, I decided danger finds you. I do not know what we are going to do with you, boy." She does her impression of a country pronunciation of "boy."

PATRICK ABBOTT

"Ha, that is what you think of me, eh? Since trouble finds me, I guess that means I could die at any time. Am I banned from riding on your ship because of that?" He smiles playfully.

"Funny you should mention getting a ride. I am indeed banning you from my craft for the rest of this mission. No reason, really. It does conveniently align with the order from Mon requiring you to ride with her, though. She wants a full debrief of your conversation with the governors before the militia members show up. Just wait next to me; her aide Sahreb will come for you soon enough. Have you met Sahreb before? He is a nice enough fellow, likes studying Terrans, probably has a lot of questions for you about your youth."

Brendan takes a position against the wall next to her. For a moment, he enjoys the music while doing a little people-watching. All the Sabia in the lobby are busy running about doing their own thing. Each time Brendan catches a new Sabia face, he prepares to greet them as Sahreb. However, no one comes for him. Instead, he tries to enjoy the waiting, but it proves difficult. His mind keeps replaying the awkward morning with Esfirs. Once then twice, he looks over at Berina, hoping she will register his angst; however, she does not.

"So, besides dressing up as a pilot, what did you do during this trip?" The question is as much a distraction from his anxiety as it is a genuine interest.

Without turning, she says, "Oh, you know, classified Sabia business. I enjoyed scaring some poor farmers. They pointed at my craft and said, 'Ooo, ooo, ooo! Look ma; it is one of them UFOs!'" She laughs at her own mockery. "Next time, you should join me on one of my fun runs. We can steal a cow together." More laughter.

"I think I will take you up on the offer—always wanted to scare some farmers in Russia, China, and North Korea. Where should we go first?" He smiles slyly at her.

"You tempt me, Brendan."

She grins at him, causing them both to break out laughing. They then go back to watching the room. People-watching, or alien-watching, with Berina, proves to be enjoyable. Memories of hurry-up-and-wait deployed moments come to mind. How many afternoons were spent with friends, just living life together, waiting for orders that never came? *If only moments like that would happen again. The positive memories of deployment are worth more than all the gold in the world.* While watching, he imagines backstories for the Sabia he doesn't know. Then, a small male catches his eye. Brendan notices the male's face reminds him of a now-dead friend. Soberness creeps up on him with this thought.

Soon, an older male makes eye contact with Brendan and walks up to him.

"Auxiliary Officer, greetings; I am Sahreb. Thank you for being down here. Are you already packed?"

"Yes, sir," Brendan responds.

"Very well, follow me."

PATRICK ABBOTT

Brendan playfully salutes Berina, who responds in kind, and then heads off with Sahreb. They leave the lobby and head outside to the top of a parking garage. A Sabia craft is parked on the roof, awaiting them. Brendan can't tell whether it's ready to go or not due to their silent run features. A hatch opens on the side as the two of them approach. Brendan follows Sahreb inside. There, he sees several guards in heavy body armor carrying railers. The group stares for a second, then makes room for him. Brendan notices Mon regally sitting on a bench along the far side of the vessel.

"Please, sit next to me." She motions to her left. "I am glad you are safe, Brendan. I heard you persuaded a mob to disperse before it attacked the hotel."

He takes a seat. "Well, that is a bit of a stretch, actually. Mob is the wrong term; even demonstrators would be a poor choice of words. They were more very concerned citizens than anything else when I met them. I heard them out, talked to them, and persuaded them to pursue peaceful means to obtain their goals. While they are still anti-Sabia, I highly doubt they will threaten you with violence."

Mon nods thoughtfully. "This is reassuring to hear; we cannot afford to lose any of us. Tell me, Dear Brendan, those governors who pulled you aside—what were their concerns?"

"Well"—he scratches his head as he talks—"they were first concerned about how I was treated. Then, after I reassured them that I was just fine, they wanted to know if you genuinely valued relations with humans. So I told them about how we trained together, how you took my advice seriously, and how other Sabia appreciated good relations with the governors. No problems then on those points. However, they believe the Sabia have ulterior motives."

"Why would they think this?" Mon asks.

Brendan measures his words carefully, "There are—for instance—times when I ask for details on the Sabia, and I am told the answer is classified. The UIC itself states you do not share information. Many regular people believe that you are bribing the powerful for their compliance. Many suspect you are hiding something because you do not share information. Meanwhile, we Terrans—humans—have little ability to keep things secret from you. Mistrust breeds animosity, which breeds fear, which breeds violence."

"What do they think we wish to accomplish?" Mon snaps, surprising Brendan. "Do they desire more compensation than they already have asked for?"

This is a sensitive topic. Best for me to try and disarm her. Brendan chooses to purposefully use the Sabia's lexicon to help calm her down. "Terrans like knowing the full, honest intentions of their partners. It helps to ensure no surprises will be used against each other. Perhaps, Dear Mon, you could inform me more of the agenda. This way, I could assist you in crafting a message which answers the Terrans' concerns while protecting sensitives."

Mon yanks her head away. She looks around at nothing in particular before settling her gaze back on Brendan. He has seen this sort of person before. *She is a leader in some regards, but she needs much more*

refining if she wants to make the hard calls of command.
He feels a fatigue headache forming. He wants to help.
Or does he want to get more information to report back
with? *Crap, what am I doing? Which one is pride?
Dang, I am tired. Just power through this one part, then I
will be back on the ship and able to sleep.*

"How about this," he says, rubbing his eyes,
"when it comes to knowing how we can keep the Sabia
safe while messaging the truth, let us ask for the sake of
the exercise what your mother would—"

Mon yells and jumps off her seat, startling her
guards. "Do not! Do not!" She points down at Brendan.
"You have no right to invoke her, Auxiliary." The term is
said with acidity.

"My deepest apologies." He holds his hands in a
defensive posture while hunching over to demonstrate
submission. "I was merely thinking out loud to find ways
to help you. No offense was meant."

The fire in her eyes makes them too awful to look
at. "I understand the reason for your foolish error. Never
do that again."

"Understood, understood," he responds quickly.

She sighs deeply. "My mother . . . she means
everything to me. She is not a token for you to play with
like you played those militia who threatened us." She
pauses and lets silence reign in the craft. The guards have
not moved after her initial eruption. "Thank you," she
says, much calmer, "for handling the situation with those
terrorists."

401

0-2 today. My line of work does not take
sleeplessness lightly.

Mon asks, "What else did you learn from the
Terrans?"

*Okay, I can catch that one in my fatigue. Mon
doesn't view me as human, at least not entirely.* "I
learned that, in a scheme to control Terrans, the Sabia
are in league with rich bankers, lizard people from the
core of Terra, and pedophiles."

Mon does not pick up on the dry sarcasm; her
eyes are so wide that the whites dominate everything.

"I kid you not; a crazy man gave me a thousand
pages of thoughts about the subject. Unfortunately, that is
what some people think you are doing on Terra."

Brendan notices several guards looking at him
now.

"Lizard people from the core of Terra?" Mon
repeats.

"Yes, lizard people from the core of Terra,"
Brendan replies.

"You were a Terran once—are the leaders of this
planet just as stupid as their subjects? If so, we may have
to adjust our plans."

The air crackles and the sound are followed by a
male. "*Chavenhemodidipola.*"

Brendan thinks the voice is garbled until he looks
over and sees Mon's gasping mouth. One guard pounds
on the pilot's door while another swiftly touches several

buttons on the wall. Mon quickly looks at Brendan and then a guard, who quickly nods, then barks at the button-pressing guard to open the hatch. Next, Brendan notices with alarm that they are all staring at him.

The barking guard then points at him and says, "You will wait here until someone retrieves you, understood?" While technically a question, the guard was not asking.

The senior guard then escorts Mon off the craft. The door-pounding one takes the pilot out of the cockpit and walks him off into the hangar. The rest follow close behind. This leaves Brendan all alone in the shuttlecraft.

He waits, and waits, and waits. Not possessing a watch, he doesn't know the exact time, but its slow progress begins to weigh on him. *I must have been alone for at least an hour in here.* Air circulation from the open hatch helps keep him cool, but the size of the passenger section of the craft starts playing tricks on him. *The longer I wait, the smaller this place is going to get. I will just head back to my cabin.* After pausing a moment before committing to this course of action, Brendan finally gets up and hops out.

His landing startles two Sabia females dressed in baggy black clothing and hats that look like a combination of comically large chef's hats and something out of a renaissance fair. They both look at him with wide eyes. Brendan nods and smiles in an attempt to disarm any fright.

"Sir," one of the women shouts to someone out of view, "we have a problem here." Her voice is not hostile, but she undoubtedly is sounding an alarm.

A six-foot-five, well over two-hundred-fifty-pound male in similar clothing comes into view. The beast of a Sabia then struts up to Brendan. His appearance causes the two females' posture to become more erect. *They're getting into a dominant stance. This is not good.*

The male says in an antagonistic tone, "Were you not told to stay put, Terran?"

This is really not good. "Hello!" Brendan tries to play friendly. "I assumed they must have forgotten about me because no one came. Not a problem, though; I will just head back to my cabin. No fuss, no muss." He forces a smile.

"There is a problem because I say there is a problem." The large man's palm pushes Brendan back five feet. "Want to know what we will do about this problem, Terran?"

As the Sabia speaks, Brendan notices the two females setting up flanking positions at his four and eight o'clock. *The three of them are going to bum rush me!* Brendan tries to position himself to have at least one of the females in his vision along with the male, but they keep moving with him. *This is getting really bad.* A crowd is forming; presumably, Brendan assumes, to watch the beatdown that is about to happen.

Brendan's voice betrays his nervousness. "Look now, no need for any problems. I imagine you were not told to attack me if I left this craft without an escort. No need for you to get in trouble because you decided to make a problem much larger than it had to be."

The male instantaneously relaxes and backs up as if he has received a silent cue. Fearing the worst, Brendan looks behind him and sees both females backing down. When he looks forward, he sees a six-foot man in his sixties, with a receding hairline and the same black clothing as the rest. The man merely looks at the crowd, resulting in all the Sabia returning to their business.

"You were not supposed to leave the vessel until someone retrieves you," the man says. His voice carries a heavy gravitas.

"Yes, sir." Brendan figures it's time to play up his Sabia auxiliary officerness. "I was concerned I had been forgotten. I was hoping just to go back to my cabin."

"And what would you do there, Brendan Murphy?"

The use of the surname surprises Brendan. *I am not a Sabia to this person either.* "I would go back, shower, and find time to write my report about my observations of the conference I just came from."

Tapping his foot, the elder Sabia looks at Brendan. There is no other movement. It's not a stoic act, though Brendan cannot figure out what it is. Brendan prepares for the worst. He decides not to fight off the attackers. *Best to play up being a victim when someone investigates. Man, how I wish I had Kimya here.*

The elder breaks his silence. "Go now. Down the hall, you will encounter a hallway intersection. Take a right and keep going to a checkpoint. The guards there will escort you the rest of the way."

"Thank you," Brendan replies.

The male does not respond. Brendan slowly backs up, then turns around and leaves at a quick pace. He doesn't know if the Sabia watch him go. On the other side of the exit are three black-clad guards. Brendan can feel their stares drill into him. The rest of the walk to the checkpoint is silent as the halls are empty. Upon arrival, the guards are more dispassionate than friendly. *At least they are not about to attack me.* A female states she will take him to his cabin. Oddly, she instructs him not to talk to her as they walk.

PATRICK ABBOTT

Interlude – Zalta: A Friend in Need

Zalta hums a tune to herself as she walks the halls. Rules prevent her from singing in her language, and she must be careful when a Terran or even Brendan is around, but in the Terran-free section, she is free to express herself more. *Pity we cannot share more with Brendan. He would love our songs.* Her mind wanders as she continues back from services. *Perhaps I should go to the party tonight with Nema and Nemahaz. There will be so many new people there. I would love to hear how things are back home!* She starts to whisper some lyrics under her breath. Her joy cannot be suppressed.

However, when she sees Brendan being escorted by a familiar Wing Unit guard, her joy changes to worry. It seems to Zalta that Enoshia is taking Brendan as if he were under arrest. She steps in Enoshia's way, which causes the little convoy to halt.

"Dear 'Nos, where are you taking Dear Brendan?"

"To his cabin. He was found alone in the DF hangar and unauthorized at that."

Zalta makes a fist with her right hand, then covers it with her flat left hand. Enoshia acknowledges the request for a moment by nodding toward Brendan. The medic approaches him.

"Dear Brendan, I will get Berina and Esfirs so they may straighten all this out with the Defense Force. Is there any message you want me to relay?"

"Yeah," he says with his funny, accented voice, "tell Berina she was right: danger finds me."

PATRICK ABBOTT

Interlude – The Waitress: A Bloody Night

The country band continues to sing off-key. Even worse are those who try to sing along. The waitress continues to make her rounds despite the awful music. *At least they don't notice.* Finally, she approaches a table where two men and a woman are sitting. *They seem to be a happy bunch.* As she draws near, she sees them hurriedly passing notes on napkins to each other.

"Anything to drink while you look at the menus?" the waitress asks.

"Oh!" the thinner male exclaims. All three look as if a surprise test has been dropped on them. "We will take three sodas, please."

"Sure thing, hon; what type do you want?"

The man swallows hard. "The regular soda, please. Three, please."

"The regular, of course. Tell me, hon, where you all from? I haven't seen you around this neck of the woods before."

The woman now speaks up. "My husband and I are from Louisiana." She gestures toward the thinner man. "He and his brother are going to get a job in the lumber industry here. We hear there is plenty of that type of work here."

"Welcome to Harney, Tennessee! Plenty of lumber to go around. We're a mountain away from the mills in North Carolina, but you landed on the good side, as we say. Where in Louisiana are you from?"

"A small town outside of New Orleans," the woman responds rapidly.

The waitress gasps. "My sister lives outside of New Orleans! What town y'all from?"

"Phoenix. It is a small town. Named after the bird in the fire." The woman's eyes are blank as she speaks.

Straight from memory, the waitress thinks. "Bless me and the heavens! That's where my sister lives! What street did y'all live on? Maybe you were right next to the big supercenter like her!"

There is a brief pause, after which the woman says, "Oh, Second Street. Most common street in America they say, do they not?"

"Ah, I think that may be on the other end of town. But, of course, I've never been on no Second Street. Oh well. Fantasia is her name."

They don't reply.

"I'll be right back with your drinks."

The waitress smiles and walks away. In the mirror over the bar, she sees the three of them watching her. Making her way into the kitchen, the waitress keeps a smile. She opens the back door to find several men in civilian clothes waiting for her outside.

Walking up to a man with a tractor hat on, she says, "They claim Phoenix, Louisiana, on Second Street. One of the males called soft drinks 'soda.'"

A bearded man types away on his cell phone. "There is a Phoenix in Louisiana, but there is no Second Street. I think we can call this confirmation of everything we have."

"Yep," says the tractor hat man, clearly the leader of the group. He addresses the rest of the men. "Make the little ETs bleed, but remember, those aliens don't talk if they are dead."

Four men enter through the back door while the waitress and group leader walks around the tavern's entrance. The loud music continues to play, drowning out almost everything. The band is doing a cover of a song that deserves better. Approaching the front door, they hear shots and screams. Then more shots are fired, and more screams can be heard as the band stops.

Idiots! How could they bungle this up!

The woman from the table runs through the door and down the street. Within a split second, the tractor hat man pulls out his pistol and takes steady aim. A single shot pierces the now silent night. Screaming, the woman tumbles to the ground. She tries to push herself up twice, but her kneecap has shattered from the .50 caliber bullet.

FALLEN

The fake waitress watches her companion slowly walk up to the screaming female creature. His pistol is leveled straight at its head. He towers above the writhing alien, holding its hands up while pleading for mercy. The waitress looks on as the man gives the Sabia spy a heavy blow straight to the face with the back of the pistol.

PATRICK ABBOTT

Thirty-Four – A Prophet from on High

The nights when his thoughts run rampant are always the worst for Brendan. Brendan lies there on his bed as the night lighting dimly illuminates the room. Turning onto his side fails to make him more comfortable. *No running from the memories now.*

Zalta had brought Berina as she promised, but Esfirs was nowhere to be seen. When he repeatedly pressed them about her, Berina demonstrated an incredible ability to redirect the conversation without seeming unnatural. However, this did help Brendan, as she was able to explain away the "miscommunication" and even get a black-clad Sabia to come to his room and apologize for the "misunderstandings." Truth be told, Brendan wanted company more than anything else, which Berina supplied in spades. She described her time in Montana in detail, including a museum of "old bones" she visited, the Air and Space Force personnel she teased, and even a couple of Sabia she seemingly had a romantic interest in. After recounting the trip, she even went on to organize a "Sabia card game" at Brendan's with Gul, Nema, and Zalta.

Esfirs never came. He closes his migraine-strained eyes, hoping he can sleep. It fails. The dreaded question comes: *What did I do wrong this time? Everything was going so well. She looked stunningly beautiful, wanted me to go outside to be alone with her, and then things got weird. Yeah, I got upset at first explaining things to her, but then I calmed down and gave her the benefit of the doubt. Instead of doing the same, she walks out on me and won't even give me the time of day.*

Tossing back and forth fails to get the thoughts out of his mind. Brendan ponders using his Sabia communication device to contact Esfirs, yet he feels pinned in place. *My emotions got me where I am now; why can't I beat them and message her? Even a text back would mean the world.* The more he thinks about it, the more he acknowledges the truth. *There is no cure for my brokenness. Instead, I have to heal, one day at a time.*

His slow drift to sleep is stopped by something primordial in his soul, a sense of dread reaching out to him from beyond time and space. He becomes fully awake and alert, adrenaline pumping through every vein. Warmth, the kind only felt during combat, floods him as his heart races faster. His body and soul communicate while his rational mind is left out. Suddenly, apprehension hits him. With fear and trepidation, he reaches down to pull out the handheld UIC device. Pressing the screen, a message appears.

Prophet: And behold, I have a message from on high.

Brendan exhales deeply as he reads the username. Prophet was the nom de guerre of an incredibly secretive but lifesaving colleague. Throughout the Middle East, this individual operated sources and sub-sources. Accordingly, he was likely to know everything in his area of operations, including rumors, phone calls, emails, and encrypted chats. So many times, Prophet notified Brendan about various upcoming ambushes or bad guys attempting to elude capture. Brendan even went so far as to put Prophet in for an award, describing the man as a "true war hero."

Unfortunately, the pleasant memories fall away when Brendan opens the second message.

Prophet: Your Sabia friend is in trouble.

A video attachment begins playing. The sight is horrifying. The footage reveals two dead bodies on the floor inside a building, then the camera pans to a woman with her knee blown away, screaming and crying out in pain. Her face has been beaten. A Southern voice mocks her, asking if she is in pain. The video pans out, revealing a man with a face mask and an American flag ballcap. "Brothers and sisters of America," he exclaims, "we have ourselves an assassin." He then walks over and steps on the woman's mutilated knee. She screams some words Brendan doesn't understand. Once again, the man is shown on the screen, chuckling to himself. The video ends.

Another message pops up on the screen.

Prophet: For one hundred thousand dollars, I can get an unwitting source to interview her. Two hundred thousand will get you the promised interview plus three days' safety.

Brendan swears under his breath. Prisoner-of-war and hostage situations have a reputation for quickly

415

getting ugly. If this escalates, all his work and more could be lost. He imagines the possibility of raids, reprisals, and more violence boiling over into open warfare. *There goes any chance of getting rest tonight.* "Bastards don't get rest." The words of his ROTC sergeant echo from the past. Thinking quickly, he grabs his Sabia communication device and dials Loft. No response. He swears again and dials Leleh. Nothing. Brendan swears even louder. *What about Berina? She is well connected.*

Her voice is groggy when she answers. "Brendan . . . why are you calling me?"

In one breath, he rattles off, "I got a message just now from a friend who has what looks like a militia torture film claiming to show two dead Sabia and one screaming in pain."

"Gashi!" Berina yells. Brendan can hear her get out of bed. "Just stay there!" There is then a beep, and the call ends.

Brendan quickly changes from his T-shirt and shorts to a collared shirt and slacks. Before he can put on socks, the door opens, and a very haggard Kimya enters the room along with two guards.

"Show me the video now," she demands.

He grabs the UIC device and presses play.

"Come with me, please."

Kimya wraps her arm around his back, putting him into a tight grapple. She hurriedly moves him down the corridors. Meanwhile, Brendan can hear motion up ahead. They pass the checkpoint into the more restricted part of the ship. At this point, Kimya begins to jog and then breaks into a run, still grasping Brendan tightly. He can barely keep up.

This is a part of the ship that's new to him. At an intersection of hallways, they run into Berina wearing an "I love Montana" T-shirt and matching shorts. Berina reaches out and pulls on Brendan's collar, causing him to choke. His cry of pain stops Kimya's forward momentum.

"Show me the video," Berina orders Brendan.

"We have to take him to command, Pilot," Kimya snaps.

"Now is not the time to get territorial, Kimya. Let me see the video! You know why I need to see it."

Kimya nods and tells Brendan to show it to her. Berina shakes her head and holds her hand over her mouth while watching the video. The moment the footage stops, she snatches the device out of Brendan's hand and grabs his wrist. Berina then bolts down the hall with Brendan in tow while Kimya cries foul. *Back to this again.*

"Just be quiet and let me do all the talking!" Berina yells without looking at Brendan.

They run up to a door that opens just as they are about to smack right into it. Inside, Brendan sees screens everywhere. More importantly, there is an assortment of Sabia. Some are wearing gray, others white, and a few black. Zand is the center of attention. Surprisingly to

Brendan, Mon is standing off to the side as a mere observer.

Berina stands to attention though no one is immediately looking at her. "*Dap ell me an e da Brendan!*"

Those in the room gasp and freeze in place. *Those syllables mean something. Native Sabia language that I was not meant to hear?*

Brendan decides now is the time to take the spotlight off his friend, who has helped him so many times before. "I have the video in case anyone wants to see it."

The room focuses on him as he holds out the small screen. No one moves or says anything while it plays. Silence hangs in the air after it finishes. Finally, a hoarse-voiced female council member commands the activation of "all security and defense forces." A small group moves at the command, but most remain still.

"I will burn them all. Where did this happen?" Zand's voice cuts Brendan to his core.

A gray-clad officer replies, "Palvah, Bager, and Nassri were operating in the United States of America state of Tennessee."

"Burn them all!" Zand repeats as she slams her left fist into her right palm.

"Um," Brendan interjects, "the person who provided me with this video says he can get someone to the woman and ensure her safety for three days." He hopes to be a helpful and calming influence in this situation.

"Is your source one of these murderers?" Zand drills her eyes into him. Her voice burns with rage, like a hot iron pulled from a forge.

Brendan holds up his hands, trying to calm her down. "Almost certainly not—"

She interrupts him. "You do not know. You could even be involved in this. Gaining our trust to betray us!"

"Whoa, whoa, whoa." Brendan waves his hands, trying to diffuse the situation. "I am speaking as intelligence officers do. 'Almost certainly' means the likelihood of him not being involved is extremely high, practically guaranteed. I base this assessment on knowing this person, his ideology, the language of his messages, and his past work experience. He is a good person, and I vouch on my honor this is something he would not do."

Zand looks intensely at him. Brendan feels a painful headache surge out of nowhere. *She is trying to form a Bond.* "Who is the source?" she demands.

"We know him as Prophet. That was his call sign when we were deployed together. His actions have saved hundreds of lives, both American and non-American. As a former intelligence officer, he has connections everywhere, including the militia movement."

"Is he part of the militia movement like your other friends?" Zand sneers as she speaks.

"I do not know," Brendan answers truthfully.

"What is his name?"

Brendan knows that to reveal this to a furious Sabia would be a risk to Prophet. "As an intelligence officer, I have to protect my sources. He is almost certainly risking his life reaching out to us. I guarantee you he can be trusted. Prophet says if we get one hundred thousand dollars, Prophet can buy us some time and an interview. And for the record, I would trust him with my own life."

Zand breathes hard through her nose. "And so you shall. You will assist in bringing Palvah home alive. When you fail, you will pay with your own life."

That was not a vote of confidence.

Unfortunately, at that very moment, Brendan notices Dena staring him down. No Bond is attempted, but he has no doubt she enjoyed hearing the leader's words. A chill runs down his spine.

I will not let that be the last word on this situation. "I accept that responsibility. Let me reach out to Prophet. If we brainstorm questions, we can get some intelligence from him about Palveh's situation."

"Do it," Zand commands. She turns her back to Brendan. Several council members gather around her and whisper.

Brendan whips out his UIC communicator and starts typing. He stops when he notices Berina is still standing at attention, facing straight ahead. Sweat is pouring out of her face. He tries to get her attention, but she ignores him. Trying again, she responds with a quick *ssh.* To Brendan, it looks like Berina expects her turn to be in trouble is still to come.

He goes back to typing. "Hey," he says to no one in particular, "what sort of questions do you want the source to ask?"

Leleh approaches Brendan and stands on his right, opposite Berina. She ignores the pilot while addressing him. "Confirm her name, her condition, list what they have done to her, her location, and circumstance of capture."

"Got it. I will also tell Prophet we will pay the fees. Unless you all have a bunch of cash lying around, now would be a good time to get together with the ambassador."

Leleh nods and runs off. Dena's cocky stride distracts his typing as she stops directly in front of Berina.

"Think language rules do not apply to you, embed?" She snarls her words.

Brendan interjects, "We do not have time for stupid rules. I have heard your language before and probably will again. I cannot make hide nor hair of it, so whatever you are trying to hide from me is perfectly safe."

"I am not addressing you, Auxiliary," Dena barks.

"Good to know. In the meantime, as the one person who is trying to do something productive to save the life of a colleague in danger, please do not distract me by chewing out someone who merely panicked. If it is a comfort, I can tell you no world leader thinks

American English is your native language, so Berina did not spill any secrets."

Dena gets her face within inches of Brendan's. Before she can say anything, a younger male Sabia standing toward the back of the room, asks loudly, "What device is the auxiliary officer typing on?"

Crap. Not now. "Oh, this? It is a quantum communicator. Had it for a while now."

"That is not something we would issue to you," a back-clad female says.

"Yeah, I know." He looks up to offer a teenage shrug that he hopes comes off as casual. "It is American government property." He goes back to typing.

"Who have you been contacting with that? What have you been reporting?" The female in black demands.

Brendan rolls his eyes, trying to play down the situation. "Here, take a look at the stupid thing. You will see the messages between Prophet and me, failed attempts to reach out to my mother, and my contacting the religious cleric in Montana. Oh, and a few messages to the UIC about my mental health. Know that every second you look at it is a second we do not get help to Palvah." *Why did I save those UIC messages?*

Brendan flings it to the female, who catches it with cat-like reflexes.

"He has been spying on us!" Dena exclaims. She seizes the device from the black-clad woman.

PATRICK ABBOTT

"Give it to me," Leleh commands. "We will analyze this. But Brendan, answer me now. Is it true?"

"I am not a spy," Brendan irately responds. The words don't quite feel right. He notices Berina giving him a side-eye. He looks at her, and their eyes lock. *Betrayal.* Instantly his mind screams the word. His father, Heather, and now him. A searing pain forms in his gut. Every bit of him wants to vomit. His sweat pours, and his heart pounds. Next, his vision contracts, and everything starts to go gray. Making it worse, feeling Berina's presence makes his skin crawl. He wants to run far away from her.

In an attempt to stand up for himself, he declares, "I have been reporting observations as any liaison would. So, I am not betraying trust." Unfortunately, all Brendan can think about when he hears his own words is his father's confession.

"Spy!" Dena proclaims.

"We can handle this later! We need to save our own right now," Zand exclaims. "Someone give him one of our communicators. Allow him to copy any contacts he needs. Then"—she stares with wrath at Brendan—"tell your own spy what we need to know."

Brendan notices Berina eyeing him again. "Can Berina be placed at some order other than attention? It is very distracting," he says.

Zand speaks. "Pilot, return to your quarters; we will handle your violation later."

Berina turns around and marches out of the room. For a brief second, she intensely locks eyes with Brendan. Heartburn forms and drains down into his stomach like searing acid. The words "I am not a spy" are eating away at him. He wants to collapse from queasiness. *I am what I hate, and it has cost me a friend.* To distract himself from the hurt, he focuses on finishing the text and hits send. Yet, this does nothing to alleviate his emotional pain as his chest tightens and throat dries.

A flash on the screen diverts his attention. "We have a reply," he exclaims. He relays the message to the Sabia. "Prophet has the unwitting source already on his way—that is good. Further, Prophet will get us the video with Palvah answering our questions as soon as possible. Additionally, arrangements are being made to move the Sabia to a safe place for now. I will tell Prophet to contact me on the new device."

"Brendan, what is your agenda in this?"

Zand is calling him out, and he knows it. His right leg is poised to start running away. Sheer willpower prevents him from giving in. Instead, looking directly at Zand, he bares all. "At this point, I just want to save a life."

"And what about the next point?"

"I do not know," Brendan says after a pause.

Again, a headache forms as she locks eyes with him. It's as if his body is burning up from the inside out. He mentally lies down, not wanting to hide anything anymore, and waits for a flood to sweep him away. His tiredness, combined with his own sense of betrayal, drains him. The doubts in his head are so loud they are practically audible; they should be easy for her to pick up as well.

"Remember," she says, "your fate is connected to hers."

He nods. Through the Bond, he senses a command to leave and heads out of the room. A guard escorts him to a lounge with pillows arranged in circles of various sizes. When the guard leaves, Brendan bends over and regurgitates. The discomfort of the heartburn slowly leaves his body.

The threat against his life is of little concern to him. He is as hollow now as he was when he rescued the Sabia in the metro.

Thirty-Five – The Video

Defeated. Brendan is defeated. It has taken him some time to figure it out in this empty room, but finally, he can put a word on it. Father Baldwin warned him about being broken. *He told me I had friends who wanted to help me, but I would push them away. And I have.*

Worst of all, he has become the very thing he hated. His life has been one of constant betrayal, from his birth to Heather, to the peace negotiator who was really a suicide bomber, his fellow officers becoming militia members—the list goes on. And now, he has finally completed the cycle. *Berina's look was that of someone who had been betrayed. I betrayed her.* Ultimately, looking back on his life, Brendan feels the bad he has done outweighs any previous good deeds. *The Sabia will never trust another human because of me.*

The Sabia communication device goes off, taking him out of his mind games. Looking down, he sees Prophet has followed the instructions and sent a message to the new number.

> Prophet: County jail. Halder TN. In custody of local law enforcement. All cops are local militia or Sons of Shepherd. Nearby presence is your boy Meade's Patriot Assembly.

PATRICK ABBOTT

A second message follows, which includes an embedded video. Muffled sounds are briefly heard over a black screen. Then, the image of smiling men standing around a jail cell. It looks like they have been laughing right before the recording. Shifting again, the camera brings Palvah on screen. She is crouched in fear in the corner of the cell. She has additional bruising, and her lip is swollen. Brendan recalls videos Iraqi insurgents would share amongst themselves, mocking their captured victims. The footage before him drags Brendan back to those dark times. The day has turned into hell for him.

"Hello there," says a male voice off-camera, "now we're going to ask you a few questions so we can get to know you, okay?" His voice is disarmingly kind. Palvah nods in fear. She is trying to avoid something, possibly the eyes of the person interviewing her. "What's your name?"

"M-m-my, my, my naaaaa-name is Palvah—Palvah." The stutters make her sound pathetically weak and scared. Her movements are odd, and she constantly raps her knuckles on her forehead while trying to hide her face.

"And what is your mental and physical state right now?

She briefly looks at the camera but then darts her head away, mumbling something under her breath.

With a firmer voice, the man says, "Tell us what happened to you."

"I-I . . . huuurt myself. I am fine beeeeecause you helped me. I hurt my—myself when I tried to kill people here."

"What officials did you try to kill?"

She begins to whimper. "All of them."

"All of them?" The man sounds genuinely surprised.

"Yyyyyyyyyeeeees. All of them," Palvah replies.

"Well, which ones?" The man sounds flustered. "Local government? Militias? The ice cream man union?"

"All of them! All of them! All of them! All of them!" She keeps yelling, repeating herself until another man yells for her to shut up. This causes Palvah to cry.

"Tell you what, I have a picture of the Prime Minister of America with me"—he pulls out a photo from his wallet of a young girl—"were you sent to kill her?" He walks into frame and shows Palvah the photograph.

She looks fearfully at him. "Yes, her, too," she whispers.

"Her too?" he pushes.

"Especially her." Palvah covers her face as she speaks.

"Who ordered you to kill the targets?"

She whispers something. The interviewer tells Palvah to speak up.

"Zand," she says.

PATRICK ABBOTT

"Really? Who is Zand?"

"She is . . . our commander. She has been sent here to kill all Terrans. I am here to do that mission." Palvah breaks down crying. Quickly, she becomes hysterical, and two men enter the cell to restrain her. They struggle to the point that other men come in to assist.

The camera is lowered, and motion can be seen. The scene becomes a hallway. The man holds the recording device to his mouth and says, "That woman is a beaten dog. I'm pretty sure I could get her to confess to being the Ice Queen of Mars if I tried. I'll hang around the area if you need anything more. By the way, this place is crawling with religious nuts, so unless you want her to have a shotgun to the face, I would recommend against using SOF. These freaks here want her dead. The money wired will last us a day or two, but three, man, I ain't lying; I don't think they will wait that long." The footage ends.

Brendan wipes his hands over his face. *Crap.* He walks over, opens the door, and tells a guard in the hallway to inform Zand that Prophet sent the video. The guard instructs Brendan to wait. As the guard disappears out of view, Brendan silently prays. *God, I am defeated, broken, and done. I accept that. But please don't let this woman die. Please, God.* He ends the prayer as the guard reappears and instructs him to reenter the command room.

The room is now filled with even more Sabia. The atmosphere is one of chaos as they run around doing individual tasks. A gaggle surrounds Zand.

Loft addresses her. "Varag claims he is very concerned about the situation and further states his country's wishes to know why the three victims were not known to them."

Zand slams her fist into her open right hand. "Do these Terrans not care about the crime against us? We shall make them care!"

She notices Brendan. Storming up to him, she demands to see the video. Zand's crowd jockeys for position against each other for the best view. Everyone remains silent as they watch Palvah's interrogation. The head Sabia's face flushes red as it plays.

"Tell Varag that if Palvah is not released to us, along with the bodies of the other two, in the next hour, we will punish all those we suspect are responsible. Auxiliary Officer, you are dismissed. Guard, see him to his cabin."

"If I may," Brendan says, holding up his hand, "I would like to offer a solution. We know where she is. If we could find a place nearby, we could set up a negotiation post."

Zand's voice is full of disgust. "I suppose you would keep your government abreast of our plans. Perhaps even your militia friends who are responsible for this crime?"

"Look, things got out of control. I understand why you are upset with me. You see me as a spy, and I, too, am upset at myself for not clearing my other communications with you. It would not surprise me if I end up in whatever jail system you have or worse. But please let me help get Palvah out of this situation. All I ever wanted was to help people. I screwed things up; I get that, but please let me help her."

Zand studies him from head to toe. "Fool, you are dismissed."

She starts to turn, but Brendan places his hand on her shoulder, resulting in gasps from everyone watching. "Please, you said my fate was tied to hers. Let me save her. Kill me afterward if you must. That is fair. But let me save her."

Mon steps up to stand next to Zand. "Perhaps," Mon begins, "he can be of use. Negotiating with the locals would allow us to prepare options involving their government and our Defense Force. Fortunately for us, the auxiliary officer has nowhere else to go. His own government views him as an enemy while the militia would turn on him if we revealed his hybrid status." She turns toward him. "You will stay loyal to me, yes, Brendan?"

Brendan lays all his cards down. "I will follow your orders. However, it would be beneficial if I could coordinate with the Patriot Assembly. As a sign of my intentions, you will have veto rights over everything I message."

"Very well," Zand says. "Mon, you will lead the delegation."

Mon nods. "Thank you." She turns toward Brendan. "What do you need to do?"

"First, we need to find nearby locations where we could set up camp. Then I need to reach out to the Patriot Assembly to see where they have influence. If we can find a place near where they run shop, we can be safe from the Sons of the Shepherd and maybe even work with them to ensure Palvah's safety."

"Very well, you may proceed."

"Also, we should work on a negotiation strategy. I imagine whoever we talk to is going to want to know why those Sabia were deep in militia territory."

"That information is absolutely forbidden to you," Zand interjects.

Interlude – Kimya: Preparation

Water, check. Railer deployment, check. Ammunition supply, check. Medical kit, check. Everything is there. Kimya turns off her HUD. Nearby, several guards wait for their briefing. Gastab walks to their front, and naturally, they circle him.

"Alright, listen up," Gastab starts, "we are going to a village called Red Hawk. It is very near the location where Palvah is being held. Our auxiliary officer professes the paramilitaries are different there, so they will keep out hostile elements. Additionally, he claims it is in a different state called North Carolina. I suspect this means the Terrans there are rivals. Hopefully, this means the locals in Red Hawk will help us."

"Do we believe him?" a guard asks.

"Zand has linked his and Palvah's lives together. Good enough reason for me to believe him," Gastab says.

Kimya jumps into the conversation. "He has been involved in multiple missions with us before. So he has a good record."

"Back to the subject," Gastab interjects. "There is a club for veterans in the village. This will be our headquarters. The auxiliary officer will be our liaison to the local officials and friendly paramilitaries. Mon will be head of mission. I will be second-in-command. Mazier, you will oversee security for Mon. Kimya, you have the auxiliary officer. Any questions? Good. Make sure you are all geared up and wearing your body armor. We will take two flights down to the surface. Abin and Minou will be the pilots."

This is excellent—Mon, Brendan, Gastab, Mazier, and no Defense Forces or Berina. And Terran veterans! Maybe I can meet some. They would love to hear and share stories. No one to mock me or call me names. Those Terrans will probably understand the complex decisions war requires one to make. They will also understand the purpose of conflict. Unlike Berina, flying around while we have to get our hands dirty. She started it—

Kimya notices Brendan walk into the hangar. His face is disheveled, his eyes bloodshot, and his stubble needs shaving. Examining him further, she can see his skin is as pale as the light khaki tactical wear he has on. She approaches slowly. He doesn't notice her, and she manages to put her hand on his back without any response. Brendan stirs briefly but then just looks down at the floor.

"Brendan, it will be alright. I will ensure your safety. You can get Palvah out. We would not really harm you if something went wrong, anyways." He does not move. "Brendan? Brendan? Do you need medical assistance?"

PATRICK ABBOTT

He finally snaps out of his trance. Then, with a slight tremor in his head, he looks at her. "I am scared, Kimya. I am scared."

Kimya can only stare back. She looks upon him as a man whose soul has been utterly crushed.

His whole body begins to shake. Kimya puts her arm on his shoulder. Then, in unison, they put their heads together.

Thirty-Six – Red Hawk

Brendan keeps praying. *Please, God, let no one die today. Let everyone come home. May I be an offering if it secures peace and everyone else's safety. Please, God.* No one bothers him as he slides down against the wall of the hanger. He feels all alone.

"Brendan!" a familiar voice cries. Zalta runs up to him in a lightly armored kit. "Guess who volunteered to be part of the first wave with you? However, do not get sick because it is just me. I am joking; I would be able to stabilize you. I know how because I did it before!"

Zalta is her usual, cheery self. Not an ounce of worry is visible on her countenance—the complete opposite of Brendan. Her joyful expression only changes slightly when she notices his distress. She puts her hands on his neck and moves her thumbs up and down his throat. Brendan's eyes lock with hers, forming a Bond. The shared sensation is one of compassion. He doesn't notice her putting a device on his skin. However, he registers her looking down to confirm that the gadget adhered to him.

"You need to get the cancerous mini-tumors taken care of, but"—she studies the screen—"they are not urgent. What is concerning are your stress levels." She begins to massage his shoulders and neck while keeping her eyes on the screen. "Brendan, I am going to give you some medicine to help calm you down."

Before he can object, Zalta presses the screen on the gadget. A tremendous feeling of cold flashes through his body before instantaneously dissolving. Sighing, he feels a thousand times more relieved.

She looks back into his eyes and says, "This will help, but watch yourself in a few hours. Your body may try to swing the pendulum the other way too hard, too fast. Let me know if you become stressed."

"Thanks," he manages.

Brendan wipes the sweat off his face. His breath is more controlled, and his heart no longer pounds in his chest. Enjoying a restored normalcy, Brendan listens as Zalta engages in small talk. For a moment, she has managed to get Brendan's mind off his guilty conscience.

Someone calls out, and they both look up to see Mon enter the room. She is wearing human professional clothing. To Brendan, she looks more like a bank manager than the head of an alien delegation sent to free a prisoner.

Walking up to them, Mon nods and addresses Brendan. "Dear Brendan, have you been able to coordinate with the authorities on the ground?"

"Yes, ma'am." He is surprised at how carefree his voice sounds. "The local sheriff will meet us when we land. He has secured the veterans' hall. Additionally, the federal government has promised us support when we ask for it but will stay away until we summon them."

"And do we have your loyalty on this one?"

"Unconditionally."

She nods. "Is there anything you need from me before we launch the mission?"

"Potentially." His nerves begin to rise. "The sheriff has contacted the law enforcement in league with the captors. He can set up a meeting with them. Is this okay with you?"

"By all means, that is what we hoped to do. Thank you for seeking my approval before initiating anything that could lead to direct contact."

"Well, this leads to what we are going to need." Mon lifts her eyebrows questioningly. "They are going to ask what the Sabia were doing along the Tennessee-North Carolina' border and about the Sabia's presence on Earth. If you tell me what they were doing there, I can help craft something truthful that they will buy while still protecting more sensitive parts of the mission."

Mon holds up her hand. "Zand and I have already discussed the matter. As a result, we have a strategy I have been entrusted with implementing."

"That is great. What are we going to say?"

"I will say it." Her sentence is definitive and conversation-ending.

"Okay then," Brendan offers. Mon nods as if it is an acceptance of the strategy; however, Brendan harbors his doubts. "Do you mind if I reach out to my US government counterparts to ensure their ability to assist us is online?" She nods again.

PATRICK ABBOTT

Brendan reaches down into his pocket and grabs the Sabia communication device. There is a message waiting for him.

> Jack: Dog, I'm going to be your POC in Washington, but can get you the help to get your Sabia girl out of a jam. But you need to work with us, bro. It's like you've been ghosting us.

He writes a message back.

> Brendan: Great hearing from ya, bro. Comms are not secure. Everything now through Sabia approval to ensure I am on up and up. Send support to Red Hawk veterans hall. I am going to need the bags. Also, Prophet is going to need to be paid. I will send the details as I get them. He tipped me off. I will play ball with you all. Please help me out. Responsibility for the first intergalactic war does not look good on a promotion packet!

Hitting send feels therapeutic for Brendan. Maybe it's being back in the saddle, or perhaps it's whatever Zalta gave him, but he feels terrific and focused.

Zalta taps his shoulder. Looking over, he sees her motioning to one of the two craft. "It is go time. Are you ready?"

"Whatever you gave me seems to have done the trick. Now or never, eh? Let's roll."

"I thought you stopped the horrible habit of contractions."

"It is a saying that has special meaning to us who served in the War on Terror. The great man who said it saved hundreds of lives with one action."

"Wow! How did he do that?"

"By ensuring a plane full of terrorists crashed with him on board."

Zalta's eyes widen, and she gives off a loud gasp. Seeing her surprise, Brendan reflects upon how 9/11 forever changed him and the country. It turned a Kansan computer geek into a warrior. A warrior who was then hollowed out by the wages of war and betrayals. *What would that Kansan boy think about the man I have become? He would be horrified.* The thought saddens Brendan, but he knows it's true. That kid was more tied to his family, faithful, and not prideful. Yet, in the darkness, there is a whisper of hope in his mind. His time with Father Baldwin created a slow awakening in him. *Maybe these pains are just the shipping righting itself.* Instead of healing his wounded pride, he wants to save Palvah for Palvah's sake. *And Esfirs'.*

Brendan follows Zalta boarding the shuttlecraft. *God, let us rescue Palvah. Amen.* He takes a cushion to view the others perform their pre-mission rituals. Watching everyone else, the desire to pray grows in him. *F— it. God, I give it all to you. I screwed up. There, I said it. Lead me. Where? Wherever you want. But please allow us to rescue Palvah. And let me make amends to Esfirs.* At that moment, Brendan lets out the most prolonged yawn of his life. When he is done, everything seems new to him. Like after the confession, things appear brighter, lighter, and more pleasant.

PATRICK ABBOTT

Previously, his mental breakthroughs have been minor and short-lived, but this is more real, more tangible to him.

Eager to share his emotions, he is disappointed that everyone is engrossed in their affairs. The ride is dead silent. It reminds him of why he enjoyed bantering with Berina on previous flights. Remembering her allows negative thoughts to creep back into his mind. Brendan knows she advocated for him to get greater access and acceptance amongst the Sabia. *And now I have betrayed her.* He tries to shake it off. It only gets worse when he imagines what Berina is telling Esfirs. There is a rebellion in his mind that fights against the grace from his prayer.

He looks up to see how the others are doing. Zalta's eyes are closed as she mouths words silently to herself, Kimya looks down at the floor, Mon has a thousand-mile stare, and the other guards passively wait on their cushions. Shifting in his "deployment clothes," he feels like some private military contractor without any sort of weaponry. Brendan smiles as he remembers the times Afghans said he was "CIA" or a "commando" because he dressed differently than the standard military. *Simpler times.*

The air crackles. Looking up, Brendan hears the male pilot's voice declare the craft has landed. A guard gets up and opens the door. Then, he and two other guards exit, followed by Mon and a few more guards. Brendan, Kimya, and Zalta are the last off.

Brendan sees a posse of brown-clad police officers across the parking lot where the shuttlecraft landed. He walks up to Mon as she takes in the situation.

"Do your thing, Brendan," she instructs him.

He nods and walks toward the man with the biggest hat. Assuming he is the sheriff, Brendan holds out his hand for a handshake. It is met, the pleasant American greeting ritual successful.

"Sheriff? Brendan Sean Murphy, Unified Intelligence Command. I want to personally thank you for working with us to secure the building."

The sheriff replies with a twangy southern accent, "Sheriff Jim Axe. Welcome to Davis County. Those alien friends of yours kicked up a hornet's nest. One of my boys"—he motions behind him to the general area where the deputies are—"saw the bodies. Ain't pretty."

Brendan makes a grunt of disapproval. "Things will get worse if we do not manage the situation, sheriff. I am here to make sure an intergalactic war does not start today. Let me know if there are any developments on the ground, especially concerning the prisoner, the two bodies, or interlopers showing up.

"In the meantime, I will have the Sabia set up shop in the veterans' hall. They will shack up in one room and have offices in an adjoining room for easy accountability. Now, sheriff, we will rely on you for force protection. The last thing we want is these very angry alien guards to have a shooting match with any hostiles from Tennessee here in North Carolina."

PATRICK ABBOTT

Mon walks up to them. *Bad optics to have two talking heads, Mon.* "Sir"—she reaches her hand out to the sheriff but withdraws it before he can respond—"I wish to thank you for your service to us."

Without missing a beat, Sheriff Axe wraps up his conversation. "Well, Murphy, we'll keep in touch with you and make sure y'all are safe. I don't allow any horseplay in my county by anyone." He looks briefly at Mon before walking off with his deputies.

The dig has no effect. She tries to talk to Brendan, but he whispers that they should take their discussion inside. She gives the order for Gastab to proceed forward. He, in turn, motions for two guards to take point and secure the hall. The guards wave their wrists, causing railer rifles to appear. *So they are materialized with the wrist gadgets.* With tactical movements, they enter the hall along with more guards. In less than a minute, one reappears in the doorway. He gives a wave which prompts Gastab to sound out the all-clear. Mon leads the remaining group inside.

"Why did he not address me?" Mon asks Brendan.

"Clearly, there is little love for the Sabia here. So, please, let me handle the interactions initially. I can work on warming them up for you. That way, when you talk to them, their biases against you will be weakened. Of course, feel free to stop me if you need anything or want me to handle something differently. However, keep in mind this is a challenging and delicate situation."

"I will. Thank you, Brendan."

Brendan and Mon explore the building from top to bottom. On the second floor, there are restrooms, an ample lounge area, back offices, and even empty rooms. Meanwhile, the main floor features a large hall and a commercial kitchen. Finally, they discover the basement is too cluttered to be of any practical use. After examining everything, Mon orders for the second floor to be their headquarters and barracks while the first floor serves as the negotiation space.

"Mon," Brendan starts, "may I reach out to set up a meeting with the opposing side?"

"Proceed," she says in a disdainful voice.

Brendan is unsure whether the scorn is directed at him or the militia. *Focus. She saved you from Zand. She may not trust you, but that is her right.* Brendan indicates he will conduct communication in a separate room so he can concentrate. In reality, he wants privacy as well.

Brendan: Arrived. We set up shop. Spread the world.

Almost instantaneously, a response comes.

Prophet: Doing so now.

He then messages Jack with the phone number for one of the back offices. Within a minute, it rings, and a familiar voice comes through the line. "Didn't I tell you I wanted you working on my team, not gallivanting about with space aliens?" The voice is playful, but Brendan can tell that Jack is distraught.

"Well, brother," Brendan replies, "we get to work together now. Pretty simple mission: get the girl and save the village. Classic RPG-style."

Jack laughs. "Well, Brodan—"

"Wait! Did you just call me 'Brodan'? You are going Ancient Scrolls on me!"

Jack laughs again. "You know it, brave adventurer. Bandits have kidnapped the mage's daughter. In exchange for us getting her back, we want his spellbook. Get that for me, and you can have a lodge in the country."

Brendan presses his free fist against his forehead. He shuts his eyes in frustration. *How can they be asking me to do espionage work right now?*

"Jack, I need to be honest, man. This job is too much for me to handle. I was asked to report observations and to learn more. Now you know I am always loyal, I know not only America but all of Earth needs me to report what I see. However, my . . . condition, you guys changing the mission, and multiple attempts to arrest me have really confused the heck out of me. At best, you made me a clandestine asset without any training or even informing. At worst, I became a tool to use and then later throw away in a cold cell."

Jack doesn't respond. As for Brendan, he keeps his mouth shut, hoping for something. He finds this waiting game to be painful as his anger builds.

Brendan breaks first. "Okay, I think we both said a lot right there. Is the package on the way?"

"Everything you asked for and more. My best guy is on it, brother."

More silence over the phone. *I have just closed a door. God, let it be your will. If not, do as you will.*

"What else do you need from me?" Brendan asks.

"I can get you more support if you can tell me why three Sabia were undercover in the backwoods."

"I will see what I can dig up."

Brendan hangs up. Emitting a painful groan, he slumps down in a chair. *They still want me to collect. He didn't listen to me. If one of my people had complained about these sorts of feelings, I would have pulled them immediately.*

A knock distracts him. "Brendan, are you alright?" Zalta's voice calls out to him. Seeing her look through the door is a comfort.

"Ah," he says, "Zalta. Yeah, I am fine."

"You do not look fine, Brendan. I may have underestimated the dosage your hybrid body would need. Here, let me give you something for the stress."

Brendan gets up from his chair. "No, no. A little bit of stress can be good. Some things need to be discussed with Mon. Wish me luck."

Zalta looks perplexed as Brendan walks by and pats her on the shoulder. Walking down the hall, he can hear her footsteps shadowing his. *She is probably worried.* He doesn't turn back to look at her, just continues to the main conference room. Inside, Mon and Gastab are discussing what sounds like plans to bring more Sabia to Red Hawk. Brendan clears his throat, which causes both the council member and head guard to turn toward him.

"Excuse me, Mon, do you have a moment?"

"Of course, Dear Brendan; what do you need?"

She used "Dear Brendan." Looks like I am not wholly in the dog house. "I wanted to tell you I have established contact with the federal government's lead liaison. He has told me they can promise additional resources in retrieving Palvah if we can relay why she and the two others were in Tennessee."

"What is it to them? A hostage is being held! Why do they not care about her?" Mon throws her hands up in the air and then puts them on her hips.

"Well, the government liaison's tone leads me to believe he was completely unaware of the Sabia's presence on Earth. In intelligence, we call this an 'illegal' operation, just for your situational awareness. Governments on Earth do not take kindly to this sort of thing because they believe it usually is done for some nefarious purpose. Illegal"—he makes air quotes around the word—"operations can sometimes be causes for war. If we could give them an answer as to why these three Sabia were here, it would likely calm them down and give us additional means of saving Palvah." Brendan hopes his phrasing is enough to crack Mon's resistance.

Mon pauses before she speaks. Brendan can see her eyes move as she thinks. "Thank you for explaining to me the position of the federal government. I understand the difficult situation this places you in, but the purpose of the mission remains classified. This is not something done against you personally, but to protect the operation."

Brendan nods with his right hand over his heart. *This is an impossible task.* "Ma'am," he says, "very well. Would you allow me to reach out to others to form backup plans? I would not ask for any classified information to give them. Instead, I would focus on getting their logistical help."

Mon glances at Gastab and then at Brendan before replying, "Of course." Her voice sounds abnormally wavy.

On his return to the back office, Brendan passes Zalta, still standing in the hallway. She tries to say something, but Brendan walks past her. Then, realizing how this comes across, he stops to face her.

"Zalta, thank you for your concern. I am sorry, but I do not have time to talk to you right now."

Once he gets to the back room, he closes the door. Then, pulling out the Sabia communicator, he starts typing.

Brendan: Jack, no dice.

Jack must have been waiting for a response because the reply is immediate.

Jack: Sucks to be you.

Glad that is how we help each other in difficult situations, friend.

PATRICK ABBOTT

Before Brendan can even sit down in a chair, the office phone rings. Expecting Jack, he eagerly picks up.

"Jack?" he asks.

There is a pause on the other line. "No, this is Lieutenant Colonel Judah Carpenter of the Tennessee Committee of Safety. Who is this?"

"Oh, sir, my apologies. I am Intelligence Officer Murphy of the Unified Intelligence Command and liaison to the Sabia."

"Uh-huh," the backwoods voice declares. "Well, Murphy, as I said, I am a member of the Committee of Safety here in Tennessee, and I was told to reach out to you to discuss the matter of the assassin we captured."

"Excellent, sir. What do we have to do to ensure the safe exchange of—"

Carpenter interrupts. "Sir, we are a collection of patriots who realize the threat these aliens pose to the people of our republic. You work for the federal government, which is irredeemably corrupt. It has betrayed us all to the globalists and their alien allies. The prisoner is best handled—"

"Colonel"—now Brendan interposes—"the whole point of capturing prisoners is to gain intelligence. I imagine you have gotten intelligence out of her. After getting intelligence, holding prisoners is to exchange them for something. Otherwise, they sit there, eat your food, tie down your men for guard duty, and attract unwarranted attention. Exchanges are the universally recognized solution to this problem. As a person working both government and extraterrestrial angles, I can work to obtain what you need, but I need to know what you want."

He hears the sound of facial hair rubbing against the receiver. Brendan thinks he can make out murmuring voices.

"Sir, the committee representing the people of our fair state is merciful. We are willing to exchange the assassin for five million dollars and full alien acknowledgment of her mission."

Crap, I hope Mon is ready to have a conversation with people who will not take "classified" for an answer. "Please allow me to work with the Sabia to gain their acceptance of these terms." Brendan writes down the colonel's number and then bids the officer wait for another phone call within the hour. Placing down the receiver, he sighs. *Crap, crap, crap.*

Yet again, Brendan heads back to the conference room. Inside, Mon is studying a map of the region hanging on the wall while Gastab communicates via his wrist device.

Brendan knocks on the open door to get their attention. "Mon, I have made contact with a group that purports to have Palvah. They say they will release her in exchange for money and information on her mission. If you desire, I can try to acquire the money from the federal government, but we would need to message the militia what mission was being conducted in their backyard." Brendan waits with a mix of hope and despair for Mon's reply.

PATRICK ABBOTT

Mon straightens herself out proudly. "The money will be no issue—Delegate Loft will supply the funds. In the meantime, tell the Terrans we agree to their terms. Have them come here with proof of life. I will tell them what they need to hear," she says.

Brendan is astonished. "Really? I thought her mission was classified. What are you going to tell them?"

"Oh, that is classified for now, Dear Brendan." She has a remarkably smug smile on her face. "Go fetch them for us." Then, waving him off, she goes to talk to Gastab.

Rolling his eyes, Brendan returns to his de facto office. First, he calls the militia to agree to their terms. Next, he contacts Jack to tell him that the Sabia will inform the militia of the purpose of the secret mission. Gazing at the wall, Brendan ponders what will happen in the next twenty-four hours. Then, not wholly trusting Mon's plan, he types out a new message on his device.

Brendan: Malcolm. Open network. At Red Hawk veterans hall. Need your help with the backup plan. Yeah, *the* backup plan.

Thirty-Seven – The Bag Men

Brendan and a man in a black suit are standing in the parking lot by themselves a little after midnight. It was a minor miracle he managed to persuade Kimya to wait inside. Brendan had to agree she would always have a clear view of him through the door crack. *Right now, she's probably aiming her railer at this dude.* A six-foot-four hulking mass, the dude is a UIC agent who refuses to share his name despite Brendan's best efforts.

The agent nods back toward the open trunk before he speaks. "It's all there. Never saw five million dollars in cash before tonight. Kinda cool if you ask me. However, don't think about stealing any of it or trying to make change with whatever you got. All the serials are marked. Moment someone tries using these, we'll know."

"Good to know," Brendan replies.

"Still blows me away that I drove all this way with five million in the truck. That's enough to bankroll a small army."

"For about five days, I imagine." The agent makes a *huh* sound at Brendan's little remark. "Inflation the last few years has made five million less than what you or I remember. Plus, these hillside warriors are more corrupt than the Taliban. I have a feeling they will tear each other apart over that much cash. That, or they will steal a good chunk of it to buy themselves extra-large televisions. Either way, we save the budget of whatever an intergalactic war would cost."

The man nods. They admire the trunk's light reflecting on the black canvas duffle bags in silence. The still, warm air of the night combined with human contact provides long-missed Earth experiences for Brendan.

"Can I ask one question?" the man says.

"Sure."

"You live with those things full time. What are they like? I've heard . . . stories, man."

Still looking at the bags, Brendan ponders his answer. "On a personal level, they are like us. Some are okay, some awesome, and some bad. For example, I know a guard who I think really hates me. As a species, they undoubtedly are keeping secrets from us. Their full motivations are something they will die on a hill to protect. I have been with them for months, but they still will not give an inch on that one."

"Do you think they'll lift that veil of secrecy to save the girl over there?" He motions across the hills toward Tennessee.

"I have my doubts," Brendan replies, as much as to himself as to the agent. "That is why I ordered an M4 carbine, M11 pistol, and three magazines for each weapon." Then, after a moment, Brendan nods and gives off a soft "yeah" at the thought of what he said. "Should arrive here before dawn."

The agent looks confused. "What good will that do you? That amount of ammo would run out real quick in a firefight."

"Classified," Brendan replies with a mischievous smile on his face. "Here, help me bring in the bags. There is an unplugged chest freezer in the back we can store these in."

The agent grabs two bags while Brendan takes the remaining two. Entering the hall, Kimya is nowhere to be found. *She is here, somewhere; she probably has a bead on the poor guy.* Together they make light work of stashing away the cash. Noiselessly they exit the hall and head back to the agent's car, where they stand, staring off into the night sky. *Beautiful. Hard to believe I have been living up there for so long now.*

"I've heard," the agent says, "their women are hot. Is it true?"

The question forces his mind back to Esfirs. Both the currents of longing for her and the pain of the last few days combine in his heart.

"Have a good night, agent." Brendan makes no effort to answer the question.

The agent just shakes his head and then gets into the car. Without another word, he drives off into the dark. Brendan's mind remains on the question as he stands in the parking lot. Doubts about his relationship with Esfirs grow as he recalls her behavior at church, her exiting the hotel room, and now his sort of spying on the

PATRICK ABBOTT

Sabia coming to light. He wonders if there's anything worth saving. *What chance does a messed-up guy like me have with her anyway?*

Just then, a vision of her eyes pops into his mind. Recalling the warmth he felt when they formed a Bond that night in Montana, he thinks of one word: love. *If only I could talk to her right now. I could explain everything.* Brendan sighs. *I am in way too deep, to the point everything is FUBAR.*

Night air begins to nip at him. *Time to put the insurance plan in order.* He gets out the Sabia communication device and types a message to Malcolm.

> Brendan: Open network. Hope you are coming. I arranged a motel room for you across the street under the name Malik Sham. I guarantee your safety. My own is another matter. Stop by if you can after the morning meeting. Hope to hear from you soon.

A dog barks in the distance. Brendan looks up toward the hill, or "mountain," as the locals call it. *Palvah is on the other side.* His eyes then lift back up to the stars. How beautiful they are. Thinking about the nights of his youth, he remembers what it was like to be a kid wishing he could go into space. *Now people up there are deciding my fate. I can live or die with that. But I don't want to be alone again.*

"Your night sky is pleasing," a voice behind him class from the darkness.

Brendan lets out a yip of surprise. Turning around, he sees Kimya walking into view. "Ah, I did not hear you approaching."

"Is this the same night sky you would see where you grew up?" She replies.

"Yes, same hemisphere, so same stars. We are close to the same line of latitude, so the stars here are in almost the exact same position as in my hometown. When I was a kid, I liked to look at them and wonder if anyone was looking back at me."

"Ha. No Sabia were looking back at you, sadly." Brendan gives her a surprised look. "You have to be in your Southern Hemisphere to see where we are from."

"I am surprised you told me that."

She shrugs. "Some consider you a spy. But I read all the things you messaged. There were no secrets. The Unified Intelligence Command will not respond to you because they are exploiters, like most other Terrans. But tell me, Dear Brendan, why will your mother not respond to your message?"

"My life has been a burden to many family members. After a while, I decided it was better for everyone if I left. I . . . I cannot blame her for not wanting me back." Brendan looks away as he finishes speaking.

"I told my mother I hated her," Kimya confesses. Brendan looks back at her as she continues. "We fought over me going to a special unit. It was different than hers." Kimya pauses. "I never came back home after that. I did meet my husband, Mehr, in the new unit, though." She offers up a smile.

Brendan feels a warmth inside him. It takes a moment for him to realize a Bond has formed. A wellspring of emotions bubbles up, primarily love and loss. Her mind has opened up to him. Brendan sees Mehr, feels Kimya's passion for her mate, and then a dramatic sense of loss rocks him. *She is a widow!* Images flash, revealing the guilt she carries about his death. He thinks sympathetic thoughts of his own pain from Heather's betrayal. The hurt she caused became a defining factor for Brendan. For a moment, Brendan thinks about what Baldwin told him about not forgiving and moving on.

Brendan's thoughts are disrupted when he notices how Kimya longingly looks at him. He feels an intimacy with her formed out of heartache. His very soul aches for a fellow suffering spirit. Slowly, he begins to move closer to her. She reciprocates. Hot breath from her mouth washes over his face. Through the Bond, he can feel his breath on hers. It is intoxicating. Soon, their faces are inches apart. Then, he sees her point-of-view; instead of him, it's of someone else, with the Sabia's iridescent skin.

No! They both snap their heads away from each other. Shame flushes over Brendan.

"I think I need to go to bed," he says nervously, wanting to get away from her.

"Yes, good idea. I will stay up." She speaks while continuing to look away from him.

I nearly betrayed Esfirs!

"Would you," he begins, "wake me up in four hours? I need to make sure a package is delivered."

"Of course," she quickly replies, then walks off to a far corner of the parking lot.

Crap, crap, crap. I emotionally was ready to—Crap! Crap! Brendan clenches his fists in frustration as he walks back inside. He makes his way to a makeshift bed he made in the recreation room.

That night, Brendan struggles to fall asleep. *I was going to . . . give in. I was prideful, ruined my reputation with the Sabia, and basically betrayed Esfirs.* He swears audibly. *I am worse than those I rebelled against.* He tosses and turns, racked with emotions. Tears stream down his face as he pulls the blanket over his face. It is a titanic struggle to keep his whimpering to that and not outright wailing.

As if from beyond, he hears the memory of Esfirs humming to him. He stops his soft crying and shifts to humming the tune himself. The memory of her song calms him. *She sang to me because she loved me.* Then, feeling the weight of his eyes, Brendan closes them as he keeps humming the few lines he remembers.

An abrupt shaking causes him to open his eyes back up. The room is noticeably brighter except for the blur immediately before him. Brendan closes and reopens his eyes thrice to allow his focus to return. Kimya is kneeling with her arm on his shoulder.

"Brendan, it is time to wake up. It is eight in the morning."

PATRICK ABBOTT

"What?" he shouts as he props himself up in a state of alarm. "You were supposed to wake me up in four hours."

"Your package arrived soon after you went to sleep. I accepted it and put it right by your feet." Brendan looks down to see the heavy-duty weapons bag. "The officer who came was not given much choice." She smiles briefly. "When I dropped the bag off, I attempted to wake you, but you would not stir. You needed the sleep, so I decided to let you rest."

Brendan nods. "Today is the day, then. One way or another, we will get Palvah back. So let us embrace it."

Thirty-Eight – Pouring Out the Wrath

"Well, to be fair, I was estimating the effectiveness of the medicine, as it has never been applied to a hybrid before," Zalta says with an uncertain tone as she holds her left arm with her right. "It has still had the same effect on you as expected, for the most part, but I am worried because the withdrawal symptoms have only appeared intermittently."

"I am fine, Zalta. Thank you for your concern, though," Brendan pushes back. "Look, whatever you gave me did a great job calming me down yesterday. Yes, there were times when I felt emotionally volatile like you described, but those came and went. Maybe my weird hybrid body managed to burn through the stuff without the side effects you feared."

"Brendan, it should not work that way—"

He holds up his hand to stop her. "Regardless, we are going to have visitors very soon. The last thing we need is me being drugged."

Brendan turns and walks out of the building. He can hear Zalta say something to Kimya as she follows him out, but apparently, it has little success, as the guard doesn't respond. Looking down at his watch as he walks across the parking lot, he sees Malcolm on the outside walkway of the motel's second floor. His former friend is sitting in a plastic chair smoking a cigarette. He has been there for hours, and his lack of direct communion is perplexing and upsetting to Brendan. Malcolm didn't even message his arrival. Instead, he merely took the room and sat down to watch what was happening across the street. They peer at each other from a distance. *So close yet so far. Maybe I need to be the first one to reach out. No, I have done a lot to set this up. But is more needed?*

An old, beaten-up pickup truck with "Bell County Sheriff" written on the side pulls into the lot next to Brendan. Rolling down the window, a deputy spits out the window before asking, "You Murphy?"

"Yep," Brendan replies, straight and to the point.

"Get ready; the representatives are about two minutes out."

"Roger that, thank you, Deputy."

The deputy studies Brendan. "You serve anywhere?"

"Iraq, Afghanistan, and Syria primarily, along with some short-term assignments in the Middle East and Eastern Europe. Got wounded my last time out. How about yourself?"

"Uh-huh, I was doing supply runs from Turkey to all over. Maybe you got some of the bottled water we hauled." The deputy laughs. "What service you with?"

"Unified Intelligence Command."

"Uh-huh," the deputy says before he spits again and turns away from Brendan, ending the conversation.

It's a response he gets half the time from armed services members who regard the UIC as a bunch of civilian LARPers. Under his breath, Brendan calls the deputy a jerk. Maybe the officer heard Brendan because he suddenly pulls out of the parking lot.

Almost instantaneously, another pickup, this one red and even more beat up than the deputy's, pulls in. It comes to a stop about ten yards away. The driver is first out of the vehicle. He reminds Brendan of Santa Claus due to his big, bushy white beard, large belly, and bald scalp with long hair forming a Hippocratic wreath around his head. *But jolly Saint Nicholas did not wear a flannel shirt with bib overalls like this guy.* Brendan judges the man to be in his mid-sixties. A woman who seems to be in her early twenties exits on the passenger side. Her white button-down shirt and pressed black dress pants give the impression she's there for church, not a hostage negotiation. As she approaches, Brendan notices her skin is of a tone that could be either dark white or a very light-skinned black. Seeing her, he can't help but think of his own mixed identity and wonders how people view him.

The two militia representatives stop, look at each other, and say a few words before approaching Brendan. Santa Claus reaches out and greets him. "Jason Argabright, marshal around these parts." Brendan takes his hand and shakes it.

"Federal Marshal?" Brendan's surprise is evident in his voice.

PATRICK ABBOTT

Argabright laughs, holding his belly, much like his lookalike. "Oh goodness, no! I am a marshal for the North Carolina Home Guard. We volunteer to protect the peace out here, keep everyone safe, and prevent assassinations."

Brendan ignores the dig at the end and mirrors his friendly attitude. "Ah, I see. Please allow me to introduce myself. Brendan Murphy, Unified Intelligence Command Officer for the good ol' United States of America." He holds his arms out wide to demonstrate a claim to the spot where they're standing and the surrounding area. Then, turning to the woman, he holds his hand out for a shake.

She responds by folding her arms. "I don't shake hands with godless Marxist tools who work for the Globalists."

Brendan forces a smile. "Well, good to know; if I see any, I will ensure they do not attempt anything." He holds his hand out for an extra second to see if she will take it. She doesn't. Dropping his smile, he decides he needs to build commonalities with her. "Say all you want about the government; that is fair. Heck, attack me for my faults, cool. However, please do not call me godless. I may not be perfect, but I am trying to get right with God. And that, I assure you, has been hard." Brendan pauses, causing both the marshal and the woman to look at him intently. "It has been hard." He nods at his repeated phrase. Brendan fake coughs to buy time, unsure how to recover. The two representatives seem to be confounded by the slight emotional break.

"First Sergeant Jo Werth," the woman introduces herself. "Children of the Lion." She does not offer her hand though her voice is now much less hostile.

The group is unknown to Brendan. He decides it must be a new Protestant militia. He makes a mental note to research it later. His attention must remain focused on the matter at hand.

"Thank you for the introductions." He nods at both of them. "I take it your groups are aligned with the Tennessee Committee of Safety—"

The marshal interrupts him. "Whoa there. I am with the North Carolina Home Guard, and Jo is in a group that recognizes only Jesus Christ's sovereignty. Like I said before, we are here to keep the peace. Our groups have agreed to arrange negotiations between the aliens and humanity."

Wiping his nose, Brendan hopes to assert the legality of the mission. "Marshal, I assure you, I am here to represent the people of the United States. As a liaison to the Sabia, I have also been entrusted by them to open talks for their formal representative. You are here to arrange the transfer of the prisoner under pre-agreed upon terms. Are you willing to abide by that?"

"Are you willing to give us what you promised?" Werth lashes back.

"What I promised was the Sabia's willingness to answer for what their agents were doing here and provide the bounty for the exchange. The money is ready to go; the Sabia are willing to talk, but do you have proof of life?"

PATRICK ABBOTT

The marshal nods while putting his hands on his belly. "We do. Let's proceed with an adequate exchange. Once we hear a satisfactory explanation, we'll hand over proof of life, you can deposit the money with us, and then we can go secure the little lady."

A friendly term for Palvah; so far, all is going well. Brendan agrees to the arrangement and offers to take the two representatives inside. Argabright happily accepts for both him and Werth, though Brendan can feel her eyes drilling into him. They walk toward the building in silence. *Please, God, let this go well.*

Holding the door for them, Brendan keeps up a smile to project confidence, to himself as much as the militia representatives. When he enters the main hall, Brendan finds Mon standing in a red gown with Sabia-style yellow symbols. Her costume is attention-grabbing; it reminds him of what various mountain people would wear in northern Iraq. Brendan is so focused on her that he barely notices the four guards, including Kimya, surrounding her.

Mon gives a theatrical wave with her left arm. "Greetings, friends. Dear Brendan, would you introduce these guests of mine?"

"Of course, Mon. These two representatives are members of independent groups not directly connected with the killing of the two Sabia and seizing of the other. This"—he motions toward Argabright—"is Marshal Jason Argabright of the North Carolina Home Guard." Argabright does a gentlemanly bow. "And this here"— gesturing toward the obviously xenophobic militia member—"is First Sergeant Jo Werth of the Children of the Lion." Werth does not move in the slightest.

Mon looks above the heads of everyone and says, "Most excellent, thank you, Auxiliary Officer. I am the delegate for the Sabia. You may have the honor of referring to me as Mon." Her voice carries lofty airs thick enough to crush an elephant.

Brendan intrudes, trying to control the conversation before the Sabia sense of diplomacy alienates the representatives. "Thank you, Mon, for that introduction." He tries to be polite while also showing the militia emissaries his own thoughts. "Now, if you would take your seats at this table, I think we can all—"

Another dramatic wave from Mon causes Brendan to go quiet. "I shall address Jason and Jo now," she declares, much to Brendan's horror. "Ambassadors from the Home Guard and Children of the Lion, a grave crime was committed when the murder of two and torture of another peaceful Sabia occurred. These Sabia were on leave and decided to observe Terran customs in person while traveling incognito. As you now know, the actions of your fellow travelers were a grave injustice. Please, provide the proof of life. Once it is satisfactory, I will order my auxiliary officer to release half the money to you. You shall receive the rest when the hostage is returned to us along with the bodies of the other two."

Brendan's eyes widen in shock. He struggles for words, feeling as though his voice has been stripped from his body. Werth, meanwhile, drops her jaw.

Marshal Argabright takes several deep breaths before replying. "Umm, perhaps, Mon, could you—

would you please explain these cryptic notes your kin were writing at the time of the incident?" He pulls out photos of napkins with odd runes on them.

Brendan is impressed with Argabright's poise, thinking he would have made a skilled intelligence officer. *When faced with a transparent lie, he is diplomatic, probing the false statement while allowing the other side to come clean.*

Mon avoids looking at the photos; instead, she clicks her tongue before speaking. "The ciphers are merely their own shared observations. As I said, they were traveling incognito, so they would not have desired to have notes that anyone could read."

Both Werth and Argabright look at each other and then slowly turn their heads toward Brendan. Werth even silently mouths, "Do you really believe this crap?" Meanwhile, Brendan feels himself zoning out. He feels a migraine building while simultaneously suffering a sudden surge of pain in his molars.

A calm voice comes out of him. "Will Marshal Argabright and First Sergeant Werth please excuse the Sabia and the American representatives?"

Werth's jaw drops even further this time. Argabright gently starts pulling her toward the door.

"I think it would be best if you two had some more time to iron out the details," Argabright says, a tremble in his voice. "We really must be getting back— and we have to file our report." The moment he approaches the door, he quickly turns to open it. He practically throws Werth through the doorway. Then, looking at Brendan, Argabright says, "Too bad you could not make it work. But then again, who could under these circumstances?" With that, he leaves.

They are going to kill her. A feeling of failure overwhelms Brendan. Zand's earlier threats combine with taunts from Heather. Negative voices tease him saying he should have died in Afghanistan, that he is a fraud.

In the background, he can hear Mon calling him. Her voice is just incomprehensible noise. Ignoring her only causes Mon to make more sounds. Brendan erupts with rage, letting out a massively loud swear word. Mon steps back in surprise, and Brendan takes a step toward her.

"You liar," he screams. "You incompetent liar! Did you really think they would believe that and let her go? Your lies are going to get Palvah killed. How many people are going to die because of you, liar?" Mon and the guards look on, stunned. "I asked you a question, liar. How many people are going to die because of your stupid lies?"

Mon remains speechless, causing Brendan to swear again. Zalta comes running down the steps with a medical kit in her hands. She stops dead in her tracks as Brendan points angrily toward her. No words need to be exchanged. *Now is not the time for drugs!* Instead of waiting for the stupefied Sabia to say something, Brendan picks up the weapons bag by his bed in the corner. Throwing its strap over his shoulder, he makes his way to the door. As he passes Mon, he swears again.

PATRICK ABBOTT

As he approaches the door, he hears Mon call out, "What are you going to do?"

He stops in an unnatural pose. Looking at Mon, he sees her discomfort. "Because of you"—he pauses before continuing—"they will go back and tell their leaders you are a liar, that all their worst fears about Palvah being an assassin are valid, and then they will recommend killing her. Then, with Sabia blood on their hands, there will be an ever-increasing series of strikes and counterstrikes which will kill humans and Sabia. All because of you and your lies. This is happening because you thought you could get away with lying makes me sick, physically sick. I imagine it ends with your technology killing billions and the world throwing every nuclear weapon at you. I must do my utmost to stop this, not for you, but every other human and Sabia. And you know what? I probably will not be successful. Most likely, I will die. I only hope my death trying to rescue a Sabia will be enough blood to satisfy the coming storm. Maybe, just maybe, it will buy time so that Palvah can be saved. There is a small chance it will stop the war you started today." He points at Mon before turning his thumb on himself. "The bill for my death has finally come, something which should have happened a long time ago. All because of you."

The words weigh heavy on Brendan's soul. This is despair talking. All he needs to do is get close; then, he can go down in flames. In his mind, there is no hope for success. Brendan remains at the doorway for a moment with his hand propping the door open.

Mon calls out to him. "We are dying, Brendan." He freezes in place. She repeats herself. He breathes in and out for a few seconds, not willing to say anything but not willing to move. "As a species, we are dying. And I am scared. I have been scared for years. I never asked for this role—I wanted to stay home and have an elder be the leader of this mission, but it was not allowed. So I had to go to Terra despite not knowing what to do."

He turns his face towards her. "What does that have to do with anything, Mon?" He needs clarity before he can do anything else. The negative voices are telling him to verbally attack her, attack anything.

"If anyone were to find out about what we are doing here, we would lose all advantage. Instead of being valued for what we can offer Terrans, we would be picked apart like prey by scavengers."

Mon steps towards him. "I swear to you, Brendan, by the divine, the Watchers, and your divinity, Palvah is not an assassin. We are not invading Terra, nor are we a threat to Terrans. I promise you that, Dearest Brendan. But, please, I beg of you, understand I cannot compromise the Sabia by giving any clue to what she and the other two were doing here." Brendan can see the tears forming in Mon's eyes. "So please, do not tell anyone what I just told you. Even I could get in serious trouble for telling you. I fear"—Mon looks at her guards and Zalta—"it may even be too late for that. But please, for . . . the ones you . . . love, please do not tell anyone."

He turns his face to the door. "We will see if I even get the opportunity." He says with a dry chuckle. With that, he opens the door and exits the veterans' hall.

PATRICK ABBOTT

Crossing the parking lot, he hears a set of footsteps behind him closing in fast. Then, suddenly, a mighty yank on his right shoulder spins him and the bag around.

Kimya forces a Bond on him. "I am not letting you go alone."

He shakes his head no. Part of him wants to have her play a role in some sort of firey redemption. *No, this is not her fight.*

She steps back, tears forming in her eyes. Through the Bond, he can see her husband's body, displaying all the natural features of the Sabia, bleeding out on red clay ground.

"Goodbye, Kimya. May you have even a moment of healing. Mine was great while it lasted."

Tears flow from her face.

Brendan turns back around. When a man has lost everything, he can go back home. If he has lost his home, he can go to his friends. When there are no friends left, he can go to an ex-friend. That's what Brendan is going to do.

Interlude – Malcolm: A Friend in Need

Malcolm notes Brendan's bloodshot eyes and the prominent dark bags underneath them. His lips are chapped as well. Seeing that Brendan is constantly swallowing, Malcolm can tell his old friend suffers from a dry throat. Malcolm feels sorry for him; to be stuck between a corrupt government and cryptic aliens has to be horrible. However, what eats at the militia leader is the suffering in Brendan's voice. *The man sounded better when he found out that tramp Heather was sleeping around. Heck, when he was blown up, at least he was too high on drugs to feel anything. These aliens have used him and now have set him up for failure.*

Brendan's tale of woe hits Malcolm hard. A government that did not provide support mixed with threats and praise to pressure a man who was ultimately thrown into a situation way over his head. The Sabia, on the other hand, used him as a tool, as they do everyone else. *And this pitiful man actually thought the common good was a thing.*

Now Brendan is here asking for help to "get close" to the alleged assassin. If Malcolm believed the alien to be a threat, he would tell Brendan to take a hike. However, since Prophet shared the video with General Meade, it is apparent to any rational person that the thing

PATRICK ABBOTT

was saying anything to stop the torture. Brendan keeps calling the alien "Palvah," which Malcolm finds amusing. *They ain't people like you or me, man.*

"So." Malcolm finally speaks up, causing Brendan to step back and take a breath. "You're telling me those aliens lied themselves into a hole. Your girl is gonna get capped because of it, and the logical assessment is things are going to get real ugly real quick?"

"Unless I can stop it," Brendan says pitifully. "One man cannot get her and the bodies out, I get that. But I can go down in flames so bright it could cause everyone to reset. So all I am asking is for you to point me in the right direction. We never were the same after— after it all went down. I ask you to let our friendship end in a way that gives the world one last chance."

Putting a cigar in his mouth, Malcolm lies back on the cheap motel bed. "Brendan, my boy. I never liked those Evangelicals and moonshiners. Neither does Meade. You promise me the cash, and we'll do you a solid."

Interlude – Esfirs: A Second Remel and Namziah

The large hall is a scene of commotion. *The chaos before battle.* Esfirs is well familiar with the lead-up to combat. *First, there is the hectic mess of preparation. Then follows the calm of being left behind, waiting for the guardians' return. Some fools, usually the immature ones, say waiting is the hardest part. But the hardest part of the cycle is what happens next. Having to treat the injured. Those who have never heard the screams of the dying have never known the real pain of war.* Esfirs scans the biotechnology and equipment ready to save lives. *If only time were not a factor.*

She walks back and forth between tables preparing kits for the medics. Her focus on the task is fleeting as her mind wanders back to the horrible news she heard when she was called down to this miserable planet: Brendan has gone rogue. *Brendanshe is out there, alone, trying to sacrifice himself in his foolish errand.* Putting down the kits as she loses focus, Esfirs watches the guardians equip themselves for the upcoming mission. *Kill them all. These Terrans are murderers.* She closes her eyes and offers a prayer. *Oh divine and my Dear Delkash, if the Terrans harmed Brendanshe, I will offer my meals for a week to the fire if you will make them suffer.* Her anger feels like a comforting blanket.

PATRICK ABBOTT

Gradually, the memory of holding Brendan in Montana intrudes into her thoughts. She recalls his opening up to her after the New Year's celebration. *Please, oh divine and Watchers, bring him back to me alive. I will serve the divine as Remel served the divine. Please, return him to me.*

Meditating on prayer, she daydreams about flying over the planet and finding Brendan. She swoops in, picks him up, and soars with him into space. There they visit the moons and planets he always wanted to see. Then, finally, they fly through space to where she was born. *Home. I will take you home, Bredanshe. Away from all these horrible people and places.*

A female's shrieking voice pierces the air. "I do not know you! I do not know you!" Before Esfirs can turn toward the screeching, a male voice responds, "Lady, you've already said that."

When she finally faces the yelling, she's met with a shocking sight. An extremely bloody Palvah is being dragged into the hall by two Terran men dressed similar to, but not quite like, Terran soldiers. A gaggle of guards, guardians, and medics swarm the three of them. Commanding everyone to make way, the head doctor for the Defense Forces pushes through the Sabia and seizes Palvah from the Terrans.

Esfirs notices as several other Terrans enter the room and head toward the back. In a few seconds, they return with four heavy-looking duffle bags. An odd urge to follow them compels her to go outside. There, she watches the Terrans toss the bags into a truck while someone else slowly walks away from the vehicle and into the night.

Another man standing by the truck yells, "You're a fool if you think you are anything but what you are, Brendan!" After a brief moment, he gets into the truck, which drives off.

From her vantage point, Esfirs can tell it is indeed Brendan moving away from the veterans' hall. She rushes toward him. "Brendanshe!" She does not care if anyone hears her.

Brendan turns around, revealing his blood-soaked clothing. "Esfirs." His voice is hauntingly hollow.

"My Dear! You are covered in blood!"

"Oh... it is not mine. It belongs to a kid and his mother. They would not let us rescue Palvah. I . . . I killed them, Esfirs."

My divine, his voice is so hollow and haunted. Esfirs pats him down, looking for wounds. She finds none. Touching the blood, she can tell it has been on him for at least an hour. *He would already be dead if this were his.*

Brendan continues, "I-I need to get away, Esfirs. This is just too much for me. The threat of arrest from my own country, my ruined relationship with the Sabia, especially you, my body trying to kill me, and the people I've... I've... I have killed; it is just all too much." He looks behind his back toward the dark road leading out of town. "Esfirs, I am so scared."

PATRICK ABBOTT

She puts her arms on his shoulders. Taking a deliberate breath, she then exhales on his face as Remel did. "Feel my breath, Brendanshe." Esfirs again breathes on him, this time even slower. "Feel my breath."

Brendan relaxes as his body loosens up. Esfirs uses the opportunity to form a Bond with him. His emotions are all over the place. She slips into his thoughts. Slowly but surely, his mental activity calms down.

"I love you, Brendanshe."

His emotions surge, causing discomfort in Esfirs. "I love you so much, Esfirs." He begins to tear up. "It pains me how much I failed you and became what I hated. I strived so hard in my life to be an honest man a wife could take pride in. Heather was right, though; she always was—"

Esfirs silences him through the Bond. She chooses to communicate telepathically. *You do not have to be in pain anymore. There need be no more worries. Leave all those things in the past. Will you let go of all which ties you down?*

A weak "how" emanates from his lips.

Marry me. Let go of all those obligations and finally trust me to free you, my love, my mate, my Brendanshe.

Thirty-Nine – Life-Altering Choice

Guilt. Exhilaration. Horror. Anguish. In the end, the emotions are just symptoms of the pain.

Brendan checks his twelve o'clock, then three o'clock and nine o'clock. Malcolm is directly in front of him, yelling commands. To Brendan's left, a son is trying to wake up his unconscious father while the woman of the household screams. Simultaneously, on his right, three Patriot Assembly militia members watch as a fourth kicks open a door revealing a screaming Palvah.

A gurgling sound seizes Brendan's attention. Shifting his gaze, he sees blood coming from the mouth of the father. The son yells, "Murderers!" and leaps toward Brendan as if to tackle him. Two unthinking shots from his carbine put the kid down. Now it's the woman who shrieks something about "her baby." Brendan thinks she is making a move toward him, so he lets loose five shots into her. Palvah's screams drown out the noise from the spastic writhing of the mother. Her blood sprays everywhere as her body contorts on the floor.

Esfirs' melodic humming snaps Brendan from his flashback nightmare. Above him, she looks down with a sweet smile. She gently caresses his hair as they mutually form a Bond. She shows him different memories. First, he looks shocked at her proposal and awkwardly replies, "I do," as if it were the ceremony itself. Next, he remembers Esfirs taking him back to the cabin, removing his shirt, and smelling the overpowering scent of blood. He notices that her reactions to the memories differ from his. Brendan's embarrassment at the "I do" is countered by her mirth. The recalling of his bloodied clothing does not elicit disgust but rather honor from her. He senses she esteems him as a warrior rather than the murderer he knows he is.

Stop it, Brendanshe. She places her thoughts in him. *No more of this, no more feeling sorry for yourself. You saved Palvah, and the Terran authorities were tipped off where the bodies were hidden. You have no reason to be upset.*

Brendan shudders. Feeling Esfirs probe inside his mind, he decides to show her the memory of the horrible day at the ballpark. Brendan is sitting next to his father at a baseball game. The sun is out, yet the day is mild, and there's a breeze. To many, it would be the epitome of Americana; the best humanity has to offer. Instead, for Brendan, it is the day his life changed forever; it is when he decided he had to leave his home. Baseball players run around as he asks his father why his mother won't tuck him in like she does his sisters, Mary and Bernadette. Nonchalantly Joseph tells Brendan that Alexandra is not his mother—he is a bastard from a one-night stand with a Rhodesian coworker. Alexandra agreed to raise him to save the marriage but refused to treat him equally to the two girls. Joseph remains indifferent to his son's shock, just sips his beer and laughs off "the woman's terms." The words "I saved my marriage while you got a stable home, didn't you, boy?" collapse Brendan's world.

Next, Brendan shows Esfirs the night he yelled at his dying dad. "I will be different! Everything I do will be honorable! I will not inherit an ounce of betrayal from you!" All Joseph can do is hold up a tie as a peace offering. The father is sobbing as he apologies for what he did to the family. Brendan scoffs. *I thought he was beyond redemption. It was then I came belief-broken; people were hopeless. I laid the seeds of my damnation then.*

Brendan's memories shift to his confusion about what to do with the UIC and Sabia, reporting to the UIC in anger when he was upset at Esfirs. There are also memories of him being too cowardly to tell her about his covert work and the murders he committed rescuing Palvah. Lastly, he shows himself entertaining the temptation of Kimya. *I am the embodiment of everything you hate about the Terrans. Hate me, please, hate me. My actions killed a mother and child! Hate me!*

Dear Brendanshe, take an honest look at who you are. What sort of man is willing to sacrifice himself for the hope of peace?

He tries to look away, but his eyes fail to obey. Instead, he remains transfixed by Esfirs' eyes. An attempt to shift on the bed also fails to initiate muscle movement.

A whisper emanates from his mouth. "What sort of man?" He can tell she caused him to say the words. This time he doesn't panic.

PATRICK ABBOTT

You, she telepathically says to him. *Look at your own memories. You strived to do what was right. My love, you were willing to sacrifice yourself for us. While you fought to destroy in the metro, here, you fought to save. Brendan is dead, my -she lives.*

I do not understand.

Brendanshe! The divine took you away from Terrans for a reason! Your Watchers sent challenges to break the remaining illusions of your Terran self. You were given to me so I can remake you like Namziah.

Baldwin's words about breaking ring in Brendan's head. *What are you going to do?*

We will get rid of the last bit of Terran in your body. Your Watchers will guide the hybridization to whatever the divine chooses. But first, we will end the harassment from the Terrans once and for all. They need to know you are no longer something they can torture with threats. The Legion will adopt you, and you will be entirely and solely one of us.

A feeling of ultimate vulnerability enters Brendan. He realizes he may never see Kansas or Earth again.

Have no fear, for nothing will harm you anymore. You are my husband, and I am your wife. Esfirs' thoughts cause memories of Heather to burst through. *No! She is gone now. I am your wife. You are my husband. We are a family now.*

Brendan nods his head once. He can tell she has released his muscles. Their eyes remain tightly locked together.

They message each other the words *I love you.*

Esfirs now speaks vocally. "Close your eyes, Brendanshe. Picture yourself alone in the dark. There is nothing. Only a cold emptiness surrounds you. You cannot see yourself. In the darkness, you hear an audible voice come from within you. Listen to it; know it is our voice. Not my voice and your voice but our single voice. It sings our song. Listen to it. Feed it with your strength. Let it build inside you like a fire. Feel the voice inside you. As it moves, realize it is a fire inside you. Let it out, Brendan, let the fire consume its way out of you, become a bright light that lightens the dark. Release yourself, become the light."

He envisions an overwhelming flood of light consuming his entire vision. Time flows smoothly in the whiteout, with Esfirs' singing echoing in Brendan's mind. Several times he feels a warm breeze blanket his body. Everything is comfortable.

Slowly Brendan opens his eyes, revealing he is back in his bed, alone. An unknown urge persuades him to get out of bed. Putting on a button-down shirt and black slacks reminds him of getting ready for work. He studies himself in the mirror. It takes him a few moments to realize he enjoys checking himself out. *Am I still under the influence of the Bond?* He calls out, "Esfirs, are you in my head?" Silence reigns.

He heads out to the living room to catch the news from Earth when he suddenly senses something. *Esfirszan.* The thought of her name with the suffix makes him smile. Saying it out loud once leaves a honeyed sensation in his mouth. He looks around the room. *Are you still with me, Dear Esfirszan?* He says the new name out loud several times. It makes no difference whether she can hear him; it is an act of love.

The door chimes and Brendan invites the visitor to enter. Kimya slowly steps inside. "Brendan," she says, "Leleh has summoned you. I am to take you to her." Brendan can hear her shaky breath and notices she is avoiding eye contact.

"Very well," Brendan says, "lead the way."

Kimya reaches for Brendan's wrist but stops herself. Gracefully she turns her outstretched hand to an open palm, inviting him to proceed forward. He responds by nodding. Regardless of whether he is still Bonded with Esfirs, Brendan decides to avoid any touch or cozy conversation with Kimya.

However, she has other plans for their walk together. "You should have let me go with you. Anything could have gone wrong with those hostage-takers."

"Kimya, two people got killed."

"Yes, thank goodness you were able to put those two attackers down. But what if there had been more? You could have died."

Brendan sighs at her indifference to the dignity of those who died. "They were mother and son."

"Everyone in war is daughter or son to someone else. Having the family there is what happens when these . . . these—what is your animal?—rats try to hide." She sighs. "I do not want to argue with you, Dear Brendan. Just tell Leleh what happened. Mon, well . . .

apologize and only apologize. You are in trouble with her."

They arrive at the conference room where the council previously engaged with Brendan. Kimya opens the door by hitting a button on the wall panel. The sight inside causes Brendan's heart to stop: Leleh is standing to Mon's left.

"Greetings, Brendan. Please come in." Leleh's tone is not hostile though it isn't warm either.

Brendan addresses them both by name and does his Afghan greeting. Kimya closes the door behind him as he enters. Once inside, he notices there is no pillow for him to sit on.

Leleh's interrogation begins with a question he does not expect. "Why is the government of the United States asking for the return of five million dollars?"

"Leleh, that is an excellent question." His hands begin to shake, so he places them behind his back. "The group referring to itself as the North Carolina Committee of Public Safety originally demanded five million dollars as part of their conditions to secure the release of Palvah. As such, I acquired the money as part of my role as the federal government representative. However, Mon . . . excuse me, negotiations between Mon and the militia representatives failed. A comment from the male representative indicated to me their intention to kill Palvah. Since we were unable to secure Palvah's release, I decided we needed to rescue her. I brought in my former colleague Malcolm as a backup plan. The money was used to secure his aid in rescuing Palvah."

PATRICK ABBOTT

The Sabia intelligence officer taps her foot. "The Terran authorities are upset with what you call the rescue mission. They say crimes were committed. What crimes do they speak of?"

"Malcolm was able to acquire intelligence indicating Palvah had been moved from her holding location to a cabin in the mountains. We approached it at dusk. One of Malcolm's men was known to the household, so we were able to approach and enter without alarming anyone. Once inside, Malcolm declared our intention of taking Palvah. The head of the household tried to contact his leadership. One of the cooperating militiamen reacted by punching the man in the throat. In the chaos, the injured man's son attempted to tackle me. I—I gunned him down. Things got intense, and I had to shoot the kid's mother, too. I assume the government is upset at these homicides."

Leleh remains impassive and asks, "Do you believe your colleague will use the money for anti-government, anti-Sabia purposes?"

"Without a doubt," Brendan replies flatly. "Some money will be lost through corruption. However, there is no need for anyone to worry. That money is marked; they cannot spend it without it being tracked."

"Then how can you justify your actions, which work against both the government and us? Would it not have been better to use the militia to rescue Palvah but prevent them from seizing the money?"

"That would have been very bad. Because we gave Malcolm the money, the Patriot Assembly has no problem being credited for the raid. They are using the opportunity to demonstrate themselves as a reasonable player who will clamp down on the most extreme elements. Additionally, the extremists are upset at the Patriot Assembly, not us. Denying the Patriot Assembly the money, or worse, seizing them, would have resulted in alienating everyone."

"What about your behavior toward Mon?"

Brendan nervously gulps. "That I own completely. I am sorry for my harsh words. The stress of thinking I would have to die to save Palvah after the failed negotiations got the best of me. Lashing out was wrong. The pressure on Mon must have been intense. It was a critical failure of mine to target her during my blow-up." He turns and looks at Mon. "I truly am sorry. Nothing I can say can take back my offense." He nods nervously.

Mon tilts her head. "The knowledge you gained during this mission would be precious to your government and General Meade. Perhaps it would be enough to secure a position within the so-called Patriot Assembly. Yet we know you did not tell anyone. Additionally, your own secret communication device comprises messages of you seeking help and open communication. The only information you shared was already known to them. And you came back to us versus attempting to obtain sanctuary elsewhere. What is your motivation?"

"If you asked me when I first arrived, I would have given you some answer to protect my pride. I would have believed my own crap, too. However, since the New

PATRICK ABBOTT

Year's celebration and Montana, I have been experiencing moments of clarity." He chuckles. "Clarity on what is the right thing to do – not that I always do it. Like when I was in Montana, I realized I needed to keep my emotions under control. Heck of a lot of good that did me in North Carolina, eh?" Brendan notices Leleh and Mon eyeing each other. "Never mind about that. Down there, I was thinking more about saving Palvah than myself. I thought about all the people on Earth and . . . and the people here who—" He stops himself from finishing his sentence. Brendan averts his gaze from Mon and looks at the floor.

"People here who what, Brendan?" Mon asks.

Brendan takes a moment to commit himself. "I love."

Mon rises from her pillow. A slight nod from her causes Leleh to exit the room. The council member watches the intelligence officer leave before locking eyes with Brendan. Unlike previous Bonds, this one feels neither overwhelmingly oppressive nor comforting but like an empathetic bridge between the two.

"Command is difficult, Brendan. I hope the heavy burden of it passes you by. Since my youth, I have had to carry it with everyone expecting me to be like my mother." Mon remains silent as Brendan sends her an apologetic thought. He believes he feels a sense of acknowledgment from her.

She continues. "That is all we need to discuss of the past for now. Let us confer about the present and future." A smile flashes across her face for a second before disappearing. "Esfirs tells me you are now affianced to her. Is this true?"

Brendan panics. Mon quickly and forcibly blocks his anxiety through the Bond.

"Congratulations. She came this morning to discuss matters with Zand. Her concern for you focuses on your physical and mental health. She tells us your combat illness has not been treated. I believe she attributed this primarily to your own fear."

Brendan grimaces when admitting to the accuracy of the diagnosis. "I am more familiar with the term 'post-traumatic stress disorder,' but, yes, that would be an accurate assessment."

"Of course it is—we Sabia have outstanding doctors." Brendan is unsure of whether there is levity in Mon's words. "Before I allow such a union, I have three demands. First, you agree to medical treatment to heal your combat illness. Second, remaining with the Unified Intelligence Command is unacceptable. We will arrange for you to file a report to close out the North Carolina mission, but you must resign. Finally, you will be adopted into the Legion and thus subject to our laws. Do you agree to these terms?"

Brendan thinks back to the times he's made life-altering decisions: not attending his father's funeral, leaving Kansas for college, volunteering for his first deployment, marrying Heather, and arranging the peace conference on the military base in Afghanistan. Maybe two of those were good choices; the rest backfired. Now in front of an alien, something he didn't even know existed a few years ago, he is at another turning point.

"Yes," he says, "for Esfirs."

"And for yourself?"

"Yes."

"Very good," Mon says. "Esfirs will arrange for your adoption. This way, you will have full rights and responsibilities as a Sabia. However, you must be free of all past obligations to your former masters before any rites are conducted."

Mon shakes her head, smiling. "I do believe Loft will take some pleasure in telling the new ambassador from your . . . previous home we will not be taking you to the Pentagon for a debriefing as she demanded. Imagining her shock brings me a small amount of pleasure."

Brendan remains quiet. Leaving the UIC may be one thing, but he doesn't have to enjoy the bashing of the organization he has served for years. He feels probing in his head and assumes it is Mon trying to read him. *Probably best to be transparent.* He does not resist her efforts.

"Have you thought about the consequences of marriage?" Mon asks.

"I was married before. Learned a lot of lessons from that failure. Making things work this time will be my main priority."

"There is no doubt in my mind Esfirs can control you, Dear Brendan. However, she will expect you to think of yourself as a Sabia, not a Terran. Are you prepared for that?"

He is not. The issue has been a point of tension, but one that he's always been able to maneuver around. Now, he will have to work on communication and emotional control and accept that he is Sabia in law and biology.

"Things to consider, Dear Brendan. You are dismissed." Brendan begins to pivot but feels the sudden urge to stop. "One last thing. Deputy Commander Sainas has placed you on leave because of the stress your body and mind have taken. However, in a few days, I have a reception with the House of Representatives and Senate committees that oversee our relations. No one can order you to come, but if I could have a trusted advisor to—informally—prepare and accompany me, I would be grateful."

She is giving me another chance to be trusted. "Of course, Dear Mon. Thank you for considering me a friend after everything that has happened."

"Dismissed, Dear Brendan."

He turns around. *That went a lot better than it could have.*

As he leaves, his worries are replaced by thoughts of Esfirs. His mind creates a daydream of her awaiting him in a prairie field. She is holding something—a bundle. When he is close enough to touch her, he sees the mystery object is a baby wrapped in a blanket. Brendan tries to look at the child, but his mind resists the effort. *Is it a boy or girl? Does the child have Sabia skin? What color are the eyes?* He can't tell.

PATRICK ABBOTT

His solitary journey back to the cabin is blissful. Walking through the halls without escorts dragging him about and the daydream make for a beautiful experience. The hallways are more inviting, homey even. This observation stops him in his tracks. Never did he think this deployment could be permanent. *Permanent.* The secondary effects of accepting Esfirs' marriage proposal have yet to register with him. His family left Ireland to create a life in America. The importance of America and what it represented was drilled into him as a child. *Can I leave that behind?* *"She will expect you to believe yourself a Sabia and not a Terran."* Brendan needs to pray.

Interlude – Zand: An Unorthodox Union

Zand sits on her cushion. *I am getting too old for this.* On her left, she sees Mon, as usual, struggling for words. Mon's moment of uncertainty reminds Zand of her overall mission here. *Mon is going to need her handheld for the rest of her life. To serve on this ship of the damned is a punishment. It is not the honor of service my family has held for generations. Thank goodness Defense Force leadership is coming. Soon, I may be allowed to go home—if I prove to them Mon is competent.*

Having had enough of Mon's bumbling, Zand takes over the questioning. First, she clears her throat to gain everyone's attention. Next, Zand taps her chin with her index finger. Finally—the most crucial bit—she locks eyes with Esfirs without forming a Bond. *Simple intimidation to establish dominance. Watch and learn, Mon.*

"What part of you thought it was okay to propose to an auxiliary officer?" *Keep it open yet leading.*

Without a moment's pause, Esfirs responds. "What does it matter to you, or anyone? He serves in an officer role for the Legion."

PATRICK ABBOTT

"Legally, he is a Terran." *Facts are the best counterargument. Note, I have no set position yet. Always test your subject.*

"We know medically that is not the case. Brendan—"

"The auxiliary officer is a hybrid. Not Sabia." *Double down.*

"That is what we tell him. Keeping his cancers at bay has allowed the hybrid process to morph into a Sabization. He is becoming more Sabia every day."

"Yet not Legion. You must mind the laws we have set." *Triple down.*

"What do they matter to me?" Esfirs yells. "Since I was a girl, I have been mocked, disowned, and called horrible things. They called me 'joonbaf' to my face!" Her voice becomes wobbly. "That is why I am on this mission. So, what does it matter if I am with him?" A fire glows in her eyes.

Mon holds her hand up. "Dear Esfirs, what we mean is no one here faults you for having Brendan first as a diversion and then a paramour. Marriage, though, is sacred. We are not the Zeshita."

Good reframe, Mon.

Esfirs holds her hands as if in prayer. Engaging in an obvious Bond, she remains silent.

"Speak to the whole assembled gathering, Dear Esfirs," Zand says to interrupt the private communication.

"My apologizes, Zand." She closes her eyes and breathes deeply for a few moments. "The Watchers gave us adoption for things like this. The laws apply to Brendan as he is no longer Terran and is arguably more Sabia than some of the children of Dravisp."

That makes sense. "That answers religious concerns. However, we also live in a demon-haunted cosmos. What does the Defense Force think about this?"

Zand turns to her right. A Defense Force member in black, grand regalia—a puffy hat, harem-style pants, and a tucked-in robe along with black ceremonial light body armor—does not turn to acknowledge Zand. Instead, she studies Mon with the eyes of a Watcher.

"Having him could prove disastrously dangerous or highly beneficial. There are ways to weigh this out before any ceremony." The Defense Force member turns to face Zand. "As deputy commander, I have no objection to Esfirs moving forward under her proposed timeline."

"Very well." Zand stands up. Now forming a Bond with Esfirs, she addresses the doctor. "It is an unorthodox union. But one we will support."

Zand knows without looking that Mon wants to object to Zand making the final call. She does not bother glancing at her ward before leaving the room.

PATRICK ABBOTT

Forty – Brin and Nasha

Esfirs guides Brendan's hands, gently touching the strange bush's flowers. With delicate movements, she has Brendan feel the waxy petals. Their thumbs glide over the smooth surface together. She instructs him to hold a stem with one hand while he picks off a petal with the other. It is more challenging than he imagines, so he must tug twice. She laughs at his efforts, yet it does not bother him. For the first time in years, he is enjoying the simple pleasures of domestic life. Esfirs commands him to place the petal with the others into a vase, which reminds him of a hookah. At the same time, she reaches over and sets a dish with a flaming liquid at the bottom of the vessel. They watch the flame sitting side by side on their pillows.

"It will take a few minutes to boil," Esfirs tells him. "It is customary for husbands to make *brin* for their wives at the end of the day. Not every day, but most. I have memories of my father making brin for my mother. It will be good to have these moments together." She hugs Brendan from behind.

After she lets go, Brendan bites his lip in apprehension of what he wants and needs to do. *Just*

*keep it together. These things are better settled than
eating me up on the inside.*

"Esfirs—"

"Esfirszan," she corrects him.

Brendan claps his hands together in a eureka-like
moment. "Were you in my head after you left my
room?"

"Not really. Think of it as a recording. A gift to
you, Brendanshe."

They share a smile. For a moment, it helps break
the tension.

"Esfirszan, when I am adopted into the Sabia, can
we at least respect my Terran heritage? I understand that
I am cutting ties with the UIC and more, but I want us to
always remember where I came from. My religion, for
example, is something I cannot live without. I do not
want to lose it, not again."

Esfirs remains still for a few seconds, exhaling
deeply through her nose. "I understand where you are
coming from, Brendanshe. I am willing to let you . . .
keep certain traits which you value."

Sighing deeply, he breaks out in a big smile.
"Thank you so much. It is no secret you do not see
much good in humans. But thank you for valuing me."

Nodding, she remains silent.

"One more request, if I may, Dear Esfirszan."

Stoically, Esfirs gazes at him with her head silently
tilted up. "Proceed."

"Thank you." Brendan's throat tightens. Again, he feels the desire to run. "I . . . had a very . . . nice daydream today. In it, umm . . ." Brendan's face turns red. "No, what would you . . . think . . . if any of our children—"

Esfirs jumps up. "Children?!"

Alarmed, Brendan scoots back on his pillow. *The thought was foolish. She is an alien, for crying out loud!* "I am sorry; I did not mean to ruin the mood. It was a silly question, us being different species and all."

The pain in his forehead indicates that Esfirs is searching his thoughts. This time it feels frantic. Purposefully, he recalls his daydream, hoping it's what she wants to see. Suddenly, the pain stops.

Her smooth, stoic face morphs into one that shows the wear of age. Lines run around her mouth, and the bags under her eyes seem more prominent. To Brendan, it's as if she's aged more than a decade.

"-she, I—" Esfirs breathes in deeply. "I am barren. Do you remember the memory I gave you of me crying when I was a child?"

"Yes."

"That was the night the doctors said I could never have children. After that, no boy wanted to be my friend, and other girls thought I could infect them. My own mother called me 'dirty.' She would yell at me to get away from her. She stopped being my mother that day. No more would she play with me, take me to work with her, or even . . . make my hair. Brendanshe, she would not even touch me for a year!" Silent tears stream down her face.

"I should have told you, my love. At first, I did not think it would matter—you were a Terran. Despite Berina's observations, I did not think we would be anything more than an expedition fling. However, as I began to love you more, the night of the new year . . . I wanted to explain it to you." Her eyes plead with him. "But every time I wanted to tell you, I became terrified you would hate me because I was dirty." Esfirs looks down at her lap. "If you want to leave, I understand. If I were in your situation, I probably would."

Brendan stands up to look at her. "Not being able to have children does not affect my love for you one bit. I am not going anywhere, Esfirszan."

She lets loose a loud *bah*. "But why stay? You mentioned wanting children before! Well, I cannot give you that. So are you looking for something else? Maybe you want to stay here to get access for your militia friends?" The question is accusatory, and her tone reflects a level of uneasiness.

That is something I would say in her shoes. "Because I love you." He feels a whip-like sensation through the Bond. "We both have a lot of pain in our souls. You are helping me through so much, saving me from what would destroy me. Please let me stay. I want to help you heal, too. Will you take my hand and promise me that you at least will let me show you what I mean?"

Esfirs loses it. Crying, she puts her left hand over her face and collapses on her pillow. Brendan knows the

Bond should be severed, but it doesn't take a telepathic connection to understand her emotions. He embraces her.

They sit there for what seems like an eternity.

When Brendan finally pulls away, he sees that her eyes are not bloodshot but the natural golden combination of the Sabia. "-she," Esfirs says hoarsely, "can we finish making the brin? It will overcook if we do not watch it properly."

Brendan nods his head. He moves over, and Esfirs examines the hookah-like vase, taking off the top and peering inside. She instructs Brendan to pour its contents into little handle-less cups and, once done, takes a sip. A worn smile indicates her approval. Brendan sips from his cup but immediately spits out the brin.

"It tastes like hot mouthwash!" he declares.

Esfirs bursts out laughing. "Do you not drink mouthwash hot?"

"No!" His voice is incredulous. "Mouthwash is medicine we use for dental purposes. It is meant to be swished around and then spat. It tastes disgusting."

"Maybe your tastes will adjust." She pinches his right cheek. "Making and drinking this is an important rite in families."

He takes another swig, forcing himself to swallow despite its revoltingness. Esfirs fingers gently move across his cheek in a soothing motion. Then, unexpectedly, she leans over and smells his neck. The feral action surprises Brendan. Not knowing how to handle it, he stays still.

Courting rituals are essential in every culture. I don't want to mess this one up.

"Calm, be calm, Brendanshe. I smell fear, not love."

Esfirs leaps backward when the door opens. Brendan looks up, ready to challenge the intruder, but seeing Berina causes him to freeze.

"How did I miss a betrothal? Nothing happens on this ship without me knowing! Well, it did not until Mr. Unified Intelligence Command came aboard."

Brendan winces. "I want to apologize for everything."

"I read your logs. Wish you could have trusted me with what you were going through. I have to be honest—that hurt. However, putting the timeline together, it is apparent you were not working against us. Can you promise not to do anything like that again?" Berina places her hands on her hips as she finishes.

He nods and puts out his hand. Berina playfully gives him a low five instead of shaking it. "Ouch. Guess I deserved that." She nods. "Yes, I will not be working for the UIC again; going to resign, in fact. But on to other important things—did you get in trouble for speaking your native language in front of me?"

She laughs. "I have been chewed out before. We saved a Sabia; that is the only thing that matters to me. Speaking of your actions out there—this killer Brendan, where does he go when you pretend to be a person who prefers talking out differences?"

PATRICK ABBOTT

His face drops. Pondering the differences between the Sabia's and his views of his homicides creates a knot in his stomach. Berina seems oblivious to Brendan's emotions while Esfirs reaches over and touches his back, gently rubbing up and down his spine.

Esfirs whispers to Brendan, "We can talk about this in the future." Then, turning to Berina, she says, "Would you want to join us for a meal?"

Berina readily accepts. She squeals as Esfirs pulls out a towel containing large, round pieces of bread from her bag.

"*Nasha* is a unique bread, Brendan. It is made only by women. This nasha is from Nema," Esfirs declares as she passes it, first to Berina, then to Brendan. Both take a piece.

"Berina," Brendan starts, "I just made some brin. Perhaps you would enjoy some?"

"Whoa there, boy! I do not think your fiancée would appreciate you pouring me a cup of brin."

Esfirs snaps an angry look at Brendan. His fearful reaction is enough for her gaze to turn more sympathetic. "Brendan," she says, "men only pour brin for their wives. Berina can pour her own cup."

Berina laughs as she does so. "Training him well, I see. Let this time be your education, Brendan. Use your medical leave wisely."

Esfirs speaks for him. "We will. First, a day or two of rest, then we will start the remaining medical procedures. Those will take maybe a week. After that, I hope to have some time alone with him."

"I do not think that schedule will work," Berina responds. "Three days from now, I am taking Mon and your man to the United States Congress. There is a nice little reception for her and someone else who just got put on the fly-down list."

"What?" Esfirs stands up, angry. "Who authorized this? I specifically ensured he was placed on medical leave!"

Brendan sheepishly raises his hand as if a cloud of guilt hangs over him.

"What?" Esfirs asks him.

"I, um, volunteered to help Mon. She asked me to be a trusted advisor for it. I did not want to let her down."

Esfirs' olive complexion becomes red. She holds her fists so tightly Brendan can hear her knuckles begin to crack.

"Esfirs? Esfirs?" Berina calls to her. "Esfirs!" This snaps her out of her rage. "Esfirs, nothing will happen on this trip. It will be a calm one. Three craft are going because Mon is taking extra guards. Officially because of the militia threat, but I know she is considering the safety of Brendan as well."

"I was hoping for some time together before I"—Esfirs turns to Brendan and then back to Berina—"go on leave."

PATRICK ABBOTT

Her comment catches Brendan off guard. "Another home leave?" His mouth hangs open.

"Yes. Home leave. I must go away for a short time. Mon dragging you away ruins our time together."

Berina waves her hands dismissively. "It should be only one night, Esfirs. I am sure it will be uneventful."

Forty-One – Delilah at the Party

Brendan observes Mon as she works the room. *Gray blazer over a red midi-dress. Abnormally casual, but when you are a space alien, I guess you can get away with wearing anything.* Representatives and senators gather around her, smiling at everything she says. Brendan takes in the rest of the reception; plenty of politicians and their staffers mingle in the ballroom and on the outdoor patio overlooking Washington. Strategically placed Sabia guards stand out in their gray, padded body armor.

He approaches one of them and asks, "Hey brother, how many times have you been to Earth?"

The guard gives Brendan a skeptical look. Then, after a few moments of sizing him up, the guard turns his attention back to the crowd.

Another non-talker. Brendan's mind flashes back to the pre-briefing before the party. Several things indicated to him something was amiss. First, Berina was replaced by a pilot named Qarden. He then discovered a female guard named Hasti had replaced Kimya as his security detail. The only time she addressed him was when she said, "Brendan will notify security of any situation that alarms him or would result in him leaving

the ballroom." The use of the third person strikes him as
odd.

Mon's speaker-amplified voice fills the room.
"Hello, everyone. Dear Senators and Representatives, I
wish to thank you for hosting me here despite the late
hour. Because of your wise leadership, I am honored
and humbled to consider all the people of these United
States friends. Here on Earth"—she smiles at Brendan—
"you have many ingenious inventors. These women and
men remind me of the heroes of my civilization that I
learned about during my tutoring. We have decided,
with your approval, of course, to work with some of your
most elite minds to improve your transportation
infrastructure. At no cost to you, we can ensure a
technological evolution that will forever change how
people and goods transit this planet. Our cooperation
will result in greater efficiency, wealth, and lifesaving
opportunities."

The politicians clap with rapt approval. Mon
places her right hand over her heart and nods. *She's
learning. Way to go, way to go.* Guards return to their
positions, flanking Mon as she moves back into the
crowd of various legislators and other Capitol Hill
staffers.

A firm pat on the back causes an involuntary jolt
from Brendan. He sees a balding but fit man in his mid-
fifties wearing a black tuxedo. The well-dressed man puts
out his hand. *That is a firm handshake.*

"You don't remember me, do you, Officer?" the
man asks.

"I am sorry, sir, I do not."

"Senator David Blair, Missouri. You gave a briefing to me, or, well, the committee I served on about the situation in Afghanistan. That was about two years ago. I would say 'if I remember correctly,' but to be honest, one of my staffers had to point it out to me."

"I hope the briefing was helpful to you, sir."

"The name is David, not sir." The man holds his hands out, making a gesture downplaying the formality.

"Murphy," Brendan follows suit.

David does a double-take. "I thought your name was Brandon."

Brendan laughs. "My apologies. My first name is Brendan, sir."

"Well, Brendan, I'll call you Brendon, and you can keep calling me, sir." He laughs. "I don't remember the details from your briefing. However, I remember you saying, 'things bad, getting worse.' That little rule of thumb proved to be quite an adequate guide when developing foreign policy. Thanks for that."

"You are welcome. As I probably said then, I wish I could have given you much better news."

"No worries, Afghanistan is Afghanistan. But, hey, would you mind if I introduced you to my good friend here?" He motions to a well-dressed woman but does not wait for Brendan to respond. "This here is House Majority Leader Christine Poirier of the decent state of Louisiana."

Christine laughs. "Keep that up, and you won't get my endorsement for president." She gives David's arm a fake punch, then turns her attention to the liaison. "Brendan, David tells me you have been working closely with the Sabia."

Brendan acknowledges Christine with a quick headshake and a hard blink. *No one introduced me tonight. Someone has prepared them.*

"Ha! Don't worry, Brendan," David says. "Both Christine and I are on the intelligence committees. We won't be asking you anything which would put you in jeopardy; we just need to know a few things. Can we ask you some questions in a quieter setting?"

"Uh, I basically put myself on leave after some recent events." Brendan's eyes dart around the room as he pats the back of his head. "So let us keep things informal. How about that empty corner over there? We would not want our Sabia friends to think I ditched them."

"Fair enough," David eagerly replies.

Brendan quickly excuses himself to notify a Sabia guard of what he is doing. This guard is as indifferent to Brendan's presence as the first one he talked to. Once his due diligence is done, he jogs over to the standing table in the corner where David and Christine have set themselves up with two drinks and some appetizers. Approaching them, Brendan sees they did not grab anything for him.

David leans in. "Okay, Officer Murphy, give us the truth. What do you think about the Martians?"

507

"Thankfully, the Sabia have not been hostile, and I have managed to make some good connections. Their tolerance of me has been most appreciated, especially when things could have developed very differently. Mon over there has been especially interested in giving a positive impression." Brendan gestures toward Mon with his thumb.

Christine leans in to whisper, "Is she the one who messed up in North Carolina?"

"I have never commented on that," Brendan attempts to deflect. *They must have a good collection on the North Carolina groups.*

Christine snaps. "Come on! Meade's boys are going helter-skelter down there, knocking off anyone who opposes them. They are claiming independent groups' poor discipline is a risk 'to be solved.' Brendan, a well-organized group growing a monopoly of force that can easily be turned against the government, is unacceptable to the American people. The Patriot Assembly will use any Sabia misstep to grow in power. We need to know what happened out there, Officer."

Brendan's heart begins to race, and his hands start to tremor. "Ma'am, this is an intelligence matter. Please wait for an official report."

"And when will that happen? I hear the Sabia won't let you talk to us." Christine leans in even closer.

"Representative, that is not true. For months, my efforts to talk to our diplomatic presence on the ship have been met with silence. Meanwhile, various domestic organizations have tried to arrest me. As a result, I have been working on high stress and limited sleep for months. Tomorrow I have a rest day. After that, I will reach out to the diplomatic presence on the ship yet again. Please help me help you by having the ambassador or staff contact me. Good day, madam." He turns to walk away.

"Brendan, stop," David calls out. He examines his drink as he fiddles with the glass. "What else can we do to make your job easier?"

Brendan sighs. "What is with the mixed messages? I am told to report in, called out for running so-called illegal operations, pushed to toughen up when I ask for help, threatened with arrest, and now politely asked what can make my job easier. What the heck, man?"

"Thank you for your insight, Brendan. I'll see what I can do." The senator puts on a friendly facade. "Now, if you'll excuse us, we have hands to kiss and babies to shake."

Brendan sighs deeply as they walk away. His body feels like an energy vampire just sucked everything out of him. He mutters, "How many more hours do I have to endure these jerks?"

A soft voice floats into his ear. "You're at a party full of politicians—what else did you expect?"

He sees a short woman with long Irish-red hair wearing a scarlet bandage dress with a plunging neckline. She walks over and takes David's spot. *I cannot get away from this table.*

"I am unaware of Sabia customs, but here on Earth, men still introduce themselves first, Officer Murphy."

Brendan remains on high alert. He eyes the woman as prey would a potential predator. "Well, you know my name, but I do not know yours." After a moment, he decides to give her the benefit of the doubt. "Sorry about that. I am Brendan."

She looks into his eyes and does a little curtsy, giving him a view from which he diverts his eyes. *This woman knows what she is doing.*

"A pleasure, Intelligence Officer Brendan Sean Murphy. My name is Emily Kelly. Friends call me Fee, though. You may, too." Her eyes linger on his for a moment too long, Brendan thinks.

"Hello, Fee. You are right about this party. Guess I need to grin it and bear it for another hour or so, eh?" Brendan's head turns to look at the crowd as he speaks.

"Mmm, I don't really agree with that resignation thinking. Hey, tell you what"—Fee perks up, causing Brendan to face her again—"let's go for a walk. Tell your babysitters I am an old friend and that I want to show you my office. They'll let you go."

This is not right. "I think I really have to be going."

Brendan steps away from the table, but Fee manages to obstruct his path. He attempts to maneuver around her, but she mirrors him, ensuring his exit is blocked. A few more quick steps, which would rival those in any English period-piece dance scene, are matched point-for-point by her.

"I was thinking we could go somewhere a little more intimate," she says.

What the heck is going on? "I am not interested in that sort of thing, lady."

"Not like that." She bites her lip seductively. "Something like a SCIF would be a place where we could talk safely."

"And what could we discuss in a SCIF which we cannot here? The only classified I know are all out-of-date stuff about old wars."

She dips her head and laughs. "No, no. I don't care about that. I'm interested in what those politicians were trying to find out. However, they didn't know where to take the conversation. I do, Brendan." She scans the room as if checking to see if anyone is paying attention to them. "Would it surprise you to learn the sheriff in Red Hawk is a trustworthy individual? That he could be the type of patriot who would plant a bug in the veterans' hall for us? We know you and Mon had one hell of a falling out. I lost count of how many times you called her a liar. But unfortunately, something knocked our mic right as things were getting good. Through the muffled sounds, we can tell she told you something. Whatever it was, it quieted you down. Let's just say it doesn't take a genius to figure out it was important. So come with me, Brendan, and I promise you—promise—all the threats of legal problems go away."

Emily's tone has gone from flirty to deadly serious. Brendan thinks her body posture displays a hunger for information, a drive that makes the best collectors. This operative is allowing him to close one door and jump headfirst through another; however, Brendan's brain kicks in. Remembering the bathroom message at the UIC and having not identified Emily's affiliation, he decides to trust the system.

"Emily, I look forward to being debriefed by you. First, working with my hosts, I will file an official report and get it to the ambassador. As I told the senator, please use your contacts to ensure the ambassador will talk with me."

"Gonna be like that? Before you go"—she pulls out a business card from her clutch purse—"contact me tonight. The number will only work for so long. I'll take any message from you as a sign you're willing to talk. I'll take care of logistics." Emily places the card in Brendan's shirt pocket and then pats him on the chest. Walking away, she turns and gives him a sly wink.

Brendan returns to the gathering of politicians and Sabia. "I have returned," he tells a guard. The guard gives Brendan an incurious look.

As he watches Mon interact with various politicians, the crowd forms a gap, giving Brendan a direct line of sight. Noticing she is motioning to him, Brendan approaches.

"There he is. Senator Juan Prats—my friend Dear Brendan," Mon calls out. "Brendan, this legislator told me there are large snakes in Florida. Did you know this?"

PATRICK ABBOTT

"Yes, Mon, there are huge reptiles in Florida. Especially in the southern part of the state known as the Everglades."

"Dear Juan, would it be possible to obtain one of these snakes? I would very much like to tease Brendan with one."

The crowd of politicians and staffers laughs uproariously as if it is the most hilarious thing they've ever heard. *A bit forced, guys.*

"As you servants of the people clearly see"— Brendan's words garner more laughs—"your continued support of the diplomatic mission to the Sabia has fostered such friendly relations that they feel comfortable teasing me."

The laughter is honest this time, with even Mon getting in a moment of mirth. She smiles warmly at Brendan.

A congresswoman in her sixties with thick glasses speaks up. "Brendan, tell us something we don't know about the Sabia."

Both Mon and her guards stare intensely at Brendan. The question basically stops dead the music in Brendan's mind. Quickly, he goes through various stories and weighs their potential impact. Finally, crossing his arms, he says, "I will say something which may not be fascinating to you but has been a delightful surprise to me." The crowd goes silent. "As you may already know, the Sabia were kind enough to not only save me but rebuild my injured body." He feels a headache from a Bond being forced on him. "Their medical care was incredibly generous. However, what touched me has been the friendship they have given me. Several of them have been exceptionally kind. They are true friends."

The audience's anticipation dissipates as shoulders slouch and people back away. Brendan's headache vanishes as well. *Better to disappoint them than anger Mon right now.*

For the next hour, he becomes a wallflower, enjoying the night. People come and go—mostly go—as the clock continues to move. Brendan yawns and rubs his eyes several times as he awaits the night's end. The activities finally wrap up close to midnight.

At last, the Speaker of the House takes the microphone. "Fellow representatives and senators, I want to thank everyone for coming to our little after-hours get-together. Please join me in giving our honored guest, Mon, a warm ovation." The crowd claps furiously. "Thank you, Mon, for allowing us to get to know you. May we have even more fruitful exchanges in the future with our Sabia friends, in the form of trade and other economic opportunities!" The crowd hoots and hollers. *Good thing Esfirs is not here. She would be giving me a disgusted "I told you so" look.* The crowd breaks up with everyone going in for one last handshake with Mon. She is visibly not comfortable with this gesture yet. *Something we need to work on.*

Looking around, the lady in red is nowhere to be found. All the guards are also unknown to Brendan. *Where the heck did this crew come from? What gives with their behavior?*

PATRICK ABBOTT

Mon's voice from right behind Brendan causes him to jump. "May we have a moment together?" Brendan turns to face her. "I am sorry—I did not mean to startle you."

"Not a problem, Mon. I was just deep in thought."

"What were you thinking about?" She looks at him with a mild scowl.

"Oh"—*please do not scan me with a forced Bond*—"I was just thinking about how you were going to tease me with a large snake. Have to be careful, you know."

"Glad to know you now learn the price of failing me." Mon's serious tone is undermined by a smirk. "Come, Brendan; I want to walk and talk with you outside."

She offers Brendan her left hand, which he takes. Together they step out onto the patio. The early winter night air is crisp and nips at his face. For a few moments, they watch light traffic slowly make its way down the far-off streets, a few tourists' cameras flash in the distance, and a plane descends towards a nearby airport. Brendan thinks about the evenings he would spend in the city when he first came to Washington. Those were fun nights for a young man fresh out of college. Then came dating, and those were even better. Next were the nights back from deployment, the attempts to distract himself from the pain of war, pretend that he was fine, and ignore the warning signs of his mental decline. After that came the married nights. How many of those had he wished he was anywhere else? Later on, there were the post-deployment, post-betrayal widower nights. Those nights he didn't even live; he just survived. Now he was back in Washington, wishing he could live those early nights again, but this time with Esfirs. *Esfirs* . . .

"Dear Brendan, when we filed the guest list with Congress, we received a message back from the ambassador claiming the government would seek your arrest. For them to back down, Zand had to state that any action against you would be considered an attack against us."

Brendan waits for more. Instead of continuing, Mon goes back to gazing at the nighttime metropolis. He shifts his head around several times to gain her attention but fails to.

"Mon, what was the point of telling me that?"

"Oh"—she turns around with an almost surprised look—"I thought you should know there is a standing threat from these people against you."

With that, she walks back into the ballroom alone. Brendan instinctively feels his shirt pocket and notices the woman's card. Having received mixed messages from the letter, Brendan finds himself frustrated. He is overwhelmed by choices and temptations, actions, and consequences. *A text to the woman might buy me some leverage.* But then the thought of losing Esfirs forever causes a sour taste in his mouth. *No, file a report about the relevant parts, keep Mon's trust—everything secondary can be brought to light at an appropriate time after assuring the Sabia of our good intentions. This way, nothing is jeopardized.*

PATRICK ABBOTT

The guard, Hasti, approaches Brendan as he walks back inside. With a flat voice, she asks, "Did you encounter any problems while you were here?"

"Besides some uncommunicative Sabia? Nothing I could not handle," he replies.

Hasti studies him for a second and then walks away without a word.

Weirdo.

Forty-Two – Nemesis

Writing the report is somewhat enjoyable for Brendan because of Berina's struggles to sit still in an Earth-made chair. It's not cruel schadenfreude, just the guilty little pleasure of watching her fish-out-of-water moment. This amusing sideshow originated when the new United States diplomat, Ambassador Sandra Fie, demanded Brendan be debriefed on Earth. Delegate Loft managed to negotiate it down to Brendan filing a report and a debriefing afterward on the Sabia's mothership. Brendan is to announce his resignation from the Unified Intelligence Command at this meeting. This initially made the North Carolina after-action report emotionally challenging to write. Thankfully, Berina's fidgeting and moaning during her battle with the chair make things more doable. Brendan watches her from his desk as he types on the laptop.

"Why do you have to keep the Terran custom of sitting in chairs?" She maneuvers some more, trying to find a comfortable spot. "You know, Esfirs will not allow you to have chairs when you move into her cabin."

"You do not need to be here," Brendan replies with a wry smile. That is a bit of a lie; Berina almost certainly has been ordered to be here. She claimed her schedule was clear for the day and that she was bored.

PATRICK ABBOTT

He initially appreciated her offer to help him draft the report, but then the questions came. Berina was interested in everything Brendan was going to say. She even offered "tips" on how to word things.

After struggling some more, Berina finally gives up. "Nope!" She gets up and moves the chair to the corner. She leaves only to return a minute later with a pillow that she promptly places on the ground and sits on.

Brendan tsks, purposefully loud enough for Berina to hear. "I have had to adjust much here with you Sabia, but you cannot even handle a chair. I do not know what that says about you, Berina."

"Guess who I have been talking to?" Berina asks, ignoring Brendan's pointed statement.

"Let me guess: Esfirs."

"Wrong! Your friend Dear Baldwin." Brendan stops typing and looks at her. "Oh, that got your attention. I wondered how I could assist with your upcoming married life, so I decided that helping you on your faith journey would be a place to start. Let me tell you, Brendan; he had things to say about that."

"You told him I was getting married?" Brendan stops typing. *Oh, Father Baldwin is not going to be happy with me.*

"You are welcome." She laughs sardonically.

"What did he say?"

Berina claps her hands playfully. Then, with a sly smile, she replies, "Many things."

"Stop playing!"

"Let me think. What was the most important thing the priest told me? Oh, yes, I remember now." She acts out her thinking with overly dramatic gestures. "He said you need to contact him immediately so the marriage can be regularized."

Brendan rakes his hand through his hair. "Berina, if he knows, it probably is only a matter of time before the government knows. I have not had time to prepare anything."

"So what, Brendan?" Now she crosses her arms and makes an aggressive face. "You are going to quit the government and marry Esfirs. You asked me to help you spiritually, so I am. You need to reach out to him."

Brendan checks himself. His emotions are torn between the panic of losing control of the narrative and the relief of taking one step closer to marriage. He swallows hard. "Thank you. Thank you, Berina."

Berina makes an exaggerated hand motion which Brendan takes as mocking homage. "You are most welcome." She becomes more serious. "I know Esfirs is excited about the wedding. How are you, though? You have been through a lot lately. I often worry that my friend Dear Brendan gets little say in what is happening."

He sighs. "Thank you, Berina—really this time, thank you." Brendan pauses with another sigh. "That actually means a lot." Brendan closes the laptop. "To be honest, I think my 'I do' was said in an out-of-mind state.

That does not mean I made the wrong choice. I do very much look forward to marrying her. However . . . I think my main emotion is apprehension."

Berina repositions herself. "What are you apprehensive about?"

"Lots of things. What if our cultural expectations of each other are so foreign that we eventually decide it is too difficult to love each other? What if she hurts me as my past wife did? What if I cannot be the husband she needs? What if—what if I hurt her?"

"Brendan," she says in a soft voice, "would you stay up in the middle of the night to care for Esfirs if she was sick?"

"Yes, of course." *How could she even ask that question?*

"Would you abandon her if she was dying?"

"What? Never!" Brendan responds as if his honor had been challenged.

"Brendan, she would do the same for you. So you have nothing to fear. Choose to love her every day, and she will do the same."

He goes silent with self-reflection. Heather had mocked him when he had anxiety attacks. When he was away, she went to bed with other men. A functional marriage was something he had grown to think was beyond his reach. *Not anymore. Esfirs loves me.* He smiles at the thought.

"When I was a kid," he begins, "I thought the happiest people in the world were adventurers. Those who got to travel the world and do daring things were my definition of heroes. That is what I wanted to be. So, I found a skillset that gave me that opportunity. Europe, the Middle East, and Asia. I went to war in countries throughout those regions. Worked with tribes, getting them to fight the bad guys, even became a 'war hero'"— he sets this in air quotes—"taking a series of bridges. And after all that, I became a shell of a man. Only after it was too late did I realize I wanted a family to love. Now that I have that opportunity, I am worried about losing it."

"Welcome home." Berina smiles at him.

Her response truly touches Brendan. He puts his head down and nods. Even without a Bond, he can feel Berina's care for him. *It really feels like it. How I missed being "home."*

"What about you? What did you long for when you were a child?" He asks while looking at his screen.

A familiar voice answers, "Answers about pre-arrival life experiences are classified."

Brendan looks up. To his shock, he sees Emily Kelly, the redhead from the party, standing in the doorway. Now though, her skin is not pale Irish but Sabia olive, and she is wearing the black uniform and floppy hat of the rather hostile Sabia from the mystery hangar. Brendan turns his gaze to Berina only to see her at full attention.

Emily looks at her. "Leave us." In a flash, Berina runs out the door. Emily folds her arms and looks at Brendan with a triumphant smirk on her face.

"Stand up, Intelligence Officer Brendan Sean Murphy." He does so and walks out from behind the desk. In turn, she removes her hat. "Please allow me to introduce myself. My name is Fahime." She pauses. "I must admit you disappointed me."

Brendan feels like a deer in headlights. "Oh, how so?" He nervously chuckles.

"You were supposed to contact me last night or this morning."

He chooses to remain quiet.

"Ah," she remarks, "where are my manners?" Fahime walks over, grabs the chair Berina moved, and places it beside Brendan. Next, she goes to the desk where Brendan had been working and sits in his chair. "Sit down, Dear Brendan."

Brendan looks at her. *That is a convincingly dishonest smile.* "You are in my seat."

"Oh"—she acts surprised—"my apologies! I was under the impression it belonged to the Legion. And now I must confess my disappointment in myself. You require friendship from those you submit to and roll over for." Her friendly tone and manner, combined with her cruel words, are disorienting to Brendan. "Do you know why your failure to contact me disappointed me? All I needed was one little message from you. It could have been a single letter. Then your disloyalty would be on full display. Hell, as you Terrans say, you could have denied encountering me. Instead, you hide behind 'nothing I could not handle.'"

Brendan controls his words but makes his tone forceful. "You are in my chair. You are insulting me. You are not in any chain of command I recognize. Leave now."

"Oh, Dear Brendan, you misunderstand." She places her right hand over her heart and bows slightly, mimicking his Afghan gesture.

He cuts her off. "Do not mock that gesture of friendship!"

She laughs, this time not hiding her mockery.

At this moment, Kimya comes bursting into the room with Berina, positioning herself on Brendan's left side and glowering at the Defense Force member. Fahime responds silently, looking Kimya straight in the eye. *Bonding sure is versatile.* Brendan watches as Kimya's rage faces down Fahime's defiance.

"No need for such aggression, Kimya. I would not want you to end up like the others." Fahime releases a cruel cackle. Brendan notices that Kimya takes several steps back. Then, Fahime looks at Brendan with a soft, deceptively calm face. "Thank you, Dear Brendan, for bringing such entertainment. Never did I think I would see this pair together. I hope to catch you soon." Again mimicking the Afghan gesture, she locks eyes with Brendan and transmits pleasant emotions to him. "Good day." On her way out, Fahime stops and makes the same gesture at Berina.

PATRICK ABBOTT

"What was that?" Brendan asks angrily.

"Counterintelligence," Kimya responds.

"Why is there a counterintelligence operative targeting me?"

With her eyes fixed on the door, Fahime exited; Berina replies, "Some are still not persuaded you are trustworthy after the communicator incident."

Brendan turns toward her. "Carrot and freaking stick, eh?"

Berina looks puzzled. "Vegetable and wood? I do not understand, Dear Brendan."

"'Dear Brendan,'" he mocks. "You wanted to help me with the report? Hardly. You were really spying on me just like Fahime was when I was on Capitol Hill!"

"What? Not like that!"

"Just like that!"

"Like what? A spy?" Berina takes a step towards Brendan as her voice rises. "Do I need to remind you that you were the one writing back to those people who wanted to dissect you like an animal? What did they need to offer you for you to give up our friendship?"

Kimya screams, getting both of their attention. "Stop it! She is trying to poison your mind, Brendan."

He opens his mouth to speak, but Kimya seizes him. Lifting him several inches off the ground, she forces a Bond on him. *This does not feel enjoyable.* To make matters worse, her overwhelming will echoes the words "stop it" in his mind. His anger is forcibly shut down. It is the Montana experience with Esfirs all over again, but it's definitely a violation this time.

Meanwhile, a sensation of light develops and hovers above him like a lightbulb just out of reach. His mind grasps at it as if it were a life preserver. Slowly, Kimya puts him down. Closing his eyes, Brendan breathes deeply for a minute. When he finally opens them again, he is much calmer.

"I am—good. I am good." He looks around. "I need to sit down." Brendan allows his back to hit the wall as he slides to the floor.

"The reason I wanted to help you was because I wanted to make sure nothing you wrote would jeopardize your future with Esfirs." Berina holds her hands good as she speaks.

"Look, I am sorry. There are times I—I really mess up. Goodness, it is so easy to hurt others and myself. I am sorry." He buries his face in his palms.

A strong pair of hands pull his head up. He can see Esfirs as well as Kimya, Berina, Zalta, and a new woman also wearing a black uniform.

Esfirs sits down next to him. "Brendanshe"—her use of the diminutive in public surprises him—"how long have you been sitting on the floor?"

Brendan looks at her as if she asked a stupid question. "What do you mean 'how long?' Not even a few seconds. How did you get here?"

Esfirs nods thoughtfully while Zalta's eyes widen. Brendan looks around, searching for a clue as to what is happening. Esfirs forms a Bond with him and quickly sends a message of love before standing up and then slowly backing away. The unknown woman then approaches and sits directly in front of him. She smiles as she crosses her legs. As their Bond forms, Brendan can feel her flow into him. He senses her smoothly progressing deep inside him without causing him any discomfort.

"Hello, Brendan." Her deep voice adds maturity to her forty-some appearance. "My name is Sainas; I am the Chief Medical Officer and the Deputy Commander here for the Defense Force." Brendan's head begins to spin. "You have been on the floor for quite some time—longer than you would think, I suspect. If you would allow me, it would be my pleasure to assist you."

"Assist me with what? I do not understand what is going on." Brendan's voice is agitated.

Sainas gently places her hands on his wrists. Instinctively, Brendan loosens his grip and realizes he has been digging his fingernails into his biceps. Through the Bond, he feels Sainas' concern for him. Nodding, he allows her to take control of his hands. She guides them to her face.

"You had what we would refer to as a symptom of combat illness," she says.

Brendan's heart drops. *Did I just have a PTSD blackout? I am doomed.*

No. Brendan can hear Sainas' voice in his head challenge his dread. *You are going to be okay. Trust me, friend. Come with me.*

Slowly he lets go of her face, and then they both stand up together. She reaches out her hand. Nervously, he takes it.

PATRICK ABBOTT

Forty-Three – FOB Robertson

It is indeed a comfy couch. It is a Sabia couch, though, making it feel like a mattress on the floor. Brendan sits on his backside while Sainas sits cross-legged on a separate sofa, facing him. Brendan's head is swimming from the earlier encounter with Fahime. Running his hand through his hair, he feels his scalp is dampened with sweat.

"I can only imagine the mental angst you are feeling right now. Would you like me to explain what is happening, or would you prefer some more silence?" Sainas' voice is surprisingly deep yet feminine. It reminds him of Eastern European women speaking English but is even deeper than that.

Brendan rubs his eyes, struggling for words. "I— the . . ." He makes several attempts, but thankfully, Sainas doesn't rush him. Finally, coherent thoughts start forming in his mind. "Could you please introduce yourself? I like to have context when I talk with people. It helps me understand what is happening."

"Of course." Sainas rocks herself once on the couch. "My name is Sainas. As I said earlier, I am the Chief Medical Officer and Deputy Commander for the Defense Force assigned to this mission to Terra. But let me think of something I have not told you." She puts her left index finger on her lower lip and pauses for a moment. "You are the first person born on Terra that I have met. Previously, I saw some in the realm of North Carolina, but I did not talk to them. So I am intrigued to get to know you and learn about Terran culture."

"Well," Brendan says, leaning away from her on the sofa with his arms crossed, "it is nice to meet you, Sainas. No, sorry"—he sits up—"This should be done more formally. Thank you for introducing yourself. Really, thank you."

As Brendan talks, Sainas' smile transforms into a somber expression Brendan can't place. He looks at her expecting a Bond, but none comes. In a sort of discomfort at the silence, he pulls his knees to his chest and holds his legs tightly. "I yelled at a friend today. I—hell—can I be honest with you?"

"With patients, I have a straight talk policy. You are free to say whatever you want. So please, feel at liberty to always be honest with me."

"Ever since I got here, with the Sabia that is, my life has been a painful cycle of trauma breaking me down, coming to some resolution that resolves the problem, only to then experience new trauma. Again and again and again, I make the same mistakes." Brendan buries his face in his legs.

"How do you feel about being in this cycle?" She asks non-judgementally.

Brendan replies without lifting his head. "I hate it."

PATRICK ABBOTT

In his self-created darkness, Brendan feels a weight to his right. Looking over, he sees Sainas sitting next to him. He instinctively looks her in the eyes. As a Bond forms between them, she puts out her hand. Without thinking, he takes it.

The next moment he finds himself in a courtyard surrounded by Hesco barriers. The sun is out, the air dry, and the surroundings oddly silent. Heavy military gear weighs him down. Touching it, he feels the textures of his vest, ammo pouches, helmet, and more. He briefly panics as he looks for his firearm. Then, suddenly, as if out of nowhere, he realizes a carbine is strapped to his shoulder, and his sidearm is in its holster. This allows Brendan to partially calm down, although he doesn't understand how he got here.

"You are the one who brought us here." Sainas' voice calls from his right. His gear slows him as he turns to face her. The voice remains bodiless until she suddenly appears out of nowhere. She stands next to him in what looks like Russian combat armor. "We have two different uniforms on. Why are we wearing this?" She asks.

"This is a place from my past," Brendan says. "Why are we here?"

"We are in your mind, Brendan. Where we are is how you feel about your current situation. You brought us here. Tell me more about this place, please."

"Oh, this is a terrible place. FOB Robertson is where I arranged for a peace talk with Taliban militants. However, they sent a suicide bomber instead of a negotiator." Brendan points to a black mark on the ground. "It was right there where he . . . I nearly died. My life changed after that. No more deployments, no more missions; my marriage ended while I was in the hospital. I was never the same." Tears form in his eyes. Brendan tries to back up and divert his gaze but finds himself paralyzed, staring at the ground.

"How do you feel about being back here?" Sainas asks calmly.

"I want to run away."

"What makes you want to run away?"

Brendan looks at her with disbelief. "This is a dangerous place." He tugs on his chest to demonstrate the body armor. "Look at this—even with this, we are not safe enough."

"Not safe enough? Should we go into one of the buildings?"

"Sainas, did you not hear me? We are not safe anywhere. The best we can do is hunker down and defend ourselves. If I can get on a radio, maybe I can get us a ride out of here."

She holds up her padded hand. "Remember, Dear Brendan, this is in your mind."

My mind? Yes, I'm not here. Here. But this is so real. My mind. Remember, I am in my mind.

"Be calm, Brendan. I wanted to see how you envisioned your current situation. But unfortunately, your mind is associating your current situation with this corner of Terra." She motions to the empty forward operating base. "What I see is someone who senses danger constantly. You put on this armor because you feel threatened by almost everything. The need to fight interferes with your friendships." She leans in to examine him. "Your time with us has even damaged your armor." Brendan can feel her fingers against his skin as she prods what looks like shrapnel damage. "You cannot act on your decisions to change because you are still in combat and at risk of being hurt." She looks at him intently. "How does what I say land with you?"

Brendan wants to hide like a turtle within his armor. He frowns in acceptance of Sainas words. *She is right.* The weight of this realization causes him to lower his head in shame.

"There is no shame in knowing such things," she continues. "What we need to do is to work on healing. Tell me, why am I in different armor? Perhaps this is for your females?"

"No, it is, um . . . for another country."

"Friendly or enemy country?"

"It is complex."

Sainas studies her armor for a second. "What country is Complex? Is that a slang term for the official name?" Her question causes Brendan to laugh. "I see you still have your sense of humor." She briefly smiles. "Your mind put the armor of another country on me. You fear you are surrounded by enemies that you cannot trust anyone. What do you need from me to show the Sabia and I are not a threat to you? How can we make sure you think my time with you is like combat?"

"No offense, Sainas, but I do not think there is much you could do that would ultimately end in better mental health for me."

"Brendan, thank you for your opinion. However, I am asking you, no, I am pleading to you"—she presses her hands together as if she is praying—"to try. If I may offer a recommendation, is there anything you tried to get from or learn from a Sabia who denied your request?"

This is a waste of time. Brendan throws his hands to his sides. "Heck, I do not know—tell me how come the Sabia speak perfect English."

Sainas matter-of-factly explains, "For nearly seventy Terran years, our probes have acquired media signals from your planet. Using artificial intelligence, we could determine and differentiate your various languages. As soon as it became evident that English was the language of the planetary elite, we developed a rigorous philological training and enculturation program."

Brendan stands there with his mouth open in disbelief. In response, Sainas takes a step forward, places her hands on her hips, and asks for another question.

"Umm . . ." He tries to buy time while he thinks of something important to ask. He remembers his conversation with Berina about UFOs. *What would she say about possible early trips and spying on Earth?*

Without waiting for him to vocalize his question, she says, "Besides the probes, we did send small teams into the general population to gain insight into how Terran society worked and how it would react to first contact. I can deny the claims that we infiltrated governments, though. Additionally, while we did have craft insert and exfil small teams on Terra, I have no idea what the various UFOs Terrans claimed they saw were. Our shuttlecrafts have outstanding stealth capabilities."

Brendan can only stare at her; she entrusts him with classified Sabia information. What she has just revealed is epic but not surprising.

"May I ask one more question?" Sainas tilts her head in acknowledgment. "I-I—" Brendan closes his eyes. Taking a moment to regroup, he presses forward. "I have to ask—are Berina and Esfirs real friends? Or have I fallen for some sort of confidence operation? Their kindness really has meant a lot to me. I-I do not know."

"Berina originally was assigned to report on your activities. She continues to do so. However, her care and friendship have been self-evident since revealing your hybridization. As for Esfirs, do you truly need third-party verification of her love?"

Crap. Brendan's mind flatlines. "My behavior has jeopardized everything."

"That sounds bad. How can you save 'everything'?"

"Apologizing is just a first step—I have already done that. I need to—I need to . . . get out of this mindset I have been in since I got here." A mental dam opens. The words flow freely. "All this time, I have been reacting to pain from my previous marriage and deployments. Doing all that made me think there is no one I can trust. I have been putting on this freaking armor that separates me from others. No more combat for me, just healing. Then maybe, just maybe, I can focus on helping others. Until then, though, no more."

Sainas walks up to him and places her hand on his shoulder. Their armor is instantly replaced with civilian Earth clothes.

"Very good," Sainas says as she smiles. "What is the first step toward accomplishing this?"

"I need to apologize to Berina."

With those words, Brendan finds himself back on the couch.

PATRICK ABBOTT

Interlude – Berina: The Goodbye

Brendan is holding back tears right now. However, he is much more composed than I thought he would be. If this had happened earlier, he would be bawling his eyes out on the floor. Little bugger has toughened up. Good for him.

Oh, here is the apology. Yeah, Brendan means it, no doubt about that. Is this where the tears come in?

Nope, Esfirs for the save. You always were a softy inside, sister. I bet he really needed that pat right now. Just make sure you have the patience to bring healing to him. Who knows, maybe his caring heart can temper your strong will.

He is wrapping up. Yeah, I will accept it, Dear Brendan, you need not fear that. I will let you think I am pondering whether to accept the apology only because I want you to enjoy Esfirs' hug for an extra second.

"I will not deny your words hurt," she finally says. "The harm in them was not the words themselves but the emotion you had toward me, a friend who has advocated for you and even taken heat for you."

She looks at him with a stoic face. *Terrans are too emotional for their own good. It allows Brendan to do his thing with other Terrans, but Esfirs should help balance him out. They have their own philosophers who practiced ending the reign of emotions over them. So why do Terrans ignore their works? Sadly, that is not the only time their species has made the wrong decision.*

"I know," Brendan says. "And"—he begins to choke up before stopping himself—"I know I ruined everything, but . . . just know I will always be thankful for the friend you were. The destruction of our friendship is totally my fault. Thank you for everything, and I wish you the best. Goodbye, Berina."

Yep, he meant that apology. "Never did I say the friendship was over, Brendan. We are still friends."

Before she can continue, he puts his head in his hands. He takes a sharp breath before looking back up at her. *Good for you, Brendan, dominate the panic.* He thanks her "from the bottom" of his heart. *I do not need a Bond to know he means it.*

Brendan now begins talking about the next steps for his own healing. Much to Berina's surprise, he discusses the need for closure by returning to the Unified Intelligence Command to resign. The words "sooner rather than later" set Esfirs off. She demands Brendan not to go to Washington. In response, Brendan indicates he does not want to work on the after-action report with the diplomatic presence on the ship but instead wants a "one and done" meeting with his command to end everything in person. Esfirs, meanwhile, is insistent they spend the remaining days she has before she leaves together. *This is not too hard to fix, Esfirs, calm down!*

PATRICK ABBOTT

"You both are acting like a bunch of Terrans." Unfortunately, Berina's joke falls flat as Esfirs bares her teeth in anger while Brendan looks on, confused. Having gotten their attention, Berina does not let this suppress her smile. "Esfirs is right, Brendan. You need to rest now. Plus, she will soon be your wife, so you should listen to her." Esfirs peacocks haughtily. *Oh no, you do not!* "As for you, Esfirs, he needs to do this for his own healing. So I will take personal care of him while you are away. I will ensure he continues sessions with Sainas, is included in social events, and has a safe trip to his old comrades to resign."

Esfirs moves to object, but Berina cuts her off with a stern look. Through a speedy Bond, Berina stresses the importance of ending the conversation there. *Stick to your mate, Esfirskhan.* The doctor lowers her head in submission.

Thankfully, neophyte Sabia Brendan is unaware of what is occurring around him. Esfirs helps keep him in this state of bliss by gently stroking his arm. He leans into her as she holds him. *If only you two knew how lucky you were. If my birth had been different, maybe—*

Esfirs starts talking about her plans for the next few days. Brendan asks if she really must leave. With a simple "yes," Esfirs tries and fails to be stoic. Finally, he asks if he can go with her. *Let her go, Dear Brendan; you will see her again soon.*

Berina looks into Esfirs' eyes. *Do not worry, friend; I will make sure everything is ready.*

Forty-Four – A Feast of Fools

Soothing sounds of gentle rain serve as white noise to their conversations. Brendan finds them particularly calming, though unnecessary. His visits with Sainas have been enjoyable throughout the past week, and Brendan recognizes their effectiveness. Despite their brief length, discussions with her have helped him deal with his stress. Yesterday's session was incredibly beneficial. With just a few questions, Sainas coached him into developing a strategy for coping with potential future harassment from those who distrust him. *Prove them wrong with actions, and any future behavior will only demonstrate their foolishness.*

It is Brendan's turn to start with a joke for today's session. "Sainas, do you know what the greatest warning about the quality of military intelligence is?" She raises her eyebrow inquisitively. "The fact that the military makes shirts with zippers and pants with buttons." Brendan chuckles at his own joke while Sainas forces a laugh.

"Well," she says, "you do have humor. I am glad such observations of Terran habits bring such lightheartedness to you."

"Trust me; it is funny if you have lived it." Looking at her, it's apparent to him she doesn't understand the joke. This causes Brendan to laugh even more.

"I see you amuse yourself. Are you willing to be part of an exercise I have thought up?"

"That is why I am here. Let us begin." Brendan says as he shifts on the couch.

"Very good. I want you to examine these images and tell me your thoughts about them."

Brendan nods in acceptance. Sainas reaches down and pulls out a thin silver plate-like object, which she hands to Brendan. He views a photograph of a teenage-looking Sabia woman with iridescent skin and golden eyes of multiple hues. Her long brown hair reaches her shoulders, covered by a gray robe. Brendan thinks he sees a cockiness in this youngster. Something about the smile turning into a smirk comes across as a prime example of youthful arrogance. Additionally, the way she looks into the camera gives Brendan an impression of one who seeks to dominate all that she encounters. Like a high school student who thinks she knows how the world works. He wipes his face as he ponders what to say.

"Just tell me initial thoughts." Sainas leans in and squints at him.

"Well,"—Brendan takes one last look at the image before looking up at Sainas—"I think this girl believes she can take on the universe—as we say on Earth. I would suspect she is rather a handful. Personally, I would feel bad for the mother who has to deal with her." He chuckles.

"How would you feel if I told Berina what you thought about her first Legion portrait?"

"This is Berina." Brendan is hit by a wave of mirth, knowing he can use this photo. "Ha!" He laughs and slaps his thigh. "Oh, my goodness, I am so going to make fun of her for the long hair. But, looking back on this image, it makes perfect sense. This is the photograph of a pilot, all right."

Sainas grins. "I will ignore you not answering the question. Here is a second image I want you to look at."

Brendan accepts the portrait and gasps. This young girl's features are instantly recognizable. First, he focuses on her dark brown hair, held in a particular style with a clip in the back. Next, he observes the lushness of her lips and, finally, her golden eyes, which radiate intelligence. *Esfirs.* Closing his eyes, he holds the picture to his heart. A short hum from Sainas reminds Brendan that he is not alone. Putting down the image, he awkwardly chuckles.

"Fairly obvious I already miss her, eh? It is amazing how beautiful she was already, even when she was young. Man, has it been only four days since she left? Look at this"—he shows the picture to Sainas—"can you not see her now in this image? Her maturity, kindness, and beauty are so self-evident." He shakes his head in awe and puts both plates down on the couch.

"I am in no doubt about your emotions and thoughts toward that portrait," Sainas says. "There is one more I wish to get your reaction to. This one is what you call a photograph."

PATRICK ABBOTT

The doctor extends a thin, 8.5 x 11-inch glossy photograph. Brendan reaches out to accept it but freezes when he sees the image. Brendan shudders when viewing it and his hand slowly begins to shake.

"Where did you get that?" he demands.

"Could you tell me why your reaction is such—"

"Please"—Brenda's voice cracks—"no."

Sainas leans in. "Brendan, I promise you there is healing if you do this exercise. No doubt it can be painful, but please try. Take the image and tell me what you think."

Finally accepting the photograph, he can barely bring himself to look at it. Twenty-one-year-old Brendan is lanky and still has traces of teenage acne on his face; he exudes youthful energy. Brendan's breathing becomes heavier as he stares at his younger self.

"Brendan? Have you disappeared on me?" Sainas shifts on her couch.

"No," he whispers, "I am still here."

"What are you thinking, Brendan?"

"I am thinking about a ghost." He pauses. "Memories of me being happy, trusting, ready to take on the world." Brendan pauses. "However, that was only how I thought about myself, not what reality was."

"Who were you?"

"Nothing more than a fool. I was a dupe who loved a woman who did not love me. Nothing more than an unwanted kid who was his father's mistake..." He wipes his mouth. "I wish the things I thought at the time were true. So much. But they were lies." Then, exhaling deeply, he puts the photograph down on his lap.

The chief medical officer silently studies him. Both Sainas and Brendan shift on their respective couches. A desire for an emotional connection drives Brendan to look into her eyes. Instead of a Bond, however, he gets a look of pure sympathy. Together in the stillness, they stare at each other.

Brendan feels a desire to open up more to Sainas. "You know," he says, "I have long had these opinions about myself. That is why I never liked to have my photograph taken. Every time I saw myself, I would see through the facade I put up. Even if it was just for a second, I knew the truth."

Sainas stretches out her legs to recline. "Brendan, your words are heavy. May I share what Berina and Esfirs said about the portraits?"

His eyes widen. *Oh no, they saw what I was and realized what I have become!* "Of course, I would—" He stops himself from lying. "No, but I would . . . Yes, please, tell me what they said."

"Their thoughts about each other were humorous, at least to me. Esfirs remarked that Berina was always overconfident. Meanwhile, Berina stated Esfirs was not dating at the time because, and I quote here, 'she is not wearing ribbons in her hair to attract the attention of boys as she did for Darai and Nek.'

PATRICK ABBOTT

"It may surprise you how they discussed their own portraits. I will quote Berina again because she provided such good quips. First, she said, 'Ugh, humble yourself, girl.' Then she requested I not show you the image. Her worry was you would think her immature. When I reminded her that she had volunteered for this exercise, she became somber. Would you have guessed she saw herself as having to create a facade as well? The fear of not living up to her mother drove her to express confidence when there was none. Esfirs, on the other hand, started reminiscing about her happy childhood but stopped mid-sentence. She threatened to leave when I prodded about her reaction."

Poor Esfirs. You must have thought about not being loved by your mother.

"And," Sainas continues, "do you know what they said about you?" Brendan shakes his head. "Well, Berina first threatened to make fun of you for how you looked if you mocked her about her portrait. Therefore, I advise you to watch how you interact with her. Then, when I pressed her, she said she could see the Brendan she knows, who eagerly served his people.

"It was Esfirs, though, who gave the emotional response. She pried the photograph from my hands when she realized it was of you. She said—and again, I quote—'My Brendan, my Dearest Brendan. Look at you, my love.' She felt the paper and said, 'How happy his eyes were, even back then. I will make them even happier.'"

Brendan crosses his legs. He lets out a "huh" before putting his hand over his mouth. "It is something, how we see the worst in ourselves yet the best in each other. It could be we choose to ignore each other's errors. I do not know." He shifts again. "But maybe I do. Man, I cannot believe Esfirs said 'even happier.' She still sees my eyes as happy?" Brendan starts to tear up. "Maybe I see—maybe I am not so messed up? Maybe there is hope for me? Is there?" His posture opens toward Sainas.

"Exactly," she says with a smile. "The answer is for you to decide what it is. I simply wanted you to know how people see each other. We think what we perceive is reality even though we really only see our biased perception of it."

Brendan fights back the tears. "She thinks I still have happy eyes. I mean – she really – loves me. She wants me to be – happy. It is okay for me to – trust – her." Brendan wipes a tear from her eye. "I think – I know – I am ready to trust again."

"Same time tomorrow, Brendan. Next time I will tell the joke; with any hope, we will both find it amusing."

The slight put-down goes over Brendan's head as he remains transfixed by his fiancée's words. Then, getting up, he awkwardly shakes Sainas' hand before leaving. *I should offer a class on handshakes.*

Walking down the halls is an exhilarating experience. Brendan's racing thoughts build positive momentum within him. *Maybe they see the real me while I am the one with the screwed perspective. She said I have happy eyes. They blew up their own perceived negatives when I know those are so inconsequential. Maybe I do the same. Yes, I do. Things are not as bad as I let them get in my mind!*

Brendan greets Gul upon arriving at the cabin. After a vigorous conversation, Gul agrees to watch a baseball game with him tonight. Entering his room, Brendan claps his hands out of enthusiasm. He looks up at the ceiling. *Thank you, God, for giving me a woman who says I have happy eyes!*

Interlude – Asal: A Terran Heresy

Asal is absolutely stunned by the creature in front of her. Two days ago, she arrived at Dors Station near what everyone was instructed to call "Terra." And now, sitting across from her, is a living, breathing Terran.

She studies the male Terran as if he were one of the creatures from the mythological stories her mother would read to her before bed. *It has dull, monochromatic skin absolutely covered in hair. The fur on the chest and shoulders is noticeably visible underneath its "T-shirt." Its sickly green outfit with its banner printed on the sleeve is supposed to identify this Brendan as an elite, but all it does is show off its animalistic traits. How a priestess such as Berina can associate with this Terran without going through endless cleansing rituals is indeed a scandal. Just look, everyone, it has no shame in being like that! Why are we letting it— a creature the divine has for some reason protected as a hybrid—defile the genetic material of heavenly beings by living as a Terran? Someone must stop this.*

"Hello," she meekly says to Brendan. *Hello? Hello? First contact with a creature from this planet, and all I can manage is a 'hello'? Well, maybe I should not be too hard on myself. The briefing Fahime gave on him is enough to warrant caution.*

PATRICK ABBOTT

Brendan puts down the weights on the metal pol, then nods and wipes his sweaty head with his shirt. He huffs on the workout bench, smiling again at the gaggle.

Ahdin speaks up, grabbing everyone's attention. "Sir, may I inquire about something pertaining to Terran religion?"

'Sir'? Being overly polite to the natives, are we? Just the other day, you were talking about demonstrating a position of strength, Ahdinshe.

"Yeah, boss, you can ask whatever you want. I hope I can give you an answer. If not, I will do my best to get one for you." The Terran uses his hand to wick even more sweat off his hair. "And by the way, you can call me Brendan. On the other hand, if you want to be all formal in a human manner, call me Murphy. Either one is fine."

Why have all those names? And what about the other name? The one in the middle—Juan or Won or something like that? What is the point of a name if you do not use it or selectively use it in various settings?

Ahdin chuckles. "In a briefing, I was told the main religion of Terrans teaches that men own their wives. Is this true?"

Ahdin! Asal shoots her love a furious look.

Meanwhile, the hairy Terran makes a moaning sound while leaning back in his chair. Grinning, he rubs his chin for a few seconds. His eyes briefly appear to be looking beyond everything and everyone to a much more distant horizon. The grin morphs into a pleasant-enough smile. "Not too long ago—Ahdin is it?—I was talking to a cleric friend of mine." He nods toward Berina. "He and I actually talked about what you have asked. In the main holy book on Earth, it says wives must obey their husbands. That is, 'obey,' not 'are property of,' mind you. However, the next section is about how husbands must love and serve their wives with their whole being, even up to death. So, the wife is not the husband's property; instead, they become intertwined partners willing to give up their own needs for the sake of the family they form."

"And there it is," Berina interjects, "you really have been talking to your Dear Father."

What does his father have to do with the cleric? Did his father have to explain what the priestess said? Is Brendan one of the lower-level members of his faith? Maybe his mother should ask for permission to present more of the religion to her child.

A younger medic named Zalta asks, giggling, "Will you demand obedience from Esfirs?" Several Sabia, including Berina, laugh.

What? How can a cleric laugh at such a statement?

"I would love to see that," Berina says. "Can you please do it in a public area so we can watch? Plus, we will probably need Zalta on standby to give you medical aid. All that will be left of you is your left hand."

How can you make light of such a thing! Brendan is by adoption a child of heaven. We killed apostates for far less!

PATRICK ABBOTT

"I do not suppose you could rebuild me from a hand, eh?" Brendan laughs at his own joke.

And you think this is funny? No wonder your civilization can barely travel to its own moon. Terrans are backward, ignorant heretics.

Ahdin comes up to Asal. He whispers in her ear, "Perhaps we should see how their culture works on this matter? Might spice up some things."

Virus! Terran culture is a virus!

Forty-Five – Partings

The shakes are growing sharper and more dramatic. Whether they are due to stress, the hybridization process, or something new is a mystery. They first occurred when he was practicing a breathing technique with Sainas. She noticed them before he even realized what his body was doing. A slight tremor would start in his fingers when he was thinking about something else. Then, even once he was paying attention, it would continue for minutes. At first, Brendan tried to downplay it as him being tired, but Sainas would have none of that. For two more days, she observed the shakes during their exercises. The next day, she took Brendan to a medical bay he didn't recognize. A dozen other doctors, all deferential to Sainas, watched Brendan shake as they studied various monitors and displays. Of course, they shared none of their findings with him. The next day had been even worse. The whole process repeated, but this time, Mon avoided conversation with Brendan while the doctors took more measurements. And now the shakes have begun again, but this time it lingers longer than Brendan can remember.

Descending to Earth reminds Brendan of the time he rode in a police car as a kid. That trip ended with him spending a night in a jail that people euphemistically referred to as "juvenile detention hall."

PATRICK ABBOTT

Back then, he made a series of poor choices in reaction to his father's latest affair. *Am I now making similar mistakes?*

He is drawn back to the present moment by the cool touch of Zalta's firm hands. She presses her thumbs hard into his wrists. Brendan feels a Bond form, and an almost pleasant tickle flows through his body. As the sensation reaches his hands, the shakes cease.

"Thanks," he says.

"Esfirs would not like you so nervous. Let your mind be kind to your poor body; it does not know how to be Terran and Sabia." She lets go of his wrists.

He wonders what is behind the current round of tremors. *Some sort of new fight my last few Terran cells are putting up? Maybe my hybrid biology is unstable.*

"Be calm, Brendan, calm." Zalta's echoing of Esfirs' calming phrase has its desired effect. Brendan exhales deeply and sits down on the floor against the craft's hull. Looking away from Zalta, causing the Bond to sever. The temptation to remain in it is appealing, though it lacks the all-embracing warmth of Esfirs'. With Esfirs' Bonds, she fills him, and he flows into her. *It has been weeks, my love; come home. "Home?" Yes, home.*

He hears Berina's voice in the air. "One minute to landing!"

Kimya breaks off from her group of guards and approaches Brendan. Her arrival elicits a huff from Zalta, who walks away. Heavy-looking armor adorns the guard. Looking down at Brendan, Zalta offers him her hand. He takes it, and she pulls him up with ease.

"Remember," she starts, "wait on the craft until I confirm the prearranged conditions have been met. Only after I am satisfied will I give the all-clear to Ishan. You may come out once he gives you the signal. But, if at any time you feel unsafe, run back to the craft immediately. Do you understand, Brendan? Come back to us as fast as you can. I will cover you."

Brendan lackadaisically focuses his eyes on her. Then, with a downward motion of the hand, he signals for her to calm down. "Got it. Just—let us keep calm, okay? I know these people. I trust them."

Kimya lets out a sigh of exasperation. "These people want you arrested and dissected. Do not trust them."

"We know my government has tried to arrest me before, but not these people."

"The Terran government is not 'your' government, and 'these people' make that government hostile to you. Seriously, Brendan, you need to realize this!"

Berina's voice cuts through the air announcing their arrival at the Unified Intelligence Command's landing pad. Two guards automatically flank Kimya. She touches a panel, which causes the hatch to open, and the three of them hop out, the other two guards following shortly behind. While watching them disappear into the morning light, Berina walks to Brendan's side.

PATRICK ABBOTT

"Forget her, Brendan." She tugs on his arm to get his attention. "If you trust your friends, that is fine. We all get how hard this is for you; we also are so thankful for you doing it." Brendan doesn't respond. "Your better half says she loves you for who you are. It is why you are part of us and why there are people on this planet who want to harm you." She points toward the clear field tent next to the landing pad. Letting out a shudder, she continues. "However, take all the time you need to process and make peace with what has happened. Let me know if you need to leave now and redo this some other time." Her voice transitions to one of levity. "If you want to leave Kimya behind, I am fine with that."

"What is with the hostility toward her? I have not heard her say one cruel thing about you, yet you only indicate disdain for her."

Still looking at the guards outside, she ignores the question. "Look alive—they are coming back." Berina heads back to the cockpit.

Kimya jumps back into the craft. Panting, she catches her breath before pivoting toward Brendan. Her face is red, a telltale sign she got into an argument. However, she composes herself before speaking.

"They are a bunch of liars. Those Terrans wanted to take you inside 'just to talk to' you, but I said no. Can you believe they were even threatening to walk if I did not let them take you out of my sight? However, those primates"—she stops herself—"those people were not expecting me." Tapping her chest, she betrays a moment of pride and ego. "I got them back to the original agreement."

"Thank you, Kimya. You did not threaten them or anything, did you?"

She replies with a playful shrug. *Great, this is going to be a hostile interview.*

"Remember," she says, "stay within my line of sight. Just walk toward the clear plastic tent. Once there, you can enter and discuss whatever you need to. Make sure you come back to us quickly. I will be back here, ready—"

"Kimya, thank you again, but you already gave me this rundown. Cover my back, and all will be fine." Brendan says while patting her on the shoulder.

Brendan jumps out into the Virginia morning air. Ahead of him lies the clear plastic tent, meant to be a place for secure conversation. *It is hardly a secure SCIF.* Beyond that, he sees three individuals in suits, one of them his old friend Jack. *Friend or abandoner?* They give each other a nod of recognition. As Brendan approaches, Jack breaks off from the group and heads toward the tent, but Brendan makes sure to beat him to it. Instead of going in, he holds the flap open for Jack.

"You don't call; you don't write—I'm so lonely, babe. Where did you go?" Jack's tone is teasing, but Brendan senses an accusation behind it, causing his anxiety to spike.

Instead of replying, Brendan enters the tent ahead of Jack. Letting the flap close behind him, he quickly realizes this probably was not the best first impression for the meeting and turns around to apologize. Jack, though, to his surprise, has a disarming smile on his face.

PATRICK ABBOTT

"Okay, buddy, I hear you want out. Tell me, as a friend, what's going on." Jack's words provide a warmth that Brendan has long missed.

Brendan lets out an unintentional moan which echoes in the greenhouse-like environment. The length and depth of it take both Brendan and Jack by surprise. They look at each other; locking eyes without forming a Bond is surprising to Brendan. *Oh my gosh, I forgot this little bit of humanity.*

"Hey man, just take it slow. No pressure, you know? How are you doing?" Jack asks.

Taking a big breath, Brendan decides to cut to the chase. "I was not prepared for this mission. The pressure of being with an alien race is one thing—I was embedded with foreign cultures, so I think I could have handled that. But constant threats of arrest, having my cries for help ignored, and"—his voice begins to crack—"and having my own body change like this. Dude"—Brendan shakes his head—"if it were not for them, I probably would have blown . . ." Brendan stops himself. His words alarm him. "As you can see, brother, I need some rest. I-I am getting married. To one of them. Can you believe that? I really think she could be the one. There is . . . love between her and me. She cares about me. And I love her. And listening to myself, I think I need her to heal."

Jack laughs. "Yeah, we all know about you and Isfurs or whatnot. Loft told the ambassador about it two weeks ago. Hey, how about one last debriefing? For me, buddy?"

Every bit of Brendan wants to sink to the floor. *Not here in front of Jack. Why could you not have helped me when I needed it?* Brendan resists the urge to collapse. *This is the time to dominate the stress, not let the pressure dominate me. Plus, I can help my country without betraying the trust the Sabia have in me. That is what I signed up for in the first place.*

"Okay." Brendan wipes his brow. "The most important thing to know is the security apparatus has been penetrated. When I was at Congress, a woman approached me. She tried to get me into one of the congressional SCIFs to discuss what happened during that Appalachian hostage situation. Turns out she was a clandestine Sabia agent."

"Holy crap." Jack covers his mouth before crossing his arms. "Did this alien compromise anyone or anything while you were there?"

"I honestly do not know. However, the Sabia might have access to a SCIF. If that is the case, who knows what support networks they have established and how wide the breach is."

"This is going to be one hell of a write-up. But you know, there is a way you can help with the big picture. What happened out there? Sources say you told Malcolm about a falling out. Yet you went back with them right after. Later, you say a clandestine Sabia agent asks what happened when you are at a party—with the same Sabia leader you were with in North Carolina. That leaves the powerful question: what is the event everyone knows more about than us humans?"

PATRICK ABBOTT

Brendans' desire to provide intelligence clashes with memories of Mon pleading to him to keep the secret. *I cannot betray that secret. I am not like my father or Heather.* Closing his eyes, Brendan thinks about holding Esfirs. *What can I do for my family? Something that will respect both of our backgrounds.* Brendan nods slightly to himself.

"Mon told the militia representatives the Sabia were on an undercover vacation. It was obvious to everyone that it was a lie. So I blew up at her and stormed out."

Jack squints. "Uh-huh. That matches what our sources told us. However, I was hoping you could give us more details."

Brendan shrugs.

"Well," Jack continues, "you did give me one last debrief. If it means anything, the director thinks the National Security Council completely FUBARed your case ever since we learned about your medical situation. Personally, I would have pulled you out under the pretext of a debriefing or even saying we needed to reverse your hybridization. Some people really wanted you back safely; others wanted to cut you up. I honestly have no idea which side would've won out if you'd come back to us.

"All that being said, here are your orders direct from POTUS: stay with your girl, get married, make sure she doesn't give you some weird alien disease down you know where. You don't want to become the example case for SPACECOM's General Order Number One."

Brendan laughs. "Yeah, I will look into that. But, no one seems too shocked or concerned about my upcoming nuptials. That must mean something about our two species. What that is, I have no clue."

"Let's shake hands." Jack puts out his hand, which Brendan takes. "Now smile." Jack's voice becomes serious. "Listen quick," he says in a hushed tone, "I am joining the militia movement in two months. Most people will think it's because I am upset about politics, but really I'm going deep undercover, I mean ultradeep. I may have to do some things to earn my way to the top, but I am loyal to America one hundred percent. Now, I need the same from you. Do all the right things and be that happy family man I know you always wanted to be. But, if you ever hear anything we need to know, find a way to tell us. I am not asking you—I am ordering you. Our country is being corrupted by Sabia buying off the business, cultural, and political elites. This isn't some conspiracy stuff; we're tracking it. The two big presidential contenders have been bought off already. These aliens are up to something rotten. Our country needs us to save it from all threats, whether domestic, foreign, or extraterrestrial. We respond to the call, Brendan." Jack lets go of his hand. "I am going to walk out of the tent looking peeved. Make up a story of you and I having some major disagreement. It will give both of us cover."

Jack abruptly turns and storms out of the tent. Brendan looks on in shock. *Oh, come on!* Closing his eyes to recenter himself, the image of holding Esfirs comes back to him. Peace flows over him as he calms down. *Esfirszan, how I love you.*

PATRICK ABBOTT

A rustling draws his attention. Turning, he sees Kimya open the tent. The guard winces as she pokes her head in.

"Brendan," she says, "why are you still in this stuffy room? Did that Terran say something upsetting? One minute you were shaking hands, and the next, he left with the most malicious look on his face."

Brendan chuckles dryly. *Another opportunity to live a masked truth. I will not be able to escape this life. Maybe I need to accept that all I can do is minimize it.* "Just lost in my own thoughts, Kimya. You are right—the room is stuffy. Let us leave."

She gives him an odd look as he walks out. The contrast from the stale tent to the fresh air is pleasant. As he begins walking toward the vessel, Berina steps out wearing a dark blue jumpsuit with gold piping. Brendan's inquisitive look is met with an impish grin. Zalta also comes out in matching clothing. Her face is one of pure, innocent joy.

"Matchy-matchy uniforms for you both. What gives?"

Berina lifts her eyebrows for a brief moment before lowering them. "Terrans tend to view our standard uniforms as aggressive, according to a recent study," she says. "In fact, in Montana, one soldier said we looked like 'space invaders.' That sent command into a tizzy. So now we wear a slightly lower-profile uniform whenever we go out in public. So, people get to see aliens while we get less protection. Everyone wins!" Her voice is thick with sarcasm.

"Our leadership put zippers on shirts and buttons on pants, so I guess that is sort of to be expected." Brendan laughs at his familiar joke.

Zalta looks confused, but Berina waves her finger. "You claim to be a Terran with me, kid, but your wife will not approve of her Sabia husband talking like one. Now, come, we are going out."

"Where are we going?"

Berina doesn't respond, instead playfully offering her hand like a debutant. With an exaggerated gesture, Brendan takes it. She leads the way to the edge of the landing pad, where two Secret Service types in suits are standing motionless.

"Wilbert. Kimo." Berina does a mock curtsy and semi-twirl as she addresses them. "Is everything ready?"

"Yes, ma'am," one of the well-dressed agents' replies. "Right this way, Ms. Berina." He motions with high decorum.

Berina rolls her eyes and places her hand over her heart.

Is she using things she learned from me to influence people? Or is she genuinely flirting with them?

As Brendan ponders the question, Berina speaks into his ear. "They all love being flattered. No wonder you succeeded in your job."

Her words chill Brendan. He can't tell if he is reacting to the joy she takes from manipulation or her perception of what he did in his role for the Unified Intelligence Command. *Either way, it is terrible.* He's not sure which is worse—the suggestion of a future of alien exploitation of humanity or the damning indictment of what he is trying to get away from.

Berina yanks Brendan's hand, indicating for him to follow. The two walk toward a parked SUV while Zalta and the two agents pull up the rear. Berina makes small talk with everyone about the weather, but Brendan remains silent. One of the agents runs up to Berina to pass off an envelope, then keeps pace at her side. The other rushes forward to open the SUV's back door. Berina enters, followed by Brendan, then Zalta. It has been years since Brendan has sat in the middle of any vehicle. He squirms to fit in the not-quite-full seat. Putting on the seatbelt is a struggle; Zalta and Berina ignore their respective safety devices. One agent takes the driver's seat while the other sits shotgun.

Berina pats the driver on the head and then turns toward Brendan. "A couple of days ago, I was looking at the agenda for this meeting, and I noticed Wilbert and Kimo would be present. So I thought, 'What can my lovely friends Wilbert and Kimo do for me?' Well, I reached out to them to arrange for a great morning for you, Dear Brendan." She smiles warmly.

"Wait, how do you know these two?" Brendan asks, puzzled.

"I have visited every spaceport this country has to offer. There are only so many Terrans cleared to man security at these sites."

"But how did you reach out to them?"

"Everyone has a phone," she replies nonchalantly.

That is a mindboggling breach in security. Does Berina flirt with people because that is her personality, or could it be a collections thing? How deep am I in this? His doubts begin to arise anew. *This has been a horrifying trip.* As Brendan ponders the ongoing events, the vehicle starts to move.

Zalta makes a short, sharp humming sound. "Why are you not asking where we are going?"

Brendan looks up at her. Seeing her serves as a bit of a distraction from his worries. "Want me to play your game, eh?" He smiles as he asks. Simultaneously, a memory of being on a road trip with his sister when he was young comes to the forefront. *Good times, how I miss them.*

"We are going to a restaurant for a morning meal!" Zalta squeals with excitement.

"Ugh," says Berina, "it was supposed to be a surprise! So just act surprised when we arrive at an Irish pub for brunch, okay?" Berina then goes back to chatting with one of the agents.

The rest of the fifteen-minute ride takes them into the District of Columbia. Zalta's excitement surges as she witnesses tourists milling about the various museums. She points out families, remarking how many children they have. Additionally, she repeatedly asks if buildings are zoos. When told the zoo is miles away, she asks Berina if they can make another trip to the menagerie. Berina waves her off. "Maybe next time."

Reaching the East Capitol Hill neighborhood, the SUV stops at Reynolds Park across the street from the

Navigator Irish Pub. The driver rushes out of the vehicle to open the door for Berina. Zalta receives a slightly more subdued but still attentive treatment from the other agent. This leaves Brendan alone in the SUV. Somewhat awkwardly, he shimmies over to exit the vehicle. Berina compliments both agents for their "job well done" and "making her wish come through." The fakeness, which seemingly goes over the humans' heads, sickens Brendan. *Am I being played too, and just do not see it yet?*

Brendan and the two Sabia females enter while the guards remain outside. The first people Brendan encounters inside the pub are members of the Washington police. Berina engages the cops in conversation. Again, she treats those who appear to know her as friends, while she spends extra effort to impress others. Brendan can't help but notice all the men are gathered close while the two female officers glare at Berina, standing back with their arms crossed.

"Tell me, boys, what do you prefer: flight suit, armor, or jumpsuit?" she asks, posing like a model as she lists each outfit.

The cops laugh.

"We'll take you to your table, ma'am," one declares. The policeman then takes Berina's arm like a prom date.

Seeing this, Zalta mimics her motions, and another cop takes her arm. Brendan follows alone. The group is led to an alcove, where a table is set for three. The cops leave as Brendan, and the Sabia take their seats. Brendan faces Berina and Zalta, who have been given the park view through the tinted window.

"I cannot figure out what game you are playing here," he says to Berina.

"Why, Brendan, what do you mean?" She obviously feigns shock.

"You clearly planned this side trip, police waiting, knowing you, and we are at an Irish pub named after my namesake." Brendan squints his eyes at her. "So, I ask, what are you up to?"

"Normally, I would attribute your paranoia to some Terran psychosis, but this time I will confirm your suspicions. I thought your meeting with your former comrades would be difficult. Because of that, I decided this trip to Earth"—she pauses while giving him a thumbs-up—"should end on a high note."

Brendan is silent for a moment as he takes her words in. Again, his anxiety flares as Jack's words ring through his mind, but he decides to confront it this time. "Berina, thank you for caring about me, but I need to be honest. I have fears sometimes." Berina leans in. "And I know these fears are unjustified based on the lengths you have gone for me, but sometimes I worry that I cannot tell the difference between the . . . behavior you show towards"—he motions to the police in the back—"and me." His hand tingles again as it starts to shake.

Berina reaches her hand across the table, and Brendan takes it. They lock eyes. He senses her comforting presence but does not feel her entering him through the Bond.

He lets out a low snort of disapproval of himself. "Sorry, I let my mind ruin things."

Berina forces her way into him through the Bond. "A sister in pain is a gift. Comforting her allows you to love her more." She rubs his hand. "That is one of our proverbs. It was wise for you to voice your fear. Doing so allowed you to see how stupid it was. It also gave me the ability to love you more."

He closes his eyes and reaches down to the deepest parts of his memory. "Here's wishing you a rainbow after showers and miles of smiles for golden hours. Shamrocks at your doorway for luck and laughter too. Hosts of friends for days on end, may God give to you."

Removing her hand, Berina asks, "Was that from your religion? It was beautiful."

"It is an Irish poem my father would recite when I was a child in bed."

"Never stop being Terran." Her words cause Brendan to smile. He looks at her. "Do not get me wrong. Heal from your combat sickness and get accustomed to being a Sabia male for Esfirs. But never, ever forget that you are also Terran."

He stares at her in silence. Finally, they nod to each other. Even without a Bond, Brendan can sense they each know what the other is thinking.

"Thank you," he says.

Zalta squeals and claps her hands as the waiters arrive. A brunch comprised of eggs, toast, fruits, and salmon is laid out before them. Brendan takes a bite of a strawberry before realizing he has forgotten something. He sheepishly stops to say a quick prayer. Both Berina and Zalta wait patiently.

"I just want to say," Brendan begins, "thank you for being you." Zalta looks confused, but the smile on Berina's face speaks volumes.

Before they can resume eating, Zalta shrieks so loudly that a police officer rushes to the alcove to see what has happened. She points out the window at what looks like a class of elementary-school-aged students in the park.

"That woman has over a dozen children!" Zalta exclaims.

"Zalta, you are creating—" Berina starts.

Zalta ignores Berina, "How many Terran women have that many children, Brendan?!"

"Uh—" Brendan takes another look before continuing. "I think that is a school group. Maybe one of the local Montessori schools, judging by the size of the class."

Zalta grows increasingly excited. She starts talking about the children's ages and wonders aloud if any of them are brothers or sisters. She makes such a scene that Berina has to yank her shoulder hard. Berina's expression remains fierce as Zalta meekly slides down in her chair. *The pilot clearly got the better of the medic this round.*

To break the tension, Brendan returns to eating. Berina starts on her toast but doesn't take her gaze off Zalta, who somehow manages to slouch down even further. Brendan tries to comment on the salmon but gets no reply from either. The rest of the meal is passed in silence.

Finally, Berina says it's time to go. She glares at Zalta one last time before the two females get up. Watching the silent exchange, Brendan follows them out of the restaurant. *Who is footing the bill?*

Berina's demeanor changes when she meets the Secret Service types at the SUV. During the drive back, she once again flatters the agents while Zalta sulks, paying no attention to the passing tourist families. *What the heck was Zalta and Berina's little tiff about?*

Instead of the Unified Intelligence Command headquarters, the SUV travels to the Pentagon's spaceport. There, a Sabia shuttlecraft surrounded by guards awaits. It is a low-key departure, with Berina hugging both Secret Service agents as Zalta smiles slyly at each of them. Neither agent addresses Brendan, and no one from the UIC is there. *Years of service and not a friend to see me off.*

Sitting on the floor, Brendan closes his eyes and begins to drift off into a daydream. He imagines Esfirs and him at the pub sharing a meal, listening to live music, and talking about their day. There are no snide remarks about Terrans or complaints about not being trusted, just a conversation between a husband and wife. In the fantasy, they take a long walk through the neighborhood, past the park full of children, and down to the river walk. She nuzzles him as the sun sets.

Suddenly, he feels pressure on his head and a heavy cloth rubbing against his face. Opening his eyes, he can't see a thing. Instead, there is a jolting sensation of being grabbed and lifted. A solid punch to the head jars his consciousness for a second and leaves his ears ringing. The next feeling is one of being slammed to the floor.

PATRICK ABBOTT

Forty-Six – Cana

Brendan breathes heavily through the cloth mask, his pores now clogged from perspiration. His feet dangle behind him as he feels himself being dragged down a hallway. Brendan is about 90 percent sure the Sabia have imprisoned him, though this might be some sort of Unified Intelligence Command smash-and-grab. *Hell, this could be some trade between the two. I wonder what I'm worth to the Sabia.* He recalls the brave Afghans who aided the United States in the twenty-year war. The cook who served him ice cream one rainy night in Ghazni, in particular, comes to mind. *I didn't get you out... now it's my turn to suffer. Justice works that way.*

Brendan feels a pinch on his right inner thigh, and the sharp pain causes him to jump. Letting out a war grunt, he turns in what he believes to be the direction of his assailant. Brendan tries to jolt forward, but people on both sides restrain his arms and pull him back. A hard slap to his outer left thigh adds insult to injury. The throbbing, stinging sensation makes him leap. A second blow, this blow to his back, knocks him down to the cold floor. Lying face down, Brendan slowly pushes himself back up. A rage now builds inside him as he hates. *I am going to slam myself into the first one who touches me. The second one I will fight off.*

His plan fails immediately. Someone slams their weight directly into him, forcing him to fall onto his back again. Brendan can feel the unknown assailant grind their knees into his stomach, so he cries out. The pain is unbearable. Then, suddenly, the pressure eases, providing significant relief. Scolding whispers from male and female voices buzz around him. As he tilts his head to hear more, the voices suddenly become silent. Unknown hands are slowly and gently placed on his arms, and very deliberately, the anonymous helpers pull him up off the floor. Brendan regains his footing, and they let him go. He feels pressure on his back, a signal to march forward.

The lengths of the hallways, combined with the predictable twists and turns, convince Brendan he is on the Sabia ship. *My reward for my friendship and trust in them. Well, I won't go down like a punk.* He thinks about his next steps, debating whether he wants to kill at least one Sabia if it looks like the end. Anger pounds inside him, ready to break out.

A push on his shoulders brings him to his knees. *So this is it, then.* He works up a powerful stare, preparing to glare down the person standing in front of him.

Brendan's face drops in awe as the hood is removed, however. An incredibly alien Esfirs, sitting on a pillow, smiles bashfully back at him. Her golden eyes glow magnificently, her iridescent skin radiates, and slick, smooth, dyed gray hair hangs down to her shoulders. Her hypnotizing gaze relaxes him and causes him to forget all about the very recent assault. Studying her more, Brendan becomes enraptured by her deep red lipstick and her heavily shaded eyebrows. The longer he looks at her, the more the world fades away.

"My love," Esfirs says, "we have been apart too long."

Words trip over themselves as Brendan tries to say something. "What," more as a statement than a question, is all he can get out.

Laughter fills the room. Turning around, Brendan can see Berina, Loft, Gul, and a host of other Sabia. Even Zand and a few—but not all—of the council members are there. Everyone is wearing colorful, draping clothing except for Berina and Zalta, who are in their blue jumpsuits.

Brendan's blinking and blank stare gets Berina's attention. "Nothing like a little husband kidnapping," she says. "They do that with the wife in some places on Terra." Then, becoming more serious, she says, "Sorry for going a little too rough on you."

With her right hand, Esfirs turns his head back toward her. "You are forever mine. For as long as the stars burn, you are mine."

Brendan's eyes begin to water. The desire to love and be loved has always been with him since . . .

"She is gone"—Esfirs intrudes on Brendan's thoughts—"I am here, not her."

He nods. "I am sorry—" he says, realizing Esfirs is not Heather, nor could she ever be. Instead, Esfirs is more than he ever dreamed possible. His love from the stars.

"No more words -she."

Esfirs rubs the side of his head. Then, turning her face to the crowd, she nods and gently rises. With a slight motion of her hand, she signals for Brendan to stand up. As he rises, Berina approaches, wearing a sheer white mantle over her jumpsuit. The two females lock eyes and exchange broad smiles. Berina then turns to Brendan.

"My friends down on Terra were able to secure this for me." She pulls a letter out of her jumpsuit. "It contains authorization for your marriage to be considered valid by your church."

Opening the letter, she passes it to Brendan. The ecclesiastic writing reminds him of all the seminary papers he had to write. The meaning of its contents is crystal clear to him. Keeping his Catholic faith and a monogamous relationship until the death of one of the spouses are listed as requirements for a valid marriage. The only thing expressly forbidden is a prenuptial agreement. *Like I have anything. I guess birth control wasn't even considered with aliens.* At the bottom of the letter is a signature: Father Baldwin, FSL. *Thank you, friend.* Father Baldwin's pastoral care for Brendan and Berina's support of his messy religious growth touches him deeply. Without thinking, he looks at Berina and thinks of his gratitude to her. She smiles back. *Did I form a Bond?*

Berina turns to face the audience. "We will conduct two rites. The first will appease Brendan's Terran religious requirements. Once that is complete, we will seal the marriage as instructed. Then, of course, we will celebrate."

She about-faces toward the couple. "Brendan"— her voice becomes somber and heavy—"have you come here to enter into marriage without coercion, freely and wholeheartedly? Are you prepared, as you follow the path of marriage, to love and honor Esfirs for as long as you both shall live?"

"I am," he responds. It feels so surreal to him.

"Esfirs," Berina now addresses her, "have you come here to enter into marriage without coercion, freely and wholeheartedly? Are you prepared, as you follow the path of marriage, to love and honor Brendan for as long as you both shall live?"

"Yes, I claim him for me." Esfirs beams while Brendan suppresses a laugh at the disconnect between how they both interpret the vows.

Berina continues. "Brendan, do you take Esfirs to be your wife? Do you promise to be faithful to her in good times and in bad, in sickness and health, to love her and honor her all the days of your life?"

This is really happening. "I do."

"Esfirs, do you take Brendan to be your husband? Do you promise to be faithful to him in good times and in bad, in sickness and in health, to love him all the days of your life?"

"Yes." Esfirs rolls her eyes.

No honor in her vow. I wonder what Berina thought when she decided to drop that line. A hint of doubt grows in him. *Heather did not honor me.*

Berina looks behind her at the group and then back at Esfirs. "Claim your husband."

Esfirs pulls Brendan to her. The warm, intimate kiss is the most loving thing he has felt in years, if not his whole life. The warmth surging through him longs for him to give in to his passions. Slowly Esfirs pulls her head back. He gazes into her eyes as they form a Bond. He messages the word "Esfirszan." Her voice in his head answers back. *Brendanshe.*

Berina approaches and places her hands on both Brendan and Esfirs' arms. Meanwhile, Brendan feels Esfirs suck him deeper into the Bond. Blackness grows from the edges of his peripheral vision as she becomes more prominent. She is brighter, her features more detailed and appealing, and the background blurs and fades as she appears to inch closer. All sound is drowned out except for their heartbeats. Her lips part, revealing polished white teeth and the most pleasing smile he has ever seen. The darkness now consumes everything but Esfirs. Brendan wants to drown in this sensation.

Then, in his vision, his arm with blood pouring out from the wrist rises toward Esfirs. She takes it and presses the open wound to her mouth. Before he can realize the danger, Brendan feels a steady sucking from his own wrist. His heart aches and quivers as Esfirs sucks down more of his blood. It is as if his essence is being drawn out of him. He tries to pull away, but Esfirs digs her talon-like nails into his arm, the pain combined with her iron grip keeping it in place. Animal-like grunts come from Esfirs as she speeds up her consumption of his blood. Then, everything slowly fades to black.

PATRICK ABBOTT

Brendan is on his back in Afghanistan. Looking at his wrist, he can see that shrapnel from the suicide bomber has cut his artery wide open. Additional entrance wounds on his chest begin to pool blood. The sun is already baking his skin. He looks to his right; only the bodies of his friends who trusted him are nearby. Brendan sees Michael Neuhouse twitch his last painful spasms. He attempts to apologize but is too weak to form the words. His music-loving friend expires—whether from exsanguination or choking on his own blood will forever be a mystery to Brendan.

This is the end. I'm going to die. Brendan wonders why he had such strange visions of life after Heather. It was a life without joy, one of pain, until aliens, of all things, came to Earth. *And of all things, one of them fell in love with a PTSD me. Ha. It is now my turn to join Neuhouse and the rest. Time to die.* Brendan opens himself up to let his soul go. *Soul?* Thinking back to his vision, he pictures Father Baldwin at the church in Montana. *Did God just give me a chance to convert? Did I blow it?*

Suddenly, something comes flying down and eclipses the hot sun. Brendan sees it has feathery wings coming out from all sides. From its center, a golden eye surrounded by fire peers down on him as the creature descends. Despite his labored breathing, Brendan gasps, awestruck by the entity. He even forgets about letting himself die.

The mystery being hovers above the ground in front of him. Its wings overlap each other and the eye, forming a feathered halo. As he looks on, it morphs into a biblical-looking angel bearing the features of one of the aliens he dreamt about. She holds a clear, blue ball of what looks to be water in her hand. Bending down, she tilts his head back and presses the water to his lips. He instantly feels electricity coursing through his body. The iron-like zing from the water jolts him. As he drinks, the angel extends her wings to form shade around him. It cools his burnt exterior while the refreshing liquid warms his insides.

Looking at the angel, he sees her eyes are golden, like those of the alien from his dream. Their eyes lock, and Brendan can hear her thoughts in his head. She urges him to drink, live, and be with her forever. Then, as he stares deeper into her eyes, his whole field of vision is drowned out.

First, everything is golden. Then different hues of gold, some lighter and others darker, begin to appear. These morph into featureless shapes. Slowly but surely, the forms start to develop meaning. One is a woman kneeling in front of him. With her arm extended toward his face, she looks directly into his eyes.

Suddenly, Brendan realizes what he is doing—he is drinking blood. His eyes widen in terror as he sees Esfirs holding her wrist to his mouth. Immediate revulsion forces him to spit the blood out, and Esfirs withdraws her wrist. Brendan screams.

"Calm, Brendanshe," Esfirs says. "It is my gift of life to you in exchange for what you gave me. We are wife and husband forever. Just rest, my love."

Brendan remains too shocked to say anything. Nothing makes sense to him. As he struggles for

PATRICK ABBOTT

meaning, his new wife says a few indistinguishable words to the crowd. He hears laughter from an audience he cannot see as he gazes toward Esfirs. She, in turn, lowers Brendan's head onto a pillow. Now, only the ceiling is visible. After a moment, he hears Zalta's voice mention biotech. It appears Brendan has already received it because as he looks at his arm, there is no wound.

Time moves slowly during the celebration. Brendan begins to feel cold on the inside. Instinctively, he reaches out toward Esfirs. Someone takes his hand. Turning his head, he sees Sainas. She moves closer and lies down next to him.

"I was back in Afghanistan . . . dying," he manages to say weakly.

"Hello, Brendan," Sainas whispers. "Sabia wedding vows and gifts most seem strange compared to what you are accustomed to. Do not worry; I will stay with you until everything is finished. Some men fall asleep after the gift of life. There is no shame should you want to fall asleep."

Brendan's guts begin to twist, pull, and contract. He moans. "My insides hurt."

Sainas nods. "Esfirs' blood is flowing in you. We have seen how this can stress the inner organs in some lab tests. How bad does it feel?" Her eyes express kind concern.

"Like the worst gas I have ever had," he manages to get out.

She looks at him sympathetically while also suppressing a slight smile. "Do not worry. Esfirs would never do anything to hurt you, especially now, Esfirshaz. That means 'husband of Esfirs.'" She waves at something behind him. "Hold on; this will help."

Zalta kneels next to Brendan and lifts his head. She is holding a vial of black liquid. Out of apprehension, Brendan attempts to shake his head free from her grip. Twice she tries and fails to feed him from the vial.

"Stop, Zalta." Sainas' commanding voice is powerful without being loud. "Brendan, it is medicine. It will help you recover. I promise you it is not blood."

Brendan stops resisting. The medic gently pours the liquid down his throat. Within seconds, the pain in his gut ceases, and his insides cool. Zalta places his head back on the pillow and walks out of sight. For a minute, Sainas and Brendan stare at each other. He attempts to form a Bond, but she does not reciprocate. Finally, giving up the effort, he sighs. He feels a restored strength. *I think I can sit up now.* With a quick swing of his body, he sits next to Esfirs, albeit with a dizzy head.

"Esfirshaz! You recovered quickly," she declares.

Brendan nods.

Esfirs looks toward a group of women seated next to her. Then, in very broken English, she says, "Mother. New blood. Esfirshaz. Your blood."

A woman in her sixties wearing a solid gray robe scoots over to a pillow next to Brendan. She studies him with a stoic look. "Esfirshaz," she says, "I. Is.

PATRICK ABBOTT

Asterdaadeh. Esfirs. Is. Blood. Asterdaadeh. You. Is. Blood. Asterdaadeh."

Brendan's mind registers Asterdaadeh's poor English skills. *Definitely just started.* However, Brendan can't reply as his head is still recovering from passing out.

Leaning over, Esfirs whispers to him, "Asterdaadeh is my mother, the reason I am a doctor. She said you are her son now. Welcome to the family."

Brendan can only place his hand over his heart in response. Asterdaadeh gives him a broad smile.

Two more hours pass. Plenty of laughter, drinking, eating, and conversation occurs between the guests and Esfirs. Strangely, apart from one short conversation with Berina and frequent check-ins by Sainas, the crowd ignores Brendan. Throughout the evening, more people arrive, causing the party to grow in size and intensity.

Berina breaks the celebration with a strange war cry. The audience turns to her. "Our Dear Esfirs now has her Esfirshaz!" Male and female Sabia cheer. "But now we all know it is time she enjoys her prize!" More laughter. "Gul, Nema, and, um—Farbod! I will take his left arm; you take the rest!"

The three named Sabia, along with others, approach Brendan. They seize him and pick him up off the ground. Joyously, his captors lead him out of the room and into the halls.

Forty-Seven – Afterward

Shadows dance on the wall as the flame flickers in the dark room. Brendan watches the shapes move while Esfirs embraces him. Her eyes and skin glow, reflecting the urn's flame, giving her an eerie prominence in the otherwise dark room. She runs her nails over his shirtless torso while softly humming.

The memory of what happened during the wedding threatens the peacefulness of the present. He can't get the blood ritual out of his mind. The tasting of her blood gave the wedding a creepy vampire vibe. Sainas' care aside, the sanguinary experience is becoming mental cancer.

"Esfirszan-" he begins, almost afraid to address her, "may I ask you a question?" His throat dries up. The old enemy anxiety is alive and well.

"You just did, -she." Esfirs laughs. Her voice has taken on a deeper tone that almost seems to echo. She gently scratches the front of Brendan's chest, like a cat playing with a mouse it has captured.

Brendan swallows hard before building up the courage to speak again. He starts to form words, but suddenly his jaw clenches shut. Initially, he tries to move his muscles, but nothing responds to his synapses' commands. Esfirs, meanwhile, lets out a laugh. Brendan's right hand stretches out toward her face with the index finger raised. Then, with a mischievously curved smile, Esfirs makes a shushing sound. The alien rolls onto her back, wrapping her arms around herself in a tight embrace. Nerves across Brendan's chest and shoulders respond as if he is being hugged. The feeling is restricting as it is terrifying.

Brendan's body wants to cry in terror. However, he chooses another option—with a robust mental push, Brendan thinks the word "no." Esfirs responds by loosening her arms and turning to look at him. She frowns. All his muscles suddenly relax.

Finally free to speak, he says, "It is not right to take control of my body. I-I . . . I know there is much for me to learn about how you need me to be as a husband, but to do that robs me of my independence. If I am not free, I cannot freely love you."

She winces as her eyes focus on him. Then, with the voice of a woman spurned, she says, "You do not want to be in everything with me, Brendan?"

Brendan, not -she. Her choice of name stings hard.

"Of course, I want to be intimate with you. It is just . . . to rob me of freedom—I cannot defend myself."

Her pupils dilate. "-she, I would never hurt you. Never. You will always be my love, deserving of protection and care. You have always been under my care, ever since I first saw you bleeding on my operating table. Let me show you what you mean to me."

Brendan feels sucked into her. His vision becomes what she saw that day. From her point of view, his bloody body lies in front of her, staring back, breathing its last breaths. *It is okay, go ahead,* Esfirs' thoughts echo. Slowly, Brendan reaches out. Looking at what remains of his left hand, he uses Esfirs' hands to rotate and then squeeze it.

"No"—Esfirs is speaking out of his body—"everything was in motion long before. The divine shaped you into the person who would come to aid beautiful creatures in peril. You were rewarded for doing the will of the divine. I know it is hard to believe, but at least see the reward in being with me, -she!"

Back in Esfirs' cabin, Esfirs-in-Brendan's-body places his body on top of Brendan-in-Esfirs'-body. Brendan's left hand is placed upon Esfirs' cheek. "-she, I love you," Esfirs-in-Brendan says.

Suddenly, a mental whiplash moment occurs, with Brendan back in his own body. Esfirs grabs his left hand and studies it in the flamelight. When Brendan looks over at his hand, he sees the iridescent Sabia skin.

"Oh, praises to Borzu! Oh, praises to Befhar! Oh, praises to Sheherbaraz! Oh, praises to Pashfi! Oh, praises to Rouzbah!" She repeats the litany twice more." Remel! Remel, thank you for listening to my prayers." Tears begin to form in her eyes. "-she, it is just as I prayed!"

What?!

PATRICK ABBOTT

"Oh, -she, my own Namziah!" Ecstasy soars in Esfirs' voice. She looks up at the ceiling with her arms outstretched.

Brendan regains his composure. Reflecting on the names she listed, he uses this moment to learn more. Remel and Namziah are familiar, while the rest are not. "Esfirszan, you thanked Remel for listening to your prayers. Is Remel the divine you mentioned who you think led me to the Sabia?"

"What—" Esfirs says before quickly recovering with a stern shake of the head. "Oh, no, -she. Remel is— how would Terrans know them as . . . like an angel. Namziah was . . . a woman. Simply a woman."

"You mentioned she created the Sabia Legion?"

She sits up. "No, Dear Brendanshe, they begat the Sabia. A thing cannot be equal to its maker. However, a child begat has all the honors of mother and father. Before Remel and Namziah's children, there were no Sabia."

"So the Sabia are mixed race?"

"Do not talk of such holy things with such vulgar language. We are pure; we are the beautiful ones."

"Sorry," Brendan sheepish replies, knowing he has pressed too hard.

"No, no. I owe an apology, my love." She pushes him gently back on the sheets. "I will talk to Berina about evangelizing you. There is much for you to know." Her eyes dart around as if she is looking for someone. She leans in closer and whispers, "Remel saved Namziah by

585

feeding her his blood. Later, she fed him her blood so they would always be a part of one another." She takes a big whiff of Brendan's torso. "I can smell myself in you, -she."

Brendan looks at his hand again. The Sabia effect is visually appealing but troubling at the same time. *I should talk to Sainas about this.*

"Do not worry, -she. Your hand is becoming perfect. Here"—she gently strokes his cheek—"tomorrow we will go to the gardens and join my mother and friends for a meal. But for now, forget all the things which tomorrow will bring. Be with me tonight."

PATRICK ABBOTT

Interlude – Esfirs: The Gift

Esfirs' new husband gently strokes her hair with his right hand. His back is against a carpeted wall while she rests with her head in his lap. Her eyes grow heavy as the rhymed strokes slowly numb the reality around them. The effect is amplified by Brendan's humming some Terran tune. Reflecting on the moment, marriage for her is all that it could be and more.

What a marvelous three days. The well wishes and gifts from all my friends. I really will be spending weeks thanking everyone. The clothing Berina gave Esfirshaz is probably the best, though—the sooner I can get him out of Terran rags, the better. Mother likes him a lot too. Esfirs chuckles at the thought of her mother at dinner earlier. *Teaching her the word "son" has proven to be helpful. At least she is not talking about blood anymore.* She communicated using the word "son" repeatedly but in different tones. *Remember when you said I was the sad end of the family, mother? Now, I have a husband, and he is your son. Oh, divine be praised.* Her thoughts then progress toward the future.

She looks around the darkened room and notices Brendan's hand has stopped rubbing her hair. *He must have fallen asleep.* But turning toward him, she finds his eyes are watching the flame in the lamp. *Oh, divine or watchers, are you communicating with him? Please be so!* Esfirs allows minutes of silence to pass, wondering what to say. *It would not be a spillage to tell him more about Namziah now. He has yet to be formally adopted— talk about a headache there—but he would not betray the truth to the Terrans. He has kept the words of Mon to himself. Cursed Fahime even knows that. Maybe . . . no, better to play it safe. The adoption will be the right time.* She goes back to watching him. *How lovely he is.*

"You are beautiful." Her words apparently startle Brendan, who looks down at her suddenly. "I did not mean to scare you, love."

"It is alright, Esfirszan. I was just thinking about a lot of stuff. Life, really. It has been more than a year since I arrived here, but I still need to learn so much more. And not just about the Sabia, but myself, too."

She places both hands on his cheeks. "Oh, Esfirszan. Ask me anything. Anything at all, and I will answer." Her voice is melodic and smooth.

He nods once, twice, then three times. *Poor thing is scared.* Before she can speak to reassure him, Brendan seems to push through his mental block. "Thinking back on everything with—no, let me start again. How can I be the husband you deserve and want?"

"You selfless man." She pulls his face down to hers and kisses it. "All I ask of you is to trust me. I will never hurt you, I promise." She removes the glove covering his left hand. *Why do you think the blooming Sabia nature of your body is something to hide?* Admiring his ever-expanding Sabia skin, she kisses it.

PATRICK ABBOTT

May you cover all of him. "And trust the divine. All this is happening for a reason."

He nods silently. Locking eyes with him, she initiates a Bond. *Promise me you will trust me.*

"I will," he replies. "I want to show you trust now," he adds. "Ask me anything. Nothing is off-limits. Anything, seriously, I will tell you. Even things—even things I do not want to answer."

How can I be the wife you need me to be?

Without a moment's pause, he says, "Just be honest and communicate with me. I will obey you knowing you are open and truthful with me."

I will.

She gently ends the Bond, leaving Brendan with the sensation of her pleasure. She turns toward the flame. *Oh divine, what else can I ask for but all the blessings you have already given me?*

A sharp pulse rips through her body. *What? Can it be? Now? Does it take hours? I thought—*

Brendan repositions himself to look her over. "Honey, what is wrong? You jolted and became as tense as a log."

"I just need to get up, take a stretch, you know." She grabs a piece of cloth and wraps it around her sleeping robe. "I will be back shortly. I think I just need to walk it out real quick."

Brendan starts to get up, but she stops him. Before he can object, she is already out the door and moving down the hall.

He asks for truth and communication, and the first thing I do is tell him a lie. No, no—it was not a lie. This could be considered a bodily function. And he is not even adopted yet. What I did was justifiable. I just . . . lied. Something I have done to him before . . . Well, he has done it to us! Ugh. He is one of us. I must mean that! She stops. *I need to talk to Sainas about this later.*

Continuing her run through the hallways, she makes her way to Berina's room. Finally, past three corridors, she arrives.

The door flies open, revealing a partially eaten dinner, Berina in her nightclothes, and a young guard without his shirt. He and Berina jump off their pillows with alarm as Esfirs rushes in. A Sabia program is on, and while Esfirs tends to enjoy an Old Colonial War drama as much as anyone, her mind is on other matters. The youthful guard runs out, leaving his shirt and kit behind.

"I was about to have a great night with Kianush," Berina declares, annoyed. "Should you not be with your husband now and leave the rest for us?"

Everything in Esfirs wants to snap at Berina. *He is below your caste for crying out loud!* She bites her tongue, though, because there is something more important than that. However, the words fail to materialize at this critical moment. Esfirs stands in shock, unable to convey everything swarming in her head.

PATRICK ABBOTT

"What the heck is going on? Are you going to stand there just gawking at me, you married bird?"

Esfirs closes her eyes and counts to ten. She then bends her knees, tilts her head forty-five degrees to the left, and holds her palms out to her sides.

Berina leaps back, gasping. "We need to get your mother!"

Forty-Eight – Multiple Layers

Walking down the hallway through formerly restricted Defense Force space is nerve-racking for Brendan. Fears of being grabbed, cornered, or even having another encounter with Fahime play on his imagination. Yet, no black-clothed Sabia are seen. He wonders if their absence is because they dislike him. On the other hand, Brendan thinks perhaps it could also be mere coincidence or even Sainas' doing. Whatever the reason, he chooses to deal with his fear by pressing on instead of letting it control him.

He finally locates a door marked with a piece of paper that reads "Welcome" in penciled cursive. Touching the panel next to the door, he hears. Sainas' voice crackles in the air. "Enter, friend!" The door swooshes open, revealing a living room the same size as his own but much different. The floors are carpeted like in Esfirs' cabin, but instead of solid red, they are patterned with yellow, green, and red stripes that overlay a surprisingly vivid gray.

The walls are covered with tapestries depicting Sabia in what appears to be a wintery wonderland with green forests. *How odd that it's winter, yet the vegetation has green leaves.* Brendan stops to take in the images.

"It is from a historical story." Sainas' voice draws Brendan's attention to her. In the opposite corner, she stands in a dark button-up shirt, gray pants, and a gray blazer.

"What is the story portrayed?"

"Nice open-ended question." She smiles. "Heavenly beings saved the Sabia from a catastrophic flood by relocating us to a safe forest known as The Garden. There, the Sabia were protected from those who sought our destruction."

Brendan studies the various tapestries, showing Sabia and larger figures flying above the Sabia. "Fascinating. Did you know flood narratives are common throughout Earth? In my own religion, The Flood plays a major role in salvation history."

"Really? How interesting." She puts her arms down and assumes a formal, attentive posture. "So, what shall I call you this session? I must admit Esfirshaz is a beautiful name, but I suspect you are still partial to Brendan."

He chuckles. "Yeah, I would prefer that." Sainas offers her hand, which he shakes. *Very natural handshake—she must be practicing.* "Did you know that, in my culture, Esfirs' married name would be Esfirs Murphy? She could even be referred to as Mrs. Brendan Murphy."

"Ha!" Sainas crosses her arms. "I would not tell her that."

"Oh, I did. She called it a stupid custom." Brendan looks down. "And then she apologized." His voice trails off in a slight mutter.

"What about that incident caused an emotional reaction just now?"

Brendan makes an uncomfortable noise and looks down, rubbing his shoe against the carpet. His past experiences with Heather weigh on him. No amount of effort can break the floor's hold on his eyes.

"Brendan," Sainas says, leaning in and cocking her head to see him better, "what is wrong?"

"Well," he starts while his view remains fixed on the floor, "We have talked about Heather before. She would belittle me a lot. She never apologized, though, so Esfirs apologizing was really touching. It is just—just—" He takes a moment to gather himself again. "I am apprehensive about being hurt again. There is little doubt in my mind that Esfirs does not want to hurt me or that she would enjoy it. Though, look—I am going to be honest—I worry that she will keep disrespecting human elements of me, which is pretty much everything when you consider the mental and emotional. I really do not want to be hurt again. I simply cannot be hurt again. It would destroy me, Sainas."

"What emotions are you feeling right now?"

"Scared. I am so scared. Even more, than I was in combat." Brendan thinks he has only a few bits of physical humanity left and worries how his new relationship might cause him to lose any remaining ties to his past identity. Without realizing it, Brendan is panting as an anxiety attack forms.

Sainas puts her hand on his shoulder and slowly guides him to the floor, where they sit on their knees. There is no Bond; instead, Brendan feels the comfort of a friend. He lets loose a long and loud sigh. When finished, his chest feels relieved of a tremendous pressure.

"Brendan, I promise you Esfirs will hurt you." He looks up at her with a look of disbelief. "Additionally, I promise you that you will hurt her. What matters is both of you work hard to reduce the number of times you hurt each other, and both of you apologize quickly when you do. Life is full of pain. Your religion is one of suffering. Not out of cruelty, but because it proves you like metal in fire. Love, communicate, apologize when you do wrong, and forgive Esfirs when she apologizes to you. Do that, and this marriage, with its ups and downs, will be the best thing to ever happen to you."

No words are needed to express Brendan's thanks. *Father Brendan was right. He was so right that this alien who barely knows me gets it.* Shutting down at the first sign of trouble prevented him from restarting his life in DC and settling down at work. *I would have run away from here so many times if it had not been for Esfirs and Berina.* Looking back at Sainas, he nods in appreciation for the revelation she helped him see.

Sainas picks up Brendan's gloved left hand. She initiates a Bond as they hold each other's gaze for what feels like an eternity. No words are shared, but compassionate thoughts comfort Brendan. His anxiety dissipates like fog in the morning.

"Show it to me when you are ready," she says.

Carefully, Brendan removes the glove. The fingers and entire palm shimmer with iridescence. *Sabia skin, not mine. Everything started with this.* Looking away from Sainas causes the Bond's soothing effect to wane while his emotional turmoil grows.

With soft hands, Sainas delicately flips his palm face up and gracefully rubs her fingers into his hand. Brendan watches as the rainbow-like pattern changes in the light. Next, her thumb slides nimbly toward his wrist. Brendan worries that she will drag the Sabia skin down to his artery, but it effortlessly crosses over to the human-looking skin. *It looks human, but it really is hybrid flesh.* Finally, the doctor stops over the central vein on his wrist, and Brendan can feel his pulse meeting her thumb.

She smiles. "You became very nervous, dear friend, when I started touching you."

"Oh yeah," he replies, "I understand that I am different now, but it seems I am losing more and more of my humanity. Is there anything you can do?"

"There is a surgery we can do to place blockers under your skin. This, along with radiation, would stop the cancerous growth while allowing you to keep human cells in your bone marrow. We obviously have not been able to test it properly, but it should be better than your current treatments. Additionally, you probably would want to start taking steroids to restore the Terran appearance of your skin. You would not oppose this route, would you?"

Brendan is a little taken aback by the seemingly easy answer. *Why wasn't this proposed before? Esfirs . . . no, she wouldn't have held this from me.*

"I—" he begins.

"Excellent! We will perform the operation tomorrow. After the first morning chimes, one of my staff will escort you from your new residency. Esfirs can assist me in the procedure. You will be under my protection and her loving hands."

"This is rather sudden. Would she not need time to prepare? Plus, she is rather territorial—I think she would want a say in what happens to me."

"We already talked," Sainas replies instantly. Brendan thinks the smile on her face is forced.

Brendan's face is a combination of confusion and surprise. *Conprise. I need to get that into a dictionary somehow.* "Okay," he says, "I will get together with her and, yeah, prepare for tomorrow." He shakes his head as if agreeing with his own statement.

"Oh," Sainas interjects, "Esfirs will be occupied with various reintegration activities for the rest of the day. Once the procedure is complete, I will ensure you get time with her to make up for what this will cost you. In the meantime, you will need plenty of rest before the surgery." She turns to look at the ceiling. "Paknessa! Dedar!"

The door opens, and Brendan lets out a soft chuckle as the Defense Force members, two of the youngest Sabia he has ever seen, enter. *These are kids. ROTC kids.* It's hard to square their diminutive stature with his imposing stereotype of black-clad bullies. He sees the male's face has pimples, and the female looks like she could be as young as fifteen. Even her black uniform appears too large as if they didn't have one in her size.

The girl lifts her arm to shoulder level and points toward the hallway. "The hybrid will come with us back to his cabin."

Sainas rises from her seated position. Locking eyes with the female, she firmly states, "Paknessa, what has given you leave to address a future officer of the Legion with that indirect tone?"

Paknessa gives Sainas a deer-in-the-headlights look of terror, her eyes darting back and forth between Sainas and Brendan add to the panicked effect. Meanwhile, the male, presumably Dedar, looks straight ahead. *Playing the enlisted, eh?*

"Dedar," Sainas snaps, "how should one address the Sabia officer sitting next to me?"

Dedar's nasal breathing becomes louder and louder. Brendan watches as he grimaces and begins to sweat. *Poor dude is having an abort, retry, fail experience.* Brendan decides he has had too much of this gotcha moment. He begins to stand but is quickly shut down by a snap of Sainas' fingers. She points to the floor without even looking at him. *Yes, ma'am.* He sits down and crosses his legs.

PATRICK ABBOTT

"Did they teach you two nothing?" Sainas' words burn even Brendan. She reminds him of certain generals he had to work with. Then, realizing that she is as much a Defense Force member as a doctor, Brendan makes a mental note not to cross her unless absolutely necessary.

Paknessa is the first to budge. With shock in her eyes, she steps forward, opens her palms to Brendan, and addresses him. "Esfirshaz, we have been summoned to escort you back to your cabin. Will you please accompany us, sir?"

Standing up, Brendan acknowledges the request and agrees. Before leaving, he thanks Sainas with a hand-over-the-heart bow, which is reciprocated. The youthful Defense Force members step out into the hallway, allowing Brendan to join them there. He nods at them, although they do not reply.

Paknessa repeats her earlier arm-to-shoulder-level point. "Your room is this way, Esfirshaz."

They walk down the hallway together. Brendan tries engaging in small talk, but neither one is responsive.

When they reach the end of the Defense Force's section of the ship, both Sabia stop, displaying nervousness. *These kids are out of their league.*

Brendan decides to relieve them of this task. "Thank you so much; I can see my way from here. Paknessa and Dedar, it was a pleasure meeting you." Brendan adds his now customary hand-over-heart bow. Then, he turns and begins to walk away.

"Sir, a question," Paknessa says.

Brendan stops and turns around. "Yes?"

"How many siblings do you have?"

Odd question. "I have three. Two sisters and a brother. Four kids, not bad for my parents, eh?"

Dedar makes an odd noise while putting his hand over his mouth. Paknessa asks, "Is that common for Terrans?"

"Where I am from, yes. Most couples have between two to four kids. However, many in my religious faith have up to seven or more."

"How many become fighters like you?"

Brendan wonders where this is going. "About 10 percent of the adult population of my country is either in our military or has been before doing something else." He is skeptical of the question. "Why?"

The girl looks down, her eyes darting as if she is doing mental mathematics. She starts nodding her head slowly. "I am not scared," she says.

Brendan understands her meaning as a former grunt himself. "Are you telling yourself or me that, soldier?"

She takes his question as a challenge. "You laughed at me when you first saw me. I may be younger than you, but that does not mean I will get scared in combat."

"Your words tell me you never saw combat. Let me tell you, if you are not scared in a fight, you are dead. You need to know what to expect, or the cognitive

PATRICK ABBOTT

dissonance will mess you up. Trust me, I know."
Brendan pauses to consider his words before continuing.
"I thought combat was going to be an adventure. Instead,
it was the dead bodies of men, women, and children.
Some of them friends. You must prepare for the fear
and the pain. It is what you do with it that matters, not
lying about having no fear. Now tell me, what combat are
you expecting?"

She looks at him, trying to put on a stern face, but
fails.

It is here that Dedar speaks up. "Terrans are
killing Sabia now. We were told to prepare for—"

"Go back to your mothers, you runts!" Kimya's
voice cuts through the air.

Both Dedar and Paknessa run back to their
section. At the same time, Kimya rushes up to Brendan
and takes him by the arm. Looking both ways, she opens
a door and drags him into an empty cabin.

"What did Sainas tell you?" she demands.

"Kimya, what is going on?"

"What did Sainas tell you?"

"That bad things happen, and I need to accept
that and communicate with Esfirs to ensure we do not
hurt one another."

"What did she tell you about tomorrow,
Brendan?" Her voice is extremely impatient.

"What is this all about, Kimya?"

"We do not have time! Berina will be looking for you if you take too much longer to get back. What did she tell you about tomorrow?"

"I have surgery tomorrow to stop the growth." He waves his ungloved left hand in front of her face.

Kimya nods. *She is thinking about something. What is it? Asking another question will probably just set her off.*

"You will be okay, but you need to get your wife to talk to you about this. Demand to know everything, and I mean everything, okay?"

With that, Kimya opens the door and rushes out. Brendan is left alone, standing in the empty room. He gawks after her, trying to figure out just what exactly happened. *I will talk to Esfirs before the surgery. I should be okay, right?*

Brendan shakes his head to clear away his growing anxiety. It does not work. Instead, he decides he should rest back in Esfirs' cabin, his new home.

As he approaches his new home, Berina walks out of it. A friendly veneer quickly replaces the concerned look on her face.

"There you are! What took you so long?" Berina asks.

"Oh, you know, stuff."

A sense of danger tingles within him.

PATRICK ABBOTT

Interlude – Berina: Wrath and Lies

Praying with the flames has always been relaxing for Berina. That is, it was always relaxing before she had to minister to Esfirs during one of her rages. Every time the mid-level minister closes her eyes, Esfirs starts muttering about her mother again. *Are you timing your rants to interrupt my peace?* Berina waits for Esfirs to calm down before attempting to pray again. However, after only a few short seconds of pause, she begins again. Berina's attempt to close her eyes and drown out Esfirs' ranting fails. Sighing and tilting her head also fails to distract Esfirs from her anger.

"How do you expect to hear your Watcher when you spout such ire, dear sister?" Berina is pleased with how stoically she poses the question. *Prayer time is essential, do not ruin it with your own emotions.*

Esfirs turns toward Berina, her iridescent skin refracting the light, her golden eyes bloodshot. "I followed the law; I am fine. It is Asterdaadeh who needs to pray. My presence here is to offer thanks for all the blessings I have."

"That is borderline blasphemy. Take it back now." Berina is unwilling to play any word games.

The doctor snorts before replying. "Fine. I need to pray as much as my mother. Our prayers are different, however. There are many blessings for me to give thanks for. She, meanwhile, sinned against her daughter and the Legion itself with her challenges to my authority."

"And you had her sent back. Quite a long punishment. Harsh too, when one considers she will miss the adoption of Esfirshaz and what will come next."

"Oh, stop playing such an impassive Atenam!" Esfirs snaps back. "You are not ministering to a slave; there is no rule against us having passion."

"You bite back at a priestess?" Berina's words have their desired effect. *Even Esfirs can be reeled back.* "In the end, I care little how you address me; our friendship is too deep for your uncontrolled passions to ruin. However, my love for you forces me to remind you that the flame is lit. We are in the presence of something our own beings can barely understand, in a situation we hardly expected, with a Terran given to us in a manner not even Farzena could foresee. And this Terran has been given up to you of all people. This means you have an epic responsibility. The divine is amongst us now; Dear Esfirs, pray that you will be guided well. Something like, 'Woman, listen!' would work just fine."

Esfirs runs her hands through her hair. The ironed straightness has mostly been lost, curls calling her hair back to its natural form. Soon she will have to clamp it back up again. Meanwhile, the gray wedding dye is fading as the deep brown begins to show through. She raps her knuckles on her forehead twice. With a quick grimace and shake of her head, Esfirs regains her composure.

"She said I was a bad wife. Me! Then she said I was betraying Brendan." Esfirs gulps. Her voice becomes more haunted. "My own mother said I was building my marriage on lies. Then . . . she said I did not love him."

There is the underlying pain. "Sister," Berina says, "how much do you love him?"

"Why would you even ask that?" Her voice is more pleading than questioning. "I love him with my entire heart, and now the love is alive in me."

Berina reaches over to place her hands on Esfirs' shoulders. "Then you love him enough to protect him. Brendan—sorry, Esfirshaz—can easily get overwhelmed. We should give him bits and pieces of the truth as time progresses. If we told him everything now, he would have one of his panic attacks and naturally reach out to Terrans. We would have to permanently cut him off from his old friends to protect ourselves.

"We protect him and the future of the Legion doing it this way. He will, of course, have difficulty with this when we tell him. But by then, so many more things will be better. He will understand, sister."

Esfirs peers into the flame. "I pray he does."

"We will make him."

Both females watch the fire in silence. Berina is too lost in thought to realize this deep contemplation was what she wanted. Instead of being relieved, Berina ponders the fate of the Terran-turned-hybrid. What will happen to him weighs on the priestess. *He is a dear friend. Watcher Sapind, help Esfirshaz. Please watch over him as you do me.* She envisions Brendan lying in the gel-filled tank. Sainas said he would feel nothing and be okay when he woke up. Still, the exploitation of him seems wrong despite his lack of awareness.

"When is he scheduled to be through the procedure, Esfirs?"

"In two more days."

Berina raises her eyebrow, still gazing into the fiery urn. "He was told it was going to be a simple surgery. Not something that would take five days. How will you explain this to him?"

"With another lie."

PATRICK ABBOTT

Forty-Nine – An Interior Burning

Everything hurts. A migraine tears through Brendan's head while the bones in his limbs ache. To make matters worse, extreme hypertension in his crotch has forced him to recline on the floor out of fear of further aggravating things. Lying down, however, worsens the flashes of heat which flow from his heart through his body. *Simple surgery, huh?* Even his teeth hurt, which in turn is what Brendan thinks is causing the sharp pain in his ears.

Thankfully, Esfirs begins to gently pet his hair, causing the whole world to melt away. His pain is replaced by waves of soothing love with each soft tap. When he woke up in the medical bay that morning, there had only been darkness and pain at first, but affection superseded all negativity when he saw his bride. Her beauty was magnified, her now browning hair held back in the clamp like normal while her golden Sabia eyes and rainbow-like skin remained.

Recalling how Esfirs said he'd been out for five days, Brendan remains amazed but not troubled. Her deep eyes had such concern for him; he'd known then and there that he was safe. *She must have been so worried—her singing seemed to calm her more than me.*

Oh, how beautifully she sings. If listening to her is the price of surgeries, I would undergo a thousand more.

"How is the play, my love?" Esfirs asks. "Enjoyable, I hope."

Brendan takes in the gathering from his pillow. Actors stand on the stage at the front of the hall, performing their lines. He doesn't understand the plot even though the Sabia actors are speaking English because of the constant distractions from the audience. At first, the audience was saying many lines along with the actors; however, audience members began their own conversations within minutes. Because of all this, the plot is incomprehensible. Things are compounded by an endless stream of Sabia visiting with Esfirs to wish her congratulations. Each time an audience member comes over, Brendan is made to sit up despite being practically ignored compared to the showers of praise Esfirs receives.

He looks up to view the performances. The Sabia, who Brendan assumes is the main character, is having the worst day of his life. It's hard to tell, but the actor's exaggerated actions indicate constant rejection. Very little emotion is displayed; instead, everything is said in what appears to be bold declarative statements.

"Well, Esfirszan, honey"—he struggles to sit up again—"I have to admit I have no idea what is going on besides that guy has just been shut down by everyone else on stage."

She laughs. "That is not what is happening at all, - she! But what about everything else? Are you enjoying the company?"

PATRICK ABBOTT

Brendan winces as pressure down below mixes with another hot flash. He tries to speak again, but the pain in his arms causes him to weaken, and he must lower himself back on the pillow.

"Hey, married man, you do not look well." Berina pops into view above Brendan. Her cinched, colorful tunic reminds Brendan of the Sabia's skin. She smiles in an attempt to cheer him up.

"I really do not feel alright," Brendan says while shutting his eyes tight, which helps with the migraine. However, increased tooth pain undoes any relief. Even Esfirs running her hand through his hair does not alleviate the situation. The feeling of weight shifting on his pillow implies Berina has laid down next to him. Gathering strength, he opens his eyes and finds her face next to his.

"I can go get you some medication for the pain if you want," Berina says with compassion in her voice.

"That might be good." Berina begins to sit up, but Brendan stops her. "Berina, thank you—seriously, thank you for everything. You always had my back, even when I doubted you. I am sorry for all those times I was not as good a friend to you as you were to me."

She lowers her head back onto the pillow. Her smile reminds Brendan of all the pleasant times they have spent together. "You know," she starts, "I had to put myself on the line for you several times. A couple of them were close calls, but for what we have, it has all been worth it.

"When I was young, Esfirs and I vowed we would be sisters. On that day, -she—she had a horrible day. We became ever close that day. Later, when—when it was my turn to have a horrible day, she was there for me. So, being there for people always works out for me."

"With Esfirs being my wife, does that make you my sister-in-law?" He gives her a playful smile.

A tap on the top of his head grabs his attention. "I am not ready to share my sister," Esfirs says. Berina chuckles. "You, Esfirshaz, need to watch yourself talking to women." Esfirs leans over him and kisses him on the lips.

"Ah, true love," Berina says dramatically.

Clapping on the stage gets their attention, with Esfirs and Berina looking eager for something to happen. An actress recites a line, pauses, and everyone shouts another line back at her. Laughter erupts in the audience; even the cast can barely contain themselves.

Brendan dry-coughs several times during the commotion. Although Esfirs pulls him up and pats him on the back, the coughs keep coming, and his face grows red. Tears form as he struggles to control his fit.

"Berina, look after him while I go get something." Esfirs gets up and walks away.

The pilot starts patting him on the back even though the coughing has stopped. Brendan attempts to wave her off several times before she realizes the hacking has ceased.

PATRICK ABBOTT

"Hold on, brother; she will be back soon with some medicine. Let us get your mind on something else. Who do you want to conduct your adoption ceremony next week?"

He attempts to focus on her as the pain in his body increases. "Esfirs told me you were going to do it."

She rolls her eyes. "Just flatter me a little—I think I have earned it."

He chuckles, then winces from the pain. "Okay"—another wince—"I want you to conduct my adoption ceremony."

Waving her hand theatrically, Berina feigns surprise. "Oh! Thank you!"

"Hey," he says with a trembling voice, "can I ask you a question? It would help distract me from this pain."

"Of course, anything."

"I asked Esfirs, but she shut me down immediately." Berina shifts, looking intrigued. "Why is Kimya not invited? She has been kind to me and—"

"Stop it," Berina snaps. Locking eyes with Brendan, she sends a powerful feeling of odium through the Bond. This strong emotion causes Brendan to cower. But, at least her passionate hate diverts his attention away from his aching body.

The arrival of Esfirs, Zalta, and two male Sabia break the tension. As Zalta bends down, Berina gets up and leaves. Esfirs calls to her, but the pilot does not respond.

"Brendan," Zalta excitedly exclaims, "this is Arshis and Zarqosh." She motions to the two males, using her free hand to dig into a pack on her hip. "They are new to the medical crew on the ship; I have told them we are terrific friends."

Both males nod. "Zalta says you can get us access to the Washington zoo."

Brendan looks at Zalta, who winks back at him. "They were learning about all our adventures together when Esfirs came over. Arshis and Zarqosh are going to be my guests at your party."

She is using me as bait to get guys. Ha, never thought I would be the eye candy.

Brendan feels a slight pinch in his left arm as he thinks those thoughts. Promptly, relief flows from the site, where Zalta has pressed a tac-like device on his skin. Brendan watches as the disk absorbs into his skin. A coolness calms him from the center of his limbs to his crotch. He stretches to test his body and finds he again has full-spectrum mobility without discomfort.

"Just like new! Come by medical tomorrow, and we can do this again. Plus, you can tell Arshis and Zarqosh how I saved your life when we first met."

How you saved my life? "Sure thing."

Zalta turns toward the two men she is wooing. "Normally, he would spend more time with us, but being married, he has new responsibilities."

PATRICK ABBOTT

Dang, girl.

Brendan sees Esfirs' eye roll, which he feels matches his own sentiments. The newlyweds playfully wink at each other. Through a short Bond, he can sense Esfirs' laughter.

Esfirs dismisses Zalta with thanks. Watching the three of them walk away, she sits on his lap.

"How are you, -she?"

"Much better, Esfirszan. Thank you for getting me help; it means a lot to me."

"Of course, love. Do you know why Berina left so suddenly?" Her voice is more curious than anything else.

Considering whether to tell the truth, a lie, or a half-truth, Brendan decides he wants to be honest in this marriage. "We were asking each other questions to help distract from my suffering. When it was my turn, I asked why Kimya was not invited to my adoption. She got upset, but she would not say why."

Esfirs' face momentarily mirrors Berina's wrath, but it quickly dissipates into sadness.

"-she, I know Kimya befriended you. She probably thought she could trick you into liking her because no one here is fond of her."

"I get she is not very popular, but why?"

"She was not originally in the guard service. Originally, she was in the Defense Force. On her last mission, she killed her husband and several Sabia. Everyone knows it was intentional, too. Through some lies, she managed to avoid the death penalty. However, the Defense Force wanted nothing to do with her, so the Legion moved her over as a guard. No one wants a murderer at your ceremony."

Brendan remains speechless. He nods his appreciation and looks away. *Kimya a murderer? That doesn't make any sense. Everything she told me indicated she loved Mehr. She even thought about me as Mehr.*

A shadow hovers over Brendan throughout the rest of the play. Another hour passes of well-wishing for Esfirs, the yelling of lines, and people mostly ignoring Brendan. The solitude allows him to reflect on what he has been told about Kimya. A younger Brendan would try to gather more intelligence and manipulate the situation. Instead, the current Brendan decides to find out the truth for friendship's sake.

PATRICK ABBOTT

Fifty – Adoption into The Fallen

Brendan slips on a Christian scapular over his torso. Closing his eyes, he says a quiet prayer, asking for God's guidance and for his married life with Esfirs. Once finished, he opens his eyes and nods. Zalta accepts the sign, picks up the tunic, and throws it over Brendan's head. He, in turn, works to shift the piece of clothing to fit him correctly. Zalta takes a moment to study the tunic before yanking it hard, adjusting it to her liking. Finally, she takes a step back, admiring her handy work. She smiles approvingly.

Once dressed, Esfirs enters and stands immediately in front of Brendan. Her golden Sabia eyes examine him up and down, eventually settling on his hair. Slender yet toned iridescent arms reach for the top of his head. As she fixes his hair, Brendan feels Esfirs' warm breath on his face. The flowing exhalation is intoxicating. His entire being wishes she would do this forever.

She smirks, admiring her craftsmanship. With a quick head gesture, she calls Berina over. In contrast with Esfirs and Zalta's bright, sari-like outfits, Berina wears the heavy and thick gray hooded robe she wore at Brendan's welcoming party. The ladies share a few short words in Sabia before laughing. Esfirs playfully rolls her eyes and grabs Brendan's hand. Next, Berina starts humming a tune to which Zalta and Esfirs add lyrics. Brendan can't make out what syllables are linked together to form words, but it sounds like "tis le bis key dog lo be di ro gos is nee tee ran nak ah dul ush." Brendan remains transfixed throughout the short song.

"What are you singing?" he finally asks.

Berina stops to answer. "Think of it as a psalm." Brendan raises an eyebrow. Berina continues, "It is from our religion, yes, but we are not forcing it on you."

Brendan means to simply nod but instead lets out a massive sigh.

"Do not worry," Berina responds, "your wife and you are meant for each other. Though I can only imagine how you will wrangle over how to celebrate holidays."

Esfirs ceases singing to reply. "With communication," she says, looking at Berina sternly.

Her words comfort Brendan. *Esfirs willing to work with me, not just shut me down.* Meanwhile, he finds a particular pleasure in watching Berina raise her hands in a defensive position. In response to her victory, Esfirs gives off a triumphant sound. Then, she turns to Brendan, places her hands on his hips, and begins to sway him back and forth, singing verses that sound like "*tee rip ee it see rat om satk me lee ag har a pee dar cha.*" He leans in to kiss her, but Esfirs yanks her head away. Slowly, he pulls back, only for her to quickly peck him on the lips. They smile at each other, and a Bond forms between them.

What is amiss, -she? Brendan feels his wife in his mind. *Ah, her.* Esfirs' voice gains a tone of hostility. *Mother had to . . . go.* She bites her lip while looking at him. *-she, you know what sort of woman you married.* She tries to pass it off playfully. *My mother and I are too alike sometimes, that is all.*

Brendan responds vocally, "What happened?"

I do not wish to relive it. Esfirs turns away for a moment, severing the Bond. Then, after some quick exhales, she turns back toward Brendan and reforms the Bond. *Can we not be happy today? You are being adopted into the Legion. No more limits will be imposed on you. You can even come home with me—when we are ready.*

There will be difficult conversations in the future, he knows. *But let the future worry about the future.* He imagines Esfirs keeping the eye lock while resting her head on him, which she does. Suddenly, his perspective changes to Esfirs' view, looking up at him. The thought of Esfirs nuzzling her head on his chest is instantaneously acted out. He hears her voice in his head say, *Thank you.*

"Am I controlling you?" Brendan ponders the words, but they are said out of Esfirs' body.

Esfirs' view fades from his mind as his own perspective comes back into focus. Meanwhile, his wife's body is animated with new energy. She gently pulls away, still maintaining the Bond. Her voice echoes in his head,

617

saying, *I have you, -she. We will explore your nature together when you are more comfortable.*

Putting her hands on his arms, she verbally asks, "Are you ready?"

He looks down to examine himself. All he is wearing is a tunic that runs down to his knees. His feet are bare on the cold ground. Brendan then looks up at Esfirs, shrugging to indicate uncertainty.

"Do not mind me," Berina's voice declares from behind him.

Brendan's view goes dark. *Another hood over my face. Joy.* He lets out an audible sound of displeasure. A pinch on the inner thigh is the stinging reply. The sudden pain causes him to leap.

Six firm hands are placed on him. *Berina, Zalta, and Esfirs, check.* The hands guide him to turn 270 degrees, then forward. Barely audible mumblings stream forth from the Sabia women. Worries of forced blood-drinking enter his mind, but he tries his best to dismiss them. *If that happens, I am going to stop this ceremony.* His mind gets stuck on the dark memory from his wedding.

Brendan is then pushed forward, up five steps of stairs. He feels for a sixth but can't find it. Before he can stop, he is yanked back to the edge of the top step. One set of hands removes itself from his back only to be immediately placed over his ears, hard. He can't make out words, but the bass of someone's voice is audible.

Despite being robbed of sight and sound, Brendan senses a freeing breeze meeting his skin. The air and floor are painfully cold. He supposes the ambient temperature could be close to freezing. Uncertainty now begins to dominate him. Muffled voices yelling "Esfirshaz" bring him back to the immediate reality.

One set of hands—the feel of them implies Esfirs—now press on his back. He takes it as a signal to move forward, walking about twenty feet before a gentle tug commands him to stop. The sound of footsteps tells him the presumed Esfirs is walking away while another person is approaching from behind. Then, straining his ears, Brendan can hear something like water stirring.

Time seems to pause as nothing happens. No hands are pressed on him, nor does anyone attempt to rob him of hearing again. Suddenly, everything changes. Mid-yawn, Brendan feels an overwhelming, compelling force thrust into his upper back, launching him forward and down. Brendan belly-flops into a startlingly cold pool of water. Shocked and horrified, his involuntary scream of pain causes water to flood his body.

Interlude – Brendan: The Ghosts of FOB Robinson

Drowning, Brendan opens his eyes. Expecting to see what a water death looks like, he is instead shocked beyond belief to find himself back at FOB Robinson in Afghanistan. Once, twice, three times, he turns around in panic. Nobody else is there. Looking down, he finds himself wearing a fresh set of body armor. *Oh crap, I'm dead.*

"You are very much alive, Brendan."

Brendan turns to face the anonymous voice. It's neither male nor female, young nor old. *Why am I back here?* "Sainas!" He calls out. Nothing. *Or am I dead? Crap, I'm dead.* "Show yourself!" He spins around a couple more times, looking for the voice, expecting trouble to appear in front of him.

A slight tap on the shoulder makes him spin-jump 180 degrees. In front of him stands Sainas wearing Russian body armor.

"Sainas, is this your doing? How did we get here? I am supposed to be at my adoption."

She smiles at him. "Yes and no. That answers your first two questions. But, let me answer them clearly. That should address your third."

PATRICK ABBOTT

Brendan takes a step back and clenches his fists. "No riddles, Sainas. What is going on?"

"Peace, friend." She holds up her left hand to motion for Brendan to stop. "Let me speak, please. First, I am not truly Sainas."

"What are you? Some sort of demon? I am dead, am I not?"

The Russian-armor-wearing entity rolls its eyes. "No, I already answered that question. Please, let me explain." It waits a moment before continuing. "Think of me as an imprint, a facsimile, or even a memory of Sainas. My purpose is to guide you in your healing during this adoption."

Brendan stands silently, observing the faux-Sainas.

"May I continue?" she asks. Brendan nods. "Thank you. Your trauma from earlier in your life ties you down to past events and allegiances. It is time to let go."

"How? I-" Brendan scans the empty FOB – "I do not understand."

The imprint eerily and slowly lifts its hand and extends its finger, pointing to something out of Brendan's view. He cautiously turns his head toward the direction. There, in the middle of an otherwise empty lot, is a bleeding-out, dying Brendan.

This is the suicide bombing. "Why have you taken me here?" Spittle flies from the real Brendan.

"I have already told you," the imprint says, "it is time to let go."

"And I said no riddles!" Everything overwhelms Brendan. He closes his eyes as he presses his palms against the sides of his head. A slow stream of tears forms in his eyes.

"Please, be calm, Brendan; there is no intent to upset you. Sainas imprinted me with only the purpose of helping you during the water ritual of your adoption. May I instruct you on what to do?"

Brendan's vision is now blurry. He wipes his eyes, resulting in salty tears and perspiration coming into his mouth. Unable and unwilling to speak, all he can do is a nod at the apparition.

"Thank you. That imprint of you is dying. It represents all your past pain with Heather, the Unified Intelligence Command, and those who would seek to harm you. Go over there and give it the relief of euthanasia. Kill it, or, at the very least, watch it die. Allow yourself to be reborn."

Instantly, Brendan is transported over to the dying imprint. Looking down on himself, the sensation of wanting to heave comes over him, yet whether he can stop himself from doing it—or whether this illusion will allow him to—remains unknown.

The Sainas imprint at his side addresses him. "He will die in two minutes. You can passively allow this to happen, or you can control the situation and end it. How you choose to let go is your decision, and no one will judge you for it."

PATRICK ABBOTT

Brendan looks at the Sainas imprint in horror. But then a revelation suddenly dawns on him like a new day. "You are an alien, Sainas, and I have changed a lot, but you know what?"

"What?" the imprint asks with a raised eyebrow.

"All these changes have made me more human. To you, there may be only two choices. But there is a third. And call it humanity or Christianity or whatever you want—I will show it to you."

Brendan leans down to the wounded imprint of himself. Then, with his right hand, he grabs the bloody left arm of his alternate version. "Listen up, buddy."

"He cannot hear you," the Sainas lookalike intrudes.

Without skipping a beat, Brendan continues, "You are going through a lot right now. You will blame yourself for this and a helluva lot more that will happen to you. But guess what—it is all going to be okay. Focus on what is essential, remember friends and family, and always do what is right. This will not stop bad things from happening, but it will help you heal.

"Most importantly, down the road, there will be someone who loves you for who you are. Even when you do not love yourself, she will love you. So stay in the fight, buddy; you will not die today." Brendan gulps. "And forgive your father."

Brendan's imprint locks eyes with him, and they give each other a nod of recognition.

"An interesting coda," the Sainas imprint says.

Suddenly, the sting of cold water hits Brendan like a thousand needles as he is washed away from the scene.

PATRICK ABBOTT

Fifty-One – Adoption into The Fallen, Continued

Brendan surges back to reality. Struggling not to panic, he feels hands pull on his tunic, yanking him out of the water. Another set of hands removes his hood. Despite regaining his vision, everything remains blurry and pale white. The suddenness of the event, coldness of the water, and stinging air all overpower him. Two body-shaped figures rush up to him and take him toward what looks like a fire. As he approaches, Brendan can feel the warm heat emanating from the dancing flames. The sharp rise in temperature feels life-savingly good. The two figures set him down next to what forms into a sizeable flaming urn.

Blinking repeatedly helps clear and refocus his eyes. While he can now firmly make out his surroundings, his ability to process what is going on is still significantly degraded. Only as he warms himself next to the fire does he realize his body is shivering violently. *Sttttooooppp sha-sha-sha*—He feels his stuttering call for help. Tears well up as the pain becomes unbearable.

He watches but does not register Zalta running to his right side. The next sensation is that of her pressing a device against his skin. Quickly, cool relief flows once again through his body. Though still cold, he's no longer in pain. His breathing returns to normal, and the shaking stops.

Minutes pass as the heat dries Brendan off. Waiting proves relatively easy since being close to the fire has become an enjoyable experience. Pleasant thoughts begin to flow through his mind. *This is good. It might be the medicine influencing me, yeah, but I want to feel more like this.* However, slowly but surely, something becomes amiss in his mind, like music skipping notes, as he remembers . . . something . . . from when he was in the water. But whatever it is, mental clouds interfere with his recollection.

I only wish Esfirs was here. With that, he calls out his wife's name. As if it were a magical spell, she appears, kneeling at his side. He turns his head and gives her a sedated smile. *I can finally be with her. No more worries.*

His new bride is practically glowing. The fire magnifies the iridescent rainbow effect on her skin. Additionally, the glowing light amplifies her golden eyes. Brendan notices the walls are a black, marble-like rock, making her colors even more prominent. What is most beautiful, however, is the love she physically displays. Studying her, he sees Esfirs is trying to contain something inside her that makes it seem like she is about to burst. Finally, Esfirs reaches out and takes Brendan's hand. Carefully, she moves it to her abdomen and slowly begins to rub it across her stomach.

"Her name is Roxin," she says.

Brendan's haziness instantly dissipates. "Wait, what?"

PATRICK ABBOTT

"We have a daughter," Esfirs responds, beaming like a peacock.

Incredulous, he demands, "We have only been married for two weeks. How can you be so sure?"

She chuckles. Again, she rubs his hand over her belly. *She truly believes what she said.*

He can't stand her silence any longer. "Esfirs, how can you be so sure?"

" I have sensed her since her conception. Our love has become alive. When you go to sleep, I sing to her."

Tears begin to flow from his eyes as he instinctively realizes she is right. *I am a father.*

"Do not cry, Esfirshaz, do not cry. Instead, rejoice with me. You are Sabia and have a daughter. You honor me in all ways." She reaches over and embraces him. Then, she pats him hard on the back as his cries intensify. "Be strong," she whispers. "Now, you must learn about us."

He slowly withdraws from the hug in time to see Berina placing a pillow on the white, marble-like floor between him and the urn. Her disposition is stoic. *This is one of her serious moments.* He nods to her as a sign of respect. Placing her hand over her heart, Berina bows. *Thank goodness they could pick up that friendly gesture.*

"Hello, Esfirshaz, welcome home." Berina pauses for a moment. She gives him a curious look, then reverts to a stoic expression and continues. "You previously asked many questions about us. For the most part, we were unable to answer them to the depth you desired. Now, however, as a member of the Legion and a Sabia, we can tell you more about us." Her voice lacks any of the friendliness Brendan is accustomed to. "Here are the most important things about us: We believe in one god, the divine, the giver of all life. We believe in the Watchers. They have watched over us, protected us from misfortune, and advocated for us to the divine. Your religion's concept of angels is somewhat similar to the Watchers.

"In terms of us as a species, we are the Legion. All Legion are Sabia, but not all Sabia are Legion. We are the Legion, a wholly unified command organization designed for our race's protection, unification, and advancement. Of all the Sabia, the Legion is the purest. Now you are an officer in the Legion. As a Sabia, your entire life will be ordered for the benefit of the species and you."

Brendan rubs his arms to keep warming himself as he listens. "Our expedition to the planet the Terrans refer to as Terra or Earth, and what we refer to Namziahga, is peaceful. I promise you there is no hostile intent other than the desire to merely protect ourselves from those who would harm us out of ignorance or intra-Terran feuding. It is an honor to be part of this mission for the Legion because while Remelga is our main planet now, Namziahga is our original home."

Berina's words cause Brendan to do a double-take. His mind quickly adds everything he learned together into a surprising revelation. *She just said Earth was the original home of the Sabia.* As he struggles to speak, Berina keeps her emotionless gaze on him. Then, quickly, she raises her hand, silencing him.

"Yes, Esfirshaz, we Sabia are the children of Garmands, our word for Terrans, and the Watchers. For a while, both Garmands and Sabia lived on Namziahga. However, strife between us led to hatred and violence. After seeing their children being murdered, the Watchers took us to Remelga to avoid a series of catastrophes which the divine released on Namziahga." Here, Berina stops, exhales deeply, and begins to show curiosity on her face. "Do you understand, Esfirshaz?"

They're space-alien hybrids. I am married to a freaking human-alien chimera. Brendan gasps in shock at his subsequent realization. Remembering Montana, he recalls how the Bible mentioned fallen angels marrying women. *Namziah was a woman who married the Watcher angel Remel. Does that mean the Sabia are evil? Oh God, what have I done?*

"What have I done?"

"-she?" Esfirs calls out to him. "What do you mean?"

Brendan eyes both women in front of him nervously. Their efforts to create Bonds with him force Brendan to defensively dart his eyes away. For further protection, he closes them hard. He retreats within himself. *I need to think this through.* A moment of silence gives him a grace period to think. However, the revelation acts like a raging torrent through his thoughts, rocking the peace he ever so recently had.

Rubbing his eyes, he catches Berina and Esfirs in an eye lock. Both of them immediately turn toward him. Berina begins to speak first, but Esfirs rapidly and furiously talks over her friend.

"It is that *gawur* religion of his. I told you, Berina, about the book—"

"Silence!" Berina's voice scalds like boiling water. She slowly turns to face Brendan. Closing her eyes, she shakes for three full seconds before reopening them. They look calmer now. "Esfirshaz," she says shakily before closing her eyes again. The next time she speaks, her voice is much more tranquil. "Esfirshaz, you know Esfirs and me well. And the others, such as Zalta, have innocent hearts. You know there is nothing to fear in us. So please, be at ease with us."

Brendan can only stare at Berina. He is trembling, not from the cold but from fear. In his heightened state, he can't stop staring at the threat his mind has determined Berina to be. However, the fear of a Bond being formed and his thoughts being betrayed becomes paralyzing.

A hand on his cheek turns his face toward Esfirs. She looks at him with pleading eyes. "I am not a monster, and neither is your child. She is our love—so intense that it became a living girl. "

Before he can resist, he hears Esfirs singing in his head. Panicking, he attempts to look away to break the Bond, but he can't. *She has control of my body. Let my body go, Esfirs! Let it go!* Rage and fear directed at her flow from him.

PATRICK ABBOTT

Esfirs' thoughts resonate in his mind. *-she, you are going to frighten her!*

A loud popping sound goes off in his head. Then, Brendan senses a third presence in the Bond. No coherent thoughts, not even full emotions—instead, the presence makes itself known through a long, continuous hum. Brendan mentally reaches out toward the third entity, which responds by humming louder.

Roxin senses you, -she. This is the first time she has sensed you. Esfirs begins to mentally hum a song. While not a match, the third entity's adjustment of its hum is seemingly some sort of response.

"Is that her?" Brendan asks aloud.

Yes.

His emotions break like a dam. Simultaneously, he wants to laugh, cry, jump for joy, and curl up into a ball. Roxin now independently starts adjusting her hum.

"She is singing to you, love," Esfirs says.

Brendan places his hands on his head. Tears flow from his eyes. Within a second, Esfirs comes over and embraces him. She says words of comfort while Brendan ponders his future. *Between their human origins and Mon's statement that they are dying, something is horribly wrong. I will do everything I can to ensure Esfirs and Roxin have a peaceful universe to live in—for both Sabia and humans. I will make sure these two sides do not harm each other. Somehow we are all connected. Our futures are intertwined.*

Fifty-Two – The Future and the Past

Another moan cuts into the darkness. *This is the tenth or so sleeping wail from Esfirs in the last hour.* In response, Brendan sits upon the bedding. Yawning, he reaches over and rubs his sleeping wife's arm. His fingers brush away condensed sweat from her Sabia skin and whispers loving commands for her to rest.

She responds with a loud belch and says without opening her eyes, "Let me rest, -she. If I do not rest, I might lose the baby." Esfirs fidgets and then rolls over, showing Brendan her back.

Again with the overdramatic statements. They have been coming fast and repeatedly for the last few weeks. What is more worrisome, though, is how Esfirs' health had been going downhill the past month. Constant visitors expressing their well wishes for the pregnancy initially prevented Esfirs from resting. First, fatigue set in, and now she is becoming feverish. Thankfully, she took the situation seriously with daily trips to medical, but Brendan remains concerned.

He stands on the fluffy, pillow-like rug that serves as their bed. He can barely make anything out in the dark except Esfirs in her golden sleeping gown. Slowly, he maneuvers off the Sabia mattress and makes his way to the living room. Opening his bag, he pulls out a loose

PATRICK ABBOTT

T-shirt and gym shorts. Slipping off his pajamas, he puts on the gym clothes and heads out to work out.

The hallways are empty as Brendan traverses them. *It must still be pretty early.* However, his yawning indicates it is still late at night for him. The only Sabia he encounters are at the checkpoint. Gul's and Ishan's familiar faces are there to offer welcoming smiles.

"Officer Esfirshaz! Things have certainly changed since the first time we were at your place for a party," Gul says.

"They certainly have," Brendan replies. "Tell me, is your name Gul or Nemahaz?"

Gul bashfully looks away with a red face. "You figured it out. Family information is classified, so we do not use married names with Terrans. But truth be told, it was a bit depressing. When we interacted with you, it felt like I had to deny my wife, and she, me."

"Huh, interesting. I do not know if I will ever get used to Esfirshaz; for now, I think I will hold onto Brendan." The guards give each other a glance. Reading their discomfort, Brendan decides to lighten the mood. "Hey, if you want to have some fun, call Esfirs by her Terran name: Mrs. Brendan Sean Murphy."

Ishan and Gul burst out laughing. "No, no," Ishan barely manages to get out, "I do not think we will be doing that."

Once the laughter dies, Ishan asks, "You are up early. Everything okay?"

Brendan rubs his eyes. "Not really, no. Esfirs is having another restless night. I cannot sleep either due to all her moaning. So, I figured I would go see if the gym in the hangar is still there."

Neither one of the guards responds. Instead, their attitude becomes somber when Brendan mentions Esfirs' condition.

"Well, Officer," Ishan begins, "the hangar, medical bay, and dining hall are open to you. Just stay away from the Terran delegations. I do not believe you are authorized to deal with them."

Brendan makes a mental note about the last sentence. *There goes the covert route. If I am going to make sure my family has a peaceful future, I will need to somehow get the Sabia to give me access to the United States again.* He nods and thanks the guards.

Once he makes his way to the hanger, he enters it expecting to find it empty. However, on the far side, several Sabia in gray uniforms look over toward him, only to lose interest within a few seconds. After ensuring his presence is not a disruption, he notices that all the machines, weights, and other workout equipment are still there. In fact, there is a new chest press device. *This is awesome. I was worried the Sabia would get rid of it during my honeymoon.* Despite some weariness, Brendan decides to do a complete workout on the elliptical and bench press.

An hour later, he is done in more ways than one. *That dang well near killed me.* Out of sheer exhaustion, he collapses on the bench press surface, closes his eyes, and reaches a peaceful rest. Ever so gently, his brain shifts to a state of sleep. Finally, an extremely vivid dream of Esfirs breathing on him completes the transition.

Suddenly, a blast of hot air straight into his nostrils wakes Brendan up. Two large brown eyes are staring right at him. All he can do is gaze back in paralyzed surprise.

"Boo!" the face in front of him screams.

Brendan presses his back into the padded bench, giving off a yipe of terror. The head above him pulls back and gives off a hearty laugh, and Brendan realizes Berina was looking at him.

"Berina!" Brendan says in only half-calmed down terror.

"Do not tell me she is making you sleep in the gym, Esfirshaz." Berina puts her hands on her hips. Cocking her head to the side, she says, "Esfirshaz or Brendan. Wow. I guess it really comes down to how I am interacting with you. Right now, this is definitely a Brendan moment."

Brendan glowers. "Glad to know what your opinion of me is."

She responds with an overexaggerated Afghan thanks. "You are welcome. Since Esfirs is like a sister to me, I guess that makes you my brother." She steals a quick wink. Next, she takes a more conventional stance. "Say, everyone has been all about Esfirs and Roxin, but what about you? How are you doing?"

Brendan sounds tired as he speaks. "Esfirs has not been sleeping well. The symptoms are close to fever and—"

Berina holds up her hand to stop him. "I asked how you were. Pregnancy is more . . . intense for Sabia. She will be fine—I have no concerns about her. You are the subject of my curiosity right now."

Old memories of being manipulated come to mind. *She wants to get leverage over me. No! Stop! She is asking as a friend.* "Truth be told, I am worried."

Berina sits down next to him. Her face is now troubled as she wraps her arm around his shoulders. "What is wrong, Esfirshaz?"

He takes a deep breath. *Here I go.* "If the Sabia are descended from ancient humans—and I do not doubt you—this is not just a trip to visit another intelligent species. I am willing to bet those three in Tennessee had something to do with the real reason. And what truly worries me are not some abstract thoughts about peace between two powers, but that the hidden truth is putting my family at risk."

Berina focuses on Brendan like a hawk. He can see all of her intelligence being used to study his body language and formulate a response. She shows none of the signs of friendliness or concern he is used to. *Unfortunately, this is becoming a more common experience.*

"I think you are tired," she replies with an edge. Then, to make matters worse, she gets up and folds her arms across her chest.

PATRICK ABBOTT

He appeals to her as a friend. "Please, do not be like that, not after everything we have gone through. I am not attacking anyone. All I am doing is worrying about my family."

"Go get some rest—you are tired. That is an order, Officer."

Brendan's heart sinks as she stands there with her arms crossed. All he can do is nod his head and leave. So he stands up, snaps to attention as he would for a human officer, and makes a beeline straight for the door.

"Brendan," she calls to him with emotion in her voice. The use of his name catches his attention, so he turns around to look at her. "Do not tell anyone else those thoughts. Promise me that."

"I promise you no one here will hear my worries."

He pauses to take a serious look at Berina. Her expression is one of puzzlement. With no response from her, he turns and heads out of the hangar. *Now I know the lay of the land. That was close.*

Back in his new cabin, he takes a shower while Esfirs remains sleeping. Deep in prayer, he eases himself into the warm water. *God, I need you now. I will not betray anyone, but I need to find out the truth. Let your will be done, not mine.* Turning off the water, he stands there alone in his thoughts. *I can't work against the Sabia on this one. Everything will have to be above board.*

"-she, why are you still in the shower?" Esfirs' achy voice calls out to him from the bedroom.

"Just thinking about things, my Esfirszan," he shouts back.

First, there is a moan, then Esfirs snaps at him. "I am not property. Terrans speak that way, not us, -she."

This will take some time for both of us to get used to. Brendan decides it's best not to respond. Instead, he dries off and goes to his wife. She remains in bed, somewhere between awake and asleep.

"You left the bed," she softly accuses.

"Sorry, love, I wanted to work out and did not realize the time. Go back to sleep, now."

Esfirs closes her eyes. Immediately, Brendan sees the muscles in her body relax. *She must be asleep.* In the still silence of the room, Brendan uses his fingertips to rub her stomach. This time, Esfirs smiles and turns her head to face him.

Within seconds, a flashing light on the wall panel catches his attention. He kisses his wife and gets up to check the message. Pressing the panel, he reads the text.

> Fourth Class Officer Esfirshaz is summoned to a third chime council meeting. Senior Officer Fahime will retrieve Esfirshaz from his cabin at a time Fahime chooses. Council members will be given the full dignity their station requires.

Brendan screams in frustration.

"What is it?" Esfirs surges awake in a state of alarm. "Is there something with Roxin?"

PATRICK ABBOTT

"Crap," Brendan says, "I am sorry. Looks like I have my first meeting as an officer. It is with the council, and get this, Fahime is the one who will escort me to the meeting."

"-she!" Esfirs sits up, still looking feverish. "You must be careful. No yelling, challenging, or combating the council members. Be subservient, answer their questions, and accept whatever they say. How you behaved with Mon when preparing for the meeting of Terran governors will no longer be tolerated at your rank." Her face is pleading. "Promise me you will behave, -she. Roxin and I cannot lose you now."

Lots of promises are being forced on me today. "I promise you I will be subservient, answer their questions, and accept whatever they say." He leans down to hug her. "Rest now, Esfirszan. Everything will be alright. I will even be polite to Fahime."

Letting go, he watches Esfirs nod in agreement. Quickly, he gives her a loving peck on the forehead. She starts to say something but stops herself. Instead, she just shakes her head, trying and failing to repress a slight smile. *So you like some Terran parts of me. Terran? Dang, now they have me doing it.*

The rest of the morning is spent anxiously waiting for his retrieval. Brendan makes brin for Esfirs while he tolerates a breakfast of nuts and nasha. As he eats, Esfirs chooses a meal of hydroponically grown greens. Brendan uses the silent moments during the meal to observe his wife. *She is tired but does look better. Hopefully, Sabia pregnancy difficulties are limited to the night.* Once finished, Esfirs dresses in her gray doctor's uniform.

Esfirs begins to talk about the day ahead when the door chimes. Her eyes widen, and Brendan steels himself for what is about to come. Breathing deeply, he opens the door. There, standing in full black regalia with the floppy hat, is the redheaded Fahime. Her posture is perfectly erect. *Fahime is obviously well trained. She is practically the model of professional and personal appearance.*

"Ma'am." Brendan snaps to attention. "Fourth Class Officer reporting for duty."

The greeting must have thrown Fahime off her guard. For just a moment, her face becomes one of bewilderment before assuming an air of condescension.

"Do not greet superior officers like you would one of your Terran friends, Brendan." She puts extra emphasis on his original name. Esfirs starts to make a sound, but one quick look from Fahime silences her. "Now," Fahime continues, "we have places to be."

Brendan feels pain as Fahime grabs his right bicep. She yanks him out of the cabin and into the hallway, her steel grip becoming even tighter as they walk down the corridors. The pain forces Brendan to clench his teeth hard; he looks at Fahime only to see a smirk on her face. Fortunately, she suddenly swings him into an open room. Unfortunately for Brendan, several other black-clad Defense Force members are waiting there. None of them look pleased to see him.

"Here is your second order," Fahime says with disdain. "Sit down." Brendan complies by taking a seat with his back against the wall. "I know who you are and what you are, spy." She starts to pace back and forth.

PATRICK ABBOTT

"The moment you try to contact the diplomats on the ship, we will be on you. When you try to leak secrets to your Terran friends back home, we will grab you. And when you decide it is time to commit sabotage, oh Terran, that is when we take the gloves off." She stops pacing and steps up to Brendan, towering above him. "So, here is my offer to you. I promise you, honestly, that if you confess here and now, my friends and I will not beat you to a pulp. Instead, we will arrest you, hold you in detainment, and maybe, just maybe, your government will do something that will result in your exchange." She crosses her arms. Then, as if she has another thought, she smiles and holds up a finger. "Tell you what, I am not cruel. We will allow you to see your hybrid child – somewhat periodically – in exchange for your immediate admission of guilt."

Berina's warning, along with Esfirs' words about deference, gives pause to Brendan as he formulates his response. *Looks like everything today was building up to this.*

"Look," he starts, "I am not going to pretend to know how to properly address you, so please forgive my lack of chain-of-command deference. The failure is mine, and I need to work on fixing it. All that being said, Senior Officer Fahime, the fear you have is false. I am not a spy. What I am is a father who will do everything for his family. My wife is undeniably Sabia, even by you. She would not stand for me doing anything which harms the Sabia, so I will mind myself there. What I will do is be honest in whatever I am assigned to do. Additionally, I will advocate for what truly, honestly is best for those on Namziahga and those from Remelga." Fahime winces at his use of Sabia place names. "Does that include things you personally oppose? It probably does. But what I will not do is betray anyone by doing those things you mentioned. So please, drop the smart interrogator technique and take your friends where they can do something productive."

Fahime looks back at a thin male Defense Force member. It looks to Brendan as if they are in a Bond. As this transpires, there is no movement from the other Sabia. Finally, after taking some time, she turns back toward Brendan. With a motion of her hand, she summons him to stand up. No words are exchanged between them. She motions to the door. Brendan nods.

Together, they walk the corridors in silence. Fahime signals each turn with her hands. Next, they pass a routine checkpoint and then another. Counting the minutes, Brendan realizes this is the farthest he has gone into the ship. Even the hallways become more elegant, with what looks like smooth stone walls. He even thinks—but is not sure—that he smells incense. Finally, they turn a corner, allowing Brendan to see a gathering of people by a large set of doors.

"Fahime, a second, please," Brendan says. She stops and turns to him, her face emotionless. "Look, I get you, and while I have a personal dislike for how you treat me, I respect you. You are using all your training to do your job. However, I assure you I am not a spy. There is no way you will believe me now; I get that. All I ask is you keep open the possibility of me being truthful to you."

"No." Her stoic reply is as cutting as it is short.

Brendan shrugs. In reply, she motions for him to approach the gaggle of Sabia alone. He can feel her eyes on the back of his head as he walks away. The dozen or so Sabia turn toward him with looks ranging from curiosity to disinterest. As he approaches the group, the familiar figure of Leleh pushes her way through them.

"It has been too long." She awkwardly holds her hand out, which Brendan promptly shakes. "It has been so long since we have talked that you have become a Sabia and have a new name, Esfirshaz."

"Great to see you, Leleh. I was wondering what happened to you."

She chuckles. "I was promoted out of Loft's command. Now, I am an aide to councilmember Nazteb. So it was great to learn you would be brought before us today." She shifts back slightly. "Did you see the last part of my order to you? The one about respect?"

"That was you!" Brendan laughs and smiles. "Oh yes, I got that. You should have no worries about that; I will comply."

"Excellent. However, we should go now." She motions for him to move forward.

A memory of Esfirs pleading with him to be respectful pops into his mind. Deciding to heed her advice, he keeps his mouth shut about what just transpired with Fahime.

The group of Sabia part for them as they make their way toward the doors, which open automatically as they approach. Inside is the most opulent room Brendan has seen on the ship. A plush red carpet provides the base for a room full of pillars, tapestries, councilmembers, and an audience. The council is in its familiar seated semi-circle while the audience stands along the sides of the room. Zand occupies the center with Mon to her right and a man in Russian military camouflage to her left. Meanwhile, invisible incense dominates the room to the point where Brendan coughs. Leleh motions for him to stand in front of the council.

Zand looks up with an impassive stare. "Esfirshaz, greetings." She looks at the camouflaged man. "Iraj, please proceed."

The man speaks without a Russian accent, surprising Brendan. "I am Commander Iraj, newly assigned commander of Defense Forces Forward – Namziahga. You are already familiar with my number two, Sainas."

"Yes, sir," Brendan replies.

"I will not waste your or my time any more than I have to. What I need from you is an assessment." Brendan nods in anticipation. "The European Union and the Russian Federation are concerned about the security degradation in Ukraine. We have offered our services in securing peace, which both sides have agreed to. The Defense Force will occupy a buffer zone around the Southern Bug River and establish the Transitional Authority in Ukraine in three days. Councilmember Tanimah"—a raven-haired female in the semi-circle nods—"will run civilian affairs while Defense Force Assistant Deputy Commander Zur will oversee security."

PATRICK ABBOTT

Brendan does not see anyone respond to this name. "My question for you: how will anti-Sabia forces on your planet—" Mon coughs hard. "My apologies. How will anti-Sabia forces on Namziahga react to our"—he emphasizes the plural first-person—"presence in Ukraine?"

Brendan uses all his mental strength to keep his jaw from dropping to the floor. Sucking in his lower lip, he bites down hard to keep his emotions in check. Then, he reaches down to reply as he would have back in the Unified Intelligence Command. "Anti-Sabia forces will flock to Ukraine. They will use insurgency tactics to conduct hit-and-run and no-contact attacks against the Defense Force presence."

"How soon will things occur?"

Brendan does some quick mental calculations. "The first week will probably prove to be a shock. The chance of violence in the first seven days is low. However, after that, for the next four weeks, small-scale, target of opportunity attacks likely will occur as domestic forces seek revenge against the Sabia, whom they will blame for occupying their land. Then, after a month or so, we will see a rise in international groups moving into Ukraine. It will take two to three months to establish themselves before launching open operations."

Tanimah leans forward. "How united will the international groups be?"

It will be like Iraq and Syria all over again. "At first, they will be independent of one another. The first initial attempts at joint action will fail. Then, however, one to three unified commands will emerge. Eventually, these commands will de facto unite various groups into one organization primarily based on ideology and country of origin."

"What about your own former commander, General Meade?" Brendan turns his head to confirm Loft himself asked the question. *They're adapting to use surnames, interesting.*

"He is smart. This will be a domestic opportunity for him. He will use it as a talking point to further unite the various anti-Sabia and populist groups, both political and paramilitary, under his command. He may even openly seek political power for himself. I suspect he will attempt to seize power through legitimate political means. However, after meeting with a prominent Patriot Front member in North Carolina, senior advisors of his will very likely advocate for violent means of seizing power."

"As for Ukraine," Iraj starts, "where would the international groups come from?"

"Primarily from Europe. However, with Turkey being a player in the conflict, Ankara possibly will enable Middle Eastern and, to a lesser extent, Central Asian groups to enter the fight. The last group to possibly have a presence would be from Australia. Meanwhile, only a few low-level fighters would come from North or South America. I cannot foresee African factions getting into the fight."

Iraj covers his mouth to yawn. "Alright. Nice to know our analysts came up with the same assessment as you did. We can take them out piecemeal. You are dismissed."

Strong urges to challenge the plan rise within Brendan. *This is insane. People are going to die because of this.* The promise he gave Esfirs pulls him back, but just barely. All he can do is thank everyone for their time and walk out. Leleh takes him outside. They talk, but Brendan has a sort of out-of-body experience in which he is unsure of what is being said. He must be saying the right things because Leleh is friendlier to him than she ever has before. Soon, Loft comes out to join the conversation. Everyone is all smiles. Inside, though, Brendan feels defeated.

Once they're finished talking, both Sabia leave Brendan alone. Looking down the hallway, he realizes he can't remember his way back. He makes his way to the first corridor intersection, where he sees a full-body-armored Kimya fiddling with a panel on the right sleeve of her suit.

"Kimya!"

She looks up, surprised. "Brendan! I mean Esfirshaz. It has been a while." She takes a small step backward. Meanwhile, Brendan notices she is not smiling at him.

Time to end this awkwardness. "Hey, can we talk alone for a moment?"

She looks both ways; only a few Sabia stand by the council chamber's doors. "I do not think it would be appropriate for us to do that."

He looks her dead in the eyes. Though he is unsure whether she will take him up on the offer of a Bond, he makes a mental plea to talk. Suddenly, he telegraphs the desire to walk down the hall and enter the first room on the right. However, he is unsure how successful his telepathy is because Kimya does not respond. So, he starts to make his way to the room. Once at the door, Brendan realizes Kimya is following him at a distance. *Got to admit, this is pretty cool.* Entering what turns out to be an equipment room, he finds it is perfect for their private meeting.

When Kimya closes the door behind her, Brendan gets to the point. "Look, I have heard stories, but you are still a friend to me. Why are you being so distant? You were there for me in the past, so let me be here for you."

Kimya's shoulders slump. Grimacing, she turns and opens the door. Brendan has to yank her back to prevent her from leaving.

"You cannot do that to a superior officer," she rebuffs him.

"I will do that to a friend. And I will keep doing it until I learn why a friend who cares so much about me pretends she does not."

Kimya's eyes begin to water. "Your wife told me I was not allowed to talk to you anymore. She threatened to tell you everything about my past if I did."

Brendan puts both hands on her shoulders and, for the first time, forces a Bond. *Kimya, you were there when I needed you. You have looked out for me. Poor*

life decisions have robbed me of my own flesh-and-blood
family. I do not want to lose people who have formed
new connections with me. Tell me what separates us,
sister. Rob your fear of its weapon.

Brendan is sucked into her memories. He sees
Mehr again. Flashes of romance between Kimya and
Mehr occur. Then, orders are received in the field. Mehr
and Kimya disagree. Mehr tells Kimya to disobey them.
Then, Brendan sees the horror of Mehr and others
kneeling on the ground. Kimya uses her railer to cut him
and the others down. The next memory is Kimya being
praised for her work. The memories then flash forward
to Kimya talking to a cleric next to a fiery urn. Kimya is
expressing remorse for her role in the deaths.
Unintelligible words are shared. Kimya is offered the
ability to disown her words, but she refuses. She is
arrested and sentenced to death. Finally, on the day she
is scheduled to die, she is given the option to be a guard
on the Namziahga mission because of her "condition."
She accepts.

The Bond is severed. Kimya throws Brendan
against the wall. "Get away from me!" she screams.
Though his eyes are still adjusting to the light, Brendan
can see a glare on her face, rivers of tears flowing from
her eyes.

"Kimya," he calls out sympathetically.

"I am so sorry" is all she manages to say before
running out of the room.

Brendan sits down on the floor of the equipment
room. Alone with his thoughts, his mind naturally shifts

to faith. *God, any time before, I would have lost it at this point. I would have shut down. But you have seen me through everything. So whatever I am supposed to do now, may I do it well.*

PATRICK ABBOTT

Fifty-Three – The Room with the View of Things to Come

It's so beautiful! God's gift to his creation. The stars Brendan is staring at fill the window. Never has he seen so many of them, not even during the camping trips out west with his father. *Dad, they are so beautiful!* He looks for the familiar constellations and the ones he and his father made up while stargazing. This proves impossible, as the known patterns are drowned out by the sheer number of visible stellar objects. For a whole minute, these stars have nullified all his worries. Watching them, he feels their splendor moving him to the point where a single tear forms in his right eye.

In the back of his mind, he hears Mon call to him. "Billions of fiery altars praising the divine. Amazing, is it not?"

"Thank you," he barely gets out. Then, still staring out the window, he adds, "Truly, thank you, Dear Mon, for letting me see this."

"You are authorized for personal time off. Spend a day on a spacewalk or visit one of the nearby planets. In fact, the other day, I spent a few hours meditating while I floated nearby the ship. It was good clearing my head."

Brendan does not reply. Just looking out the window has reduced his stress levels to near non-existence. A few more minutes with the window, and he will be like a lotus eater.

"But tell me, Esfirshaz," she continues, "Deputy Commander Sainas informs me you are now doubting your use to the Legion?"

This gets his attention. He turns around to face Mon. He admires the fine cut of her tailored, black pantsuit. *Something diplomatic is coming up.* She perfectly fits the stereotype of professional and feminine beauty. "Yes, ma'am. Now that I have accepted a commission and citizenship with the Sabia, which automatically ends my service with the Unified Intelligence Command, I fear my ability to liaison with those you need me to is at an end. Heck," he says, partially flustered, "you will not even allow me to talk to the diplomats here, let alone go back to Earth, so I do not know what I can do for you. The Defense Force has its own analysts, so there goes that angle as well."

"Dear Esfirshaz, you have no need to worry. Your expertise will be required as things progress. Our success in Ukraine is fostering closer integration between major Terran leaders and our on-the-ground experts. There will be opportunities there for you. Additionally, your former friends, Javier and Malcolm, are a growing concern for us. Last night, we heard of a poll stating Javier is already the frontrunner for the presidential election next year. And, how many militia groups have now signed up with the Patriot Assembly?"

PATRICK ABBOTT

"In the last week, over two dozen. That figure includes the New Sons of Freedom, the Nationalist Sons of Freedom, and six of the eight major factions of the Sons of the Shepherd. Combine that with the political endorsements, and the way I figure it, he pretty much has over two hundred electoral votes already locked."

Mon laughs. "See, only you would know what that means. When trouble begins to form in the United States, you will be able to spot it, and together we will neutralize anything that threatens us. Now, Esfirshaz, how are Esfirs and Roxin doing? It must be pleasing to finally be a father."

Opening his mouth, he decides to gamble everything. "Dear Mon, permission to be blunt?"

She rubs her chin, giving the appearance of pondering her decision. "Very well, proceed, Officer Fourth Class."

That is a warning. "Back in North Carolina, something important was discussed between you and me. It was a secret I did not dig into out of respect for you. However, now with me being in the Legion and Roxin—" He pauses, realizing he is becoming emotional. "I have to be honest. I will do anything and everything for my family. If there is a risk to her, I need to know."

Mon takes a deep breath and slightly shakes her head. *She is trying to control her anger. Dang it, I should have listened to Berina on this.* He counts to five while watching Mon. His mouth dries, and his stomach churns. The familiar sensation of his despised friend, anxiety, returns once again. But then Mon opens her eyes, this time with a light air about her. She seems even younger, almost carefree.

"You have kept it to yourself. You have not shared it with anyone here, even your wife. That is commendable. What truly is touching is that at no time alone with your Terran friends did you transgress our trust." A sly smile forms on her face. "We would know." She drops the smile. "But no. There is nothing your rank needs to know."

Brendan nods his head. "Okay. I am sorry for having pushed the envelope. It is hard being a first-time father while dealing with interstellar politics. That is all. Look, I have probably taken enough of your time, so if you do not mind, I will go out and start putting in requests to create a network of people who I can talk to about the upcoming election and—"

"Stop." She holds up her hand. "Everything we are doing here is to ensure the Legion, including our beautiful Roxin, has a future. The sacrifice of the reconnaissance scouts in North Carolina was not in vain, nor were . . . your provided services.

"We have experienced good and bad times together, Esfirshaz. Being patient with each other has been the key to success—and no one dying. I ask the same person who was a liaison to us, then our auxiliary officer, and now full Sabia, to trust us in the dark for a little while longer."

"Okay," he manages to say. "Okay, I put my family in your hands for a little longer."

"Then let us shake hands. I need the practice, anyways."

Brendan reaches out his right hand first. Initially, Mon looks apprehensive, but after a quick laugh takes his hand with hers and heartily shakes it. *She's learning well.*

"And I promise you, Esfirshaz," she says with a smile, "we will kill everyone who threatens the future of Roxin and the Legion."

Interlude: Sainas – Playing the Long Game

"Why do you insist on dressing like one of them?" Fahime does not bother hiding her contempt. To make matters worse, she doubles down by repeating the question.

She always was her own worst enemy. Not answering her question, Sainas replies, "What gets me is your insistence on always pushing your luck. You find something, daughter of Sharh, and you always think you must exploit it to the utmost level. However, opportunities often close up when you apply too much pressure to the situation. So instead, think about how you can be the water that gets into a small crack. Freeze, thaw, and refreeze. In time, you can break the mightiest boulders."

Fahime gives off a *hmpf.* "Okay, I will take that as advice. But why are you always wearing Terran clothing?" She crosses her arms and leans toward Sainas.

If I could roll my eyes a thousand times, I would right now. "Fahime, you are a fine protector, but you could be great if you only listened."

Throwing her arms up in the air, Fahime exclaims, "What are you talking about? I only asked why you wear that type of clothing."

PATRICK ABBOTT

Sainas raises her finger, which silences Fahime. Then, ever so slowly, she blows on her finger to signal the need to be quiet. "Lesson time, my student. Your latest encounter with Esfirshaz—what was the motivation for your little escapade?"

Her face becoming strained, Fahime slowly says, "I—the reasoning was to quickly win against an assessed spy. I—"

"And what was the outcome?"

"He knows the next time he commits espionage, he will be arrested." Fahime straightens her back and lifts her head slightly up, displaying her proud success.

"No." Sainas' immediate refusal deflates Fahime. "You ensured he will increase his operational security. Additionally, you closed doors of coopting him or having him ever open up to you. I was under the impression that, as a protector, you would do anything to neutralize threats. Did you never stop to think that you could gain his trust and then use it against him?"

The counterintelligence agent looks down to the floor. Her sulking speaks louder than anything she could say.

About time you are silent. But this is not an exercise to embarrass you, dear friend. "Put your head up, Officer. Everything is not so bad. Your misjudgment led him to come to me about it. I listened, offered words of encouragement, and reinforced his feelings of friendship for me. It would not surprise me if the odds of him including me in any of his plotting remains about one in a trillion; however, he makes himself more susceptible to influence for our greater plan. And like a farmer sowing crops, he will be harvested again and again in time. And maybe, just maybe, he can even be a tool given to us by the Divine to redeem our true leadership."

No words are said for over a minute. Instead, both women look into the candle sitting on the table. *There is a simple beauty to it. Knowledge, wisdom, and purpose are all summed up with fire.*

"Will he really be that useful to us? Every day he remains, he will learn more, increasing the risk of him reporting back sensitive intelligence to the Terrans."

"That risk exists, but every day, as I indicated, he becomes more and more vulnerable." Sainas studies the flame. "Take, for example, his adoption. It went awry in a small way. He would not kill or even watch his old self die. Instead, he comforted the memory of his dying self."

"He told you this? Wow, he really does trust you."

"No, I doubt he will tell anyone, even his wife. He believed I was an imprint."

"What a foolish creature."

"Ignorant, and that ignorance is our key to having him be the tool we need. I am clearing with Defense Force leadership back home a few more interactions between my 'imprint' and him. Between his trust of me and Esfris' miracle, we are in a very good place."

Fahime goes silent as she watches the flame. "I am sorry for not performing the best I could, deputy commander. Next time, I will synchronize efforts with you."

Very good; I will have assignments for you yet. Now, your receptiveness deserves a reward. "As for your question: we are far from home—what is the point of deployment if we cannot dress up in funny costumes now and again?"

Epilogue

Our Father, who art in heaven, hallowed be thy name; thy kingdom come; thy will be done on Earth as it is in heaven. Give us this day our daily bread, and forgive us our trespasses as we forgive those who trespass against us, and lead us not into temptation but deliver us from evil.

Really God, on Earth and as it is in space. Meade's presidential run will tear the country apart, and what we humans do not do, the Sabia will finish. Lord, make me an instrument of your peace.

Brendan keeps looking down as Sabia pass him in the hallways. Fearing betraying his thoughts through some sort of accidental Bond, he figures being safe is a thousand times better than being sorry.

She practically admitted to having spy rings in the government. Jack is gone, the diplomatic staff is off-limits, and Fahime will be monitoring everything. Yet, my family is here. Man alive, I have to be careful.

Arriving at the door, he finds Esfirs standing and talking with Sainas and Zalta. The three turn to see who has come in unannounced.

PATRICK ABBOTT

"But you are right," Esfirs says, looking at Brendan, "I now have everything I ever wanted." She rubs her belly when she is done speaking.

"Very well," Sainas says while smiling slyly, "we should let you two be."

Sainas is the first to move. She whispers "congratulations" in Brendan's ear as she walks out of the room.

Meanwhile, Zalta remains at Esfirs' side. "I have more friends who want to meet him, so be sure he comes to the party tonight." Esfirs rolls her eyes at Zalta. "Hey, people do not believe me when I say that I am friends with him. Plus, he will always be Brendan to me." Zalta laughs at her own joke and walks out without saying anything to Brendan.

This leaves husband and wife together in the room. Esfirs begins swaying her hips back and forth. "Berina bought me a Terran dress for a costume party later. If you behave, I will go as Esfirs Sean Murphy for you, -she." She starts to hum as she dances up to Brendan.

Brendan feels a Bond initiate. Immediately, Esfirs stops her dance. "What is wrong, -she? Your emotions are all jumbled inside you. Is it the combat sickness again? I will go get Sainas back here."

He reaches out and holds her upper arms. "No." He gazes deeply into her golden eyes. "Everything you ever wanted is a family to love and love you back. Is that what you meant?"

"Yes," she says. Brendan can sense her trying to sift through his emotions through the Bond.

He sighs, then smiles. "I love you and Roxin more than anything in the world. Can we just spend tonight together? Let us stay here for the night with no parties, no worries, no Sabia-Terran tension. What do you say?"

"Of course, -she. Whatever you need, we will do."

"May I ask you one more thing? This is a big thing, but I need your help so badly."

"Tell me."

"Can you love me, even though I am a broken, scared, wounded man?"

"Yes—"

"A man who doubts the Legion's course of action for the Namziahga mission?"

"Of—"

"A man who will always consider himself more Terran than Sabia?"

"Brendan Sean Murphy!" Her use of his Christian name startles him. "I love you unconditionally because you are who you are. I have and always will love you. And most importantly, I will never give up on helping you heal. Please accept that. And- " she pauses - "I hope you can love me as a woman who is scared of having her first child, with my own doubts about the future, and praying every night that my husband can love me for the Sabia I am."

PATRICK ABBOTT

He passionately kisses and embraces her. Through the Bond, she transmits Roxin's happy sounding-humming.

At this moment, Brendan realizes he has what he has always wanted: being truly loved. The pain of his father and Heather's betrayal lose their sting in his soul.

The future is uncertain, and I have to find a way to ensure peace continues between the Sabia and Earth. But for today, I will love and be loved. I am not alone.

About the Author

Patrick Abbott lives near Washington, DC. He is an International Coaching Federation certified coach. When not writing or coaching, he is enjoying the outdoors, reading, and travel.

www.patrickabbott.net

t.

Made in the USA
Columbia, SC
20 August 2022